The Reunion Recipe

by Mara Moody

Paperback ISBN:
979-8-9911234-0-2,
979-8-9911234-2-6,
979-8-9911234-3-3
Ebook ISBN: 979-8-9911234-1-9

To my moon, rose, and star, my three reasons for everything. And to anyone who has been told their dreams are too much, they aren't. Lastly, to Taylor Swift, one day I hope to write as well as you.

Author's Note

Dear Reader,

I wrote this book in the midst of severe burnout during 2019 and 2020. In challenging times, I always turn to romance for comfort. I longed to read a character like myself reflected in the pages of a book with a guaranteed Happily Ever After. At the time few books featured Arab American heroines and even less in Romance. So I decided to follow in the steps of one of my idols, Mindy Kaling, and write it myself.

I was born in Baghdad, Iraq and moved to USA at 6 months old. My parents and I did not live near large Arab-American communities and due to conflict, immigration restrictions, and cost of travel, we could not afford to visit Iraq while I was growing up. So, the stories I write reflect the narrow lens of my experience as a first-generation Iraqi American which is not the same perspective shared by all other Iraqi- or Arab-Americans, nor should it be as our experiences are not a monolith. But I do hope what you see reflected in these pages is a deep, abiding love and respect for my Arab heritage. I hope you see, counter to the common depictions in Western media, that Arab-American families are as warm, loving, complex, and devoted as all families. And most of all, I hope you see that what unites us all is a yearning for happiness—to be seen as our whole selves and be loved for it.

Love, Mara

Chapter One

Marlo

MARLO SAGE WAS known for two things aside from crafting a killer pop song: terrible taste in men and an obscene inability to school her features. Every emotion wrote itself in screaming color across her face—rose red when embarrassed, ghostly pallor in shame, and rarest of all, a golden lit-from-within glow when incandescently happy. Her myriad facial contortions were unmatched, an expressway to her deepest, sometimes ugliest, thoughts. That's why she was everyone's favorite meme. And why awards show cameras frequently panned to her to catch her reactions in real time—fodder for the morning shows' body language experts.

Some people wore their hearts on their sleeves. Unfortunately, Marlo wore hers on her face.

And her face often betrayed her.

Marlo's gaze snagged on the last person she expected to see in a dive karaoke bar deep in the valley, and her facial muscles twitched. Even as she tried to fight it, her brows pinched together as her eyes rounded and her face warmed. A tableau of *what the fuck* painted across her features.

"Marlo, what's wrong…oh shit," Heather said as she too spotted the subject of her best friend's distress.

"Is that Jude Beckett?" chimed in Asha. "Damn, remind me why you dropped him. Ow—"

Heather glared at Asha after elbowing her between the ribs.

"All I'm saying," Asha continued, "is Cliff is so past his sell-by date and Jude Beckett looks farm fresh."

"Shh," Marlo scolded, but it was too late.

The entire space abuzz with drunken chatter and laughter went quiet as the last performance ended. A momentary suspension of time and noise as a collective of people recognized the moment for what it was—the most unlikely reunion in the most ironic of places.

"That's Marlo Sage in the pink wig," someone said aloud, shattering the stillness.

"And Jude Beckett's over by the bar," another answered.

Time tripped into hyperdrive. Before Marlo could even process who she'd seen, the crowd coalesced around her, nudging her forward until she stood face-to-face with her former pop duo partner.

The passage of twelve years had only rendered him more beautiful, hewed the sharp line of his jaw, thickened his tall frame with corded muscles. He hadn't even lost a damn bit of his thick hair. It still curled at his temples. Aggravating. When the corner of his mouth tipped up into a half smile, she noticed a couple of new lines bracketing it.

An ache bloomed in her chest. Jude had lived nearly equal amounts of his life with and without her. Yet she remained permanently arrested at the point he'd broken up their act.

"Nice hair, Marlo," Jude said in his honeyed velvet voice.

The sound of it still ignited an electric pulse through her veins.

She tugged the end of her bubblegum pink wig, her pitiful attempt at a disguise. Had it even bought her five minutes of obscurity?

Instead of attending the Grammys tonight as half the world expected her to, she'd decided to return the Academy's snub and skip out. Her publicist accused her of sour grapes, but Marlo thought of it as more of a self-protective choice. Art shouldn't be made with an uncontrollable outcome in mind, but after years of nominations and awards, Marlo had grown to rely on recognition for her efforts—a means of measuring the immeasurable. Logically she understood an award couldn't truly quantify an album's capacity to make its audience feel something, but her heart never listened to reason. Driven by ambition, Marlo still craved gold stars. A tangible measure of her worth.

As she continued to stare up at Jude, she regretted her choice. At the Grammys, she wouldn't be standing face-to-face with the enigma that was her first love. Fate clearly had a sense of humor.

"What are you doing here?" she asked, unable to tear her gaze from his deep chestnut eyes.

God, she missed him. Marlo shook her head. She refused to continue down a spiral that led nowhere.

"Catching up with old friends," Jude answered. "You?"

Marlo couldn't even count the ways she'd playacted running into Jude in her head, but this scenario had never entered her mind. It was oddly calm, ordinary even. Jude didn't drop to a knee to beg her forgiveness. She didn't emotionally eviscerate him with a razor-barbed remark. No tears in sight.

"Bachelorette party," she answered.

"Yours?" He asked.

Marlo spotted a glimmer of indiscernible emotion behind his eyes.

"No," she said, almost certain she saw relief wash over his face.

Marlo needed to return to her friends, but her feet remained rooted in place—magnets drawn to true north. In the background she heard a building buzz, but she was too focused on Jude to recognize it.

"They're chanting our names," he said. He'd always had an uncanny ability to read her mind.

"Oh."

Oh shit. Jude hated this type of attention. He'd been so eager to flee the spotlight when they were young that he'd left her too.

An all too familiar pain throbbed deep in her chest.

The crowd jostled behind her. Marlo turned to find her friends pushing through, similarly bewigged in eye-popping shades, to flank either side of her. Her Skittle-haired band of protectors.

"Marlo, should we have the car brought around?" Heather asked, gaze dancing between her and Jude.

"Where's your security team?" Jude asked, a furrow forming between his brows.

Marlo's shoulders stiffened. "I asked them to stay outside."

Jude shook his head as if he had any right to have an opinion on the matter.

"One normal night," Marlo added. "That's all I wanted."

She didn't owe him an explanation but couldn't help offering one anyway. She hated seeing even a hint of disappointment in his eyes. Normal disappeared the moment she'd spotted him.

"Don't you hear them?" Jude asked. "They're getting louder. We're going to have a riot on our hands here in a minute."

"What do you want us to do, Marlo?" Asha asked. "Should we leave?"

"No, what? No, we're here for Diana. I'll buy a round of drinks for the room. That will quiet them down." Marlo started to push forward, but two large hands on her shoulders held her squarely in place.

"You should go," Jude said, his mouth flattened into a stern line.

His pupils narrowed down into pinpricks as she stared back at him.

Her gaze traveled from his eyes to his lips and back. She still remembered how his kisses tasted—minty, anxious, wanting. No one had ever kissed her the same way since, not with his particular brand of raw vulnerability. Sure, she'd been kissed with passion. But with frank earnestness? No.

"You're the one who runs away," she said.

Twelve years of heartache distilled into a handful of words.

Marlo took advantage of Jude's stunned silence and squeezed past him. She stepped up to an open spot at the bar. The bartender held up a finger, and Marlo was relieved she didn't make a big fuss to rush over to her. She could wait her turn. *Celebrities, they're just like us—karaoke dive bar edition.*

"Marlo Sage," a man near her said. "Thought that was you."

She smiled tightly. *What tipped you off? The crowd chanting my name?*

"The pink suits you." He gestured to her wig.

"Thanks."

"I was going to do you tonight," he said, then sputtered. "I mean, do one of your songs."

"Look forward to it," she replied, hoping he'd move along.

"Would you consider—"

"Nope, I have a strict no karaoke of my own songs policy."

"What can I get you, darling?" the bartender asked.

"Six shots of tequila for me and my friends and a round of drinks for all."

"Wow, too kind," the stranger said, holding up his half-full beer in salute.

Marlo paid cash and tipped generously—a small investment to secure as quiet a night as possible. Though it was probably too late for that. She wasn't about to admit defeat to Jude or her friends. Marlo's team would've insisted she leave. But she hadn't even told Tara about this little excursion, so in pop star math, she figured that meant she didn't need to worry about it. Not yet. Easier to beg forgiveness of her publicist than ask her permission.

The bartender hopped onto the bar and stamped her cowboy boot onto the surface three times before delivering an ear-shattering whistle. "Everyone's next round courtesy of Marlo Sage. Now give the girl a break."

Marlo mimicked tipping a cowboy hat at the bartender before picking up her shots. As she turned away, she nearly slammed straight into Jude's chest.

"Hey," he said, steadying her by the elbows. "Hope those aren't on account of seeing me." His half smile didn't mask the concern still lining his eyes.

Marlo glared at him. She didn't need his pity. She was doing just fine on her own.

"I'm fine," she said. "Stop flattering yourself at my expense."

She'd give anything to hate him, but she and Jude Beckett had known each other since they were babies. He'd been her everything—the boy next door, best friend, first crush among other firsts. Until he was her nothing.

She didn't know what the protocol was for running into the boy who broke her heart and nearly destroyed her career at its first meteoric rise. But she was over his sudden insertion into matters he'd chosen to remove himself from years ago.

"Why don't you get back to your friends and I'll get back to mine?" She tightened her grip on the three shots she carried in each hand.

They stared at each other for several beats too long.

"The pink suits you," he said.

"So I hear."

Jude squeezed her bent arms, and it was only then she realized that he still held on to her. There was a time when she'd barely known where her body ended and his began. And now he was a virtual stranger.

"It's good to see you, Marlo."

"Is it?" Only she asked it aloud instead of just in her head

His hands dropped to his side and he studied her again. "Uh, I mean…I'm surprised to see you, isn't tonight the—"

"I need to get back to my friends," she interrupted, not about to discuss her career failures with him.

He smiled and nodded, stepping out of her path. Marlo bet he was dying to tell her he told her so. *There's no path to happiness and fulfillment here for me. I'm not sure there's one for you either.* That's what he'd said when he left her, left their duo.

Promises sworn then broken.

God, she hated that she didn't hate him.

Marlo's hands trembled so bad by the time she made it back to the booth her friends had claimed. She'd probably lost half the volume of the shots in her last few steps alone.

"Marlo," Heather said, brows creased. "Are you okay?"

"Yeah," she said. "Fine. Why do you ask?" She slammed back a shot.

Marlo swallowed back a cough as the liquid blazed down her throat. She forgot how much a tequila shot burned. She didn't drink often. It conflicted with the health management plan the label enforced. She was on a strict regimen of pre-planned meals, exercise, health supplements, and liters of water.

Her friends exchanged a look before following suit.

The media made it a game to hate her. It stung—every dig, every baseless accusation cut her to the bone. All she'd ever wanted to do was sing and entertain people. Marlo didn't anticipate becoming a cultural touchstone, a measure of how cool someone was directly correlated to how much they hated her or at least pretended to. The critics disregarded her. Art produced by a woman for a primarily young female audience couldn't possibly be as legitimate as men touring on the same album for decades well into their seventies. The hurdle Marlo needed to clear was set exponentially higher. She was expected to release a new album every couple of years and couldn't afford stagnancy, but she also wasn't allowed to depart too far from her roots.

Reinvent but don't change. Stay in the public eye but stop seeking so much attention. Be desirable but stop flaunting yourself. Think before you speak but stop being so calculating.

All of her label's and the media's impossible edicts pounded through her head. David Stringer, President of Pop Machine, sat at the ready to remind Marlo how short she fell of his impossible vision of what she should be. She'd tried to contort herself into what he demanded, but she was simply an imperfect human thrust into extraordinary circumstances.

Still, Marlo's album sales were real. People bought her records. Her concerts still sold out within minutes. Yes, she was beyond grateful for her good fortune, but she'd also earned her scars and their accompanying bruising cynicism and doubt.

Fame came at a cost—Marlo was expected to absorb all the negativity simply because she'd been afforded the opportunity to travel the globe first class, wear designer dresses, and walk red carpets. Worse, she'd had the audacity to do it not only as a young woman but as the child of an immigrant. Obviously, she owed them access to all of her, all the time—on demand humility and grace. But celebrity status didn't confer immunity to the vitriol so often directed at her for simply daring to exist and create her art.

She slapped a hundred-dollar bill down on the table.

"Who's volunteering to go buy us an entire bottle?" Marlo asked.

Diana opened her mouth to object. They all knew Marlo wasn't a big drinker, but thankfully Heather sensed what she needed tonight—to dull the razor-sharp edge of her broken heart. Couldn't she afford to be reckless for one night?

"You got it," Heather said.

The girls made it through their third round of shots before a familiar tune started playing and Marlo groaned.

"This one is dedicated to Marlo & Jude. I can't believe you're both here tonight," the woman on stage screamed into the microphone before shouting out the lyrics to Marlo and Jude's first chart-topping single, *It's All About You.*

And just like that, dozens of phones pointed in Marlo's direction. Any hope of a simple evening disintegrated before her eyes. She lifted her chin defiantly and pretended not to notice. Then the chanting resumed, first slow and quiet, barely discernible. But the woman on stage heard it. Their names, Marlo's and Jude's, a call demanding a response.

"Yes," she sighed. "How about it, Marlo and Jude?" She addressed them so casually as though they'd known each other for years. "A mini reunion for your biggest fans?"

The question hung in the air for a moment, quieting everyone. A flush crept up Marlo's neck. She adored her fans, truly. She never wished to disappoint them, but wasn't she ever allowed to mark some time simply for herself? All she wanted was to enjoy the company of her friends without having to put on a show. But her answer to the singer on the stage was inevitable.

A pathological nice girl to her core, Marlo struggled to ever say no.

"What are you—" Asha asked as Marlo rose from the booth.

Her audience always got what they wanted.

"Putting her and this place out of its misery so we can leave," Marlo said.

"Marlo," Heather repeated, her voice ringing with alarm.

"I'm a big girl. I know what I'm doing. If the audience wants a show, I'll give it to them."

She marched toward the stage, stumbling on the step up to it. One shot of tequila was more than enough to generate the buzz sizzling through

Marlo's veins, and she'd had three. Still, she was sober enough to know she shouldn't be doing this. Her friends also knew that. Especially not with Jude in the audience. Especially not on tonight of all nights.

"Marlo, I love you," a stranger in the crowd yelled out.

"I love you too!" She hooked her fingers into the leather sling of her stiletto heels and pulled them off, tossing them into the crowd. Damn it, she thought a moment too late, those were her favorite pair. Oh well.

See, a show. Marlo still knew how to deliver one. It didn't matter if her heart slowly shattered inside—she could always make the crowd smile.

The flashes and faux shutter sounds from cell phones held aloft in the crowd blurred her vision. Every step toward the microphone screamed at her: *mistake, mistake, mistake.* When they'd first arrived, Marlo could swear this place was half empty. But now it was nearly standing room only. Word traveled fast.

The crowd whooped and hollered with a healthy share of boos intermixed. Marlo pretended not to care, even trying to join in on the fun, always game to make fun of herself.

You hate me? I hate me too!

"I know, right, just can't get rid of me." She smiled, squinting at the crowd.

But the truth was that Marlo ached for approval. She had since age twelve when she and Jude first started posting videos of them performing music from her parent's living room. The likes and shares on those posts hit her like a shot of pure adrenaline. They'd almost made her feel like she belonged. Unfortunately, just like any other addiction, enough was never enough. Marlo always wanted more—more success, more legitimacy, more adoration.

Love me.

Marlo gripped the microphone, the only tether keeping her on solid ground. Before she could utter a word, another member of the crowd yelled out.

"You try too hard," he said.

Why was it that the heckler's voices echoed so much louder than the majority of the crowd shouting words of adoration and support?

That random man's critique burned even more than the rest. Of course Marlo tried hard. How else could she succeed with the sheer amount of obstacles in her way? When partnered with Jude early on in her career, he'd buffeted some of the negative chatter for her. But now she faced it all alone.

Alone.

Marlo half-curtsied and forced herself to smile. "That I do."

"There's no auto-tune at karaoke, sweetheart," someone else heckled.

Marlo suppressed the urge to laugh. Did they really think there was an insult left in the world that she hadn't heard?

The room continued to buzz with unstable energy, if she didn't bring them back around soon, she'd lose them for good.

"What would you like to hear?" Marlo asked.

The crowd answered back chanting Jude's name. Of course. She wasn't sure whose worst nightmare this was, his or hers.

"Come on," Marlo said. Her voice pinged around the room harsher than she'd intended. "Leave the good man alone."

Her gaze landed on his. She couldn't read the expression on his face, either shock and horror or shock and awe. Separated by years yet reunited by coincidence and circumstance. It was almost funny. Marlo's heart kicked up its tempo. Would she ever be anything less than a sparking live wire in proximity to him?

Pick me.

"Hey," a bouncer at the edge of the stage yelled at her. "Think you can get on with it? The crowd's getting restless."

She nodded.

"Last chance, any requests?" Marlo asked again, losing sight of Jude.

"Shouldn't you be at Grammys?" someone yelled.

Blinking, Marlo considered how to respond. It was in these unscripted, spontaneous moments she tended to get herself into trouble. With every passing year, she found it harder to keep her opinions to herself, but she'd already landed in scalding water for recent behavior. She bit down on her tongue.

"You mind?" Jude asked, bringing Marlo back to the present and slipping the mic from her grasp. She hadn't even noticed him joining her on stage.

"Hey, everyone," he said. His voice not only calmed her but soothed the crowd as a whole.

Singularly infuriating. She wanted to scream. Marlo was the one who stayed, the one who kept delivering to her insatiable fans.

He left you. He left me. Is there no justice?

"Listen," he continued, "Marlo and I will make you an offer: We'll perform one song, but that means no more yelling, no more insults, and then you let us go our separate ways in peace. Deal?"

Separate. Ways. In peace.

Each word stabbed fresh into her scarred heart.

Wait? Had he just offered to perform with her? She couldn't have heard that right.

The audience applauded. For Jude. It took everything in Marlo not to roll her eyes and kick him in the shins. She could have gotten the crowd there—she just needed a minute. Besides, she hadn't asked for his help. He handed her back the microphone.

"What do you say, Marlo?" he asked.

"Are you serious?" she said under her breath.

"Any better ideas?"

She glanced out at the sea of voracious faces. Her mind drew blank. "I guess not."

Marlo turned the stage version of herself up to eleven—all smiles and sugar.

"Ready?" she asked Jude aloud for the crowd.

She couldn't believe, after all these years, they were truly about to perform together again. In a karaoke bar in the valley, no less. She couldn't decide if she wanted to laugh, cry, or throw up. Possibly all three at once.

Jude nodded, the one mic shared between them forcing them to stand uncomfortably close. He leaned toward her, cupping the mic with his hand. "Let's give them what they want."

Twelve years, hundreds of miles, and yet she knew exactly what he meant. He was so close she could count the freckles she used to trace with her fingers, her favorite constellations stretched across the bridge of his nose.

He winked at her before relaying the message to the DJ.

The familiar tune blared on the club's less than stellar speakers. Marlo's verse came first. She shut her eyes for a moment, letting the unusual circumstances of the evening fade and giving herself over to the music. She recalled the bright, hopeful version of Marlo she'd been when she'd penned this tune, wishing she could be her again. The Marlo who wrote this song with her best friend, her first love, the one who was never supposed to leave her. Jude nearly missed his cue—she opened her eyes to find him staring at her, an inscrutable expression on his handsome face.

"Never have I ever told you how much I love you," he sang back to Marlo.

A strange pit formed in her stomach. She wished she hadn't heard the way his voice strained at "I love you."

Being on stage together cost him more than it did her. He'd hated this life, but it was her fuel. The anticipation that sizzled through the crowd ignited her blood.

Holding his gaze, they slipped back to a place she'd never expected them to ever find again—harmony.

Marlo's skin prickled at singing these lyrics with Jude again through a lens of time, distance, and hurt. It had been orders of magnitude easier singing to the boy in her bedroom who'd somehow gone from best friend to first crush without her even noticing. Love breezed into Marlo's life so early and with such ease, she hadn't appreciated what a rare gift it truly had been. She'd taken him for granted, assumed his presence in her life was guaranteed. Then he'd walked away.

Now they stood here singing like the turbulence that wrecked them had never happened.

The song continued, a sweet banter back and forth, culminating in a synchronous crescendo that perfectly melded their two voices. It was no mystery why it remained a fan favorite. It bore the promise of flirty, first love. A fantasy so divorced of reality that it punched Marlo right in the heart to sing it again. She'd unlocked the key to time travel—singing with Jude brought her right back to the complex feelings she preferred to bury deep.

The audience erupted so loudly it drowned out her thundering heartbeat. No hecklers now. Jude stood there next to Marlo, tall and broad, cheeks flushed, eyes wide with his pulse hammering at his neck. He looked every bit as shook as she felt. What had they done? Unleashed pop's version of Pandora's box.

"Encore, encore," the crowd chanted.

They'd created a spectacle, and Marlo would surely hear about it from her team. But just like the first time, she found herself unprepared to say goodbye to Jude Beckett. Another oldie but goodie of theirs started to play overhead.

Jude raised his eyebrows at her. Their stage shorthand still intact. She nodded her assent. This time, Jude's verse came first.

"You're my yesterday, today, and tomorrow," he crooned, easing seamlessly into the melody as though they'd never stopped performing together.

Her Jude Beckett *was* back. He reached out with his free hand and acting on pure instinct and probably some adrenaline Marlo slipped hers into it. The tender contact nearly caused her to miss her next line. Her first impulse was to pull away, but there was something about the way he looked at her. Marlo weaved her fingers through his instead.

Home.

"You're mine for today, tomorrow, and always," she sang back to him, drawing out the final note.

No matter how good it felt to share a stage again, it couldn't last. He'd been clear about this point—he didn't want this life and she did. An insurmountable impasse. They both knew it.

Years ago, she'd been convinced Jude Beckett was her soulmate, but they were too young and naïve then to know that love alone wasn't enough. Life was far more complicated, and that was even before accounting for the celebrity factor.

Marlo pulled away first this time.

"Bye, Jude."

Chapter Two

JUDE

HE COULDN'T BELIEVE he'd taken Marlo's hand like he had any right to it. More alarming, she'd let him. The old magnetism between them resurged with a vengeance. He didn't know what compelled him to tempt fate this way. Tequila? Beer? *Pining.* It was impossible to tamp down the typhoon of emotions coursing through him while singing love songs with the girl he'd once let push him away.

Now she looked at Jude with her deep, mournful brown eyes, and all he wanted to do was lay his soul bare to her in the way that was once second nature. He longed to tell her how much he'd missed her, how sorry he was for the way things ended between them, how much he looked forward to her late-night texts from tour. It was the only time she reached out to him. The miles separating them a safe enough buffer to allow her to contact him.

Jude hated to think about Marlo lonely on the road. No matter how often he considered texting her or calling her of his own accord, he allowed Marlo to initiate contact. It was only fair. He was the one who'd walked away, so the prerogative to call belonged to Marlo. Maybe it was cowardly, but that's what Jude did when faced with difficult situations—avoid them.

He wished he'd captured the moment they'd just shared under glass. But Marlo was already walking away, and this time he was the one left on stage holding the mic. Karma, he supposed.

"Uh, you've been a great crowd. That was fun," he said to the audience. Jude's voice cracked as another flood of emotion walloped him. It wasn't that easy being up here without her. It never had been.

Marlo turned back and eyed Jude curiously.

Thanks, he mouthed to her.

"Enjoy the rest of your evening," she sing-songed, just loud enough for him to hear.

Marlo had always been a beautiful girl, but lately she brooded in most of her pictures, an uncharacteristic seriousness clouding her typically sunny features. Tonight, seeing her brighten again, even if briefly, had been refreshing. She even smiled at him at one point the way she had after their first kiss under the fairy lights in Jude's backyard. But like memory, the moment slipped away, right through his fingers.

Marlo held his gaze for a brief moment longer before adopting her expressionless mask again. Jude hated that her memories of him were wrapped in caution tape and barbed wire. He shouldn't be back in this place, where it all fell apart. When he left their duo, Marlo wordlessly laid claim to Southern California, and he'd taken Northern—the unspoken terms of their break up. Jude should have kept it that way, but the reason he was back was too good to pass up. He simply needed to return to his own business and forget tonight ever happened.

Goodbye, beautiful girl.

~

The next morning, Jude Beckett surveyed the outfits spread out around the hotel room and shuddered. Having his clothing picked out for him while a stylist fussed with his hair brought back memories he preferred to bury deep in his chest or layer into the flavors and textures of his latest pastry concoctions. Memories far too accessible after last night's impromptu reunion. Of all the ways he'd imagined reconnecting with Marlo, a surprise opportunity to perform two of their greatest hits at a run-down karaoke bar was not one.

He sighed. It was his baking after all that brought him back into this mess. Worse, he didn't exactly hate the public recognition for his chef skills. Not the way he'd hated it during his brief pop ascendancy. Strangely though, this morning everything was tinged with guilt. The fact that the magazine hired a rising new country star to do the shoot with him only worsened the sensation. It was too close to history for comfort, and it made him itch to get back into his kitchen to engage in some baking therapy.

The stylist pumped product into the center of his palm and massaged it through Jude's hair, bringing it into a low swoop across one eye. Jude couldn't help himself—he raked his fingers through his hair, allowing it to settle back into loose waves pushed back off his face.

"Hey man, I'd rather just look like myself." Jude scanned the room again, tension bunching between his shoulders.

"Do I come into your kitchen and tell you how to cook?" The stylist pouted.

"Fair point, but I don't cook. I bake."

He arched one well-groomed brow at Jude. "You're the talent."

Suze bounded toward him across the hotel suite. "Jude, heavens, don't you look gorgeous!"

Even after all these years, he still hadn't figured out how she managed to move so quickly in her four-inch spiked heels or where she'd picked up her unique drawl. It was like second-rate theater southern accent and valley girl had a baby. Suze Bunko was born and raised in Fresno, California. Her parents were second-generation Japanese immigrants. None of them had spent a minute in the south. It only made her all the more endearing.

“Hey, Suze. This is a bit much.” Jude gestured around the room.

“Just a little photo shoot, darlin’,” Suze cooed as she knelt down to brush her lips across Jude’s cheek. Her lavender-dyed hair tickled his face.

“I don’t know if this is the right strategy,” he said. “Also, what is a country singer doing in a photo shoot for a culinary magazine?”

She softly swatted his shoulder. “Oh-em-gee, I told you. Her father comes from a multi-generational line of bakers, so it’s like a little cutesy star-crossed thing.”

Jude groaned. “I wasn’t a country star. And this girl’s father isn’t a pastry chef. He owns a cookie shop.”

“Sweetie, your snobbery is peeking through. She’s practically a child. Be kind.” Suze patted his arm. “You of all people should remember how overwhelming all of this can be.”

Suze was like a second mother to him. A career mother. She’d ushered him into the celebrity life, guided him through it, and then helped him walk away. She had his best interest at heart, and he knew it. It wasn’t fair to lash out at her for his own issues.

He hadn’t told her about the run-in with Marlo last night. She still harbored a soft spot for his former partner. Again, he ran his fingers through his gel-slicked hair, ignoring the stylist’s shriek.

“Sorry,” Jude said, “I told you I want to look like myself.”

Suze placed a placating hand on the stylist’s arm and whispered in his ear. Head drooped between his shoulders, he walked away. Then Suze turned her attention back to Jude.

“No worries, hon. We’ll get you in front of that camera and out of here in a wink.”

“Do I really need to pose with the singer?”

“Her name is Kaylenne, and this is her first magazine shoot. You were once totally where she is now. Don’t begrudge her this moment.”

“That’s exactly what bothers me. I don’t want to be reminded of where I came from. This is supposed to be about my act two.”

Suze paused and studied him for a moment. "Seriously, bud, I get it. I'm sure all the stuff with your dad plus the madness last night upset you on top of everything else."

"What madness?" He wasn't sure why he played dumb.

Talking about last night with Suze would make it real in a way he wasn't sure he was ready to deal with at the moment.

She sucked in her lower lip, her teeth grating on her lip ring. "The pictures, the video of you two. All the news outlets have been playing it on a loop, like endlessly. Did you think I wouldn't find out?"

"Suze," he said, searching for but not finding the words to explain. "I wasn't trying to hide anything. It was nothing."

"Didn't look like nothing."

Someone caught a two-second clip at just the right angle, when he'd leaned in to sing a harmony with Marlo, which made it appear like he stole a quick kiss. It had spurned an internet frenzy with forensic levels of dissection.

Jude pulled in a deep, slow breath. He couldn't ever quite shake Marlo. She was his own personal version of that billboard in *The Great Gatsby*. Her dark eyes bored into him with that penetrating gaze from social media posts or magazine covers at the grocery store. Her presence omnipresent. She was a chronic illness—when he least expected it, she flared back, and try as he might to ignore her, forget her, he couldn't.

Marlo Sage was the permanent albatross around his neck.

"It was nothing more than a little crowd control," Jude said.

He softly pounded his fists into the side of his head. This wasn't a time to lose himself in thoughts of Marlo. Not after all the years they'd spent in rooms just like this, preparing for shoots that were so effective in making them look like an indivisible pair that he'd fallen for it too.

Jude wished he'd explained to Marlo why he was back in town. He hated to think of her reaction when she saw this photo spread. "You know what, Suze, I can't talk about it now."

Suze pursed her lips. "Here for you when you need me."

Pressure built behind his eyes. Though they'd worked together for nearly half his life, even Suze didn't understand how much his heart broke every time he spoke about Marlo. Every mention of her name brought him back to that moment twelve years ago—a kiss he hadn't realized would be their last. He'd laid his soul bare to Marlo and begged her not to go along with the label's publicity campaign.

"Choose me," he'd pleaded. "Choose us."

Marlo cradled his cheeks in her hands and said, "I wish I could have it like you do, where everyone wants me perpetually single. But I have to be seen as desirable if we want to sell our records. We can't afford to date behind closed doors only. You made your choice. I'm making mine."

She brushed her lips against his. He knew when he felt it that it was a goodbye, but he'd still refused to believe it.

"I want you," he whispered into her mouth.

Marlo pulled away and placed her finger on his lips. "Jude, you only want me backstage or in hotel rooms. You said yourself that you didn't want to date under the glare of the flashbulbs. But that's where we live. David Stringer said we need to be focused on the album, and the best thing for the album is for me to be seen dating Bay Stevens."

She stared at him with those large, bright brown eyes, and he watched the hope evaporate out of them and crystallize into something harder as he remained mute.

He should have said something, he'd desperately wanted to, but he hadn't. No words seemed adequate to capture the immensity of his emotions.

Instead, he'd let her push him away.

The best thing for the album is for me to be seen dating Bay Stevens.

The words remained imprinted on the darkest recesses of his mind. He couldn't rid himself of them no matter how often he concocted recipes to exorcise those demons—black sesame cakes with a lemon chiffon and bay leaf-infused mousse or black forest cake served with sage gelato.

He'd watched her walk away and then returned to his rented condo, packed his bags, and moved home.

Marlo didn't follow Jude and ask him back. She'd called a few times and cried. She'd sent him a few ranty texts, but in the end, Marlo Sage had chosen her career over Jude. They were so young and he couldn't really blame her, but it hurt all the same. He'd known from the start that the music meant more to her than it had to him. For Jude, it was a distraction of youth. A chance to live a charmed life of travel and room service and performances with his best friend. It had never been his dream. He'd simply been lucky to share the ride with Marlo for a couple of years.

"Ready?" Suze asked, bringing Jude back to the present.

He followed her downstairs to shoot location at the hotel pool. The crew had transformed the space, constructing a shabby chic mini pastry stand that displayed artist-rendered reconstructions of his desserts. Strands of multicolored flags crisscrossed overhead. A dream transformed into life. A dream coated in all too real memory.

"Jude, stand here, and Kaylenne across from him with the guitar," the photographer instructed.

He gave the girl he'd met minutes ago a tight smile. She looked a mix of eager and anxious, tugging a chord of sympathy within him.

"Pretend no else is here," he whispered, compassion winning over his apathy. "It's easier that way."

"Sorry, this is a lot," Kaylenne said, dropping her gaze.

Jude couldn't help himself. He'd always had a weak spot for a girl with a guitar and a desperate dream in her heart. But Kaylenne was no Marlo. She was a generically pretty blonde, industry standard type. Her almost colorless blue eyes weren't windows to the depths of her soul, not like Marlo's were. But he was biased.

“You were made for this life,” he said, giving her a genuine smile. The sooner she felt comfortable, the sooner this would be over. At least that’s what he told himself.

She looked back up at him and exhaled. “Thank you for being so nice.”

Jude wasn’t sure if the driving force behind his words was kindness or selfishness. He could say the things to Kaylenne he’d never had the chance to say to Marlo, and no one would be the wiser.

“Okay, Kaylenne, lean forward,” the photographer said, “and Jude give her a bite of the dessert you’re holding.”

Jude inhaled sharply. For a moment, the girl before him morphed into a specter of the past. Him and Marlo hiding out in a hotel room, Jude feeding her chocolate mousse. He’d perfected the art of no bake confections while they toured.

“Yes, that’s it,” the photographer urged.

After Jude had left his pop music career, he’d returned to his mid-sized hometown in the foothills of Northern California and immersed himself in baking while he attended the local junior college at the urging of his parents before enrolling in culinary school in Napa a year later.

The first few years had been bliss. He’d been so focused on learning, practicing, and dreaming that everything else fell away. His desserts were his refuge. He could speak in the language of pastries and creams, cakes, and croissants, what he couldn’t say aloud. Some people journaled their heartache, others wrote songs, but he crafted delicate, bittersweet morsels.

His business was born and he tended to it with a singular focus. It’s not that he lived like a monk during those years, but he never pursued anything long term. His bakery was his baby. He’d shielded it from wide public view for as long as he could. But as his skill improved, people took notice. Now he was inviting the world in willingly, once again making himself—and now his shop—vulnerable to judgment and criticism.

Yes, so far most of the attention was praise, but still he preferred a quiet life away from the spotlight, away from the prying journalists with the questions that struck old wounds. Away from photo shoots that recreated memories of a chaotic time in his youth. But he also wanted his business to thrive, for his talented staff to receive recognition for their accomplishments, so he accepted the less desirable facets of public attention with an understanding born of maturity.

Jude and Kaylenne continued to run through a series of cute poses at the prompting of the photographer and his staff. The young singer quickly settled into the rhythm and actually appeared to enjoy herself. At least one of them did. Jude just wanted it to be over so he could get back on a plane bound for home.

"We're ready for your close-up, Mr. Beckett." The photographer grinned, dismissing Kaylenne.

Jude wondered how often the older man had uttered the weak joke to clients. Minute by minute, Jude's patience wore thinner.

As Jude stepped into position, the photographer spoke again. "Look at the camera like it's the love of your life."

Jude stared into the lens, and all the emotions and memories surging through him came to the surface. He heard the gasp among the small crowd of assistants. He shifted his glance to Suze, and she mouthed, *Wow*. Damn it, now he'd really done it. He'd given the world a direct window into his deepest secret. His heart, after all the anguish of the intervening years without her, still belonged to Marlo Sage.

Chapter Three

MARLO

THROUGH HALF-SLITTED EYES, Marlo woke to a figure standing over her bed. Her half scream died on her tongue when she registered the familiar mop of blond hair and piercing green eyes. Had the man ever heard of a hairbrush? Though…glass houses. After last night, Marlo must've looked a wreck by morning light.

She sat up, pulling the duvet up to her chin. "Cliff, what the fuck are you doing here?"

"Just checking in on you, love," he said, sitting on the edge of the bed.

"How did you get in?"

He fished a key dangling off a gold chain from inside the neckline of his T-shirt. Marlo reached out to yank it off, but the quickness of the move made her vision swim and her stomach roil.

"Easy there, darling, hangovers are a bitch." He handed her a glass of water from her nightstand.

After a timid sip, she glared at him. "You would know. But, seriously, why are you here?"

"Saw your cute little reunion last night. Stepping out on me, love?"

Marlo groaned and debated dumping the rest of the contents of her water glass over his head. "Not that we were ever really a thing, but we're definitely over."

"Are you talking me or him?" Cliff grinned, revealing cigarette- and wine-stained teeth.

"Funny," Marlo said, swallowing hard. "You know exactly what I mean."

"It's not too late to change your mind. We haven't officially confirmed the rumors."

"I'll convene a press conference right now," she said.

"Might want to shower first. Happy to lend a helping hand."

Marlo shuddered. She couldn't believe that, when their publicists had set up their first date, she'd actually thought there might be potential for something real between them. Being a hopeless romantic was a real bitch. How many times had she broken her own heart with an overactive imagination and a wish for the best despite evidence to the contrary?

"Cliff, seriously, why are you here?" she asked again.

He rubbed the back of his neck. "If I promise to do better, could we renegotiate our arrangement?"

Marlo laughed, gagging on the rancid odor of her own breath. "The last time you were here, I found you in my bed with two other girls and a guy. Have you already forgotten?"

He rolled his eyes. "Marlo, normal shit is so boring. Open your mind."

She pursed her lips. He was like an oversized chihuahua—constantly nipping and yapping.

"Being sexually promiscuous doesn't make you deep," she replied.

"You're already getting heat for skipping the Grammys, and everyone is calling the stunt with Jude a desperate attempt for attention." He put his hand on her bedding covered leg. "Do you really want to add a messy, public breakup to the mix?"

Marlo kicked his hand off. "It doesn't have to be messy. There's no love lost here. Just two grown-ups parting ways."

"Oh yeah, until you eviscerate me in lyrics a year from now? I know how you operate, love."

"Stop calling me that, and you know nothing about me." Marlo bit her tongue. The audacity of thinking he even registered as significant enough for her to write about. Men like him were a dime a dozen in Hollywood.

"I know everything about you, and if you insist on ending things, who knows what I might share."

Marlo caught him unaware, shoving him right off her bed. She cackled when he tumbled to the ground.

"You should see your face," she said, unable to stop laughing.

He jumped up and brushed himself off. Handsome by objective standards, but Marlo knew him too well to see anything but a crass, overgrown cad. Cliff tugged the key on a chain off his neck and tossed it at her. He spun his wrists in a flourish and tipped his head to her.

"I warned you." He smiled at her, a rough glint shining behind his emerald eyes.

"Are you threatening me? In my own house?"

"Calm dawn, princess. It's not really yours. You're just renting."

Realization dawned on Marlo. "Oh my god, you don't have anywhere to go, do you?"

His gaze dropped to the floor. Like so many actors before him, Cliff often succumbed to the darker temptations of the industry.

"That rock 'n' roll lifestyle is gonna kill you, kid," she said, quoting a line from one his biggest box office sensations, annoyed with Cliff for the weak threat but overcome with empathy for his situation all the same.

Cliff's eyes flicked back up to hers. "You're not half as funny as you think."

"I'm not trying to be funny. I'm trying to be a friend."

"I don't do friends," he said, pouting like a petulant tween.

"Yes, you do."

He dropped his chin to his chest and huffed out a laugh. "Yeah, okay, I do."

"Listen," she said. "In all seriousness, if you need a place to stay, I'll have Tara book you a room at Marmont."

"You'd do that?"

"Yeah, we're friends."

"Friends," he repeated. "It's only temporary. I'll find another gig. Franco Santorini is a tyrant. I didn't want to work with him anyway."

Marlo tried to still her face, but it was too late. Santorini was who everyone wanted to work with. His films were nearly guaranteed to win Oscars.

"It's not a big deal," he said. "Stop looking at me like that."

"You haven't spent it all, have you?"

"No, of course not, I'm not an idiot." His gaze flitted around the room, avoiding connecting with hers.

This town was about to swallow Cliff Rochester whole if he didn't change his ways, but his reformation was no longer Marlo's pet project.

"You need to take care of yourself," she said.

"So do you, love," he said, bending forward and placing a kiss on the top of her head. "Seriously, though, get in that shower. You smell foul."

Marlo laughed. "Goodbye."

"Bye," he said, standing back up. "Guess you're taking me off the security roster now?"

"You know the drill."

"Let me know when Tara gets Marmont squared away, doll."

"Will do. Bye, Cliff."

Fake dating had its perks. It made for easy, breezy breakups.

Chapter Four

MARLO

TARA, MARLO'S PUBLICIST, folded her arms across her chest and stared forward, boring holes into the seat back before her. She'd been prickly since Marlo's impromptu karaoke reunion with Jude a couple of weeks ago, busy fielding inquiries from media outlets around the world. Video clips of that night spread virally on numerous platforms and showed no signs of abating.

"Thanks, Marlo," she'd said, the last words they'd shared. "There's nothing I love more than playing whack-a-mole."

Tara hadn't even offered Marlo more than a customary, clipped greeting when she joined her in the car a few minutes ago. She sighed loudly. It wasn't like the mini reunion was Marlo's idea. Finally, Tara shifted to face her but still didn't utter a single word.

Marlo blew out her breath. "Tara, please say something, anything."

Tara's well-manicured brows arched so high they nearly touched her hairline. "I am out of things to say, habibti."

Tara Alrasheed was of Egyptian and Iraqi descent, which is why

Marlo felt a special affinity toward her. Her own father, Sami, née Samir Rayhan, was born to Iraqi immigrant parents. Sadly, Marlo never met her grandparents. They'd died in a car accident just before she was born. So aside from her father, Tara was her only other link to her roots. Her grasp on which, a tenuous thread at best, slipped more with each passing year. Marlo's dad understood spoken Arabic, spoke broken informal Iraqi Arabic himself, but he couldn't read or write it. Marlo only knew the words he and Tara sprinkled into their vocabulary.

Marlo's stage name was another contrivance designed to obscure her heritage. Sage was the moniker the label assigned to her as a quasi play on words—a more palatable herb-related name than her father's own Rayhan, Arabic for basil, because the public couldn't possibly be expected to remember the correct pronunciation of the original.

Even before she'd earned her celebrity status, Marlo still hadn't completely felt a part of the world she inhabited. Working with Tara, though, anchored her, reminding Marlo that there were other people like her—Arab Americans trying to carve their niche in a place apathetic to them at best but, more often than not, outright hostile.

"It wasn't my idea," Marlo repeated. "I'm sorry. It just happened."

"Nothing *just* happens. Besides, are you telling me that deciding to bail on the Grammys a week beforehand wasn't your idea?"

Right, she'd been so distracted with thoughts of Jude, she'd forgotten the earlier transgression. Of course Tara was furious. She'd been stretched thin fighting brush fires on every front for Marlo. The label expected Marlo to attend the awards, and she'd defied them and chosen not to instead, leaving Tara to face the fallout on her own. She and Tara were supposed to be partners, but clearly Marlo sucked at being a partner in all things, if her past was any indication.

"The album wasn't even nominated in a single category." Tears pricked the back of Marlo's eyes. She truly didn't write music for the accolades.

Well, not only. She laid her heart bare on every record, excavating her own life for inspiration. But her latest album was an even deeper exercise in vulnerability as muse. She was deeply proud of the work. She'd pushed herself lyrically and sonically so far beyond her comfort zone that Marlo had even surprised herself. Not having her efforts acknowledged hurt in a way she hadn't anticipated. Marlo hadn't even noticed that she'd started taking the attention and the awards for granted. She'd never spared a thought for what to do if that aspect of her career disappeared. She'd never had a plan B. It terrified her.

"Like I keep saying, sour grapes," Tara said, finally looking over at Marlo. Whatever she saw softened the tense set of her features. "It was a great fucking album. The fans love it. I love it."

A tear streamed down Marlo's face. "Obviously it wasn't good enough. My next one has to be better."

"The Grammys aren't a meritocracy. It's no reflection on your value as an artist." Tara reached over and squeezed Marlo's hand.

She wished Tara's encouragement was all she needed to hear, but it wasn't. Marlo was hardwired to want more.

"I need to work harder," she said.

"Maybe you need a break." Tara resumed her forward-facing, statue-like posture.

"Any idea what this meeting is about?" Marlo asked, ignoring the last statement.

She was always urging Marlo to take breaks, but Marlo was afraid if she stepped away too long, released her foot from the gas even an inch, she'd lose it all.

"None, everyone's quite tight-lipped," Tara said. "Some whispers about asking you to mentor Kaylenne."

Marlo saw it then, the tense set of her publicist's shoulders, the way she gripped her hands together in her lap. Tara was worried. David Stringer didn't invite them to lunch without reason, especially not at Orchid & Ivy. He wanted a public record of this tête-à-tête. Otherwise he would have chosen a more discrete locale, say the actual Pop Machine headquarters, where his office occupied half of the top floor.

They were stepping into a trap.

"Ready?" Tara asked as the car slowed.

"Am I ever ready for David and his machinations?" Marlo answered, adjusting her oversized sunglasses as she pulled her hair forward to obscure as much of her face as possible.

She followed tightly behind Tara as they crossed to the restaurant's front door, both of them flanked on either side by several dozen telephoto lenses pointed in their direction by the most obnoxious paparazzi LA had to offer. At least they were somewhat held at bay by the barrier the restaurant erected to keep the path to the entrance open. A tacit agreement between the two parties: the restaurant remained a constant fixture in the papers and thus a tourist trap that could justify charging twenty dollars for a plate of duck fat-fried potato shoestrings—no one called them French fries at that price—and the paparazzi maintained a presence that typically attracted C-list celebrities, desperate for any press. But at Marlo Sage-levels of pop stardom, it was a truth universally acknowledged that not all press was good press.

"I despise Orchid & Ivy," she whispered to Tara, her hand shielding her mouth.

"David invited us here to get under your skin," Tara replied. "Don't let him."

Marlo shook her head. The president of her record label had a thing for mixing business with treachery. She had signed with him at a young age. All the contracts as vetted by her parents, and the only lawyer they could afford at the time, seemed above board, but they'd been naive to the ways a man with bad intentions and deep pockets could sink his claws into a rising star's career. He'd made it damn near impossible for her to extricate herself from his clutches. When fame was involved, there was always some degree of dealing with the devil.

The leers and shouts from the paparazzi grew more aggressive the closer they stepped to the entrance. It was tough to survive in LA and harder yet when any kid with a cell phone could land the scoop of the week. Understanding the motivations of the camera hawks didn't make stomaching their methods any easier, even after all these years.

"Can you confirm the relationship with Cliff ended due to infidelity?" one reporter shouted.

"Marlo, was that little performance with Jude an informal announcement of a reunion?" another of the shutter gnats yelled at her, his voice rising above the rest.

She'd trained for these moments like an Olympic athlete. She'd ignored the grossest of insults, the worst of innuendos. But all her restraint disappeared at the sound of Jude's name. Marlo turned around, pushed her sunglasses up, and looked directly into the smirking face of the offending paparazzo.

Damn it, I just gave him his shot.

No doubt she'd see that picture plastered all over magazines and social media for at least the next week. The birth of another meme.

"Inside." Tara spun her back around and practically pushed her into the restaurant. "Keep your cool."

Marlo wasn't sure why the photog's question unsettled her so much, other than the fact that she still hadn't truly processed the random run-in with Jude herself. It was almost as if she'd dreamed it, but they'd been inundated with proof of it. Marlo thought maybe he'd call afterward, but it had been two weeks without so much as a text. Plus, she was already agitated about this mysterious lunch meeting.

"Focus, Marlo."

Tara's admonishment reminded Marlo that her publicist was equally rattled about this meeting. There was nothing David Stringer loved more than ambushing his recording artists. Asking Marlo to mentor a new-on-the-scene country star seemed the thinnest of guises, and if it was the true reason for the meeting, it didn't make sense why it needed to happen at this celebrity cesspool.

The hostess greeted them, unfazed by Marlo's presence, and she appreciated her ambivalence. "Follow me," she said.

"Do you think he's mad that the album never hit the number one spot?" Marlo whispered to Tara. "Or about the Grammys?"

"Habibti, he could be mad that the sky is blue and somehow find a way to blame you. But he'd have a point with the Grammys."

Tara's words did nothing to settle Marlo's nerves.

They turned a corner to find David sitting in a booth with a smug grin plastered across his face as his newest acquisition, nineteen-year-old Kaylenne Daughtry, sat tucked between him and another middle-aged man. Marlo didn't often forget a face, but she couldn't quite place the man in question.

"Sweetheart, like I was saying, an angry woman behind a microphone is a bad investment. The public wants sweet and sexy. No one cares what you think about anything, isn't that right, Marlo?" His gaze fixed on her even as he continued to pet his new plaything.

An angry woman behind a microphone is dangerous.

David's perpetual mantra echoed in her head. Every time Marlo dared to speak publicly about any issue David Stringer repeated the edict.

Honey, they just want to see you prance around stage and shake your ass.

He refused to understand why she couldn't shut up and stand down. He wanted her to simply ignore the world in turmoil and not use her platform and privilege to speak out against injustice. David wanted his female recording artists pliant and reverential. Marlo's struggle to fit the tight mold he'd set for her grew into a bigger source of tension between them day by day.

Realization again dawned on Marlo. He'd invited her and Tara here to prove that she was replaceable, nothing special. A sentiment he'd never hesitated to share, even as he'd used the profits earned from her hard work to live an increasingly lavish life.

"Am I here for you to scold me because I endorsed Senatorial candidate Bettany Ruiz?" Marlo asked.

David laughed. "You flatter yourself, Marlo. No one pays you any mind. You can't even hit the top of the chart your first week out anymore."

Marlo stood taller. "I've held the number two spot for eight months straight. The tour last summer sold out."

"And yet the most positive press you've received lately was for that pitiful karaoke stint with Jude."

Marlo opened and shut her mouth as she grasped for any response. None came.

David continued to stare at her, his lips twisted in his trademark obnoxious sneer. "Not a single Grammy nomination," he said. "Remember what I told you when we heard the demo tracks? No one likes—"

"If no one pays Marlo any mind, then why ask her to mentor Kaylenne?" Tara interjected. "That is the reason you called us here, correct?"

David's eyes flared in a combination of anger and surprise. He hated being interrupted, especially by a woman. "Among other reasons. You didn't allow me to introduce my other guest."

Marlo's stomach knotted. She studied the other man's face again, unable to pull his name from the haze of her memory.

"Speaking of demos," David continued. "The decision on your latest submission was unanimous."

Marlo's gaze shifted to the young woman, who sat up straighter watching the volley between Marlo, Tara, and David. She wanted to yank Kaylenne out of the booth and give her a big sisterly chat about how she didn't need the likes of David Stringer to succeed. *Don't make the mistake I did.*

"And?" Tara asked.

His mouth slowly curled upward. "It's a no."

The floor dropped out from beneath Marlo. Maintaining full creative control of her albums was her red line. David promised that, as long as she shared her progress, the label would not interfere with her vision. She wrote and composed her own music, chose her own producers and musicians, collaborated with others on her terms. She'd played by David's rules, mostly, simply to maintain this level of control over her creative vision. Ripping it away from her was the ultimate betrayal.

"Allow me to introduce your new record producer," David was saying, "Tim—"

"Barrow," Marlo completed, finally recognizing the man in question.

"We didn't agree to this," Tara said.

"It's not your choice," David said. "Remember, Marlo?"

A sharp stab of pain lanced through Marlo's chest. How could she forget? She'd signed a terrible new contract with the label just after her nineteenth birthday—her first decision as an independent adult when she'd been between publicists and too green to realize she needed her own legal team, one that looked out for her and not the Pop Machine plant that considered only the label's interests. She'd purposely avoided seeking advice from her parents. She'd wanted to prove to everyone that she was fine on her own. A true adult with the adult capacity to make her own business decisions. But she'd made the critical mistake of trusting that David would protect her. She was his top earning asset after all.

"Your team will be hearing from ours," Tara said.

But the hollow threat meant nothing without any legal standing to back it up. David refused all Tara's attempts to renegotiate the terms of Marlo's predatory contract. He wouldn't even agree to allow Marlo to buy back her masters, no matter how much she offered. To him, this was a game of control, and so far, he'd always won.

"Did you want to tell them about your exciting photo shoot a couple of weeks ago, Kaylenne?" David asked.

Marlo's teeth clenched as David continued to torment her.

The young woman pressed herself into the booth cushion behind her as if hoping it would swallow her whole. She cleared her throat. "Uh… yes, a cute shoot with Desserts Monthly."

"I'm not familiar with it," Marlo said, unsure of the nature of David's latest game.

"That's right. Kaylenne, remind me with whom?" The way David continued to leer at the young singer made bile rise up the back of Marlo's throat.

Fully caught in his snare, she couldn't see a way out.

The girl looked down at her lap, at last seeming to grasp that she was simply present as a pawn in David's game. Marlo hated that for her. David Stringer only cared about David Stringer, and the sooner Kaylenne learned that lesson, the better. God knew, it took Marlo too long to learn it herself.

"We're done here. Thank you for the invitation, but I've lost my appetite." Marlo started to turn away, but for the second time in the span of minutes, a familiar name uttered on a stranger's lips pinned her in place.

"Jude Beckett," the young girl said.

This time, Marlo didn't glance back. She refused to give David the pleasure of seeing her reaction. Jude Beckett was ancient history. No amount of karaoke duets would change that. Questions flooded her mind, but she'd be damned before she ever asked David or his flavor of the week a single one of them.

"Former Prince of Pop-turned-baker with baker's daughter-turned-Country Music Princess. Cute, no?" David called out behind her.

Marlo straightened her back and marched out of the restaurant.

Thankfully, Tara must have notified the driver to circle back because he pulled up just as she reached the curb.

Tara caught up to Marlo just as she was about to enter the car. "Well, never a dull moment with David Stringer."

"Did you know about this photo shoot?" Marlo asked.

"Of course not. I would never have let you walk in there if I'd known." After a pause, Tara added. "Kudos to keeping your cool, all things considered. That Tim Barrow surprise was a low blow."

Marlo feigned cool, but blazing flames licked inside her veins. Now she finally knew why Jude Beckett had returned to town. She couldn't believe he'd come back to do the very things he'd claimed he hated about celebrity life like photo shoots. Worse, David Stringer rubbed the knowledge in her face. Tim Barrow? Fucking seriously?!

Sure, Tim was a successful producer, but his overbearing reputation proceeded. He didn't so much work with artists but rather dictated his vision to them. Marlo supposed for a certain subset of her colleagues his style suited them, but she wasn't used to ceding creative control.

The pressure built in Marlo's chest—an eruption looming. She tried to focus on steadying her breaths.

"Marlo," one of the paparazzi called out. "How was your meeting?"

She huffed out a tight laugh.

"Get in the car," Tara said.

Marlo hesitated, turning around before letting herself really think through the implications of what she was about to do.

An angry woman behind a microphone is dangerous.

The warning buzzed in her ears, barely louder than Tara's pleas. Marlo was tired of hiding behind the carefully constructed public persona she'd been forced to assume all these years. Signing a record deal as a green, starry-eyed teenage girl shouldn't have meant permanently signing her soul over. She was tired of hiding behind a brave smile.

“Was the performance with Jude a publicity stunt?” another man, hiding behind a low-slung baseball cap and dark sunglasses, asked.

“No,” Marlo barked back, voice thick with emotion.

“Calm down, sweetheart. It’s just a question,” he answered.

Marlo’s male counterparts never had to temper their speech publicly or privately, but she’d been forced to scrutinize every word she uttered—every tone, every item she wore, every step she took until she morphed into nothing more than a shell built of strategy and marketability and, most damning, elusive likability.

“It’s funny,” she said as the jockeying crowd of photogs stilled. “If I dare have a couple of drinks with my friends or date someone, I’m eviscerated by you guys.” Even as the words tumbled out of her mouth, she couldn’t stop herself. “David Stringer fucks over every single woman at his label, not to mention the ones he actually just fucks, every chance he gets, and he’s a hero.”

Marlo had never heard paparazzi go silent. And yet they had. Not even a click of a single shutter.

Tara took advantage of the lull to shove her into the waiting car. “Get in,” Tara said, her tone razor sharp, then barked at the chauffeur, “Drive.”

Marlo watched the buildings zip by as her phone exploded with notifications. The earlier blaze of her anger dulled into faint embers.

“What did you just do?” Tara said, fingers flying over her phone keyboard.

“I…I lost it,” Marlo admitted.

Between Jude, Tim Barrow, and her new demo being panned, Marlo’s remaining fucks exited the building the moment she’d opened her mouth. David succeeded in pushing her too far. She loved to make music, but hadn’t she already paid a steep enough price? She’d sacrificed any semblance of a normal life, she lived under a rigid regimen of exercise and nutrition, and now they expected her to yield to the label’s vision for her next album. No, she wouldn’t do it.

"I'm sorry, Tara," Marlo added.

Tara's lips flattened into a tight smile. "It's fine. We'll figure something out. At least that clip of you and Jude is still generating lots of positive interactions."

Marlo stopped herself from rolling her eyes. It was aggravating that Jude still had the ability to sway public opinion of her. "All I want is the one thing Pop Machine refuses to give me—permission to be my authentic self, battle scars, mistakes, and all. I want to make the music I want to make. I want to own my songs."

Tara pinched the bridge of her nose. "Ya wayli, you just went after the president of the label. You're not making it easy to plead your case."

Marlo swallowed hard. "I'm hardly a loose cannon. I just had a bad day."

"How many more of those can I expect?"

She didn't answer. She knew Tara was doing her job, but Marlo was a person with feelings and even she could be pushed too far sometimes. This was one of those times. She was so tired of explaining herself.

"Anyway," Tara said, "maybe consider keeping a low profile for a bit until this all blows over."

"Do you ever get tired of all this?" Marlo asked, dropping her head against the cool glass of the passenger door window.

"I can't afford to. It's my job."

Marlo blinked back tears. "I'm afraid. I'm not sure how many years of this are left for me."

Tara sighed. "I know, but you're nowhere near being done unless you want to be. You're a seasoned artist. Your best years remain ahead of you."

Marlo swallowed back the lump in her throat. She longed to believe Tara's words, but she feared her best had already started vanishing in the rear view. She could count on her hands the number of teen pop stars who continued to have a career past their thirties.

"Sometimes you have to accept that you can't affect change just by screaming into the void," Tara said. "I've been working with your lawyers to see if we have any way to get you out of your contract with Pop Machine for the last album that you owe them. I need your trust and patience."

Trust and patience were other things fame had stolen from Marlo. She'd do her best to summon them for Tara's sake and everyone else whose jobs relied on her, but she wouldn't make any promises she couldn't keep.

Marlo needed to figure out how to wrench control of her career away from the cold, dead-inside hands of the current stewards who didn't deserve it or her. She had to grab that microphone and never let it go. But for now, Marlo Sage was done. Done with LA, done with the press, and most of all, done with Pop Machine. She stared at a wall of her own making with a crystal-clear message written upon it—her pop star days were numbered if she didn't regain stewardship of her music. Maybe it was time to disappear until she was ready to come back stronger than they could ever imagine.

Chapter Five

JUDE

THE LATEST MAGAZINE feature further catapulted the pastry shop, These Delicate Delights, into the national spotlight. The store had been inundated since the positive review hit. At least Jude told himself it was only due to the food critic's kind words and not to Marlo's reemergence in his life. Clips of their mini reunion remained everywhere online. He was forced to institute a no cell phone policy in his shop to stop the recordings from being incessantly played.

In the three weeks since he'd returned home, he hadn't heard from Marlo, both a relief and exquisite torture all at once. But he wasn't about to change his rule now—if she wanted to initiate contact, he'd respond, but he'd be damned if he was the one to call or text first. Though the rationale for his stance grew weaker by the day.

"Did you see this, Jude?" his assistant chef, Penny, asked. "There are actual petitions circulating to get you and Marlo back into the studio together."

Jude groaned. "I don't want to hear it, Pen."

"Are you sure you don't want to sign it?" She teased.

He politely declined, reminding her that the shop was his safe place. A Marlo-free zone. At least it used to be. Now he was tempted to turn over the reins altogether to Penny Garner and leave town forever. Or at least until the frenzy died down.

"Have you talked to her?" Penny asked. "Since?"

"No and I don't intend to. It was a fluke coincidence, we had a moment, and it's history."

Penny's eyes remained downcast, focused on the dough she kneaded, but he could see her fighting not to smile.

"There's been no contact from her end either," he added, tone gruffer than he intended.

His cell phone rang, and he answered it without checking the caller ID first. Rookie move.

"Jude Beckett, can I help you?" he asked, as he absently inventoried the dry ingredients.

"I sure hope so," said an oddly eager male voice. "Was that karaoke concert a publicity stunt to drum up business for your bakery?"

Jude hung up. The phone at the shop rang nonstop, and Jude continued to receive offers from every daytime and late-night talk show, magazine, and podcast for interviews. Only they weren't calling to talk to him about pastries. Suze was on strict orders to tell everyone who reached out to her no as well. He was done—no more interviews, no more photo shoots unless the focus was solely on the shop. Fame hadn't been his friend before. He was happy to promote his pastry work, but he wasn't looking to reenter the public sphere the way he'd once occupied it.

Suze reminded him that, if his ultimate goal was to publish a cookbook—the dream he'd only dared share with Suze and Penny—then he'd have to tolerate the media attention and, more so, capitalize on it while it was available.

"Another interview request?" Penny asked.

"Yeah, at least this guy didn't ask if it was a publicity stunt to build sympathy for Marlo ahead of the Cliff Rochester bombshell interview. That's what I've been getting most lately." Jude groaned.

The celebrity machine had a way of taking something beautiful and morphing it into the basest of human interests. These journalists and hosts didn't want to talk to him about his love of baking or about Marlo's musical talents. They wanted to probe into their relationship and pry about why he walked away from his music career just as it rocketed into the stratosphere. They wanted him to answer for why he'd left Marlo, and the last thing Jude wanted to talk about was his complicated history with Marlo Sage. They were trying to gather evidence to indict Marlo in the public sphere once again on the heels of another breakup.

The bell over the door chimed. It played a mini jingle version of an early Marlo and Jude hit, "You're the only Sweet I Need." It was a kitschy homage to his former persona, and his customers got a kick out of it. But in light of everything recently, he'd begun to question its wisdom.

"I'll be right there," he called out from the back.

Only one tray of vegan donuts and a half dozen marionberry croissants remained. Everything else had sold out, and he was due to close in less than an hour. They didn't usually get much foot traffic at this time anyway.

Jude froze mid-step when he heard someone singing.

"Who needs sugar, when I got you, honey."

He recognized that voice. But it was impossible. No fucking way. He started moving again but in quiet, deliberate steps like he was afraid of spooking a ghost. The tray wobbled in his hand, but he managed to steady it and set it on the front counter.

Marlo Sage stood inside his shop, singing the tune that had launched them into mega stardom.

Forget seeing her in the karaoke bar—this was the singularly most unexpected place he could ever have conceived of seeing her again. Her lips curved up and it knocked the breath out of him. This was the real Marlo, no artifice, minimal makeup. He'd forgotten the power of her sincere smile.

"Marlo," he said, barely above a whisper.

He inventoried her in a way he couldn't at the crowded bar. She was the same but different. Her dark eyes looked wiser, learned in a way that made the pit of his stomach ache. Despite her bright smile, he saw sadness in her eyes. Her hair was longer and darker now than it had been when they were younger. He remembered how the summer sun painted streaks of golden red in her hair when they spent their days tubing down the river.

Jude opened his mouth to speak, but no words emerged. Marlo apparently still wielded the power to send him into multi-system organ failure.

She scanned the bakery and returned her gaze to him, pointing out the color scheme. "Teal with black-and-white polka dots."

He couldn't help himself—he smiled. The design of the shop was a less overt nod to Marlo. One only she'd recognize, his guilty secret indulgence. It was the colors and pattern of the dress she wore for their faux prom. They were touring while the rest of their high school celebrated senior prom, and he'd known she'd been sad about missing the teen rite of passage. So, he'd planned a secret mini prom after their show. It was the same night he'd given her a custom-made necklace of their intertwined first initials—his first big jewelry purchase. An unspoken promise that he'd break less than a year later.

"Yeah, it worked with the ambiance I was going for here." Jude's cheeks warmed, and he hoped she didn't notice.

She nodded and scanned the store again before stepping closer. The urge to wrap her in a hug or ask her to leave and never return warred within him. Was it possible to love and hate someone all at once? They'd shared some the best moments of his life together, but they'd also been the source of each other's deepest hurts. Whoever said time dulled old wounds was a damn liar.

"Do I get the friend and family discount?" She gestured to the tray of donuts. Holy fuck, she licked her lips.

Her presence here spelled trouble. He knew it in his bones. But he couldn't help smiling. He'd dreamed of seeing her in his shop.

"On the house," he said as he presented her one.

Her smile softened as her fingers brushed his. He wondered if the same spark at the contact sizzled beneath her skin. She sniffed the donut first, and then she took a bite, closing her eyes and sighing.

Jude's blood thundered through his veins. Unspeakable reactions cascaded through him. Watching Marlo eat his food shouldn't be so alluring, and yet he couldn't tear his eyes from her.

"Jude," she whispered, "this is heaven."

He beamed at the compliment. He hadn't realized how desperately he'd yearned for her validation. "It's called Heartbreak Hotel."

She paused, considering for a moment. "Bittersweet chocolate and bursts of berry."

Marlo understood him in a way most people didn't. Of course she'd immediately discerned the flavor profile. She'd always had an eye for detail.

Then she took another bite. She looked up at him with widened eyes. "Sage."

The word hung in the air between them. He wanted to explain, but he read the shifting emotions on her face—hurt, sadness, and then anger. How was he supposed to admit that he'd spent the years away from her trying to work out just what went wrong between them by baking it into desserts?

She set the half-eaten donut down on a napkin and stepped forward, scanning the nameplates of the long-disappeared desserts. She paused at the one at the end of the glass case and looked back at him with narrowed eyes.

"Lady Ambition," she read.

It was his most popular confection—a gravity-defying take on a mille-feuille, light layers of airy pastry filled with alternating tart lemon chiffon creme and dark chocolate drizzled raspberries, topped with a silhouette of a woman reaching for the sky rendered in a delicate wafer of white chocolate.

"Marlo," he pleaded, watching her posture tighten.

She laughed, but he heard the unmistakable chord of tension beneath it. "Well," she said, "I knew coming here would be a colossal mistake. But I guess you know better than anyone that I have trouble listening to my instincts, blinded as I am by ambition."

"Are you angry?" Jude knew the answer but asked anyway.

"This place." She gestured all around her. "It's like an entire business that exists to take digs at me."

Emotion flared inside him. "Jesus, not everything is about you."

"Oh the color scheme isn't about me? The chime over the door isn't about me? I'm a fucking flavor in your donut. But it's not about me?"

"You don't taste like sage." The words came out before he thought better of them.

They stood staring at each other as excruciatingly uncomfortable minutes ticked by. Jude wished he could rewind time and take it all back.

Storm clouds gathered behind her eyes. "You built an entirely new persona and profession designed to troll me."

"What about your songs? I've lost count of how many are about me," he said.

"Oh my god." Marlo shook her head, incredulous. "You didn't even try to deny it."

"Neither did you," he retorted.

They squared off, eyes narrowed at each other, neither uttering a word.. They'd already said too much.

"Are you sure it's me that you're mad at? Or is it yourself?" Jude said, anger thrumming in his ears.

"What is that supposed to mean?"

He wanted to say something about the Cliff Rochester interview. He wanted, needed to hear her denial, which was ridiculous because she was a grown woman and what she chose to do in a private relationship wasn't his or anyone else's business. He didn't judge the alleged behavior, maybe just her taste in boyfriends. But the Marlo he'd known would never have done those things.

Jude exhaled. No, this was simply good old-fashioned jealousy, and he didn't retain any claim to her. He didn't have the right to ask.

"Why are you even here?" he asked. "I didn't think you remembered I existed."

Damn it, he'd meant to keep his cool. What was he even saying? It didn't matter what she answered to that question. She had as much right to be here as any customer. Jude was losing his damn mind.

"I came here to let you know I'm back for a bit. It's a small town, and your parents invited us over for dinner tomorrow. I didn't want you to be blindsided. I know how our mothers are." She walked back over to him. "But obviously you're never going to let bygones go?"

Back for a bit? What did that mean? Jude pinched the inside of his bicep. Was he dreaming? "Bygones?"

"You and me." She stared at him with pitying eyes, and he couldn't take her looking at him like that.

"I'm the one who left you, remember?" He ran his hand through his hair. His brain short-circuited, causing him to say the exact wrong thing at the exact wrong moment.

Marlo plastered a fake smile on her face. "Keep telling yourself it was a good choice. Maybe one day you'll believe it."

She turned on her heel and walked out. The chime over the door taunted him. He summoned every shred of his remaining willpower not to leap up and tear it off the wall. He flipped the open sign to closed and returned to the donut tray on the counter, dumping the remaining ones into the trash.

Penny stepped out from the kitchen. "Hey, boss, you okay? That sounded pretty intense."

Jude turned around. As if the argument hadn't been bad enough, he'd forgotten Penny was still here. She obviously overheard it all, judging by her pinched expression. He prided himself on maintaining an atmosphere of civility at his shop, devoid of the big egos and toxic atmospheres that poisoned so many professional kitchens. Usually, this included keeping his personal life separate from the shop.

"Sorry about that, Pen," he said. "An old friend."

Penny waggled her dark brows at him. "You mean *the* old friend?"

Jude sighed. "Can we drop it for now and go back to the menus for tomorrow?"

She gave him the obnoxious smirk she usually reserved for when she caught him making a critical baking error. "Sure, menus."

He tried to focus on his work, but he couldn't stop replaying Marlo's disastrous visit. If she'd given him fair warning that she'd intended to visit, he would have at least mentally prepared himself. Instead, she'd blindsided him in her attempt not to blindside him.

He'd worked so hard to cultivate a life of his own choosing, and now Marlo was back. Jude wasn't sure he could easily explain to her why it had been worth abandoning her to save himself. Part of him always wished his departure would have been the catalyst for Marlo to finally see that no dream was worth tolerating David Stringer to achieve. He shook out his hands and jumped up and down a couple of times. This was the problem with Marlo—she crawled under his skin, burrowed in deep, and she was damn near impossible to excise.

Jude hadn't planned to relive the past. He didn't even want to make peace like she'd just offered. He simply wanted to forget that chapter of his life.

Liar.

He glanced around. Even in the kitchen, he catalogued dozens of little easter eggs of his pop star life, dozens of reminders of Marlo he kept near.

"I can close up if you want to take off," Penny offered after they'd finalized the next day's menus.

"Nah, I'm going to stay. I've been thinking of a new clafoutis recipe."

After Penny left, Jude fetched fresh sour cherries, amaretto, and the other ingredients he needed to create the thick, custardy batter. He laid them out on his work surface. Something was missing. He walked back into the refrigerator and scanned the shelves. Then his eyes landed on the missing piece—basil.

Chapter Six

MARLO

MARLO SHOULD HAVE known better than to doubt Tara's ability to transform a plea into action. Her publicist convinced Pop Machine to give Marlo the summer off to sort out her affairs before returning to the studio to work with the new producer on the reimagined version of her next album. Marlo's life would've turned out so different if Tara had been around earlier in her career.

Regret that tasted like tears clogged the back of Marlo's throat.

She slammed the door to her dad's sedan and stabbed the ignition button with her index finger. She'd intended her visit to the bakery to be a magnanimous extension of an olive branch to Jude, but she hadn't expected the whole place to be a living memorial to their former life.

Her temper had bested her. A real adult would march right back into the bakery and apologize. But she wasn't ready to grow up just yet.

Gripping the steering wheel, Marlo screamed as music blasted through the speakers.

She tried not to play the what-if game, but the older she got, the more she struggled to avoid it. Her fame kept her pinned to the version of herself she'd been at fifteen when she'd first garnered public attention. But she was no longer that Marlo. She'd changed and yet the label didn't want her music to refl ect her natural growth both as an artist and as a person. Neither did the media.

It stung even worse that Jude only saw her through that same lens.

"I'm not the same girl," she said to the empty vehicle, hating the wobble in her voice.

Marlo rolled her shoulders, sitting taller in her dad's beloved old Jetta. She'd offered to buy him a new car so often, but he always refused.

"I love my little Azeeza," he'd say, lovingly tapping the top of the silver car.

Marlo turned down the music and dialed Tara's number.

"Hey, are you sure I can't go hide on a remote island somewhere?" Marlo asked after they exchanged greetings.

"I'm afraid the beach isn't cutting it," Tara said.

"What do you mean?"

"How many tropical vacations have you taken? Has a single one changed your perspective on your life or career?"

"Well, not exactly—"

"This time you need to be home," Tara said. "You have unfinished business to address."

Marlo rolled her lower lip between her teeth. As much as she hated to admit it, Tara was right. Singing with Jude again at karaoke cracked open the crypt of long-buried history between them. Marlo couldn't shake the sense that their story hadn't yet reached its conclusion—it had simply been shelved.

Still, that didn't mean she was thrilled to be back in Gold Hills.

She loved her parents, enjoyed their extended visits at her house or when they joined her on tour. But returning to the backdrop of all her memories with Jude Beckett hadn't proved remotely restful or restorative.

"Listen, habibti," Tara said, gentling her tone, "take the time to sort everything out and then come back renewed and ready to work."

"Cliff keeps—"

Tara cut in. "Cliff's clock is ticking. Let me handle it. Plus, your parents are so happy to have you home."

Marlo was pop's version of Benjamin Button, maturing in reverse. She'd left home as a teen and now had to seek refuge in her childhood home as an adult. If she could even call herself one. She couldn't even manage her day-to-day affairs alone. She had a team for that.

"I have another client calling," Tara said. "We'll catch up later."

Marlo hung up the call and drove the long way home.

~

Marlo flopped onto the couch and groaned. Three minutes was all it had taken for her and Jude's exchange to sour. If she was truly stuck in Gold Hills for the summer, they needed to find a way to live companionably in the small town. Her first attempt to broker peace imploded in her face. She had to do better next time.

Heather: How's life in the Hills treating you?

Marlo: Ugh, don't ask

Heather: Miss you!

Marlo: Me too

Heather: Sorry about Cliff. If you need to talk, I'm here for you.

Marlo: I'm okay

Marlo wasn't entirely surprised that Cliff Rochester seized the opportunity to line his empty pockets by appearing on every podcast and talk show that would have him. Her survival instinct ran strong too. She simply wished he wouldn't tell so many salacious lies about their relationship. Especially since, up until a couple of days ago, Marlo was still footing his bills at Chateau Marmont.

Still, her skin hadn't stopped crawling. The louse made her out to be a depraved nympho on shows with millions of subscribers or viewers. Marlo didn't judge the sexual appetites of others, but she took issue with his lies about her and their alleged carnal pursuits. Plus, if they'd actually been in a real relationship, airing their private moments would've been a serious betrayal.

It was bad enough the whole world was weighing in on her nonexistent sex life, but the fact that her family and friends were subjected to hearing about it mortified her.

At least her family and Jude's were well-versed in sidestepping problematic press coverage about her. She just hoped they knew her well enough to know Cliff was lying. About everything. No, she did not like her toes being sucked by strangers, and she did not need at least two extra lovers in bed at once to orgasm.

Marlo pulled a throw pillow over her face and screamed into it.

When they'd spoken earlier, Tara advised Marlo not to respond to media inquiries and to wait for the story to blow over. Marlo preferred the prospect of retribution. She really wanted to expose Cliff for the damn liar he was.

"Sweetheart, you're back so soon. How was it?" Marlo's mom walked into the family room and joined her on the couch, gently nudging her legs off the couch, forcing her into a seated position.

"Cordial for about two seconds and then we just exploded at each other." Marlo skipped telling her mom that Jude looked even better than he had at karaoke. He appeared so at home in his pastry shop in his black chef's uniform. Comfortable in his skin in a way he'd never been on stage with her. The truth in that observation still smarted, and Marlo refused to explore the reason why. Then they'd started talking and it all spiraled out of control.

"Hmmm," her dad said as he hovered at the edge of the room.

Marlo hadn't heard him join them, but he tended to stick close to her mom. They were the definition of inseparable. He shared a quick glance with her mom before wedging himself in on Marlo's other side and creating parental bookends around her.

"Ugh, you guys, what? Just say it." Marlo looked between her parents.

"Well, things between the two of you ended pretty abruptly, and you never really had a chance to talk about it," her dad said.

He echoed Tara's sentiment. It was singularly annoying. Plus, Marlo recognized his *lecture incoming* tone.

"Can't anyone in this fucking town let anything go?" she said. "It was years ago."

Her mom tsked at her. She hated when Marlo cursed. This was the problem with returning home—it instantly infantilized her.

Her dad continued. "It was years ago, but you were best friends, maybe more, and there are some hurts that linger. You need to find a way to make peace."

Make peace. Why did everyone keep saying that? What did that even mean?

Besides, she'd tried. It was no surprise her parents sided with Jude. They'd always loved him. He was the one who came back, so they saw him more often than they did her. Gold Hills, though victim to suburban sprawl, remained a relatively small town, and they'd stayed best friends with the elder Becketts.

"I went there like you asked," she continued. "He wasn't even willing to meet me halfway."

Her mom nodded, chewing her lower lip but not saying a word. Her dad remained eerily silent too.

"Also, some warning might have been nice," Marlo said. "Neither of you ever told me the whole place was a weird tribute to all the ways I wronged him. I mean that's pretty fu—messed up."

"I don't think it's meant as an affront to you. I think he uses his life as inspiration for his creations. Sound familiar?" Her dad smiled.

Marlo bristled. Sure, she drew from her own life for song lyrics, but it wasn't the same. Yes, she'd written a handful of songs, including a few on the new album, about Jude, but she had a complete body of work that had nothing to do with him. He, on the other hand, had memorialized all the shitty parts of their relationship. Her parents should see the difference and just how deeply insulting it was.

How long before the rabid celebrity reporters sniffing around his shop caught wind? If that story broke, it would haunt Marlo everywhere. Especially on the heels of Cliff's stories about her. She saw exactly how it would all play out—Marlo Sage broke Jude's heart, but he found a sweet way to turn heartache into success. He'd be the media darling, even more than he already was, the wronged young man that pulled himself up from adversity. She'd be the cold, calculating career-and-sex-obsessed pop star who stomped on everyone in her path. That framing definitely sounded familiar.

Something Tara had said gnawed at her. "Cliff isn't clever enough to have orchestrated his current media blitz."

Even without evidence, Marlo recognized David Stringer's fingerprints all over this campaign to impugn her. Cliff was even implying that he'd penned a few of her latest hits. David was trying to plant the seed that she didn't always write her own songs.

She wished she could gather all the women David Stringer mistreated throughout his decades-spanning career and start telling the real stories of the toxic environment he'd created at Pop Machine. Her most frequent daydream lately. She envisioned herself standing at a podium in front of a press corps, flanked by her fellow Pop Machine musical artists, and maybe even joined by the likes of Gloria Allred. But it was simply a fantasy, and in the present, she needed to face reality.

"Well, it doesn't matter. I'm never going back there. I tried. I failed. Sound familiar?" Marlo childishly mimicked her dad's voice as she parroted back his words.

Being home brought out the petulant teen in her who'd never had the opportunity to rebel against her parents the first time around. She'd been too busy building a career.

Dad pulled her into a hug, whispering *habibti* into her hair. When he dropped his broken Arabic on her, she knew just how worried he was about her. A heavy wave of tears pressed behind her eyes.

Her mom laughed, jarring Marlo out of the moment. "Of course you're going back."

She pulled out of the embrace and faced her mom. "What? Why would I?"

"Marlo, what are you going to do all day? Hide in your childhood bedroom?"

That was exactly her plan. She'd been in the public eye for the greater part of the last decade. She deserved a bit of the hermit life.

"What do you want me to do?" Marlo asked.

The question wasn't sarcastic. She honestly wasn't sure what to do with herself. She'd always heard it was lonely at the top, but Marlo suspected it was actually way lonelier on the descent.

"I want you to live your life on your own terms for once. Take a break from worrying about record deals and tours. Stop dating creeps. Let yourself be you again. Make amends."

Marlo rolled her eyes. Okay, petulant teen mode reactivated. "Oh my god, you just want me to kiss and make up with Jude. Admit it."

Her mom smiled and shrugged. “So what if I do? Would it be the worst thing?”

“Dani,” her father gently warned her mother. Not in a chiding way but more of *a you’re spoiling our secret plan* way.

Marlo pulled her knees into her chest, wrapping her arms around her lower legs. They were obviously conspiring. If they’d cooked up a plot, she needed to squash it.

“The Marlo and Jude ship sailed, wrecked, and was lost to its watery grave for eternity,” she said.

“At least you haven’t lost your sense of melodrama.” Her mom gently poked her side.

“Where do you think I got it from?” Marlo teased, dodging her mom’s play swat. “But I’m serious, Mom. Jude made it abundantly clear that I’m the last person he ever wants to see.”

Her mom’s gaze grew distant, a strange expression passing over her face.

“Mom?” Marlo turned to her dad, who’d dropped his eyes to his lap. “Dad, what’s going on?”

Secrets brewed between them and Marlo hated being left out.

Her mom laughed nervously. Marlo caught her scratching above her left eyebrow from the corner of her eye.

It was her mom’s signature tell. Bad poker faces were genetic.

Marlo sat forward. “What have you done?”

“Nothing.” The scratch again.

“You did. You did something. Don’t lie to me.” Marlo’s heart thundered in her ears. “Dad, start talking.”

“Don’t freak out,” her dad said. “We need to tell you something.”

Marlo’s stomach twisted as she waited a seeming eternity for her dad to continue.

"James Beckett was diagnosed with Lymphoma late last year," he said quietly.

The statement knocked the breath out of Marlo's chest. No one had bothered telling her—not her family, not Jude. Was his dad's cancer diagnosis the source of Jude's crackling tension in the bakery?

"Why didn't you tell me?" Marlo asked. "Is he okay?"

"He's responding to chemo really well," her mom answered. "You had a lot going on, and we didn't want to further upset you, especially before we knew the extent of his illness."

Aftershocks continued to ripple through Marlo. If she'd known, she could have contacted the best oncologists in the world, made sure his treatments were top-notch. If she'd known, she would have reached out to Jude sooner.

"I can't believe no one told me," Marlo repeated under her breath. When had she become such a complete stranger to her own life?

"Anyway," her mom resumed, "since he was diagnosed, your father and I have been helping the Becketts raise funds for the Leukemia and Lymphoma society."

"I'm so glad he's okay. Why didn't you ask me to donate anything?" Marlo drummed her fingers on her lips, unsure why her parents brought this up now.

"You've had a lot on your plate. We didn't want to add to it," her dad said.

Marlo nodded, half listening to her parents, half lost in thoughts of Jude. No wonder he'd been so unhappy to see her. She showed up without warning, not knowing that he faced real problems. Adult-sized problems. She was such a jerk.

"And I thought, since you were home, you'd want to help out," her mom finished.

"Wait, rewind. Help out with what?" Marlo asked, realizing she missed an important piece of information.

Her mom blew out her breath, looking to her dad for fortitude. "Vinnie and I volunteered you to perform at the L&L Banquet Charity Bake-Off that Jude is hosting at the end of summer. It's a fundraiser for a good cause, and maybe working together again is a chance for you two to make amends."

Marlo jumped up. "What the fuck, Mom? You both just told me to take a break from music, and you volunteered me to perform at the end of summer? You know I can't just show up to these things. I have to ask Tara and clear it with the studio executives. This isn't a hobby. It's a profession."

The words barreled out of her mouth before she even thought them through. It wasn't what she meant to say—she'd never begrudge honoring James Beckett in any capacity. He'd been like a second father to her. The news of his diagnosis and the concert within the span of a few minutes simply overwhelmed her. Her true objection was being forced into proximity with Jude again, a guaranteed recipe for disaster. Marlo loved contributing to charitable causes, but she usually did so of her own volition and usually outside of public notice.

"Honey, relax. It's a small, local thing. Hardly anyone will even be there." Her dad took the proverbial baton from her mom.

Marlo hated these parental tag-teams. Also, the minute her name was attached to anything, it automatically became a big thing, but she didn't want to spell it out for her parents. They should know after all these years. Fame was very much a double-edged sword—she had a platform that could draw a lot of attention to matters, but with increased visibility came a media circus.

Marlo shook with disbelief. Had her parents heard of cell phones? They could have told her about Mr. Beckett *months* ago. They'd had days to tell her about this misguided scheme to force her and Jude to work together.

"Everyone will know. You saw what happened with the two songs we performed at karaoke. Clips of that night are still going strong." Marlo wrapped her arms around her waist. "Besides, Jude will never agree. Not ever, especially after today."

"Well, that's why I'm bringing it up. We were going to tell you both about it tomorrow during dinner."

"Are you kidding? You planned to ambush us in front of the person at the heart of the matter. That's low, even for you and Mrs. Beckett."

"Marlo, ayb," her dad chided. "Your mom is trying to make the best of a bad situation."

Her mom stared at her silently for a moment.

"I hoped your visit to the shop was going to go better." Her mom pushed her hair away from her face. "Given everything, we changed the plan. Vinnie is probably talking to him right now."

"You knew we'd fought before I even walked in?" Marlo turned away from her mom. Tears stung the back of her eyes. "I cannot believe you two."

It was one thing for the studio to routinely impose on her autonomy, but it was so much worse when her family did the same. Worse, all four of their parents conspired to force her and Jude back together, knowing how painful their breakup had been on both of them. Unbelievable. She couldn't possibly sing a concert's worth of those songs while Jude passed around cupcakes, not after everything they'd been through. Not after the heated dislike she saw in his eyes today.

"Just think of the cause," her dad pleaded. "Think of James. It would mean the world to him, and the money we raise directly helps patients and their families."

Marlo no longer faced her parents. Tears streamed down her cheeks. They had to understand the impossibility of this ask. They'd crossed so many lines—trust, respect, etc. She wasn't a child. She didn't need to be handled as if she was incapable of making important, meaningful decisions.

"I need to go for a walk. I need some fresh air." Marlo headed to the door, grabbing her ball cap and sunglasses on her way out.

She'd barely made it around the block when her phone rang. She answered without checking, assuming it was her mom with an apology.

"Can you believe this shit?" a familiar male voice asked.

It took Marlo a second to get her bearings. It was Jude, calling her. Just like old times. Calling her to complain about their parents. Back then, they would've met at the shared fence connecting their backyards and walked through the gate their parents had finally thoughtfully installed after all the cuts and scrapes they'd endured climbing over the fence.

Marlo cleared her throat, hoping to dislodge the memory, hoping he wouldn't hear the tears in her voice. "I mean, yes, and no."

An excruciating silence passed. Maybe he realized what a colossal mistake he'd made calling her. Marlo stopped walking and listened with a fierce intensity. She heard a soft intake of breath. Jude was still there.

"Are you still there?" she asked anyway, unsure what else to say.

"Yes," he replied, and she wished she couldn't hear the strain in his voice.

Would it always be like this between them? Old hurts and the weight of things unsaid creating an impenetrable barrier. This was why they couldn't do what their parents asked. They'd never get back to that place where they could work together peaceably.

"So, what are we going to tell them?" he asked, his tone gentler now.

We. Marlo's heart stuttered at that word.

"I don't know." She closed her eyes for a beat. "I mean, I didn't even know your dad was sick. I'm so sorry."

"He's doing pretty well, according to his doctors."

"I really had no idea what I was coming back home to."

"Home? Hardly." Jude chuckled.

"It's still home."

The line went quiet again except for the gentle rhythm of his breaths.

Marlo hated that even the people closest to her had opinions on where she did and didn't belong, what roots she could claim for her own. Gold Hills would always be home, just like being half Iraqi would always be her heritage, even if it didn't look the same as it did for other people with similar backgrounds. The Arab diaspora weren't a monolith, and her version of it was just as valid as anyone else's.

"Sorry, it's just..." he started. "After everything, it's weird to hear you call this place home."

"Don't you think I'm aware? Yeah, it's fucking weird being back. It was fucking weird being alone in LA. My life lately has been a goddamn nightmare. Do you think you could cut me some slack?"

"Marlo, I said I was sorry."

Another pause. Words danced on the tip of her tongue. But the venom of them was sharp, and if she unleashed them, the aftermath would be ugly. She'd been through way too many contentious interviews not to have learned how to bite her tongue. Ever the master of smile and placate, distract and divert. Or at least she had been until that ill-fated karaoke night.

She smiled, even though Jude couldn't see it, she hoped he'd hear it. *Fake it to placate.* "I appreciate your apology. I will make a significant donation to the charity in your father's honor, and I'll explain to the parents that Tara would not approve my performance."

"Marlo Sage to the rescue."

There was something different in Jude's words now, a hint of something like disappointment.

"Feel free to proceed with the bake-off without me. I speak solely on my own behalf." She winced as she heard the sharp intake of breath on the other line.

"Ever the magnanimous Queen of Pop."

At least in his estimation she was a queen and not a princess, even if his words dripped with sarcasm. She'd take it.

"Jude, I get it. You hate me. Go join an online forum. There are plenty dragging my ass twenty-four-seven. You could even join Cliff Rochester's Shame Marlo tour."

"I could never hate you. Don't you get that?" He said the words so softly Marlo barely heard them over the roar of her pulse.

"Well, then I guess we have one thing in common." She pressed end on the call and powered her phone off.

Her heart continued to riot. The concession, small as it is, warmed her, but rage still consumed her. She was angry at her parents, angry at her label, angry at the tabloids, angry at the whole fucking world. She was just a girl who loved to make music, and all she wanted was to share it her fans. She'd grown weary of justifying her choices and defending her value. Marlo knew exactly what she was worth, and fuck all of them for making her question it. And in particular, fuck Jude for making her ever doubt herself in the first place.

~

Two hours later, Marlo returned to her childhood home, breathless, sweat dripping from nearly every part of her body. Her walk had morphed into a punishing run and then into a furious power-walk back.

Her mom bounded off the couch as soon as she entered. "Where have you been? We've been worried sick."

Marlo belatedly remembered she'd powered down her phone after she'd spoken to Jude. "I went for a run. Sorry, I turned my phone off."

"I called you dozens of times. Tara called even more than that. She was so desperate to reach you she called here. Your dad is driving around trying to find you."

Marlo rolled her eyes. She appreciated her parent's concern, but she wished they'd start seeing her as the grown, competent woman she'd become, even if she was currently caught in a vortex of media drama.

Her mom cleared her throat. "So I spoke with Tara."

Marlo's heart stilled in her chest. Unable to ignore the tone of uncertainty in her mother's voice, Marlo didn't want to think about the conversation her mother had with her publicist, but she could almost guarantee the subject matter.

"I told her about the charity event, and—"

"Mom, tell me you didn't." Marlo curled her hands into fists, digging her fingernails into the bed of her palms.

"Tara thought it was a brilliant idea, a way for you to counteract the recent narrative that's taken hold about you."

Marlo shook her head, unable to speak. Clearly, no one intended to listen to her opinions. No one cared what she wanted for herself.

"We know you're not a dried-up party girl, cruising on the last dregs of your fame." Her mom held up her hands. "Not my words, hers."

"Actually, they're Cliff Rochester's words." Tears stung the back of Marlo's eyes again.

"If it makes you feel better, I never liked him, and I don't believe a damn word he says." Her mom closed the distance between them and offered her open arms.

Reluctantly, Marlo stepped into the hug. She was so tired. Tired of her life, tired of herself. She sobbed quietly into her mom's neck. She knew her parents thought they were helping, but they needed to understand all she wanted in coming home was their comfort, not their interference.

"Shh, sweetheart, we're all looking out for your best interest."

Marlo pulled away and rubbed her eyes with the back of her hands. "That's the problem. I have to abide everyone else's decisions for me. When do I get to make my own?"

"You always have a say, but we all really think you should strongly consider doing the show. It will be a welcome distraction from everything else. Maybe it will be a good way to remind the record executives about what you bring to the table in the first place. Tara even thinks it'll be a good idea to invite some record-label bigwigs and other clients to the concert."

Marlo sighed. "It's not a concert. You said it was a bake-off."

"If you decide to perform, it will be a concert plus a bake-off. It can be both—a perfect meld of both your talents."

She heard the wisdom in both her mom's and Tara's argument, but her heart squatted low in her chest, a panicked bird about to take flight. Behind the pretty sentiments, the underlying rationale glared—they were telling her she literally had nothing left to lose.

They were right. She'd fallen so far she either continued her descent or she needed to figure out how to bounce.

"Well, even if you convince me," Marlo said, "you still have to convince Jude to go along."

Her mother smiled and looked away.

Marlo groaned. "Of course, you spoke to Suze too, right?"

"Well, she's always kept in touch with me." Her mom's smile widened.

"Fine, whatever. You guys iron out the details. I'll show up. I don't want to fucking talk about this anymore."

"Go take a shower, sweetie. You'll feel better. I'll call your dad and tell him you're home."

Marlo shook her head. Her parents would never change. They'd always see her as the five-year-old in pigtails a warm bath had the power to fix everything for. Maybe Jude was right—coming home, if it could even be called that anymore, hadn't been the best idea.

Chapter Seven

JUDE

JUDE THREW HIS phone across the room, still in charge enough of his faculties to make sure it landed softly on the couch. He'd called Marlo already upset, and now he'd grown even more incensed for thinking it would help to talk it out with her. They no longer had that connection, and it was stupid for him to think otherwise. The worst part was her acting like participating in the charity bake-off was a bigger ask of her than it was of him. He'd be the one hosting the event, participating in judging. All she had to do was show up and sing a couple of songs. And only one of them was comfortable in the spotlight, and it wasn't him.

The prospect of working with Marlo again brought him back to a dangerous place—one where big emotions and old hurts collided. He still couldn't believe Suze and his mom conspired against him by using his dad's recent cancer diagnosis as a way to guilt him into doing the show.

Unbidden, an image of a tart meringue popped into his head. No, a pavlova with a surprise tart kiwi coulis center, drizzled in bittersweet chocolate. Jude paced the front room as he continued composing the recipe in his head. *Don't Go Breaking My Tart.* His heart rate slowed, his breathing normalized. The anger slowly faded, a sad resignation replacing it.

Maybe he hadn't been fair to Marlo earlier. He recalled his own shock when his mom first proposed having him host a charity bake-off. He couldn't imagine how surprised Marlo must have been to get the request to sing at it. Plus, he hadn't expected her to tell him how miserable she was in LA and in her cherished career. He'd always assumed she'd chosen that celebrity life over him. There were so many pictures of her at glamorous parties, smiling and surrounded by other A-listers. Those curated images and headlines sold Jude the lie he'd been telling himself about Marlo, and he of all people should've known better. He'd never considered that she might come to regret the fame.

It wasn't his place to continue down that line of thinking. Whatever was going on with her singing career had nothing to do with him.

Jude walked back to his phone. He unlocked it and stared at Marlo's number. He should call her and apologize, offer to talk it out. Just like his dad advised before. *Love might forever be out of the picture, but should friendship be?* After all, she'd visited the shop in an attempt to broker peace. Even though it backfired, he could at least acknowledge the effort.

The phone buzzed in his palm.

"Hello?" Jude answered.

"Hey, I'm sorry about earlier." Marlo's words flew out on a rushed exhale. "I was just totally caught by surprise, and I took it out on you."

Jude smiled, relieved she couldn't see him. He didn't care to admit she still held so much sway over his emotions. "I'm sorry too. I should have handled that better. I know, given your career, this was a huge, unexpected ask."

There was a long pause on the other line. "Well, I may have had a change of heart."

"What? Really?" Jude sat down.

"I talked it out with my mom, and I think maybe it wouldn't be the worst thing in the world. The charity bake-off, I mean."

Jude heard the discordant note in her voice below the forced positivity. One so subtle most people missed it. Marlo always did this. A consummate people pleaser, she swallowed her real feelings, flashed a megawatt smile, and caved to the expectations of others. He hated that Marlo's mom had likely also used his dad's illness to coax her into it.

His anger flared again. "Marlo, you don't have to do the show."

She laughed, and it tore him to pieces to hear the masked pain in her voice. "If this was just about you and your dad," she said, "you know I would have said yes without hesitation. What gave me pause wasn't the ask. It was all the other drama in my life. Mom helped me see that I shouldn't let that get in the way of doing the right thing."

Marlo was a master self-rationalizer. She almost convinced him that it was the correct move. He longed to say so much to her, but the fear of opening that door again scared him. Maintaining distance between them was the safer route.

"You do what is right for you," he said, trying to infuse his words with the gentleness he wanted her to hear in them. "The charity event will go on with or without you." *It's okay to walk away from this.*

"Jude, I am doing the show. You're welcome to join me. We can discuss the lineup at dinner tomorrow and how it works with the flow of the bake-off."

"Dinner?"

"Yes, the family dinner, remember?"

He exhaled. The distance he craved evaporated right before him. "Yeah, that's right."

For a second, he debated canceling. But something about the way she said *family dinner* tugged at his heart. He missed dodging dad jokes at the dining table with her.

“With the success of the mini reunion at karaoke, I was thinking we should sell tickets for a livestream.” Marlo switched into business mode. “I mean, as another fundraising avenue with all proceeds going to the Leukemia & Lymphoma Society.”

He knew this facet of her persona too. There was no point to arguing with her when she’d reached this place of hyper focus. The easiest course for everyone involved would be for him to simply agree to her plans. Maybe it wouldn’t be as bad as he’d thought mere minutes ago.

“If you’re in, I’m in,” he said. “My dad will be so blown away by this. He’s always respected your work ethic, and he adores you.”

Jude cringed, unsure why he overshared.

“I appreciate that,” she said, still in professional mode. “I’ll text you a preliminary selection of songs and then we can finalize the set list.”

“Hey, Marlo,” Jude broke in. Although he appreciated that they weren’t fighting anymore, he wasn’t sure he preferred this robotic iteration of her.

“Yeah.” A thread of tension tugged in her voice.

“Thank you,” he said.

“Some things are bigger than us. Sometimes I just need the reminder. I gotta go.” She ended the call before he could reply.

Jude held the phone to his ear for several more seconds as he tried to process her last statement. A confusing mix of emotions continued to swirl in his head. He couldn’t afford to get sucked into her orbit again. He needed to learn from her example and treat the charity show as a business transaction and nothing more. If he shielded his heart, he’d have a chance of surviving the next couple of months.

Chapter Eight

MARLO

MARLO INSISTED ON driving. She hardly ever had the opportunity to drive herself anywhere anymore. Plus she needed an outlet for the nervous energy vibrating through her. The enormity of a dinner with Jude and his parents after so many years apart couldn't be overstated, especially now that she knew James Beckett was ill.

She'd barely pulled out of the driveway when her dad took in a sharp breath and gripped the passenger armrest—a reenactment of their drives when she'd finally received her driver's permit at age seventeen and a half, fully two years later than most of her peers.

"Dad, I know how to drive."

"Ee, habibti, I know," he said, not easing his white-knuckled grip even a little.

For about ten minutes, her parents didn't utter a word.

"I think you might want to slow down on the curves," her mom said, dispelling the quiet.

"Okay, you two are being ridiculous," Marlo said. "I do drive myself places sometimes."

"When was the last time?" Her dad asked in his best rendition of an exasperated Tony Shalhoub character.

"Ha, ha." Hoping a change in subject would take the focus off her driving and return it to more important matters, Marlo asked, "Are you sure Mr. Beckett is up for visitors?"

"Vinnie said today was a little rough," her mom said, "so he might just say a quick hello and then retreat to his room."

Marlo locked eyes with her mom in the rearview mirror. "Should we still be going?"

"Yes, Vinnie needs the company. This has been tough on her too."

Guilt wormed through Marlo. If she'd known about Jude's dad sooner, she would have tempered her interactions with him. She would have reached out to Vinnie and James. There was a time when she'd prided herself as the mature one between her and Jude, but now it wasn't remotely true. None of her recent challenges came close to the gravity of dealing with a parent's cancer diagnosis and treatment.

"Turn left in a hundred yards," her father called out from beside her in unison with the car's navigation system.

"That would be very helpful if I had a clue what a hundred yards looked like."

"It's three hundred feet," he replied.

Marlo and her mom laughed.

"Thanks, Dad, that cleared it all up."

JUDE

Jude tried to distract himself with reading while he awaited Marlo's arrival, but after he'd reread the same sentence a dozen times, he gave up. Instead, he popped into the kitchen, even though his mom had begged him off.

"Are you sure I can't help with anything?" he asked.

She stared at him for a full minute. Little flyaway hairs had escaped her severely pulled-back ponytail, and her cheeks were flushed. He'd inherited his cooking-as-therapy predilection from her.

"Fine, I guess you can make dessert," she said.

He chuckled. Only his mom would treat his offer as a chore. Jude knew she didn't mean it that way—he'd interrupted her in the flow. He would have reacted the same if the roles were reversed. There was just something about losing yourself in the rhythm of crafting dishes from raw ingredients.

"What are you going to make?" she asked, clearing space for him on the kitchen island next to her.

"I'm not sure yet." He scanned her pantry shelves, coming up short. "I should have pulled some things from the shop."

"I have everything you could possibly need."

"You have Target brand flour."

"Oh my, listen to you, ingredient snob." She laughed.

"Remind me why we're hosting this dinner again?" Jude asked, pulling a few items and bringing to them to the island prep area.

"Dani and Sami are my friends, and their daughter is visiting. It would be rude not to invite them over. Plus, with Marlo agreeing to perform at the bake-off, we need to bring her up to speed on planning."

"Oh, don't worry. She's already taken over planning."

"See, it's all going to work out," his mom said, beaming.

She'd shed so many tears over the last few months, worried about his father, overwhelmed by the toll of caregiving—it was a relief to see her smiling again. His mom deserved a night to enjoy the company of her friends, and he'd be the last to begrudge her that, even if it came at the cost of his discomfort.

Instead, Jude worked out his frustrations by hand whisking ingredients. "Do you still have any of the peach preserves I canned for you?"

"Yes, on the shelf in the fridge door."

"Perfect, I'm going to make peach frangipane puff pastry tarts."

"That sounds delicious," his mom said, snickering.

"What?"

"I have no idea what half those words mean." She erupted into giggles.

"Okay, stop distracting me," he said, buoyed by her shift in mood. But he picked up a pinch of flour and playfully flicked it at her.

She doubled over with full belly laughs.

Baking worked its magic on him. The knot of muscle between his shoulders loosened and transported him into a semi-meditative state. He hummed mindlessly while rolling the chilled dough, folding it back up and rolling it out again. His focus zeroed in on his hands, while awareness of everything else fading into the background.

When Marlo started singing along, he jumped, nearly losing his grip on the rolling pin. He hadn't heard her and her family arrive.

"Hi," she said, waving. "Sorry, didn't mean to startle you."

"I zone out when I'm baking," he said, heat rising to his cheeks.

"I remember." Marlo smiled.

His gaze roved over her. He couldn't help himself. She wore a light summer dress and sandals, her hair loose around her shoulders, flowing in damp beach waves. Marlo always looked great, but this laid-back girl-next-door iteration of her was his favorite.

"You look nice," he said, an unexpected rough scrape in his voice.

"This old thing," she said, waving away his attention.

She'd never been good at taking compliments.

"Anyway, don't let me interrupt. I enjoy watching you." She leaned forward, resting her chin in her hands.

All his worries from earlier melted away. Marlo slotted right back into his life naturally, like she'd never been gone. He fought the impulse to close the distance and plant a kiss on her nose. He wished he'd kissed her more when they'd been together, but back then, he'd been petrified of someone catching them in moments of affection. Now that he was older, he'd do it all differently, worry less about what others thought of his overtures toward her and more about showing her how much he valued her.

Not that he'd have the chance.

He desperately tried to think of anything else to say, but her presence, her unfettered beauty, distracted him.

"Marlo," his mom called out, "Jim is awake. Come say hello."

"Okay, on my way," she responded but remained fixed in place a moment longer, just staring back at Jude, something wordless passing between them.

I know, he wanted to say. *I feel it too.*

When she finally retreated from the kitchen, she left Jude gaping behind her. He'd never met anyone else who simultaneously unsettled him and pulled him in the way Marlo did. He wasn't sure he'd ever get used to the exhilarating rollercoaster drop of spending time with her.

Chapter Nine

MARLO

MARLO ENTERED THE dim bedroom to find Mr. Beckett sitting in bed, propped up by a mountain of pillows. His sunken eyes and the hollows of his cheeks rendered half his face in shadows. The contrast to his once robust features jarred Marlo. She schooled her expression, hoping her shock at the transformation wouldn't show this once. He beckoned her forward. Vinnie stopped her momentarily, squirting a generous dollop of sanitizer in Marlo's hand.

"You are a vision for tired, old eyes," Mr. Beckett said, smiling.

"Handsome as ever yourself, Mr. Beckett. How are you feeling?" Marlo asked.

"I've had better days to be honest, but this is par for the course for this part of the cycle I'm in. How about you—how are you?"

"I'm hanging in. I too have had better days." She winked at him.

Mr. Beckett patted her hand. "Focus on what's important—your music and your heart. Everything else is nonsense."

"I'll keep that in mind." Marlo smiled again, but it was for show.

Her throat filled with brine as she swallowed back her tears. She longed to grieve for the once stalwart James Beckett, who now appeared a fraction of his former self. She wanted to cry about the dismal state of her professional and personal lives. She mourned the love story she and Jude had lost.

The acute pain of all her sadnesses intersected in this one room.

Mr. Beckett made it sound so easy to prioritize, but it was the "nonsense" that haunted her—the sensational tabloid articles, the punishing reviews, the late-night talk show host jokes at her expense when they weren't actively begging for to be a guest. Tara showed her the numbers. Marlo's appearances translated into a significant bump in viewership. But she was never shown the same deference as male performers.

"Speaking of music," Mr. Beckett continued, "thank you for generously volunteering to sing at the bake-off. You have no idea how much it means to me."

His eyes glistened, and Marlo chided herself for almost refusing to perform at the show. In this moment, she forgave her mother's and Mrs. Beckett's duplicity. She should have trusted their mothers to know what was best for her and Jude and the families at large.

"It is my absolute pleasure," Marlo said. "Your family is like my second family."

"That's what I tell the folks at the infusion center, that I practically raised you." A familiar twinkle lit up his eyes. "But they don't believe me."

"Guess we'll have to prove them wrong then, won't we?"

They spoke for a few more minutes, but when his cheeks sagged and the interval between blinks lengthened, she knew he needed to get back to sleep. The image of the mighty James Beckett unwell was so much harder to see than she'd anticipated. It was a wonder that Jude was at all functional, much less thriving with his shop. She followed Mrs. Beckett back to the dining room to rejoin everyone else, unable to shake the somber cloud that settled over her.

Jude stopped talking mid-sentence at the sight of her.

Her parents exchanged concerned glances.

"What were you talking about?" Marlo asked, sensing she'd interrupted something, and wanting to redirect their pitying looks.

A moment of quiet passed before Jude sat up straighter. "Just about everything with dad and his treatments."

Marlo shifted her focus to him. "He looks ill and tired. Are his treatments going okay, really? I can get him in with doctors at Stanford or UCLA."

"He's got a great team here," Mrs. Beckett answered.

"The doctors say they're hopeful," Jude added. "But we're in the tough part. The medicines are very rough on his body, so rest and keeping his spirits up are key."

"Can I do anything to help?" Marlo asked. "I'm available if he needs someone to hang out or take him to his appointments."

Vinnie's hand floated to her chest. "Marlo, that's so sweet—"

"We've got it under control," Jude cut in.

"Well, if you change—" Marlo started.

But he cut her off. "I said we've got it."

Marlo stared at him, surprised to see the hard glint in his eyes. Earlier, she thought they'd finally turned the corner on distrust, but the firm set of features now said otherwise. Her offer was made in full sincerity. She was the only person in the room aside from Vinnie with free time to help out. Plus, she had more selfish reasons too—Marlo yearned for some sense of purpose or direction for this summer.

"Let's eat before the food gets any colder," Vinnie said, clearly trying to defuse the tension. "Marlo, can I get you anything to drink? Wine? Beer?"

"Please sit. Start eating." Marlo rose from her chair. "I'll help myself to a glass of wine. Bottle's in the kitchen?"

"Yes, dear, on the counter."

Marlo ignored the anxious exchange of glances traded between her mom and Vinnie.

Operation reunite Marlo & Jude isn't so easy, is it, Moms?

She held her head high as she walked to the kitchen. It didn't matter if Jude wanted to keep her away from his father. She'd continue to offer to help out. She loved James too. Marlo poured a generous glass of Riesling and took a fortifying sip before returning to the dining room.

"Marlo, you must try the chicken piccata. It's perfection," her mom said.

Tension still hovered over the small dinner party. The heat of Jude's gaze tracked her every move as she served herself dinner, but she refused to look at him. She couldn't afford to cause a scene. It would upset her parents, and she wouldn't dream of inviting any more stress in Mr. and Mrs. Beckett's lives. She ate her chicken, drank her wine, and prayed for an expedient end to the evening.

JUDE

Jude struggled to chew the bite in his mouth over the bitter tang of guilt. He'd overreacted to Marlo's offer to help with his dad's treatments. He wasn't even sure why. The longer he waited to apologize, the more awkward the vibe in the room grew, threatening to suffocate them all. Marlo avoided eye contact with him, an old game they used to play when she was upset, and it made his blood boil.

Look at me, he wanted to scream. *Let me tell you I'm sorry.*

Instead, his mom, in an attempt to cover for his blunder, spoke in a nervous, high-pitched, rapid-fire clip.

"Jude, how is life in the pastry world?" Sami seized the opportunity to cut in when his mom briefly paused to catch her breath.

Jude took a swig of his beer to wash down the food he worked so hard to swallow. "Great, actually. Hiring Penny as an assistant chef a couple of years ago was the best decision I ever made."

Marlo finally looked at him. The flare behind her eyes made his chest swell. She was jealous—he hadn't forgotten how to read her.

"I've also been fortunate to be getting so much interest from culinary magazines, so—"

"Jude is on track to make his dream of a cookbook come true," his mom added, grinning.

"Well, that's the ultimate goal." He tempered his mom's enthusiasm. "But we're not quite there yet."

"I didn't know you want to write a cookbook," Marlo said.

"It's been a long time," he said. "There's a lot you don't know."

A different emotion passed behind her eyes as the room fell quiet. Of course she didn't know. They'd barely spoken over the last decade, and when they did, they tiptoed around anything too real. At least he did. Sometimes when the fatigue and overwhelm dissolved her resolve, she'd open up to him about her latest dating fiasco or tabloid troubles.

"Apologies," Marlo snapped after a moment. "I've been a bit busy."

Jude gripped the cloth napkin in his lap. He'd gone back to school, started a new career and business, and his dad was currently undergoing treatment for cancer, but Marlo thought she was the only one who'd been "a bit busy." He'd promised his mom to be on his best behavior, but he'd forgotten how easily Marlo slipped under his skin, making it too taut and itchy.

His mom jumped in again. “There’s also the photo shoot Jude flew down to LA for last month.”

“The one with Kaylenne?” Marlo glared at him.

“How did you know about that?” he asked.

“The industry is small. Word gets around,” Marlo said. “She’s David’s new pet project.”

Jude watched pain lance through her. He didn’t need Marlo to tell him. He read the truth in the false courage painted on her face—David used Kaylenne to torment Marlo with the photo shoot. The man loved a Machiavellian scheme to remind his stars they were replaceable. Jude kicked himself for not realizing it sooner. He never would’ve agreed to being used as a pawn in a game against Marlo.

“Vinnie, maybe we should go have tea on the patio and give the kids time to discuss the show,” Dani said.

“Yes, let’s do that,” his mom said.

If Jude’s attention wasn’t so fixed on Marlo, he would’ve laughed at his mom’s utter lack of subtlety.

Though the two moms leaped at the chance for an escape, Sami hesitated, exchanging a look with Marlo. She dismissed him with a nod. He walked over to her and dropped a kiss on the top of her head before exiting to the patio.

Jude took another long sip of his now room-temperature beer. “I’m sorry. I don’t know why I’m so on edge tonight.”

“I seem to bring the worst out in you,” she said, tone flat. “Always have.”

He ran his fingers through his hair. Marlo didn’t bring out the worst in him. She was a walking reminder of a terrible chapter in his life—one in which he’d failed her. He couldn’t explain it to her without confessing to one of the greatest acts of cowardice he’d ever committed. The other inescapable truth was that Marlo seamlessly fit in with his family. Her presence in their life remained second nature, which only served to make it harder to reconcile her absence over the last few years.

"It's not about you," he said. "I just have a lot on my plate, including this charity bake-off."

Marlo's gaze penetrated through his defenses. "I know you have your reasons for not believing me, but I'm serious about helping out, with your dad, the show, whatever you need."

Jude stared at her. He knew her well enough to recognize her sincerity, but that didn't mean he could explain his own hesitation. It still felt like any moment he'd wake from this dream to find himself without her in his life again. He couldn't stomach the thought of it.

"You mean until you get bored and go running back to your glamorous life?" He practically bit through his tongue, angry at himself for letting those words slip out.

"Glamorous?" She laughed. "Which part? My latest PR dating disaster? Or the part where David Stringer despises me and is actively trying to ruin my career?"

"Cliff is an asshole. And don't get me started on David."

"Guess we do agree on some things." Marlo smiled, but the sadness behind her eyes didn't fade.

"What do you mean about David trying to ruin your career?" Jude asked, suppressing a shiver at the man's name.

He'd made a deal with that devil years ago in order to protect Marlo.

She took another sip of wine, swallowing hard. "He passed on my latest album. He's bringing in a songwriter-slash-producer."

Jude's pulse throbbed at his temples. Even in the early days, Marlo had been insistent about maintaining creative control of her work. His gut clenched. He'd been the only person she'd ever agreed to co-write with, and he'd squandered that show of trust.

"Marlo," he said, her name heavy on his tongue. "I'm so sorry. Can I do anything?"

The corner of her lips tipped up. "Support my efforts to distract myself? I have until the end of the summer to figure out how I'm going to handle Pop Machine."

"What does your team say?"

She lifted one of her bare shoulders, letting it drop again. "Tara is working with legal to see if there is anything in the contract that will give us wiggle room."

"I'm sure the terms are protective of you. Suze was, and still is, great with contracts," Jude said trying to reassure her.

Her gaze fixed in the distance as she crossed her arms against her chest. Jude tried not to let his gaze linger, but the move only served to highlight her cleavage. Her silence set him on high alert. She was hiding something.

"What aren't you telling me?" he asked, his eyes flicking back to hers.

"I made some mistakes after you left."

"What kind of mistakes?"

She bit down on her plump lower lip, fighting so hard not to tell him, and then groaned. "I don't want to talk about this right now."

"Right now is the perfect time for us to talk."

"I'm not sure this is the time or place." Her gaze drifted toward the staircase up to his dad's room.

Jude pursed his lips, knowing what she meant. He dropped his voice and continued anyway. "We haven't even discussed the karaoke incident, much less what has happened since, never mind what happened twelve years ago."

Marlo absently ran a hand across the wood grain of the dining table. "What's past is past."

"If that was true, then you wouldn't avoid talking about it."

She stood up, holding her wineglass. "If we're going to do this, I'm going to need top off."

He followed her into the kitchen and grabbed a glass for himself then gestured for her to join him at one of the barstools at the island.

"So?" he said after taking a sip.

"So..."

"Where should we start?"

"David Stringer is trying to force me to breach my contract, and..." Marlo chewed on her lower lip. "And Tara thinks I need to grovel publicly to restore some goodwill so I can complete the last album I owe Pop Machine and walk away free."

Jude had his own history with David Stringer, so he knew firsthand the personal toll of kowtowing to the lecherous studio exec.

"Also, David won't allow me to perform any of my songs for the bake-off," she said.

Jude gripped the edges of his seat. Was this why she'd come to this dinner? To let him down easy? He should've known the possibility of them working together again was too good to be true. Their roads had diverged long ago. It was best he simply accepted that.

"Don't you own the songs?" he asked.

Marlo rolled the wineglass stem between her fingers. "Um, not exactly."

"What do you mean? You wrote them therefore they're yours."

She smiled but her eyes glistened. He'd been out of the music industry for a minute, but he hadn't suspected anything changed that drastically.

"Marlo, please, talk to me."

"It's complicated."

"We have time."

She sighed and dropped her head into her hands. "David made me sign some papers when I renegotiated my contract. I was nineteen and alone for the first time." Words spilled out of Marlo's mouth in a torrent. "I agreed to use one of his lawyer friends to review my contracts, and they assured me it was standard language and no different than our first one except for you being gone."

Jude fumed. That fucking bastard had tricked her. After all the hoops he'd made Jude jump through to leave, David Stringer betrayed their deal to protect Marlo. Jude had promised to keep his distance from her as long as David swore she'd be unharmed by his breach of contract.

"Why did you sign a new contract?" he asked, hating the way her face creased with stress lines.

"How far would you go if someone threatened to take your shop away from you?"

"I'd walk away exactly as I did from David Stringer."

Marlo winced. "You only got to do that because I took the hit when you left."

"What do you mean?"

"Did you really think they'd let you walk away, in breach of contract, and you wouldn't face any consequences?" She struggled to moderate her voice.

"Marlo, what are you talking about?"

"That contract I signed at nineteen—it had provisions to protect you. I assured them that I'd sell more copies of my first solo album than of any of the Marlo & Jude albums, and that profit split would be weighted in their favor. I didn't know that they'd include language that would allow them to buy my masters without similarly giving me the chance to buy them back."

The floor dropped from beneath him. He shook his head, unable to speak.

"I fulfilled my promise to the label so that you could walk away unscathed," she said. "Only I'd inadvertently opened the door for them to steal the ownership of my music."

Something unreadable passed behind her eyes.

"But I made my own deal with David and the label to protect you," he said. "I didn't walk away unscathed."

Marlo scoffed. "Protect me? You handed me to the wolves on a silver platter. I lost my masters because of you."

"No," he said. "They tricked you like they did me."

"What do you mean?"

The world wobbled on its axis. He'd made so many assumptions about how his departure affected Marlo, but he never knew that David used it as an opportunity to take the one thing that mattered to her above all else—her songs.

"Protect me from what?" she pressed. "How did David trick you?"

The air extinguished from Jude's chest. David Stringer had played them both by using their youth, innocence, and deep affection for each other against them. "He didn't have to sue me for breach of contract. My parents bought me out of the contract."

"How?" The color leeched from her face.

"The trust fund for college from my grandparents."

Marlo banged her closed fist against the granite countertop. "He played us."

Jude swallowed hard. He'd lost so much because of David Stringer, Marlo's friendship most of all. "And it wasn't just the money," he confessed. They'd owed each other these truths years ago, so he was determined not to hold anything back now. "He made me attest that I would cease communication with you."

Her jaw dropped. He swore her deep brown eyes flashed blood red for a moment. They'd shared so much over the years but never concentrated, incandescent rage. A fifty-pound weight he didn't realize he'd carried this whole time suddenly lifted.

Strangely, Jude felt freer than he ever had, even racked by the devastation of the truth.

He placed his hand over Marlo's and rubbed his thumb over the knuckles of her clenched fist. Small sparks of electricity skittered over where the pads of his fingers lay on her skin. She stilled, and he expected her to withdraw her hand. But instead, she uncurled her fingers and shifted her hand so that they were palm to palm. After so many years without being able to touch her, the simple act of holding her hand felt more intimate than it had any right to do.

Marlo's gaze skated across the side of his face, leaving trails of heat across his cheek, but his eyes remained fixed on their clasped hands.

"Jude?" she said, his name more breath than voice. "What am I going to do?"

"We're going to take that bastard down." He finally looked up at her then.

"We?" So much emotion brewed beneath the surface of her eyes.

He bracketed her hand between his. "He hurt us both, robbed of us of our friendship, stole your masters. Yes. *We*."

Marlo attempted to withdraw her hand, but when he tugged back lightly, she yielded.

"I don't want to impose," she said. "It's my fight."

"It's *our* fight. Just because you can do something on your own doesn't mean you have to."

Her eyes welled. He hated seeing her tears, but he knew from personal experience that the only prescription for bone-weary pain was a good, cleansing cry. If that was what she needed, he'd be the soft shoulder she could sob against.

But Marlo blinked back her tears, sat up taller,and fixed him with her piercing gaze. "Can I ask you something?"

"Yes."

"You hated all the baggage that came along with stardom. What changed?"

He leaned back, restoring the distance between them, and rubbed his hand across his forehead. "True, it wasn't my favorite part."

"But you're okay with the press for the bakery?"

"It's different."

"I guess I don't understand the distinction. You left me, our group, because you hated all the artifice."

"I left because I knew I couldn't stay. I didn't want to grow to resent you."

Marlo sat back and halfheartedly tried to withdraw her hand from his. But he held steadfast.

"I'm not explaining it right. Baking for me is what music is to you," he continued. "I enjoy promoting my work and the business. I love pastry enough to take on the things I hate."

"That makes sense," she said. But the furrow in her brow didn't ease.

"Talk to me, Marlo."

Her eyes softened, the veil behind them completely down. He hadn't seen her open and vulnerable like this with him in so long.

"But you didn't love me enough?"

The simple words landed a devastating blow. They had traveled on intersecting paths, only sharing a short distance together. At the time, he'd only had two options—stay and grow to hate her or leave to preserve what was left of their friendship. If only he'd been truthful and clear about his motivations then, maybe he could've spared them both so much grief.

"I loved you enough to admit the truth," he said. "What you wanted and what I wanted were not the same."

She squeezed his hand, but the light behind her eyes dimmed. Maybe he'd been too honest.

Just then the house filled with the chattering voices of their moms and her dad. Jude dropped Marlo's hand and pushed away from the island so fast it caused his chair to drop against the floor.

Marlo blinked up at him.

"We're not done here," he said, leaning in close to her under the guise of bending to set the chair to rights.

"Oh, baby, hope we're not interrupting," his mother said, joining them in the kitchen. Her tone was too bright and hopeful to indicate any sense of apology.

"Not at all, Mrs. Beckett," Marlo said. "But we shouldn't overstay our welcome."

"Nonsense," Vinnie said. "We haven't even had dessert yet."

Marlo shot a pleading look at her parents, but they ignored her.

Sami patted his stomach. "I always have room for dessert, especially if Jude made it."

Jude had never been so grateful to his mom for running interference for him. He couldn't let Marlo leave before he knew she was okay. He chuckled to himself. He'd questioned her when she'd called Gold Hills home a couple days ago, but the truth was it would always be her home and he'd always welcome her back.

MARLO

Marlo stood in the guest bathroom, arms braced on the sink ledge, staring at herself in the mirror. She studied the deep grooves bracketing her eyes, mentally making a note to bill David for her next Botox treatment. It wasn't fair to look older and yet be no wiser.

She ran her fingers under the cold water then placed them against the back of her neck. A little of the tension discharged. She pulled out her phone to text Heather Sloane. Heather wasn't in the "biz." She was a kindergarten teacher, belovedly known as Ms. Sloane by her class. She and Marlo had met in a spin class, both hanging out in the back scoffing at the far too enthusiastic instructors.

M: Hey you, I really wish I could swing by for a stitch and bitch session

*H: *crying face emoji* Me too!*

M: I am in literal hell. I'll have to call you tomorrow to fill you in on the details, but just know I'm hiding out in Jude Beckett's parents' guest bathroom trying not to freak out

H: WHAAAT???

M: Ugh, long story, we have to do this charity show together, and I think we just had one of those grown-up closure kind of talks

H: Well, I AM INTRIGUED. In my glamorous corner of the universe, a kid decided to stick gum in my hair today, and the little jerk waited until I'd bent down so it's not even at the end of a strand but at the top of my head.

M: That asshole!

H: Spoiler alert, now I have bangs. Honestly, kindergartners are so lucky they're cute.

M: Aww, you in bangs! Send pics

*H: Anyway, not to pile on but did you see this: *link to magazine article**

Marlo clicked on the link.

Everyone might be focused on a certain herbaceous-named pop star who's falling further and further into a black hole of her own making, but maybe we should be paying a little more attention to her former partner—a guy who only improves with age. Did we mention he's hot AF and he bakes? Ladies, Jude Beckett is the real deal and he's single. Here's a sneak peek behind the scenes of his recent photo shoot for a culinary magazine. That delectable dish posing with him is none other than Pop Machine's newest star in the making, Kaylenne Daughtry. Move over, Marlo Sage. There's a new pop princess in town.

Marlo rolled her eyes. Kaylenne was everything Marlo wasn't—an all-American sweetheart, inoffensive and sweet, blond and blue-eyed. Marlo took the bait and scrolled to the slideshow below the teaser. Apparently, his pastry shop really was all the rage. She suspected it wasn't only due to the delectable desserts but the hot dish who served them up.

The first picture stole her breath. Jesus fuck, Jude knew how to smolder. The intensity of his gaze singed her through the screen of her cell phone. She stared at his image for way longer than she cared to admit. She studied the shadow of dark hair on the angle of his jaw, the fine creases at his eyes. It was absurd. The real thing was just down the hall. She could just go stare at him in person, like she'd been all night.

Her phone pinged again.

H: I take it by the extreme silence that you've seen THE picture.

M: He's literally a few feet away, nothing I haven't seen before.

H: Exactly. You've seen THAT look. It's the one he saves for you.

Marlo nearly dropped her phone. No, Heather couldn't be more wrong. Spending the majority of her days with kindergartners and sunshine and rainbows made her so soft and sappy that she yielded to the slightest suggestion. Marlo clicked back to the picture.

M: You're way off

M: You've never even seen us together in person

M: You didn't even know me when we were still America's favorite singing duo

H: Whoa, someone doth protest an awful lot. I had a PhD in studying your tabloid pics. I was totally team # Judlo.

*M: Please tell me you didn't run one of those ship accounts *head exploding emojis**

M: Anyway, he barely tolerates me now

M: Plus there's some assistant chef, Penny, that he says saved his life or whatever

Heather sent back a string of variously emoting emojis that somehow perfectly captured the mood. Marlo sighed. Heather and their other friends were the only thing about Hell-A she missed at the moment.

H: You know what they say about hate, right?

M: That it's the last stop on the highway to Murderville?

H: You're dumb.

M: But you love me anyway.

H: Call me tomorrow!

M: Will do. xoxo

Marlo smiled at her screen. Her choices over the last couple of years were often questionable at best, but she at least knew a good friend when she met one.

A knock at the door made her jump.

"Marlo, are you okay, habibti?" her dad asked.

"Yes, I'm fine." She opened the door and stepped through, embarrassed that she'd lost track of so much time.

"Dessert is being served," he said, pulling her into a hug. "You know how much we love you, right?"

"I have an idea." She smiled, leaning her head briefly against his shoulder. She missed the days when a hug from her dad fixed everything.

"Yella, let's go eat dessert."

Marlo followed her dad into the kitchen. He took the seat at the island between her mother and Jude's, leaving only the spot next to Jude open. Marlo gritted her teeth and tried to forget the picture she'd just spent way too long admiring. Much to her dismay, he looked better in person.

"Hey," he said as she took the barstool next to him. "Sorry about earlier."

"No worries." Marlo plastered on her press junket smile. "What do we have here?"

"My take on a peach frangipane tart. If I'd had more time to think about it, I would have come up with something more impressive." He smiled at her sheepishly, instantly disarming her with an exact replica of the shy grin he used to give her when they were younger and he'd offer her one of his new Easy-Bake concoctions.

Marlo pressed her fork down into the tender, flaky pastry and took a bite. Her mouth filled with the taste of summer longing—tart and sweet peach tempered with hints of almond, bound by a heartachingly delicious buttery crust.

She moaned, unable to contain the noise from escaping her lips.

Turning toward him, she covered her mouth with her hand. "Sorry, I haven't had a dessert that good in a long time."

He shrugged, a soft, knowing smile teasing up one corner of his mouth. "It's just a little something I whipped up."

Marlo took another bite. She finally understood that the hype around him wasn't hype at all. Jude transformed sugar, flour, and butter into something magical, and for the first time, she saw him less as the boy next door or the boy who'd broken her heart but instead as the man who'd been unafraid to walk away from everything he knew to chase a dream. She was sick with envy.

Chapter Ten

MARLO

REVISITING THE SCENE of a crime was a bad idea, but Marlo returned to Jude's shop anyway, and again, she didn't give him any warning. The taste of that tart remained indelibly imprinted on her tongue. She wanted more. As much as she hated to admit it, These Delicate Delights had grown into a bit of a fixation for her. The shop was like a Where's Waldo of clues about their relationship, at least Jude's impression of it, and Marlo wanted to excavate each and every hint. She'd exhausted what she could achieve through studying the pictures on Google and Yelp.

As she approached the door, a petite blonde who bore an uncanny resemblance to a younger Reese Witherspoon and held a cute baby reached it just before her. She held Marlo's gaze for a moment, and Marlo momentarily panicked that she'd failed to recognize someone from her youth. It was the worst part of being home. Marlo hadn't deeply connected to most of her classmates, and as her life transformed, that piece of her past faded away. Her memories of school years outside of Jude were murky at best—renderings in shadow.

Marlo entered the shop just in time to see Jude come around the counter and give the blonde a consuming hug, and even though Marlo shouldn't care, she hated the way his hand lingered on the woman's back as he cooed at the baby in her arms.

They looked like a family.

The thought rocked through Marlo. Jude was right—she knew so little of who'd become and the life he'd built while they were apart. Maybe this was why he'd wanted to talk more the night they'd shared dinner at his mom's house.

She couldn't get caught staring but remained anchored to her spot, unable to tear her eyes away from the spectacle of domesticity before her. Jude scooped the baby up and held her overhead. The baby kicked her chubby legs and grinned toothlessly at him.

Yeah, baby, he has that effect on me too.

An ache settled low in her belly. Damn her ovaries.

Marlo backed toward the door. She'd never even bothered to ask Jude if he was in a relationship. For all she knew, he was married with a child. No, there was no way her mother wouldn't have told her. Plus, that magazine article specifically billed him as single. Still, fear lodged itself like a leaden weight inside.

Just as Marlo turned to leave, she heard Jude's voice.

"Marlo?"

She prayed her warmed cheeks didn't betray her. Waving her hand awkwardly at him, Marlo noticed the petite blonde reclaim the baby from his arms. They disappeared into the kitchen, confirming Marlo's worst suspicions. Maybe this was why he'd asked her to give him the courtesy of a warning before stopping by.

"Excuse me," another customer said behind her.

Marlo stumbled forward, growing more flustered by the second. Jude crossed the space toward her, concern creasing his forehead.

“Hey,” he said, quietly. “Are you okay? You don’t look great.”

“I’m fine,” Marlo croaked, her mouth suddenly parched. *Get a grip.*

She sucked in a shaky breath.

“I didn’t mean to interrupt.” She gestured toward the direction the blonde and the infant had taken.

“Interrupt?” Jude studied her in a way that made her want to shrivel up and disappear. Then his eyes crinkled, and the corner of his mouth lifted. “You’re not interrupting anything but a busy work day, which is a blessing. Luckily, I’m on a fifteen.”

“Oh, good timing for once, I guess,” she mumbled.

“Did you need something, or did you just stop by to visit?” he asked, gently brushing his fingers on the outside of her elbow, drawing her attention back again.

“Oh, yes. I wanted to pick up something for my parents. A thank you for letting their grown-ass daughter come home again.”

His eyes lit up. “I have just the thing.”

He started walking away, but Marlo didn’t move. Tall, lean, and muscled, he crossed the shop with graceful efficiency.

Jude glanced back over his shoulder. “Follow me.”

Another flare of heat burst across her cheeks. She walked behind him, trying not to be obvious about eyeing the goods, but it would be criminal to ignore his body, even in the middle of the day in a crowded shop full of families. His shoulders were broader than she remembered.

She had to stop ogling him. It wasn’t good for her health.

Ever since their talk and since Heather sent her those pictures, some deeply buried part of Marlo rose to the surface. The part that couldn’t stop drooling over her former flame. It was simply a way to distract herself from her slowly imploding life, she reminded herself. Nothing more.

A distraction.

Jude led her behind the counter and then into the back of the shop.

Marlo gasped when they stepped into the kitchen. Nearly double the size of the front of the shop, it featured multiple prep surfaces and a wall of ovens as well as a walk-in refrigerator. There were at least three bakers working along with other support staff. It was a massive operation.

"Hey, everyone, this is Marlo Sage, an old friend. Penny, I'll take over in ten. Sorry about holding you up."

Ahh, Marlo thought. So this was *the* Penny.

Some of the other employees looked up and offered her smiles, while others kept working. Penny, a statuesque Black woman wearing a chef's uniform matching Jude's, openly stared at Marlo. She gave Marlo a flash of smile before returning to her work. The knowing look conveyed a combination of *I see you* and *don't fuck with that man*.

Message received. Marlo flushed.

Marlo shifted her attention to the rest of the staff and marveled at their industry, some kneading or rolling out dough, others icing, and yet others delicately lifting freshly baked cakes from baking tins onto cooling racks.

Jude gestured toward the giant steel door of the walk-in. "It's in here."

Right, the cake. Marlo nearly forgot her guise for returning to the shop. stepping into the chilled space behind him, she said, "Jude, this place is amazing."

"The walk-in?"

"No, the whole shop."

He dropped his gaze, and his shy, boyish grin reappeared. "Thanks, it's been a labor of love, and I'm so lucky to have a killer crew."

Marlo shivered, the cold air seeping through the thin layers of her clothes.

"Sorry, I should have let you wait outside. I forget that not everyone is used to these babies." Jude pulled out cake box from a shelf near the back. "Here we go. This is your mom's favorite. I always try to save one for her when I make it."

Her knees softened. Jude knew her mother's favorite cake and tried to save her one. He was good with babies. Not to mention the chef's uniform. She didn't stand a chance. This visit proved an even worse idea than she'd originally imagined. The last thing Marlo needed was to fall back under Jude's hypnotic spell. It didn't help matters that his relationship status remained unclear. No, this was no time for this infatuation to roar back to life.

Suddenly Marlo appreciated the full meaning in Penny's warning glance—*tread carefully with that man, he's a good one, one worth fighting for*. Thank God it was fifty below frigid in the walk-in so that her cheeks couldn't betray her for once.

JUDE

Jude led Marlo back out the way they entered. He appreciated that his staff didn't fuss over her presence. Penny gave him a knowing smirk as they exited the kitchen. He knew he'd be in for it later. Marlo stepped up to the counter as if she intended to pay.

He reached out for her arm. "Don't be ridiculous. It's my treat."

"No, this is your business. I want to pay."

Jude noted a beat too late that his hand lingered on her arm. He pulled it away, hoping she didn't notice, but he couldn't help wanting to touch her, especially since their talk. "You're doing the charity show. Consider it a thank you."

Marlo laughed. "I'm going to be in trouble if you intend to ply me with sweets."

He wished she realized how lovely her laugh sounded—a lighthearted, carefree tune. If only her lifestyle afforded her more moments to shed her public shell. He chided himself. It was no longer his place to worry about how Marlo chose to live her life. It never had been, but old habits didn't die quietly. He handed her the cake box. She gripped it and continued to hold his gaze.

Jude shifted his weight from one foot to the other. "So I guess I'll see you soon."

She tilted her head slightly and then realization dawned upon her gaze. "Oh, yes, I promised you a set list."

"You promised me a conversation," he said. "Plus, if you need a rehearsal partner, I'm happy to help."

He couldn't pin down from what depths of his demented psyche that offer emerged. He opened his mouth to retract it, but Marlo beamed at him.

"Like old time's," she said.

"Yeah, something like that."

Jude nodded, unsure what more to say. She fidgeted with the cake box and then sucked the corner of her lower lip under her top teeth. Jude surveyed the shop. They had an audience. He trusted most of his clientèle to play it cool, but ever since his profile in the culinary world began to rise, they'd begun to attract a different type of crowd. He couldn't be sure any longer that someone wouldn't succumb to the temptation to send a snap of them to the tabloids for a quick buck.

"Please give my regards to your parents," he said, a touch too loudly.

Marlo startled, like he'd just roused her from a daydream. "Oh, yes, of course. Thank you."

She turned on her heel, and for the first time since she'd stepped into his shop, she moved with the quick determination he was used to seeing from her. She'd always known how to turn it on for an audience. He watched the door for several minutes after she exited. Her visit filled him with an ache he hated to name, simultaneously comforting and discomfiting.

Penny punched him from behind. "So are you going to tell me what's going on?"

He turned to face his business partner, accompanied by her wife and their baby. "I don't interfere with your marriage, so no grief."

Penny and Kate laughed in unison.

"Um, you do too interfere. And why do you assume I'm about to give you grief?" Penny asked.

Jude shrugged. "Guess payback."

"You saved me from making the worst mistake of my life a couple of years ago." Penny looked at her wife, her eyes brimming with love. "Consider this us returning the favor."

Jude glanced back at the door. "There's nothing there. She's just an old friend."

"Right, old friend. I've heard that one before," Kate said, grinning.

"Kate, not you too," he said. "I swear there is nothing there."

"You keep telling yourself that," Penny said, "and when you stop living in delusion, we're here for you. Isn't that right, baby girl?" She nuzzled her baby's fluffy cheeks.

Jude glared at Penny for half a second, the longest amount of time he could muster before cracking into a smile. Penny's good-natured demeanor made it impossible for anyone to stay mad at her for long. Well, no one but Kate, and even then, she caved pretty quick.

"Can I get back to work, ladies?" Jude tickled the baby under her drool-soaked chin.

"I'll be right back," Penny said.

Taking in the picture of Penny and her family, Jude's heart simultaneously swelled and ached. "Go ahead and take off, I can finish menus for tomorrow."

"Are you sure, boss?"

"Yeah, go enjoy little Evie while she still likes you both." He dodged Penny's and Kate's playful punches.

Penny didn't need to be married to work like he was. She'd built an actual life, a family of her own. He hoped to do the same one day, but in his current circumstances, it seemed an impossible dream.

MARLO

When Marlo returned home, her parents were nowhere to be seen. She set the cake down on the counter.

"Mom? Dad?" she called out as she searched for them.

The attic access ladder in the hallway was pulled down.

She climbed up the first couple of rungs, peering into the space above. "Dad, are you up here?"

"Yes, come up."

Marlo paused halfway up. "Do you see any spiders?"

"No," he answered, his voice lilting with laughter.

He knew how much she hated the cobweb-strung space. So if he lied to her, the gloves would be off. She climbed up the rungs gingerly.

"Whoa," she said, spinning around the room and shielding her eyes from the unexpected brightness of the overhead light. In place of the former solitary single bulb was a row of can lights. The attic was completely transformed with finished, bookshelf-lined walls. "Wait, when did you do this?"

"A couple of years ago, when we replaced the roof. I lost some things from water damage." His voice trailed off as he stared into the distance.

He didn't have to tell Marlo what he lost. She knew he meant items he'd saved after his parents died.

"What are you holding?" she asked.

He glanced down at the stringed instrument in his hand. "Oh, this was Jidoo's oud. I never learned to play." He ran a finger across the taut strings. "I don't even know if it's tuned."

"I didn't know Jidoo played music," she said, reaching out for the instrument.

"Not professionally like you. He was just gifted and enjoyed it as a hobby." Her dad shook his head. "I used to give him so much grief about it. I thought it was so embarrassing when he tried to play for my friends."

Marlo stopped fiddling with the strings and looked up at her dad. His eyes glistened. She wasn't sure what to say to comfort him. Sometimes he told her how much he'd struggled as a first-generation immigrant, torn between fitting in and staying true to his heritage. Then there was the grief of losing his parents at a young age, just as he was beginning to build his own family.

"Can I have this?" she asked.

Her dad chuckled, his voice thick with emotion. "Do you know how to play it?"

"No, but I can learn," she smiled, strumming her fingers across the strings.

"It already sounds better than any of my attempts," he said, wiping tears from his eyes.

"When I learn, I can teach you." Marlo set the oud down and crossed the space, wrapping her dad in a hug.

He cried quietly against her shoulder.

"I wish I met Bebe and Jidoo," she said.

"They would have been so proud of you."

Marlo's own tears gathered at the corners of her eyes. Her dad's grief was catching. Tara had recommended trying something new with her music. Maybe her grandfather's oud was the answer. Perhaps avoiding her heritage, burying it beneath an artifice of celebrity, was where she'd gone wrong. What if she tried embracing it instead?

For the first time since she'd returned home, a new goal presented itself to Marlo.

David said she wasn't allowed to perform any Pop Machine songs at Jude's show, but since the label rejected her latest demo, those songs were fair game, belonging solely to her. If she added the oud and other traditional Arab instruments like the doumbek, a wooden goblet-shaped hand drum, maybe she could create something unexpected yet entirely her own. An angry woman behind a microphone might be a dangerous investment to David, but maybe it was time Marlo started investing in herself.

Chapter Eleven

MARLO

MARLO PULLED UP in front of the Beckett household ten minutes early to find James waiting for her on the porch.

"Look at you," she called out as she walked up the driveway.

James Beckett, decked out in tour merch from both her Marlo & Jude days and her more recent solo concerts, grinned at her. He'd transformed himself into a walking billboard for her career.

"Have to rub it in all the doubters' faces," he said, beaming. "Thank you for offering to take me."

"My honor," she answered, blinking away the moisture gathering in the corners of her eyes.

She offered him a hand down the stairs, trying not to fixate on the sensation of his paper-thin skin stretched taut over prominent bones. He grew winded by the time they reached the passenger door. All her battles seemed so small in comparison to what he faced, quite sobering.

"You aren't even driving the speed limit," he said after a few minutes of riding in silence.

Marlo glanced at him and smiled.

"I'm not made of glass. I won't break."

"Sorry," she said. "Dad's given me a complex about my driving."

"You're doing great. Now give it some gas. I want to parade you around before it's time for my infusion."

She laughed. James Beckett was exactly as she remembered him, yet everything had changed. They pulled up to the nondescript two-story building adjacent to the hospital. Marlo handed the keys to the valet and again offered her arm to Mr. Beckett.

"Okay," she said. "Give me the grand tour."

He took off at a steady clip ahead of her, somehow reinvigorated.

"Hello, ladies," James said, beaming at the two women behind the reception desk. "I have a new guest."

Marlo, still working to catch her breath racing after him, waved.

"Oh my god," the brunette said, eyes welling. "I'm a huge fan."

The redhead next to her rolled her eyes. "Sorry, it's the same procedure even if you're famous." She gestured to the open pad on the counter. "Please sign in, and then we'll need to take a photo for your guest badge."

The two women exchanged a look, the brunette's cheeks flushed. "And then you need to take a healthy dollop of sanitizer and don a mask," she said, shifting her attention to Marlo.

"You, too, Jimmy," she added.

"But then how will people see my smug grin?" he asked as he slung the elastic bands of the masks around his ears.

"It shows in your eyes," Marlo said, playfully nudging him in the ribs.

Marlo followed suit, and James walked her back to say hello to a few of the administrators and nurse navigators before leading her upstairs to the infusion suite.

His pride at showing her off made her heart swell. But the reality of walking through the infusion suite and seeing the sheer number of patients dulled her shine. People of all ages and walks of life sat in semi-recliners while IV bags overhead dripped various colored liquids into plastic tubing. Marlo took her time, posing for photos with patients and signing autographs.

"The worst part about this place is how boring it is to sit here for hours," James said, when they arrived at his chair.

"How do you usually entertain yourself?" Marlo asked.

"Sometimes sudoku or crossword puzzles," he said, a mischievous glint in his eye.

"Okay, but really how?"

Mr. Beckett laughed. "I may have developed a taste for trashy reality television."

"This feels like a setup," called out an older gentleman in the bay next to Mr. Beckett's chair.

"Nassar," James said, "I'd like you to meet Marlo Sage."

Marlo waved at the man, and then her eyes landed on the object in his lap—an oud. She glanced back at Mr. Beckett, who grinned at her.

"Your dad told me you might be interested in lessons," Mr. Beckett said.

And she thought the moms were bad with their conniving.

"My Jidoo had one of those," she said, gesturing to the instrument. "Only not as fancy."

Nassar ran his knobby fingers over the mother-of-pearl inlay. "This is my special girl. James insisted I bring her today." He glanced up at Marlo. "Sometimes I play music for the other patients."

Marlo settled into the chair next to Mr. Beckett as a nurse flushed his port and connected his lines while narrating every step, likely for Marlo's benefit.

"I would love to hear you play," Marlo said.

Nassar's eyes turned misty. He flexed his fingers. "Bad neuropathy day today."

Marlo glanced back at James. "Sometimes chemo messes with the nerve endings in your hands and feet."

Nassar cleared his throat. "But I'd love to watch you play. I can give you tips."

James gently nudged Marlo. "Go on. This will be fun to watch."

She walked around to Nassar's chair, accepting the oud as he held it out to her. "It truly is stunning," she said. "Be gentle with me. I've only watched a few lessons online."

"It's a special instrument, far more ancient than the guitar. It inspired the lute. Always handmade. Oud-making is a hallowed craft passed through generations of families."

Marlo counted the strings and looked up at Nassar. "Twelve strings."

"Yes, and did you notice it's also fretless, so chords are limited but you can play quarter tones on a monochromatic scale."

Marlo smiled at Nassar. She'd never tire of talking music with another expert. "Freedom to explore new sounds."

"Exactly, every country has their own twist on styles, tunings, rhythms, and scales. Almost like a different language for different moods or cultures."

Her eyes welled with a combination of pride and shame. She came from a rich musical heritage, yet she was nearly completely ignorant of it.

Nassar walked her through a rudimentary lesson as James beamed on. As her ear learned the unique sound, her mind whirred with possibility, immediately composing new melodies. She was supposed to be here to support Mr. Beckett. Instead, he'd given her an invaluable gift.

"Amu, I don't how to thank you," Marlo said, handing back the instrument to Nassar.

"Shine your light on our music," he said, smiling. "And please, keep it. It will get far better use in your capable hands than mine."

"I couldn't," Marlo protested.

"He wants you to have it, right, Nassar?" James winked at his friend.

"From the very bottom of my heart," he said.

"I am moved," she said, her voice cracking, her heart fit to burst.

"Don't be afraid to incorporate every piece of yourself into your music," he said as the nurse unhooked his bag and replaced his port dressing.

"Thank you. Same time next week?" Marlo grinned.

"Inshallah," he said.

Marlo returned to Mr. Beckett's side and joined him in solving a crossword. She hadn't expected the infusion center visit to be such an energizing experience. There was something about the concentrated goodwill between the staff, the patients, and the caregivers that made it a hallowed space. She promised she'd give the L&L Society the performance of a lifetime. These patients deserved no less. For the first time in a long time, hope and purpose bloomed in Marlo's chest.

Chapter Twelve

JUDE

JUDE," PENNY CALLED out from the kitchen. "Back line for you."

Jude set down the tray of fresh pastries he'd just brought out, gesturing to one of the staff to take over. A call on the back line was almost always from his parents. He checked his watch. His dad was due to be at the infusion clinic right now. His heart rate kicked up.

"Hello," Jude answered.

"Hi, son, sorry to call at work," his mom said in an urgent rush.

"Is Dad okay?"

"Yes, he's fine. Have you seen the news today?"

"No, what is it?"

"A press release dropped this morning about you and Marlo reuniting for the bake-off at the end of the summer."

Jude groaned. He wished Marlo had warned him that Tara planned to do that. They could have chosen a better time than having it coincide with his father's appointment. His parents already stressed out as normal course on infusion days.

“Not entirely surprising. Marlo has to use these things to her advantage sometimes,” he explained.

“Well, yes, but apparently the infusion clinic is surrounded by the press. The parking spots are all taken up by news vans. Jude, it’s a madhouse. They’re inside, but your dad isn’t sure how they’re going to leave safely once he’s done.”

“Who do you mean ‘they’? Aren’t you with him?” Jude asked.

His mom went quiet for a beat. “Marlo took your dad to his appointment today.”

Jude’s jaw clenched. He’d never even considered that inviting Marlo to perform at the charity show might include the possibility that the media would be so crass that they’d descend upon an infusion center to badger patients and their families. He fought the urge to punch in the wall.

“Why did you let her do that?” Jude struggled to temper his voice.

“They were both so excited about it. I thought it would be a good chance for them to reconnect.”

“Mom.” He sighed.

“Please don’t make me feel worse. Help me.”

“Wait, Mom, couldn’t the clinic consider the press presence a violation of patient confidentiality? There has to be some law preventing them from camping out and filming in front of a medical facility.”

“Oh, Jude, I didn’t think of that.”

“Let me call Suze. I’ll send her over to them, okay?” He wanted to jump in his car and drive straight there, but if he showed up with all the media present, he’d only worsen the situation. Suze was the next best option. She’d know what to do.

“Thank you. I’ll talk to the supervisor about the privacy angle.”

“Call me and keep me up to date,” he said, hating the overwhelming sensation of helplessness overtaking him.

“I will.”

Jude immediately rang up Suze and explained the situation.

"Don't worry. I actually handled a similar situation for a client. Without the consent of patients, the film crews can't be on site. That's not to say we can disperse them altogether, but we can at least create a safe perimeter. I'm on my way there, okay? Don't worry."

"Thank you, Suze. I'd head over there myself, but I feel like it might make everything worse."

"Definitely. Stay put, darlin', but be on alert. They'll probably head your way next."

"Got it."

He hung up. Maybe the best course would be to cancel the charity bake-off all together. He couldn't let cancer patients get swept up in the media circus that followed Marlo like a shadow. They could just donate large matching sums to the Leukemia & Lymphoma Society and call it done. Nothing was worth inviting this tabloid madness back into their lives. Not when it impacted innocent members of their families.

Penny popped her head into his office. "We have a problem."

Jude ran his hand through his hair. He didn't even need to ask her to explain. He knew exactly what he was about to step out and find. Marlo couldn't ever separate herself from the media—they were a package deal, obligate parasites—and Jude wasn't sure he'd ever be able to make peace with that reality.

MARLO

Marlo held her phone to her ear and paced the private office she and Mr. Beckett were tucked into when all pandemonium broke loose at the infusion clinic. Suze filled her in on the unexpected fallout of the announcement of Marlo's involvement in the charity bake-off. She called on her way to get rid of the press circling like shameless vultures around a cancer care facility. It was unconscionable to disturb patients on their way to receive cancer treatment. They absolutely had no shame. A pit formed in Marlo's stomach. This was all directly her fault.

"I just wanted you to be aware that we're working on it, sweetie," Suze said.

"I can't believe this is happening." Yes, she could—it was one of those platitudes people said when words were suddenly inadequate. "Thanks for calling. I'll loop in Tara."

"Heads up, Jude is really upset."

Marlo shut her eyes and tried to steady her breathing. Of course he was upset. Not only were the paparazzi in town, but they'd targeted her and his ailing father at a treatment facility. It was lower than low, and whatever tears in the fabric of their friendship they'd mended earlier, she already knew Jude would never forgive this.

"Thanks, again," Marlo said. "I appreciate you letting me know. Is there anything I can do while we wait?"

"Stay calm. Lay low. It's going to be okay."

Standard advice lately, and it grew increasingly difficult not to take it personally. Would literally every person in her life be better off if she simply went into permanent hiding somewhere remote?

Marlo expected the glare of flashbulbs and media scrutiny to be directed at her and maybe a little at Jude, but she hadn't anticipated interest in their families. Guilt slid up her throat with the bitterest tang of bile. She was trying to help lighten Mrs. Beckett's load, and instead she'd made everything orders of magnitude worse.

"Don't worry, hon', seriously. I know you've both had a lot on your shoulders," Suze said. "We'll figure this out. I'm just so stoked to see you working together again."

"Are you?" Marlo asked, sincerely surprised to hear the admission.

"Of course. I tried to talk him out of leaving, you know. But in the end, as much as he loves you, his heart wasn't in music."

"*Loves* me?" In light of everything else going on, it was the dumbest thing to fixate on. But Suze used present tense. One letter change and the meaning of everything she knew shifted.

Jude was Marlo's first love, but when he left abruptly, she'd questioned whether she'd read everything between them wrong. Words didn't negate actions. He told her loved her in secret but pretended for all the world that they were nothing more than friends. She'd told herself it wasn't real love because real love didn't hide, it didn't fade. She should know.

"Oh darlin', yes of course. That boy is nuts about you. It tore him up to leave, and it's taken him a long time to put himself back together. But the way he feels about you, it'll never change."

Could Suze have this right? Marlo's heart lurched.

"Should I call him now to check in?" Marlo asked.

"Give him some time to process and cool down."

Marlo swallowed back the disappointment. The glimmer of hope Suze offered increased the urgency to speak with Jude tenfold.

"If anything changes and you think of a way I can help," Marlo said, "please let me know." She hated this sense of powerless inertia. Maybe Jude was right from the start and coming home had been a terrible idea. But now that she was here, she couldn't stand the thought of leaving. Not yet. Not until she set things to rights.

"You got it," Suze said.

Marlo hung up and another wave of disgust rolled over her. Tara hadn't even warned her that the press release was about to drop, which was so unlike her. They could have at least prepared, not that anyone would have seen this current scenario coming.

A thought struck Marlo just before she called Tara. She pulled out her notebook. She'd write her way through it, just like she always had.

JUDE

Since its opening day, Jude had never closed the shop early, not when they still had any items left to sell, but today he was left with no other option. Protecting his patrons and his employees from the crush of paparazzi took priority over business as usual. He reassured his staff they'd receive their full wages. They shuttered the windows and divvied the fresh goods among themselves.

"I can stay with you if you like," Penny offered.

"No, I don't want anyone here. Go home to your family, pull your blinds, lock your doors, and stay safe."

She continued to study him. "It's not her fault, you know."

He nodded, turning away and staring off in the distance. "No, it's mine."

"No, it isn't yours either."

Jude looked at Penny then.

"Even if you were the Queen of England," she continued. "you and your family wouldn't deserve this kind of violation of privacy. I wish I could do something more for you."

"Get home safely, for me. Honestly, I need that peace of mind right now, okay?"

Penny agreed and excused herself.

He pulled out his phone and called the person he least wanted to speak to at present. Well, that wasn't entirely true. He was caught in the pendulum swing of wanting to make sure she was okay and wanting to confront her about why he wasn't given a heads-up about the press release.

"Jude?" Marlo exhaled. "Are you okay? I just heard about the shop."

"I closed up and sent everyone home."

"I'm so sorry. I can't believe they've staked out the infusion clinic and your shop. Your dad wants me to tell you he's fine and not to worry."

Jude sighed. "May as well tell the sky not to be blue."

A helpless gasp sounded over the phone speaker. "Jude," she said. "I don't know what to say. I'm just so devastated this is happening to you and your family."

He paused. Fury, sadness, and guilt warred inside him. "Honestly, I want to punch a hole through something."

"My face?" She gave a little tense laugh.

"No, never that." He sighed. "It's not your fault. It's just so frustrating. I didn't ever want to be back in this position, you know?"

"Yeah, I know," Marlo said in the smallest voice.

Her clear anguish gnawed at his heart and defused his anger. He didn't call her to blame her or to make her feel worse. He simply needed to speak to someone to pass the time until he could leave and return home in peace.

No, that was a lie. He'd hungered to speak to Marlo.

He was worried about her, angry at her, and torn up that her peace was so fleeting. He wanted her to help him make sense of his conflicting emotions and responsibilities. No one else would understand.

"Jude, I—"

"You know what?" He shook his head. He was wrong. Not even she could help him at the moment. "I think I need to go and bake something. I'll call you later."

"Okay."

Jude ended the call before giving her the chance to say anything else. He retrieved the dry ingredients he needed from the pantry, then he stepped into the cooler, grabbing eggs, milk, and butter. Blackout cake soaked in bourbon with chocolate icing—he needed a cake that tasted like forgetting. He took a shot of bourbon before getting started. Measuring out the ingredients, his breathing deepened and steadied for the first time in the last few hours.

"Save some for me?" Penny asked.

Jude hadn't seen her lurking in the corner of the kitchen.

"What are you doing back here?"

"I can't leave you on your own. Kate agrees."

He smiled and poured himself and her each a shot. They toasted each other despite the somber mood.

"What are you working on?" she asked.

"Bourbon-soaked blackout cake with dark chocolate icing. Want to help?"

"Nah, I'm thinking cream pies."

"Really?" Pies were not one of Penny's favorite bakes.

"Yeah, we can toss them in some faces on the way out. Figure it'll feel cathartic."

Jude laughed. "Thanks, Pen."

"You got it, boss."

He sifted flour into the mixing bowl. His phone buzzed in his pocket with an incoming text. Then another one and another one. He wiped his hands on his apron and stepped away from his workstation. After what happened to his dad earlier, he couldn't risk not answering the phone in case of emergency. He unlocked his phone to find several people sending him links to the same article.

A Celeb Smash hit piece with Marlo's name in the headline. He groaned.

Not again.

What else did they possibly have to write about her? David Stringer's smear campaign was relentless—planting stories accusing her of everything from satanic worship to overseeing a sex dungeon. Because of the endless media bashing, Marlo remained in this self-imposed exile, but she wasn't even safe in her hometown. She pretty much only left the house when she visited him, aside from this infusion center visit. Not that it was his business to keep track of her comings and goings.

He hated giving the gossip site another click, but his curiosity won over his propriety. The page loaded pixel by pixel. A salacious headline, an unflattering picture of Marlo, which must've taken significant effort to obtain and was likely doctored to look worse, and finally the article itself.

Inside sources report Pop Machine eyes dropping arguably its most successful star. The latest Marlo Sage antics of publicly skewering David Stringer did not go over well with the label exec. And after the scandalous stories Cliff Rochester shared, Marlo Sage may be more of a liability than she's worth. Rumors are David Stringer and his fellow music industry dick clique burned her in effigy recently at a party in his swank new digs in the Hollywood Hills. Don't believe me? There are videos, people, and my Smashers did their magic to secure them for you.

Jude's jaw tensed. He'd always hated David Stringer and those other music industry executives. He remembered, when Marlo wasn't in the room or even simply out of earshot, they often made crass comments about her or how great Jude had it, a young man in his prime with "his pick of pussy." The recollection alone roiled Jude's stomach. He was a teenager, hardly a man in his prime. It was so toxic and gross, and it was a significant reason why Jude couldn't wait to leave. At the time, he couldn't name it, he just knew he couldn't deal with the pervasive misogyny in the music industry. Now the guilt of leaving her alone to deal with those bastards made him want to wretch.

He skimmed to the end of the article. The petty asshole was truly trying to blackball Marlo because she had the gall to call him out on his shady behavior in a public forum. It was wild how the music industry cannibalized its own. Marlo had put Pop Machine on the map. She'd made it a destination label for the big artists who followed.

"What's up, Jude?" Penny asked, concern lining her eyes.

He held up the video from the article for her.

"Those dickheads," she muttered, shivering at the sight of the bonfire and cackling group of old men. "What are you going to do?"

"What can I possibly do?" Jude slid his phone back into his pocket and gripped the edge of his workspace.

"Listen here, you're going to finish that cake and take it to her. Then you're going to watch her eat it while she cries on your shoulder."

Jude grunted. "That sounds messy."

"Jude, I'm not playing. That's what's happening."

A couple hours later, after checking in on his parents, and at Penny's incessant urging, Jude showed up at Marlo's doorstep with the cake and the now half-empty bottle of bourbon. It was one of those moments he knew would prove an epic mistake, and he debated leaving. Once he crossed this threshold, there would be no turning back.

Her mom answered the door before he could flee.

Chapter Thirteen

MARLO

BETWEEN THE INFUSION clinic fiasco and the tabloid hit piece, Marlo climbed up to the attic when she finally returned home, unable to even talk to her parents. She sat crisscross on the rug with her new, borrowed oud in her lap, watching video tutorials while she continued to learn to play. Music as escapism at its finest. But it didn't ease the knots and twists in her stomach. She'd been so foolish to ever think she could take on David Stringer and win. At least Tara had warned her about the story and the video ahead of time, by mere minutes so she wasn't entirely blindsided. The warning didn't dull the sting though.

Worse, Tara told her she hadn't sent the press release about the charity bake-off, so apparently it was all part of David's doings—a double strike guaranteed to wound her to the core. He was out for blood.

"Damn it," Marlo said, when she played the wrong scale. She restarted the lesson at the beginning.

She had spent years as the only woman in the room at meetings, and the animosity toward her was always a palpable undercurrent. Marlo may have been young, but she wasn't stupid. She caught all the innuendos, the smug smirks. She simply ignored them. If she didn't give it oxygen, she'd assumed it would eventually fade.

Wasn't that the lesson all girls were taught to protect themselves in male-dominated spaces? *Ignore. Rise above. The more it hurts, the bigger the smile. Relax, they're just joking. Careful, don't provoke them.* But that video of her burning in effigy really drove home just how virulent the hatred they harbored toward her was the whole time. Another wave of nausea rolled over her.

What crime had she committed?

All she'd ever wanted to do was make her music and share it with the people who appreciated it. That was her unforgiveable transgression—the desire to create and connect with others through her art. Marlo craved the space and freedom to use her voice. And to be seen as a human being, not a commodity. Pop Machine's public seek-and-destroy campaign grew nastier by the minute. All because she'd had one low moment and slipped, giving her real perspective an escape valve. She spoke truth to power, and now power intended to crush her and her dreams. The worst part was the public would likely play right into their plan to ruin her.

Because, at the end of the day, people still hungered to see a witch burn.

"Sweetheart, can I get you anything?" Her mom popped her head over the attic opening, her eyes framed by deep worry lines.

Marlo shook her head. She'd silenced her phone earlier, but it still taunted her by lighting up every few seconds with no doubt another reporter keen to land the first response from her. Earlier, Tara had locked all Marlo's social media accounts to reduce the swarms of trolls clogging her pages with hateful words and insulting memes. It was funny that so many people forgot she was one of them, a real-life person made of the same flesh, blood, and sinew as them. The words and acts of mimicked violence sliced deeper than any knife could.

"I do have a visitor for you," her mom said.

"Who?"

Her mom slipped out of view.

"Mom, I'm not in the mood for games."

Suddenly, Jude came into view. He looked at her with wide-open, sorrow-filled eyes that made her heart ache all over again.

He scanned the space. "Wow, this is cool. Too bad they didn't fix it up when we were kids."

"They probably didn't trust us to be alone up here."

Jude carried a cake box and a plastic bag in one hand. He set them next to her and then lowered himself to the ground, mirroring her folded legs.

"Is the house swarmed?" she asked, sniffling.

"There are two cars parked across the street, with telephoto lenses pointed in this direction. Sorry, I didn't think they'd get here so fast." He pulled down his hood and removed his ball cap, ruffling his hands through his hair before locking eyes with her again. He gestured to the oud. "What do you have there?"

"An oud, my Jidoo used to play, but this one is from your dad's chemo friend. I'm learning."

"That's cool. Can I try?" He held his palms out to her.

"Do you still play any music?"

"I dabble from time to time." He strummed the strings. "How are you doing?"

"Well, not great." She flicked a tear from the corner of her eye.

"I saw the Celeb Smash article." He gazed at her with such intensity, she wanted the earth to split apart and swallow her whole.

"Cool." She pursed her lips, trying but failing to stop the hot press of tears.

Jude leaned forward, kneeling before her and brushing the tears off her cheeks. Marlo tried to ignore the gravitational pull of his warmth. He was so close, and he smelled like vanilla and cinnamon. All she longed to do was lean into him and let the solid wall of muscle at his chest support her. She closed her eyes until he shifted positions and tucked her into his side.

"It's not cool. It's the very opposite," he said, wrapping his arm around her shoulder.

"Well, apparently the only thing remotely salvaging my reputation is being linked to you again, so I suppose I owe you a debt of gratitude." Marlo didn't mean to sound so bitchy, but it had been an epically terrible day. Actually, no, it had been a great day that was ruined for her. "Why did you come here?"

Jude's tight embrace was so protective that the tension between her shoulders eased for the first time all day. But it also broke the dam of her resolve. The sobs overtook her, and as she shook in his grasp, he only held her tighter.

Jude Beckett, human weighted blanket.

"Shh, I've got you," he said. "I'm so sorry, Marlo. You don't deserve this."

Marlo disagreed. What she didn't deserve was his kindness, especially since she was the one responsible for inviting the crush of paparazzi back into his life.

"I fucking hate him so much," she said.

"I do too." Jude brushed aside a lock of her hair that had fallen into her weepy eyes. "I always did."

"I mean, yeah, I was angry. I said some things. The last album didn't do that great, and by 'that great,' I mean it only spent six months at number two on the charts. A total failure, right?" She tried to slow her breathing, to steady her pounding heart. "But the thing is, everything I said about him was—and is—true. The man is a fucking creep and a hypocrite."

"For what it's worth, that album is my favorite of yours so far, and by the way, it spent over a year in the top ten album charts, even after slipping from number two to number four." Jude said. "Not a failure by any measure."

Marlo blinked back tears. "But it underperformed compared to 1977."

"That fucker. It's him that filled your head with all this nonsense, right? Your concert sold out in minutes."

She swallowed back a sob. "But I didn't win a single award for it."

From the corner of her eye, she saw Jude shaking his head, his nostrils flaring. Marlo had never seen him look so angry, but with everything that happened to his dad earlier, it had been a tough day for him too.

"Wait," she said. "How do you know all those stats?"

The tense grip of his muscles around her eased. She pushed away, out of his embrace, sadly, but she needed to see his face.

"You can't believe that dickhead's bullshit. That album is one of my favorites and not only of yours. I mean one of my favorite albums overall, ever." He dropped his head in his hands. "I tried to get a ticket to your show, but I didn't make it through the queue."

Marlo laughed. "The fan club early access queue? Jude Maynard Beckett, are you a Sage-head?"

His shoulders shook, but he kept his face hidden behind his hands. She tried to peel them back, but his grip was strong.

"Answer my question." Marlo gently pounded her fist into his shoulder until he finally dropped his hands and looked at her.

"I've never stopped following your career, and I was your first and will forever remain your biggest fan."

Marlo blinked at him for a minute, her chest squeezing tight. She had so much to say, so much she wanted to ask, but all she could do was stare into the deep pools of Jude's dark eyes.

"Thank you," she finally whispered.

JUDE

Jude pulled her back into their earlier position, with his arm caging her against his chest as her folded legs rested against his thigh. He rubbed his fingers up and down Marlo's arm absently as she railed against David Stringer—a torrent of rage she could no longer hold back now that the dam had broken. Her body alternated between relaxing into his touch and tensing as the anger welled up, demanding to be released. At the end of her last rant, Jude allowed himself a moment to process his own animosity toward David Stringer

He wasn't simply an exacting boss—he was a textbook sociopath. The coercion and manipulation of underlings was a game to him. He got off on it. Jude never appreciated the depth of David's depravity until this moment.

"Do you have any idea how awful it's been working for that man for over a decade?" Marlo continued. "Having my fake boyfriends picked out by him? Having him decide how I'm portrayed in the media? Working so hard to prove my worth to someone dedicated to never seeing it?"

Jude hugged her tighter. He never should have left her to face that monster alone.

"He poisoned my dream from the start," she said, "and now he's trying to prematurely end it. And everyone will believe whatever story he spins about me. They always have. So at the end of the day, it doesn't matter if I speak up or if I swallow all his lies whole. People are just looking for a reason to hate me."

Marlo started crying again, and it tore Jude's heart in two.

"And the worst part is," she went on, "that they don't realize that no one could hate me more than I hate myself."

"Marlo, don't say that." *The rest of us, we love you.* He didn't say that part aloud.

Jude wanted to absorb all her pain. He didn't know if any of the words he said were even adequate.

"How can I help?" he finally asked.

"I don't know. I don't think you can. I don't think anyone can." She sagged even further against him as she spoke. "Maybe I should just give them all what they want, quit and disappear for good."

"Do you remember that time you flew to LA with your mom when you were like ten years old and you auditioned to be on that children's cable network show?"

"You mean the part I didn't get?" Marlo sniffled. "You really suck at pep talks."

He tipped her chin up toward him. "Work with me here, Marlo. You came back so upset that you didn't book the job. You threw your dance shoes out, remember?"

She nodded and chuckled. "You fished them out of the trash for me."

"How did you know?"

"I know everything about you, Jude," she said.

He didn't allow himself to truly absorb those words. Instead, he returned the focus to her. "Remember how you felt those first few days?"

"I swore off a performing arts career forever. Too bad I didn't listen to ten-year-old Marlo. She was smart."

"You did that for a week, tops. Then what did you do?"

She shrugged and tried to look away, but he continued to hold her chin, firmly but gently enough not to hurt her.

"Then I signed up for more singing and dance lessons," she said. "I auditioned for a local musical."

"And?"

Marlo quirked her eyebrows. "What? That's it."

He shook his head. "No, you started writing songs. Your own songs. And what gift did you beg for that Christmas?"

She smiled and this time it reached her eyes. "A video camera."

Jude dropped her chin and pulled her into a tight hug, speaking into the top of her head. "A video camera. You came off your lowest low, and you invested in the next step. You might not have known exactly what it was or what it would lead to, but you did the work."

"It's not the same now."

"No, it won't be the same. The next few months—possibly even the next couple of years—are going to suck. But, Marlo, you will find your next path. I know you will. And I'll be here at your side to help you do it."

MARLO

Marlo's tears fell freely. She was powerless against the flood. Jude's gentle breaths tickled the side of her neck. He didn't owe her these kindnesses, and yet he was here, holding her. Of his own accord. His thumb drifted down and tipped her face back up again then brushed across her bottom lip as his gaze fixed on her mouth.

She stared into his eyes. Regret and longing warred within her. Marlo couldn't believe she ever let him go.

He leaned in toward her. She had exactly one centimeter to travel before her lips met his. Her eyelids dropped half-mast.

"Marlo," her mother called out from below the attic access.

They jumped apart, sitting opposite one another as if they were teenagers caught making out again.

"Yes, Mom?" Marlo called.

Her mom climbed up and smiled widely after a quick assessment of the scene. "Sorry to interrupt. You should probably invite Jude to stay for dinner."

"Pretty sure you just did." Marlo glanced at Jude then back at her mom. "We're not kids anymore, you know."

"I'm sorry. Did I miss the announcement that adults no longer eat dinner?"

Jude laughed.

Marlo glared at him. "Don't encourage her."

Her mother's smile faded. "Well, the thing is…" She glanced at the attic access again before she continued. "Your father just called, and it appears the road is blocked off."

"Blocked off?" Marlo stiffened.

"No, seriously?" Jude stared straight at her mother, but he reached across the floor and placed his hand on Marlo's folded leg.

"It seems word is spreading that you've returned home," her mom said, "and interest peaked with that damn video. I just got off the phone with Tara."

Okay, this habit of her mom and Tara chatting about her behind her back needed to stop.

"Do they know he's here?" Marlo glanced at Jude's hand on her leg and then back up to his eyes.

"So far, no, but Jude should probably stay until the roads clear up. Your dad went straight to the mayor's office, and Tara is doing what Tara does best—handling it."

Marlo sucked in her breath. Part of her knew it would come to this, but it was still shocking and upsetting to face the reality of it. Jude squeezed her knee, and she returned her attention to him.

"I would love to stay," he said. "It's no problem."

Marlo couldn't summon the will to say anything more. She wasn't sure if she was misreading it, but in his words, there seemed to be an undercurrent of a promise to continue where they'd left off earlier.

"I'm going to work on getting dinner ready. Can I get you two anything?" her mom asked.

"Do you need help?" Jude asked.

Marlo's voice remained muted. *No, stay.*

"No, please stay put," her mom said as if reading her mind. "You cook enough for all of us in this town. We always owe it to you to repay the favor."

Marlo caught the flash of a shy smile and a tiny dusting of blush across his cheeks. The knot in her chest eased. Her mom was so good at knowing just what someone needed. It was totally her superpower. Jude clearly appreciated someone using his own love language to care for him. A new wave of guilt washed over her again. She'd known him for so many years and yet failed to see so much about him.

"Thank you, Mrs. Rayhan," Jude said.

Her mom waved off the thanks. "Please call me Dani. Mrs. Rayhan makes me feel too old."

Then she retreated.

Marlo shifted uncomfortably, unsure how to fill the sudden heavy silence between them. Jude's gaze trailed over her skin, but she couldn't look him in the eye again quite yet. She was one raw, aching nerve. He'd read it all in the instant their eyes met. She'd always been an open book, particularly under his gaze.

"Hey, Marlo. Don't worry. We'll get through this." Jude scooted closer to her, placing his hands on her shoulders.

His use of "we," along with the physical contact, sent a dagger through her heart. She was afraid to let herself believe in the promise of "we" again. They'd grown into near strangers, and they were simply forced back together by circumstance. How long before he tired of her again?

"This is all the stuff you hated most about me," she said, "and now I've brought it to your doorstep, repeatedly."

He tipped her chin toward him. His eyes lightened into warm pools of amber-tinged brown. "I never hated you."

Marlo's heart jumped into her throat. He was so close again. The war whether or not to close the distance raged inside her. There were too many chances of interruptions while her mom remained in the house with them. And she had a feeling that, once they crossed this threshold, it would be nuclear between them—a sudden, unstoppable explosion that would permanently change everything.

"And by the way," he continued, "my bake shop brought some of the buzz to the yard."

Marlo groaned and laughed simultaneously. Jude grinned at her. Even without a kiss, he had a knack for making her feel better.

Chapter Fourteen

JUDE

A FEW SECONDS AGO, Marlo was close enough he could have kissed her, and God, he wanted nothing more. Now, she pulled away again. He wondered if he'd always experience this tug-of-war between what his heart wanted and what his sensibilities cautioned where Marlo was concerned.

Her phone rang. She covered the microphone as she rose and mouthed *Tara* at him, stepping away for the conversation. Jude took the opportunity to head back into the main house and check on Mrs. Rayhan in the kitchen, the one place he trusted his instincts.

"Couldn't resist the siren song of the six-burner stove, huh?" Mrs. Rayhan teased.

He smiled. "Marlo got a phone call."

A tiny furrow developed between her brows. "That girl just needs a chance to catch her breath."

"She does."

Marlo needed a real break, not Jude sitting in her childhood home rehashing bittersweet old memories. Actually, what she really didn't need was to be coerced into performing at a charity bake-off. He looked around the small kitchen. He still couldn't believe after all these years, Marlo's parents refused to let her buy them a newer home. A couple of years ago, they'd finally agreed to a minor renovation when their thirty-plus-year-old appliances began to die in rapid succession. Marlo contacted him to ask for his assistance in hiring contractors and selecting new equipment. He'd been more than happy to oblige.

"Can I help prep anything? I've heard I'm a decent sous chef." He winked.

"A salad would be great," she said. "Sorry it's not as glamorous as what you're used to." She pulled out a cutting board and knife, as well as the salad ingredients and the bowl to place them in.

"No task in the kitchen is too small." Jude rolled his neck, trying to loosen the tension settling there.

Chopping required the type of focus that forced him to turn off the other channels of worry and stress, and he was grateful for it. He started with a pile of cucumbers. Then he moved on to the garden-fresh tomatoes. The scent of fresh-off-the-vine tomatoes always made him smile.

"That song was always one of my favorites of yours," Mrs. Rayhan said.

His fingers stilled. "Was I humming?"

"Yes, you hum all the time. Hasn't anyone told you before?"

Jude laughed. He guessed he did. He'd never really thought about it before, and he'd never admit that it was solely his and Marlo's old hits running through his head. "I guess music is imprinted on my DNA."

She smiled. "I know you don't love it as much as she does, but there's an undeniable magic between you two, especially live on stage. I will always miss it."

Jude couldn't formulate a response, so he resumed chopping with new vigor.

“Ow,” he grunted, dropping the knife on the cutting board.

“Oh, no, are you okay?” Mrs. Rayhan grabbed a clean towel from the cupboard, dampened it, and brought it over to Jude.

“What happened?” Marlo asked, looking even more exhausted and weary as she stepped into the kitchen.

“Marlo, take Jude to the guest bathroom, and help him get patched up,” her mom said. “There’s a first aid kit under the sink. I’ll get everything in here cleaned up.”

“I’m sorry, Mrs. Rayhan,” Jude said, trying not to look at the gash on his thumb.

His face flushed. He was the professional chef, and he’d made the ultimate rookie mistake—and he wasn’t even at work. Jude’s embarrassment ran deep to his core, because in case the unforced kitchen error wasn’t bad enough, the sight of blood made him woozy. A bead of sweat broke out along his neck.

“Happens to the best of us,” she said, her eyes flicking to Marlo. “Get him squared away before he drips on our meal.”

MARLO

Marlo wrapped the towel, now streaked with bright red blood, around Jude’s thumb and led him to the bathroom. His face paled. She stifled a laugh. The sight of blood and needles always made him wilt. For someone who spent so much time around sharp kitchen utensils, it was an absurd contradiction. Marlo wouldn’t admit it to Jude, but she relished the opportunity to play the caretaker in his moment of weakness.

“Look away,” she said as she brought him to the sink. “I’m going to gently wash it out, okay?”

He sucked in a haggard breath. “Okay.”

"Warn me if you're about to faint," Marlo said, as she turned the cold water tap on.

Jude gripped the edge of the bathroom counter with his uninjured hand and sagged against her, resting his head on her shoulder and staring at the shower enclosure across the bathroom.

"Just do it," he said. "Get it over with."

"The water's cold." Marlo brought his thumb under the stream of water, and he tensed against her.

Beads of fresh blood dotted the wound as she gently explored it. Luckily, it wasn't deep enough to require stitches. After years on tour, she'd learned which injuries did and did not require a trip to the ER. She added some soap and lathered his hand as his shallow breaths tickled her shoulder in ragged bursts. She shouldn't enjoy this as much as she did, but there was something about tending to this tall, strong man that fulfilled some primal protection urge inside her.

"Almost done," she said. "Keep breathing."

He grunted and shifted. "I think I need to sit down."

Marlo guided him to the edge of the tub. He'd paled even more than earlier, and sweat dripped down the edges of his face.

"Bring your head between your knees and breathe," she said.

Dabbing his thumb dry, Marlo stepped away from him for a second to fetch a bandage. She squeezed a line of antibiotic ointment on the cut then dressed it with a bandage, and before she could think otherwise, she placed a kiss on the exposed tip of his thumb.

They both froze.

Marlo went to stand at the same time Jude tried to sit up, and the top of his head hit the bottom of her chin, stunning her for a moment.

"Shit, sorry," he said, a deep burr in his voice.

She stepped back. "No harm done, just a bit of a surprise."

That was the understatement of the year.

Luckily, some color returned to his face. She prayed he wouldn't acknowledge the thumb kiss. It was simply an uncontrollable impulse, and her new one begged her to run out of the bathroom and fling herself under the covers on her bed and never reemerge.

Jude tried to stand up, but he slammed into the bathroom wall, barely bracing himself in time to keep himself from tipping forward. Marlo reached out to steady him, and it was impossible to ignore the zing of electricity at contact with his skin. She wondered if he felt it too. But he could barely hold himself upright. No way he was thinking about her at all under his current circumstances.

"Okay," she said, "put your arm around my shoulder, and I'll walk you out of here. I think you need to lay down for a minute."

He grunted. "Sorry, my body just does this. I know it's a small cu… cu…"

Jude greened before her eyes.

"No more talking. Let's get you to the couch." She positioned herself under his shoulder, wrapping her arm tightly around his waist, and letting him use her as a crutch.

Marlo gently lowered him to the couch when they reached it, placing a pillow under his head. She returned to the bathroom and ran the washcloth under cold water. Back at Jude's side, she placed the damp cloth on his forehead. She rose again, but he grabbed her wrist.

"Stay by me." His eyes trained on her, compelling her to do as he asked.

Jude shifted, making space for her to sit by his outstretched form. "Thank you. My body is so stupid when it does this thing."

Marlo's eyes roved over his face and broad chest. "Your body is not stupid at all."

At least not in the way he meant it. It was stupid how hot his body was and how much she wanted it pressed against hers.

Damn it, she needed to stop letting these thoughts invade her mind.

He'd left her once because he knew he'd grow to resent her eventually. How could she trust it wouldn't happen again?

Jude cleared his throat. "I swear, I've been fine at every chemo appointment with my dad. The IV meds, the blood transfusions—none of it bothers me. But send a sharp medical-related object in my direction, and I collapse like a British period heroine."

Marlo laughed. "We all have our kryptonite."

He brought his injured hand to his heart. "What's yours?"

You. He'd always been and always would be her weakness. Instead, she said, "Music."

Jude moved his hand to her knee. The warmth of his palm penetrated through the denim of her jeans. "Your mom and I are worried about you."

Marlo studied his face. After all the ways she'd disrupted his life, she couldn't believe he still treated her with compassion.

"I'm fine." She smiled, but her heart wasn't in it.

During their phone call, Tara had informed Marlo that she and Marlo's father were working with local authorities to disperse the so-called journalists camped out in her neighborhood. Tara advised her that she should either return to LA immediately or check herself in somewhere with secured entrances and exits. Tara stressed that Marlo was not to remain at her parents' house now that her location had been compromised by the paparazzi.

Marlo wasn't ready to return to LA. She remained homesick for a place she wasn't sure existed. Her parents' home no longer felt like her home anymore. She was as much a guest there as she was in her personality-less, designer-decorated Calabasas townhouse. Plus, she hated that she'd disrupted their quiet lives. She wanted more for herself, even though she wasn't sure what more looked like.

Jude propped himself up on his elbows. "Talk to me."

She shook her head. "No, I've ruined just about as much of your day as I can handle."

"What did Tara want?"

"What she always wants, for me to return to LA." She stared in the distance.

"Do you enjoy working with Tara?"

"Tara isn't the problem. She's doing her job and doing it exceedingly well. I'm the problem. I have everything—well, almost everything I ever wanted—and yet I'm still deeply unhappy."

Marlo dropped her head into her palms and swallowed back tears. If Jude didn't already regret coming here, he certainly would if she dared spill any more tears in front of him. She heard him rustling then felt his hand rubbing up and down her back. He shifted again, pulling her into his chest. She was practically laying across his lap.

"You sound tired. And I don't mean you didn't sleep enough last night—I mean you sound like you're completely burned out." He sighed, hugging her tighter. "I should know. I've been there."

Marlo sighed. "No one will cover for me if I walk away. Unlike you, I don't have anything else to walk toward."

"I'm not saying what worked for me will work for you."

Jude was right. She'd suspected burnout for some time, and she had no idea what came next. She didn't even have the bandwidth to figure it out."I just wonder," he continued, "if this is the best place for you to be."

She stiffened. Was he suggesting she leave?

Then, as if he'd read her mind, he said, "It's not that I don't want you here. I just worry that this may not be the best or safest place for whatever needs to come next for you."

Marlo laughed mirthlessly. "So you agree with Tara then? I should return to LA?"

"I don't agree with her at all. I just want you to be safe. Maybe you should—"

"Dinner is ready," her mom called out from the next room.

"Sorry for how we've imposed on you this evening." Marlo adopted the detached, cool voice she used as armor. "My guess is you'll be free to leave in the next hour or so."

"Marlo..."

But she'd already stood up and started walking away. Slow, measured steps followed behind her.

Her mom pointed to Jude's injured finger. "Don't show that to your folks. They might have a valid reason to call off our friendship."

"Marlo kissed it and made it all better," he said.

A swift and deafening silence descended upon them. Marlo glared at Jude. *Why?*

Her mom cleared her throat after a few seconds. "Jude, would you like some salad?"

He nodded as his cheeks continued to redden. Marlo guessed hers likely rivaled his in color. She could only hope her dad's efforts with the mayor proved successful because if she didn't get Jude out of her house soon, she feared what would come out of their mouths next.

Chapter Fifteen

MARLO

EVER SINCE THE paparazzi had descended upon Gold Hills a couple of days earlier, Marlo was under virtual house arrest. Tara insisted she avoid visiting the bakery or the infusion center and even hold off on her morning jogs. Tara also practically checked in hourly about Marlo's living arrangements, but Marlo still hadn't decided where to go.

Gold Hills wasn't known for luxury hotels used to shielding celebrities from intense media scrutiny. At least the local authorities resurrected an old privacy ordinance that prevented the tabloid journalists from decamping on residential streets, giving her a minor reprieve. So Marlo intended to enjoy the momentary calm at her childhood home while it lasted.

Turning the corner into the kitchen, Marlo gasped. Her mom was in full Martha Stewart mode. Cookies, muffins, and scones rested on various cooling racks across the kitchen while her attention was focused on sprucing up a large wicker basket. Her dad sat at the kitchen island, chin propped on his hands, watching her mom with such love and affection it made Marlo's teeth ache.

"Mom, what are you doing?"

"Oh, just putting together a small gift for Jude."

"You're giving a basket of baked goods to the patron saint of pastry chefs?" Marlo laughed.

"Jude loves my baking. He credits me as one of his inspirations." Her mom gave her a proud little nod. "But I'm not giving it to him. You are."

Marlo choked on the bite of muffin in her mouth. Her mom walked over with a glass of water and a chagrined look on her face.

"I'm not seeing Jude today," Marlo protested once her coughing fit subsided. "Tara said—"

"It's not healthy for you to stay cooped up indoors all day."

"I jog every morning."

"Not the last couple of mornings." Her dad chuckled.

She glared at him. Whose side was he on? Never mind, she already knew the answer. "Tara asked me to keep a low profile."

"This isn't LA," her mom said, exchanging a pleading look with her dad.

"That's what makes it a little riskier for me," Marlo said. "Your house isn't a very secure location, and I'm here without my team."

Her mom and dad traded another glance.

"Oh my god, what?" Backward slide continued, Marlo felt like the teenager she'd never had the chance to be, standing in the kitchen of her childhood home and awaiting the verdict of the wordless communication between her parents.

"Go visit Jude," her dad said.

"I can't. Tara said no more visits to the pastry shop."

"He doesn't live at the pastry shop," her mom added.

Marlo huffed a laugh, her parents and their transparent maneuvers. Come to think of it, Marlo didn't even know where Jude lived anymore. Some reptilian part of her brain still pictured him living in the house behind her parents' backyard. But Mr. and Mrs. Beckett had moved years ago. She'd just visited their new home.

"I don't know where he lives," she said, her voice rasped in a whisper.

Admitting that aloud wounded Marlo in a way she hadn't anticipated. Once their lives were so intertwined that it seemed impossible she'd ever have such critical gaps in her knowledge of all things Jude Beckett.

Her mom hugged her. "Sweetheart, maybe this your chance to mend things more substantial than your image. I don't want you to miss out on a chance at happiness out of fear or misunderstanding."

Marlo groaned, not releasing herself from her mom's embrace. "A man isn't going to fix everything for me."

"That's not what I meant. I want you to find your peace, both professionally and personally. Even if you two never get back together, at the very least, you both deserve a little fun, even if it's just as friends."

"A diversion from all the ugly stuff that's going on," her dad added.

"And me delivering this basket of baked goods to Jude's house will be diverting?" Marlo asked.

Her parents traded mischievous grins.

"Maybe if you wore something cuter," her mom teased.

The thought of visiting Jude sent a panicky flutter through Marlo's veins. But maybe her mom was on to something. Maybe being home and reconnecting in an honest and authentic way with Jude was a necessary part of Project Fix Marlo Sage. She studied the basket as her mom filled it with baked goods.

"If you're wrong about this, I'm never trusting you again," Marlo said.

"I'm never wrong. Ask your dad." Her mom winked.

"Fine, I'll go change."

~

Marlo drove faster than she should, marveling at how much the perimeter of Gold Hills had changed. Former winding forest roads were widened into two lanes in each direction. Developments dotted each side of the road, which broke her heart a little—precious forest land overtaken by suburban sprawl.

She glanced at the map on the car navigation system, fifteen more miles to go. Jude lived as far out of town as possible. The roads narrowed again, and after a dense patch of trees, she turned right into a development that looked straight out of Malibu. A large, granite water feature signaled the entrance. Marlo pulled up to the large, gated guard house.

A guard approached her car, his eyes widening in recognition. But he managed not to drop his mask of professionalism.

"Name and purpose of your visit," he said.

"Marlo Rayhan, guest of Jude Beckett."

A hint of a smile played across his lips. "Oh yes, Miss Rayhan, he notified us of your impending arrival. Do you need directions?"

This time, she'd had the good sense to ask before stopping by to visit.

"No, thank you." She gestured to her navigation system.

"Enjoy your visit to Cascade Woods." He pointed to the formidable iron gate opening for her.

As she drove into the neighborhood, she grew distracted by the beautiful architecture. No two houses looked the same or even shared the same era of architectural design—a modern structure of glass and steel was followed a couple of miles later by a traditional English Tudor. Vast amounts of space separated the estates. The neighborhood was clearly private and exclusive. She couldn't believe this is where her former boy next door now called home. Everything new she discovered about Jude and about Gold Hills reinforced just how much life had changed in her absence. At least for everyone else.

Her GPS bleated frantically, indicating she neared her destination. A long, winding driveway appeared to the left. The road curved upward, and as the trees thinned, an expansive single-story French country style home with modern touches of whitewashed wood and river stone emerged. While she'd been gone, Jude had built himself a life, a business, and a home, and suddenly, Marlo couldn't shake the sense of losing a race.

Her regular daily routine included playing dress-up and living an artificial life of carefully orchestrated social outings and pairings. She rented homes, unable to commit to any property for an extended period. In fact, Marlo didn't truly own anything, not even her record masters. She remained in a state of arrested maturation, and she often forgot that her peers had grown up and started very adult lives. They didn't bounce around from rentals to hotel rooms with suitcases in tow. They bought homes, built real lives, and some even started families. In the beginning, Marlo had assumed responsibilities beyond her age. As a young adult, she'd been expected to navigate complicated business contracts, to advocate for herself in a system designed for most people like her to fail, and then somewhere along the line, she continued to playact adulthood when her childhood friends lapped her. They'd bloomed, and she remained a dandelion seed adrift in the breeze.

Marlo parked her car and took in a fortifying breath.

JUDE

Jude paced his foyer. He'd given up on hearing from Marlo and assumed she'd changed her mind about visiting. When she'd texted earlier and asked if it was okay if she stopped by, he could have sworn the San Andreas fault had opened up and swallowed him into a different dimension. He studied the space around him, suddenly nervous she wouldn't approve of the home he'd custom designed. It was thanks to her he'd been able to do so in the first place. Royalties on their early hits continued to pay him a hefty supplement to his own income. Marlo's fingerprint on his life remained indelibly inked.

When his security system alerted him to a car pulling into his driveway, it took every shred of patience not to fling the door open and greet her in the driveway. When she finally pressed the doorbell, Jude swung open the massive slab of oak to find Marlo framed in sunlight, creating an ethereal silhouette. He sucked in his breath.

"Sorry." She stepped into his house and shoved a giant basket at him. "My mom insisted."

Jude smiled. Most people assumed he wouldn't want anyone to bake for him, but it couldn't be further from the truth. He keenly understood how deeply the act of baking was imbued with love and tenderness, the purest act of care.

"Please give her my thanks. It's so appreciated." He grinned down at the giant basket.

Marlo eyed him skeptically. "Don't you own a bakery?"

He laughed. "Yes, where I bake for others. Other than your mom and Penny, no one really thinks to bake for me."

"Penny. You two seem close," Marlo said.

"She's my assistant chef and business partner. We see each other almost every day." Penny was more than that. She'd become his best friend. He wasn't sure why he'd felt the need to shield that aspect of their relationship from Marlo.

Marlo stepped farther into the foyer and seemed to finally register her surroundings. She spun in a slow circle and emitted a low whistle. "Jude Beckett, you've certainly done well for yourself."

"You've done well for me," he said.

Air leeched out of the room and his heart expanded against his ribs. Why couldn't normal ever be part of the equation when he spoke to her?

"You're a legit adult," she said.

He laughed, grateful for the reprieve. "Guess so, still doesn't feel like it most days."

Marlo's brows furrowed. "Do you live here alone?"

"Are you serious?"

"What? We haven't really discussed anything about your personal life. We were just kind of thrust together and..." Her words trailed off as her cheeks deepened, and she looked away.

Jude stepped forward, encroaching on her space enough that their gazes reconnected. "I have dated here and there over the years. My last serious relationship ended two years ago. If you're asking me if I've had any overnight guests since you arrived back in town, the answer is no."

The corners of her mouth tilted up into a smile, a familiar twinkle in her eyes. "Tell the truth. Were you a Tinder slut even for a little bit?"

Jude laughed again and ran his hand through his hair. "Were you?"

She raised a pert eyebrow at him. "I asked first, and you already know I wasn't, can't afford to be so public."

"This is going to sound bad, but honestly, I didn't have to try too hard. Local celebrity returns to hometown with his heart broken is, a—the plot to every Hallmark movie and b—apparently quite irresistible to the ladies."

Her lips flattened. Maybe he'd crossed the line. He should've tempered his honesty. For some reason, he couldn't help but be an open book with her.

"And you?" he asked.

Marlo waved her hand dismissively. "Please, you've seen Cliff Rochester squeezing every last ounce out of that dead and uninspired relationship. It's tough to find something real in the industry. Everyone has an agenda."

"I'm not going to lie—you and him together never made sense to me."

Marlo studied Jude. Clearly, she'd heard something akin to jealousy in his words.

"Oh, come on, you know how it works. *It will be good for both your careers, just a few public dates, blah blah blah.* I'm fairly certain Cliff was really dating one of the record execs before we were thrown together. Besides, he definitely isn't my type. His sexual tastes run far more adventurous than mine."

Thoughts of Marlo having sex with someone else made Jude's skin feel too tight and too warm. He needed to shift them to safer, less charged subjects.

"Would you like a tour?" he asked.

"Yes," Marlo said, the relief palpable in her voice.

Another silence descended between them as he led her farther into the house. She scanned the open floor plan centered around a large eat-in kitchen.

"It's beautiful," she said. "You probably never want to leave."

A new heaviness settled into her voice, and he wasn't sure why.

"You know me," he said. "I'm a homebody."

Marlo spun around, hurt etched into the soft lines around her eyes. "The more things change, the more they stay the same."

Only it wasn't simply banter. Danger lurked in the undertow.

Jude stopped in front of a closed door, and instead of picking up the thread, she'd just laid down, he opted for distraction.

"Any guesses?" he asked.

"Torture chamber."

"Sometimes."

He opened the door to reveal a completely tricked-out music studio. Hearing her gasp widened his smile. This room was his secret pride and joy. She was right—sometimes the more things changed, the more they stayed the same. Music might not be his great love, but he maintained a deep, abiding respect for it.

Marlo stepped into the room with a reverence most people reserved for church. He hung back near the entrance while she explored.

She turned back to him. "Explain yourself."

"I wasn't sure how to admit to you that I'd had this room built."

He watched the light dim behind her eyes at his admission.

"Have you been making music?" She picked up a guitar from a stand and played a few melancholy chords.

"I mess around sometimes, but I haven't really been in the head space to want to create music." He sighed. "I just felt like I needed to preserve the option."

For you. Crazed thoughts of a delusional man.

Marlo settled the guitar back and walked toward him. "This sounds a lot like fate."

"What do you mean?"

"I decided to write new songs for the bake-off and record a new album with the songs from the demo that David rejected, even if I simply post them for free online. I stand by my work."

"Marlo, that's—"

She quieted him with a finger pressed against his lips. He hadn't noticed her come so close.

"I don't want any advice or opinions," she said. "I need to do this. On my own."

He nodded gently, hoping not to dislodge her touch. Her soft fragrance of citrus and jasmine enveloped him.

"The studio is yours," he said, his words a promise kissed against the pad of her finger.

Marlo looked at him with eyes brimming with gratitude. He was doomed. His lips ached for hers. But it was a hunger that couldn't be sated, no matter how often they danced up to the precipice of it. Some histories shouldn't be repeated for the sake of sanity. Instead, he settled for taking her hand and completing the rest of the tour.

MARLO

As Marlo drove back to her parent's home, she tried to shake off the moment she and Jude had just shared. They'd held hands, such an innocent act for two people who'd shared so much more a lifetime ago, yet somehow the intimacy of it knocked her off keel. He'd stood so close that his scent of laundry soap mixed with vanilla still filled her nose. The more they spent time together, the more impossible it had grown to keep their hands off each other. Even if it was simply in fleeting touches, lingering hugs, near kisses, it was more than she'd dared to dream of having again. But it was a fool's game of heartbreak Russian roulette.

"Everything okay?" Tara asked by way of a greeting when Marlo called her over the car's audio system.

"I found a working space," Marlo said.

"Where?"

"Jude's house. He has a custom recording studio there."

"Interesting. And why does Jude have a personal studio?"

Marlo chuckled. She'd asked him the same. He'd given her a crooked smile and a weak explanation. "I don't know, just in case."

"Where does Jude live?" Tara was always looking out for potential PR pitfalls and optics.

"Don't worry. He lives in a secluded, exclusive neighborhood protected by a guard-manned gate."

"Does he have extra bedrooms?"

"Yeah, why?" Marlo was too focused on the road to work out Tara's thought trajectory.

"Maybe you should move in with him—secure location, secluded with a working space."

Marlo groaned. "Don't be ridiculous."

"Be honest. Would it be the worst thing to wake up in the same house as Jude every morning?" Tara's laugh echoed through the audio system, bouncing off the windshield and other windows.

Yes, if she was simply living with him in a roommate capacity, it would be exquisite torture to see him every morning and night. But Marlo refused to admit that to Tara. She changed the subject instead. "Jude is on board for Operation Debut New Songs at the charity bake-off."

"That's a terrible operational name."

Marlo laughed. "Come up with a better one."

"The Revenge Recipe."

"Show-off."

"I'm serious. I think you should consider moving in with Jude."

"I'm hanging up now, bye," Marlo said.

Between her parents' not-so-subtle urging and Tara's absurd suggestion that took it a step further, they'd succeeded in planting a seed that Marlo couldn't unearth. Could moving in with Jude and working at his studio be the solution to all her problems? Temporarily at least.

Chapter Sixteen

MARLO

MARLO WAITED A few days before reaching out to Jude about using his studio. She needed a cool-down period after the flame for him rekindled. He left a copy of his key with the guard on duty at the main gate so Marlo could use his studio at her discretion. She couldn't wait to get there to dance and sing her heart out. Despite her misgivings about the industry, she still loved to perform—mic in her hand and surrendering to the beat thrumming in her blood was when she felt most alive. Her friends weren't the only thing she missed about LA. She also missed her voice and movement craft classes.

Marlo packed up Jidoo's oud and the one Nassar lent her, a Middle Eastern drum her dad picked up for her at the Lebanese grocery store, and her guitar. She waited until half past nine before heading to Jude's house. She expected he'd be well into his shift at the bakery by then, and though she was eager to use his studio, she didn't want to see him.

Lies. She couldn't afford to see him and get distracted by thoughts of climbing him like a tree. She needed to focus on her work.

The funny thing was that Jude used to be her sounding board when she tried something new with her music, but she was no longer comfortable sharing that vulnerable part of her creative process with him. It was too intimate.

Besides, she'd outgrown the need for a partner after Jude left. In a way, his departure had been a blessing in disguise, forcing her to develop a deep conviction in her artistic sensibility and intuition. Though David Stringer continued to attack the foundation of her creative confidence, Marlo clung to her stubborn vision. The demo she'd sent him was great, but what she was currently incubating was orders of magnitude better. Her online lessons had started to pay off—she wasn't half bad at the oud. And now she was also learning how to play the doumbek, a goblet-shaped Arabic hand drum.

The new songs she smithed marked the biggest departure from her previous catalogue, American pop tinged with traditional Middle Eastern sounds—an homage to her own multitudes. Marlo wasn't sure her fans would follow her on this journey, but the rightness of it was engraved on her heart. Still, it was all so new. She wasn't ready to share it with anyone, especially not Jude.

They needed to stick to safe boundaries and stop blurring the lines between friendship and more.

JUDE

Wow. Jude wasn't prepared to see Marlo walk into his studio in his personal kryptonite—curve-hugging leggings topped with a loose tank over a colorful sports bra, effortlessly sexy. And it wasn't just the way she looked. It was the way she moved through his space with feline confidence. Jude should pop his head out of the booth and let her know of his presence, but he didn't move, mesmerized. Ever since he'd first showed her the space, he'd found himself drifting back into this room more than he ever had before. Marlo carried in a box full of instruments old and new—two oud and a small drum with the distinct appearance of something so antique he'd expect to see it in a museum display.

Marlo set everything down and eyed her surroundings then cleared space in the center of the circular room and started a series of stretches. The longer Jude watched, the more awkward the eventual reveal of his presence would be, but he couldn't tear his eyes from her.

The faint, tinny sound of music playing over her phone's speaker filtered into the booth. Jude chuckled to himself. The room was outfitted with the best of the best audio equipment, and Marlo danced to music off her phone.

Damn, Marlo.

She'd become a better dancer than he'd known her to be. Another testament to her dedication to her craft, she remained a consummate work in progress, always pushing herself, striving for better. Her muscles rippled as she danced. He didn't have to hear the music to know it moved through her on an elemental level.

When he'd held her as she cried that day at her mother's house, something unlocked inside him, a primal urge to protect her. The weight of her in his arms was so right, he wanted to keep her there forever. When she bent forward and kissed his injured thumb, he nearly lost it. Marlo had done it—cracked the deepest of his defenses. He was powerless against her allure.

As he watched her hips sway, desire flooded him. And not simply the physical type demanding to be sated. He wanted the totality of her—her thoughts, her laughs, her tears, her companionship. He wanted her face to be the first thing he saw every morning and the last he saw at night.

Damn, he was so fucked.

A shriek woke him from his reverie. Marlo had stopped dancing and was staring dead in his direction. He exited the booth, joining her in the main studio.

"What are you doing here?" she asked, rubbing her hands up her bare arms. "You scared the hell out of me."

"Sorry, I was just making sure everything was in working order when you walked in. I didn't want to interrupt. You were having a moment." He smiled, hoping the warmth flooding his cheeks hadn't translated into a deep flush.

"Why aren't you at work?"

"Penny's got the morning today. I go in soon," he answered, struggling to hold her intense gaze.

"I should have called first," she said, picking at her leggings mid-thigh.

"Mi casa es su casa."

Her eyes flicked back up to his, a light smile tipping up the corners of her mouth. "Is that all you remember from Senora Cora's lessons?"

Te quiero.

No, he remembered Marlo scrawling *I love you* in Spanish in the margin of his notebook during their tutoring session while on their first tour. Unfortunately, he'd spent more time memorizing every single one of Marlo's freckles than any of his lessons.

The way she pulled him right back into her orbit frightened him. Was there any hope of a fresh start for them when their past remained ever present, so easily accessible? He closed the distance between them, enjoying the light flare behind her eyes as he neared.

"What are you working on?" He said, gesturing to her new instruments.

She tracked his movement, her smile faltering. "Oh, nothing, just experimenting."

Once upon a time, she couldn't wait to share her new ideas with him. She'd text him to meet her in the treehouse in her backyard or, when they started touring, to meet in her hotel room. Marlo would shove her notebook with near illegible scribbles into his hands while she spoke at light speed. Her energy had always been infectious.

Jude opened his mouth to offer to bounce around ideas like old times, but Marlo continued.

"I don't want to hold you up," she said.

"Oh, yeah, I should get going." His feet remained rooted in place.

Marlo stepped into him and wrapped her arms around his neck, brushing her lips against his cheek. His eyes drooped to half-mast as he drank in her scent, one he'd recognize anywhere.

"Thank you for letting me use your house," she said.

"Anytime," he answered, hands hovering millimeters from her back as he deliberated returning the hug. Before he could, she'd already stepped away.

Learning the new shape of their relationship wasn't an easy task, not when his body reacted so viscerally to her closeness, even as his mind knew the impossibility of wanting more. He had to learn to take what she offered and be content with it. He'd lost Marlo once. He didn't dare to lose her again.

Chapter Seventeen

JUDE

EVEN BEFORE THE kitchen door swung open, Jude heard Suze's heels clacking on the shop's tile floors, heading in his direction. His heart kicked up the closer she approached. He wasn't even sure why he was nervous to see her. Marlo's presence in his studio this morning unsettled him.

"There you are," she said as she rounded his workspace.

Jude smiled. He didn't know where else she expected him to be. He wiped his hands down the front of his apron after he washed up.

"What can I help you with?" he asked, trying to ignore the crease between her brows.

Did something happen to Marlo? His dad?

"Can we talk in your office?" she asked.

His stomach knotted. Whatever she was here about was as serious as he feared. "Of course."

Instead of sitting across from her at his desk, he took the seat next to her.

"You're freaking me out," he said. "Is something wrong?"

Suze chewed on her lower lip. "Stay calm."

The caution created the exact opposite reaction, and his knee bounced in rhythm to his pounding heart.

"I don't like the sound of this," he said. "Just say it."

"I just spoke with Tara."

Jude exhaled. Not his dad, one small mercy. "What did she want?"

"Tbh, hon', a pretty big favor."

"What now?" He wiped his hands down his black canvas chef's pants. He already opened up his studio to Marlo. What more could they want from him?

"Cliff is still causing her troubles. Some pictures leaked today. He's claiming the woman in them is Marlo."

He dropped his head into his hands. Had Marlo heard about this yet? He straightened and fixed a steely gaze on Suze. "And this has to do with me how?"

"Her parents' house is surrounded by another locust storm of journalists."

The faint haze of realization appeared on the horizon of his consciousness. He gripped the wooden chair rail, knuckles whitening.

Suze dropped her gaze. "Tara asked if Marlo could stay with you until they figure out more secure lodgings."

Jude scanned the room. The light fixture overhead wasn't swaying, nothing loose on his shelves shifted even a little, yet he clearly felt the earth rolling beneath his feet.

"Suze," he said under his breath.

"It's just temporary," she said, offering him a weak smile.

Nothing about Marlo's presence was fleeting. From the moment he'd spotted her at the karaoke bar, she'd slowly taken deeper and deeper hold of his life. He dedicated far too much thought to her. He was embarrassed to admit just how much. Then she'd returned to Gold Hills, and he was nearly seeing her daily. But sharing a roof with her? He wasn't sure he'd survive sharing even generous quarters with her.

"Marlo would never agree," he said.

The admission sent a wave of nausea rolling through him. Even if his kneejerk answer to this ask was no, the thought of her rejecting him made him sick.

"She needs your help, Jude," Suze said.

He wanted to say no, but Suze knew him too well. He groaned.

"Fine." he said.

Suze placed her hand over his. "You won't regret this, sugar."

But she was wrong. Misgivings already gnawed at his bones.

"One more thing," Suze said.

He gave her a serious dose of side-eye.

"Can you swing by Sami's office on your way home and pick up Marlo's things?"

Jude shook his head. "This isn't feeling too temporary."

"I promise," she said. "This will be the best for all involved."

Easy for her to say when she hadn't seen Marlo gyrating in skin-hugging clothing this morning. He still couldn't shake the image, even all these hours later. And now she was moving in? The only thing Jude knew with certainty was how much this would destroy him. And worse, part of him welcomed the destruction.

Chapter Eighteen

MARLO

MARLO SAT, LEGS folded crisscross, among a sea of torn-out notebook pages, crumpled balls of paper, and tear-stained tissues. After Tara called back, Marlo turned her phone off and attempted to immerse herself in a creative bubble. Maybe if she simply ignored the unraveling of her public persona, it would just go away.

But that's not how life worked, not even for an A-list pop star. Everyone had been right—her parents, Jude, Tara—she couldn't hide out in childhood home forever, especially not while Pop Machine dismantled her career in front of the world's eyes. She owed her fans better. She owed herself better.

She thought she knew all of David's tricks, but doctored explicit photos of her hadn't been on her bingo card. She'd underestimated him. No low was too deep. He wasn't going to let her walk away without destroying her first—her name, her reputation, and her prospects. No amount of contrition or stretching herself creatively and subsequent success would change that. Marlo nearly choked on that bitter truth. Tara could hire all the lawyers in the world, but nothing would change so long as David drew his angry, misogynistic breaths. He'd always move the goal posts, and no matter how she contorted herself, she'd never win a game by his rules where a woman was only valuable so long as she was young and obedient.

You say you built me brick by brick,
But we both know who wielded the pen
That signed your checks

Marlo stared at the snippet of lyrics scrawled in angry strokes of her pen. She would haunt David to his dying day with her new songs, which screamed the truth her label attempted to silence. If she was going down, she'd go down screaming. And swinging. And she'd take him to the depths of hell with her.

One night livestreamed, five songs to reclaim her empire or burn it down, trying.

David might control the legal levers to manipulate her, but she had something he never could—devoted fans. She trusted if she put out the call, they'd show up for her. Still, it was a gamble, the stakes both professionally and financially devastating if she failed. But reclaiming her soul and her peace were worth the risk.

Betrayal's an old game, a slow-moving trainwreck
I gave you everything, my words, veins wide open.
In return, your suckling greed made me sick.
A devil's trick
Big, big ick
Lucky girl, so lonely
Big dreams fading slowly

Tears sprang to her eyes. She'd been carrying this hurt so long. Letting it pour from her pen to the paper with abandon cracked her reservoir, and words flooded the page almost faster than she could write them down. David was wrong—it wasn't a woman behind a microphone who was dangerous. It was the woman determined to bring him down by every means possible he needed to worry about.

Marlo continued to scribble snippets of songs, catharsis reborn in a surge of creativity. She didn't need a mailing address to feel home. When she wrote music, she was there.

When her hand began to cramp and her legs went numb, she set aside her notebook and picked up her phone. Pacing the length of the room, shaking the tingling sleep from her limbs, she began making calls to her usual roster of collaborators. Within an hour, she'd initiated the early developmental steps of creating a new album, leaving her favorite producer voice memos of the skeletal fragments of new songs.

Their enthusiasm buoyed her anew. She just might be able to pull this off.

The only outstanding item on her checklist was a favor from Jude—a big ask, given the still tenuous new friendship they were forging. Marlo glanced at her watch. The pastry shop was open for another hour and a half. She had plenty of time to grab a quick snack and refill her water before facing him.

She opened the studio door only to find Jude carrying two large cardboard boxes down the hall. Marlo opened her mouth to call out to him, but no sound emerged. Her mind whirled, trying to make sense of the scene unfolding before her. It didn't help the way his back muscles bulged, pulling his T-shirt taut in some places. Her eyes drifted lower and she couldn't help herself—she sighed.

Jude stumbled, setting the boxes down and turning around.

"Oh, hey," he said. "I didn't want to disturb you while you were working."

"Speaking of work," Marlo said. "Shouldn't you still be there?"

He pursed his lips and just stared back at her for several beats. "You haven't talked to Tara? Or Suze?"

She shook her head.

"It's not safe for you to go back home at the moment," he said, shifting his gaze to his feet.

"Are my parents okay?" Her gut twisted. She hated being handled. She should've been part of this decision-making process. "And does anyone care what I think?"

"Yes and yes," he said, closing the distance between them. "Yes, of course, we were just worried about keeping you safe."

Jude clenched his eyes shut for a second and rubbed his jaw.

"I hear it," he said, locking eyes with her. "It sounds patronizing. But Tara and Suze were truly acting with your best interest at heart."

The edges of her vision swam with too bright colors, a rainbow of slowly building rage. "I'm not some helpless damsel. You're all treating me no better than David Stringer. I'm not who I am by accident."

"It's temporary," he said.

"It always is with you," she answered, unable to swallow back the petty insult.

"Jesus, Marlo." Jude crossed his arms across his chest.

"I don't want to do this," she said, her voice dulled from a roar to a whimper.

"Is the thought of staying with me that intolerable?" He reached out to touch her, thinking better of it and withdrawing his hand.

No, it wasn't his turn to play the wounded one. He wasn't the one being coddled and managed. He wasn't the one being chased by rabid reporters or being intimately doxed by an ex in the media. She didn't want his pitying hospitality. She didn't want to be the roommate he was obliged to accommodate.

Jude gestured to the gooseflesh on her bare arms. "You're cold."

He unfolded his arms and reached for her, his fingertips grazing her outer arms. She wanted to hurl herself against his chest, lose herself in the circle of his arms.

"I'm sorry," she said, fracturing the silence after a few seconds.

"For what?" he asked, his hands absently moving in long, slow strokes over her arms.

"For imposing, bringing the circus into town."

The corner of his mouth tipped up, but his gaze remained guarded. "It's temporary."

Everyone needed a good mantra to get by. Apparently, that was his. But what brought him comfort sliced into Marlo's old wounds.

"It could be fun," he added, diverting his gaze.

"I should just go back home and put everyone out of their Marlo-associated misery."

This time, Jude committed, his large, warm hands cupped her bare shoulders. Marlo sucked in her breath, trembling at his touch, unable to control the way her body reacted to his on an elemental level. The heat of his body beckoned her closer. Maybe he was right and they could make the best of this forced proximity.

"I want you to stay with me," he said.

She could practically swim in the depths of his dark pupils. Old patterns resurged with vengeance. *Yes* danced at the tip of her tongue. Hadn't she always wanted this?

"It's just temporary," he said, a whisper soft dousing of ice-cold water.

Marlo had never hated that word more. She stepped away from him. Starved of his warmth, she stood there quivering, aching for him, and embarrassed to admit it to herself.

"I don't think I can," she said.

"Maybe this is the distraction we both need."

"And what if it blows up in our faces?"

"Do you honestly think things could get any worse?"

Losing you all over again. But she wasn't brave enough to say it aloud.

Chapter Nineteen

MARLO

ROOMMATES!" ASHA screamed.

"Are you trying to broadcast it to space?" Marlo asked as she continued to unpack her meager belongings in Jude's guest room, which was thankfully at the opposite end of the house from his.

"I think this could be the start of something beautiful," Heather added.

FaceTime was a poor substitute to actually hanging out with her friends, but she loved seeing their mugs again.

"Of course you do." Asha made an incredulous face at the screen.

"Heather, you're as bad as my parents," Marlo said. "There is zero chance anything is happening between me and that man."

"Oh, I wasn't saying nothing should happen," Asha said. "I'm just saying it doesn't have to be everything."

Marlo stopped midway through folding a pair of leggings and stared at her iPad screen. "I thought you were on my side."

"I am," Asha said. "You're there for the summer. Have some fun. You deserve it." Then her friend started twerking, her tongue hanging out of her goofy smile.

Marlo shook her head, unable to stop herself from laughing.

Fun. That word had grown into a dangerous refrain played on repeat in the back of her mind, especially since Jude had mentioned it might be *fun* for them to live together for a bit. Fun. She'd dissected and examined that damn three-letter word more than anyone had business doing. Jude wasn't summer fling material. Was he? No good would come from entertaining such an impossible possibility.

Temporary.

"Marlo," Jude called out after softly rapping his knuckles against her closed door.

Marlo flared her eyes at her friends and placed her finger over her lips in a shushing motion. They crowded the screen but thankfully stayed quiet.

"Hey, didn't mean to disturb you, just wanted to see if you wanted to join me for lunch." His gaze drifted from her to the screen of her tablet. The corner of his mouth ticked up. "I think your friends want you to say 'yes.'"

Marlo glanced over shoulder to see Heather and Asha dancing around and mouthing *yes* at the camera.

"Hi, ladies," Jude said. "Nice seeing you again."

"Hey, Jude," they sing-songed in unison.

Marlo shook her head. "You two are literally the worst,"

"Bye, Marlo, we love you!" Heather blew kisses at her.

"Have fun," Asha added before ending the call.

"So, lunch?" Jude asked, his eyes roving around the room.

"Sure, why not." Marlo placed her folded leggings on her bed and then followed him out to the kitchen.

"Settling in okay?" He asked.

"Yes, thank you." Marlo grimaced at her awkward, stilted answer.

She still wasn't sure how to adjust to sharing a roof with Jude. It felt like an O. Henry style distortion of her deepest dream—sharing a home with the love of her life—unfolding in cruel irony. But Jude wasn't even the love of her life, not anymore. He was her greatest heartbreak.

"So, your friends," he said. "Tell me about them."

"Heather is a kindergarten teacher, Asha is a tax attorney, and Diane, the one getting married. She's a professor at USC."

"Wow, a talented and educated bunch."

"They're the best," she said, her voice drifting wistfully.

"You miss them?"

Marlo nodded, a lump forming in the back of her throat. "I appreciate everything you and your family and my parents have done for me with everything going on with David Stringer, but sometimes you just need your girlfriends, you know?"

"Actually, I do. I usually spend a lot more time with Penny and Kate, but with everything going on with my dad, the shop, and…" He paused. "Everything else, I haven't seen them as much."

"Who's Kate?" Marlo asked.

"Penny's wife. You met her at the shop. Petite blonde with a baby."

"That was Penny's wife? Damn, they are an obscenely attractive family." The tension along Marlo's spine loosened.

He laughed. "You should see your face."

"What?" she said, playfully nudging him.

"Why, Miss Marlo, you look relieved." He waggled his thick fringe of brows at her.

"Shut up. I am no such thing."

"I am," he said, taking her hands.

The air in the room extinguished. Marlo wasn't sure what he was telling her and couldn't summon the words to ask.

Jude rubbed his thumbs back and forth along the inside of her palms. A small sigh escaped her lips.

"I'm glad you're here," he said. "I want you to feel at home, and whatever you want from me, you've got it."

That "whatever" did a lot of heavy lifting. It could mean so many different things, but did it mean the same thing to him as it did to her? The intensity of his gaze told her it might.

"I'm trying," she said. "To feel at home."

She couldn't look at him any longer. Her toes were at the precipice, and she was slipping. Marlo snatched her hands back and turned away from him. Breath shallow and heart racing, she tried to regain control over her faculties.

It would feel so good to throw caution to the wind
Let you hold my hands above my head, pinned.

Marlo couldn't believe she narrated this moment with song lyrics. But the more her life unraveled, the more manic her creativity grew.

Jude came behind her, placing his hands on either side of the kitchen island, boxing her in. If she asked him to step back, he would. But she didn't. He nuzzled her neck, knowing she was ticklish in that spot. Just like he used to when they were younger.

"What if we stopped fighting this?" he whispered into her ear.

Gooseflesh erupted across her skin as her anticipation heightened. "It's unwise."

"Only for the summer," he pleaded. "No one has to know."

Temporary.

"Jude, I—"

He wrapped his arms around her waist, hugging her back against his chest. Jude's touch was its own magic, one she was powerless to resist. So much of this summer had been awful so far. Why not let herself enjoy a little piece of it all to herself?

No one had to know.

Temporary.

Convenient.

Safe.

A thrill raced up Marlo's spine. She turned slowly in his arms and wrapped hers around his neck. "Are you sure?"

His pupils darkened as he nodded. Her gaze dropped to his mouth.

Marlo leaned forward, millimeters separating them.

"Kiss me," she whispered.

Jude needed no further encouragement, swiftly closing the distance and pulling her closer before crushing her mouth with his. Her lips parted, and Jude took the opportunity to deepen the kiss. Marlo anchored her hands in his hair, and they twirled in a semi-circle, angling for closeness.

He pulled away. "Follow me."

His brusque tone shot straight to her core.

Marlo clung to his hand as he led her down the hallway toward his room, afraid if she loosened her grasp on him, the moment would melt away like waking from a dream. When he stopped without warning, she nearly slammed into his back. He turned to her, lifting her up and seating her on the ledge of a carved alcove.

Now they were eye to eye. Marlo shivered in anticipation.

"I always wondered what this space was for," he joked. "I can't wait any longer."

He claimed her mouth again.

Marlo laughed against his lips, which only encouraged him to kiss her with more ardor. His attentiveness worked. She moaned and hooked one of her legs behind him, pulling him in closer. Jude's hands, previously anchored in her hair, now drifted down her sides as his thumbs brushed the outer curves of her breasts.

"Marlo, I've missed you," he said, breaking the kiss to utter the words before setting his lips to work at the crook her neck. He pushed down the strap of her tank and bra and kissed along her clavicle. "You have great shoulders."

She laughed, breathlessly. "I haven't heard that one before."

Jude gazed deep into her eyes, his finger tracing the edge of her exposed bra cup. Marlo squirmed but didn't break eye contact.

"Sorry, I pounced on you there for a minute," he said, his cheeks darkening.

Marlo bent forward, resting her forehead on his. "It's mutual pouncing."

She squealed when his eyes flared, moments before he claimed her mouth again. His hand cupped her half-exposed breast, applying delicate pressure to her nipple as he kissed her deeply. Desire flooded her, and she arched her back, pressing her breast more firmly into his hand.

Take me.

Jude pulled away, giving her a devilish grin before he tugged her tank and bra farther down, freeing her breasts entirely. He teased her nipples with his deft fingers then dropped his mouth to one. Marlo gripped his hair, anchoring him in place. The sensation so exquisite, she surrendered herself to it, collapsing against the wall at her back. She closed her eyes and turned off the ticker tape of thoughts racing through her mind.

"Jude!" someone exclaimed.

He turned away from Marlo, shielding her with his broad back. "Mom, what are you doing here?"

Marlo struggled to pull her top back up. She leaped down from the alcove and hid herself further behind Jude, clinging to the hem of his T-shirt. A prolonged moment of silence ensued, and Marlo peeked over Jude's shoulder to assess the scene. His mom stood staring blankly, her eyes wide as saucers and her cheeks reddened to a degree Marlo hadn't seen before.

"Mom, what the hell?" Jude asked, dropping his chin to his chest.

Marlo prayed for the ground to gape and swallow them both whole. Mortification was too light a word for what she experienced. She literally wanted to die.

"I...I'm so sorry," his mom stammered. "Your father didn't feel well after chemo, so I thought we'd take a little break here on our way home to let him rest."

JUDE

Jude wrapped an arm behind him, pulling Marlo flush against him. "Let's pretend this didn't happen. Mom, stay as long as you need. But please give us a moment."

"Jude, Marlo, I'm so—"

"Mom, just please, go back to the front room." A sigh vibrated through his chest.

Marlo tried to move away, but he held her close against him for another second then let her go as he turned to face her.

"Marlo, fuck, I'm so sorry. They have a key, but they usually call or text before stopping by." He took her arms, his eyes wide and pleading. His gaze drifted down to her chest, and a light smile teased his lips. He leaned forward and placed his forehead against hers. "We were just getting to the good part."

Marlo exhaled. Her darkened cheeks screamed her embarrassment, but at least she smiled at him. "I can't believe your mom just saw my breasts."

"I can't believe my mom just saw me making mouth love to your breasts."

"God, did you just say making mouth love?" Marlo slugged his arm. "Gross."

She burst into giggles and a pulse of relief flooded him. They could get through this. He pulled her into a hug and kissed the top of her head. She stilled in his arms.

He held her out from him to take another read on her mood. "Are you okay?"

"Yeah, I mean, I absolutely want to die of mortification, but I'm fine. It's pretty par for my course this summer."

"I promise I'll make it up to you."

"Jude, you don't—"

He placed a finger over her lips and then leaned down, kissing the tip of her nose. "Do you want to wait in my room while I send them on their way?"

"Don't worry about me. Your dad's not feeling well. They need you."

"I need you." The words tumbled from his mouth before he even considered the ripple effect of such an admission. Undeniably true, it was simply too much on the heels of what had just happened.

Marlo reached out and brushed her fingers along his jaw. He braced himself for an inevitable goodbye.

But instead, she smiled. "I need you too."

He leaned down and kissed her again, a soft, tender kiss. An unspoken thank you.

"If I can borrow a sweatshirt from your, I'll join you," she said. "We can visit with them for a bit."

"Are you sure?" Her capacity for grace stunned him.

"I'll have to face your mom sooner or later. May as well get it over with. Plus, I can't get back to my room without crossing their path."

Jude led her to his room and tried to keep it top of mind that his parents were in the front room. He couldn't allow himself to be distracted by Marlo's presence so damn near his bed. He pulled a sweatshirt from a shelf in his closet and walked back into the room to hand it to her. She'd straightened up her bra and tank and was bent over his bureau, studying the framed picture of her and him from the last concert they'd performed together.

"This picture is so old," she said. "We look like babies."

Jude smiled and studied the picture alongside her. "So much has changed."

"And yet, nothing at all."

From the corner of his eye, he saw her turn to face him, but he wasn't ready to look at her questioning, knowing eyes just yet. *I don't know what this is either.* She pulled the sweatshirt from his grasp and then, after tugging it on, took his hand.

"Into the frying pan," she said.

Jude's parents sat outside on the patio just opposite the kitchen.

"Marlo," his mom exclaimed. "I'm so sorry for stopping by without warning."

Before Marlo could respond, his mom wrapped her in a tight hug.

She stepped back, holding onto Marlo's hands and looking at her. "How is it possible that you've grown even more beautiful? Jim, do you see her?"

A flush of heat spread across her chest and up her neck.

His dad smiled weakly. "Hi, Marlo, if I wasn't so exhausted, I'd come over there and pull Vinnie off you."

"Stop it, Jim," she said. "I've apologized like a thousand times."

She pulled Marlo to sit with her on one of the patio benches across from the lounge chair where his dad laid down. His clothes hung loosely on his frame.

"Tell me how you've been," his dad said.

"Nothing important with me. How are you, Mr. Beckett?" Marlo asked, her gaze flitting to Jude's before settling back on his father.

She had good reason to worry. Jude knew certain days in the chemo cycles were tougher than others but even by that scale, his father looked unwell.

"They tell me I'm doing well." He shrugged and turned his gaze to the trees in the distance.

Jude glanced at his mom. She and Marlo shared the same wounded, helpless look. He still couldn't imagine how difficult the past few months must have been for his mother.

"Can't wait for another one of our chemo dates," Marlo said.

Jude marveled that after the fiasco last time she'd even reconsider a repeat visit.

His dad turned to face her. "We deserve a second chance. Plus, they were nicer to me when you were around."

"Nonsense, Jim, they're plenty nice to you, always." His mom turned to Marlo. "He's fine, don't worry." She looked between him and Marlo, a small smile curving her lips upward. "Well, we just stopped by to say a quick hello. We'll let you kids get back to catching up."

Marlo's cheeks deepened. Jude hated the sparkle he saw in his mom's eyes. Between catching them in flagrante delicto and then Marlo offering to take his dad to his chemo appointments again, Jude hoped his mother didn't think that they were together in any real capacity. They were simply answering a carnal thirst and nothing more. They didn't need the weight of family expectations on whatever this fleeting diversion between them was.

Chapter Twenty

MARLO

AFTER SAYING THEIR goodbyes to Mr. and Mrs. Bennett, Jude walked his parents out to their car. Marlo loitered in the kitchen, unsure what to do with herself. Minus the awkward interruption earlier, who knew how far they would've let things go between them? As embarrassing as being caught half naked by Jude's mom had been, it was likely divine intervention.

Marlo grabbed her phone and texted her friend group chat.

M: Jude and I may have just made out and then got caught in the act by his mom. I blame you all

Asha sent back a string of emojis that culminated in many eggplants.

H: Please tell us you're going to pick up where you left off!

*D: Our chat tomorrow is going to be *three fire emojis**

A: Finish the deed, Sage!

Marlo laughed. They were incorrigible.

Jude stepped back inside, caught sight of her, and strode determinedly toward her. Before she could say anything, he cupped her face and kissed her so thoroughly, all systems of logic failed her. There was no stopping this train.

Marlo smiled against his lips.

"What?" he asked, not breaking the kiss.

"I knew you'd taste like brown sugar and vanilla, and I just can't get enough of it."

He walked her back against the wall and pressed the length of his body against hers. Marlo anchored her hands into the soft curls at the nape of his neck. She yelped as he slid his hands below her bottom and lifted her up, freeing her legs to wrap around his waist. Now he'd aligned their bodies where they both yearned for the most friction. If she'd been capable of speech, she would've thanked him. Instead, she rewarded him with a swivel of her hips. He groaned into her mouth, and she teasingly bit his lower lip.

"Fuck," he whispered as his mouth traced along the edge of her chin down her neck.

"Bedroom?" she asked, breathless.

They were both wearing way too many clothes.

He laughed and hoisted her over his shoulder in one fluid motion, one of his hands palming her ass. Marlo couldn't complain, her view was quite nice as he strode to the bedroom. Clearly, the muscles weren't just for show.

When they reached his room, he gently set her down, gazing at her with such warmth and tenderness it made her heart ache.

"We only do what you want to do. You are in control here." The earnestness in his words and gaze sent a shot of warmth through her.

Goddamn, he was sexy.

Marlo shivered at the thought of a mature, more experienced Jude in her bed. Or more accurately, in his bed. This wasn't going to be the fumbling, exploratory sex of their youth. It would be something brand new.

Tonight, she gave herself permission to ask for, take, and give whatever she wanted.

She trusted Jude in a way she couldn't her other lovers.

"Strip for me," she said without even a hint of embarrassment. "Then you may undress me."

The corners of his mouth ticked up into a wicked grin. She appreciated this more confident version of him. He pulled the shirt over his head, sending it sailing behind him. Then he hooked his hands into the waistband of his sweats. The movement alone weakened her knees. She sat at the edge of his bed, her eyes never leaving him.

He slowly lowered the sweats over his hips, and his erection sprang from the center seam of his boxers before his pants fully dropped. Goodness, he was glorious—dark, swooping hair, chiseled jaw, all muscles, lightly hair-dusted golden skin.

Just stepped out of his sweats, now pooled at his feet, and looked down at himself.

"So much for the big reveal," he chuckled, tucking himself back into his boxers.

"Hey, no fair." She smiled. "I asked for nudity. I demand nudity."

He bent forward and kissed her. "After these come off, I demand equity in nudity."

"Fine," Marlo said. She went to pull off the sweatshirt she borrowed from him, but his large hands stilled her.

"I believe I was given strict directions to do this myself." He eased the sweatshirt and tank off her in one fluid motion, trails of heat scoring her skin where his eyes tracked over her bared skin. His hands worked quickly to release her from the remainder of her clothing. Then he cupped her breasts, his thumbs running over her nipples, creating a delicious friction.

"Fuck, me," he said in a low baritone.

"Only if you ask nicely."

Jude lifted her and settled her farther back on the large expanse of mattress. His perfect erection pressed against her lower abdomen as he lowered himself onto her. Marlo relished the weight of his strong body covering hers and the way her softer curves yielded to it.

"I don't think you should ever wear clothes," she whispered into his ear as he nibbled the soft flesh at the corner of her neck, her brain-to-mouth filter had completely dissolved.

"My house, my rules," he said, lifting up on his forearms and looking into her eyes. "If I am not wearing clothes, neither are you."

Marlo giggled. "Didn't you say I was in control?"

He growled before devouring her mouth. His tongue tangled deliciously with hers. He kissed her senseless, and when he finally broke contact to take a deep breath, he laughed.

"What?" she asked.

"Thank God, we were on the same page regarding easily removable clothing."

She slid her hands down his back to the rounded curve of his firm backside. "I remembered what you liked."

Marlo squeezed his bottom and reveled in the reward of gooseflesh erupting under her fingertips as she continued to explore the planes of his muscled body. Different but the same, a familiar terrain. She loved how he responded to her touch, every hitch of his breath, sigh, thickening of his erection, made her feel powerful.

Jude, still resting on one forearm above her, used his free hand to tuck her hair away from her face. "You are the most beautiful woman I've ever known."

Ordinarily, she dismissed such compliments as a means to an end, but the sincerity in his voice stirred something deep inside her. A dangerously familiar emotion. *Too soon.*

"You're not so bad yourself," she replied.

A lock of his dark hair fell across his forehead.

Marlo cupped his bottom again. She'd been fixated on his delectable ass since she first saw him again, so she intended to take full advantage of the access.

"Jude, I want you," she said it calmly, in complete contrast to the rioting feelings in her chest.

He leaned forward, sliding his hands above her head on the mattress, caging her between the bulges of his biceps. "I want you too."

A haunting echo of words she'd heard from him before in an entirely different context.

Jude lowered his mouth to hers again, this kiss less urgent but no less hungry than the first. He pressed his weight into her in a way that made her full breasts swell against his hard chest. She hooked her leg around his thigh, and he took the opportunity to bring one hand down and begin his own gentle exploration.

The moment he touched the core of her, she sighed. Known hands that played a familiar tune.

"My god, Marlo," he said heatedly as his fingers strummed her in exactly the right rhythm. "I've missed this."

She arched her back and he dipped in deeper. Her muscles clenched around his fingers as little earthquakes erupted through her. She clutched his shoulders and moaned his name.

Jude kissed her as she came apart in his hand. She hadn't expected to climax quite that soon, but he was clearly an expert at more than just pastries. He rolled onto his back, keeping his palm on her hip.

"That was intense," he said.

"Well, it was for me." Marlo turned on her side and propped herself on her elbow, taking his glorious form in. His cock still stood at full salute, moisture beading at the tip.

She trailed her fingers up and down his taut chest and abdomen.

Jude cleared his throat, gripping her hand. "I'm hanging on by a thread here."

A light dusting of color sprang across his cheeks.

Marlo rose and eased herself onto his lap, the wet seam of her aligned along his rigid length. He gripped the curves of her buttocks this time and pulled her closer to his erection throbbing against her core. He looked up at her, his eyes widened.

"I've wanted this again for so long," he whispered. "I never stopped aching for you."

And that tender spot in her chest flared to life again. She'd been kidding herself to think this could be a temporary diversion—a momentary quenching of a deep thirst. The connection between them was undeniable, something she'd never felt with her other couplings, a visceral understanding of his desire as though it was her own. It had been that way before too, when they were young and teaching each other intimacies. Some inexplicable part of them had always been and remained in cosmic harmony.

"I'm ready, Jude," she replied, her boldness surprising her. She'd ached for him too.

His hands traveled up her back, trailing sparks with every touch. His hands navigated the landscape of her body, and she watched him. Desire heated his eyes and his gaze undid her. It always felt good to be wanted, but being wanted by Jude empowered her in a completely unexpected way. It was like being found.

Marlo leaned forward and plundered his mouth as his hands cupped her breasts, his rough palms recreating the friction against her tightening nipples. She pumped against his length. They both groaned at the contact. Her hands skated down his muscled chest, and she relished the sound he made at the back of his throat when she touched him. Still cradling her ass, he brought her even closer to his center, her lips gliding along the length of his erection. He pumped his hips lightly, teasing her entrance but not breeching it.

"Woman, you're going to be the death of me." He rolled her off him as he reached toward his nightstand.

He winked at her. Ordinarily, she would've found it unbearably cheesy, but Jude had just the right charm to pull it off. He slid the condom on.

Marlo bit back a squeal. "I hope you have enough of those for a busy night."

"You really are trying to kill me." He placed a sweet kiss on her lips.

"Only in the best way possible."

He gestured to his sheathed erection. "Are you still sure?"

"If you are not inside me in the next couple of seconds, I may have to take matters into my own hands."

She straddled him, laying claim to his mouth again. She kissed him so deep, and he bucked his hips up against her. Marlo guided him inside her, sitting upright and struggling to keep herself from immediately orgasming again simply from the sensation of fullness. She rocked slowly, not breaking eye contact. Nothing she'd ever felt in her life compared to the sensation of this man inside her as he looked at her with…love.

The realization crashed through her.

For once, it wasn't her face spilling her secrets. Jude bit his lower lip and groaned her name.

Marlo resumed a quicker rhythm now. His hands reached up and adjusted both their positions to sitting without breaking contact or rhythm. The new angle sparked a whole new set of electric bursts through her.

She gripped the headboard behind him as he took one of her breasts in his mouth, his other hand finding her sweet spot again. They continued to move in concert, hurtling through space now at light speed. Her muscles quivered. She wouldn't be able to hold back for much longer, but she hated to take her release again before him. Then he stiffened momentarily. He was close too. She hadn't forgotten his cues.

"Together, baby. Let's let go together," she whispered into the top of his head.

His mouth found hers, and apparently, her edict was the only encouragement their bodies needed. Her muscles tightened around him, milking him until they were both wrung dry. She collapsed against him, and he held her as promised.

After several minutes, Jude finally spoke again. "Holy fuck."

Marlo giggled drowsily. "It was, wasn't it?"

"I had no idea it could get so much better between us."

She kissed his cheek and gently pulled herself off of him. He discarded the used condom, and then they nuzzled down into the bed, her head on his chest.

"It seems weird we waited so long to do this again," she said.

"Time apart made it sweeter." He gently squeezed her bottom.

"Now what?"

"A nap, then food, then round two." He punctuated the statement with a yawn.

"I think we may have already covered at least a round and a half, but I'm game." She kissed his chest and then yawned too.

A naked nap in the arms of her oldest friend-turned-newest lover sounded delightful. The big, scary questions could wait for later. For now, they'd enjoy this little bubble—just be Marlo and Jude without the baggage of history and other people's expectations.

Fun.

Temporary.

Marlo watched his chest settle into a slow, regular rise and fall, and glanced up to verify that he'd fallen asleep.

Today belonged to them and them alone. Tomorrow could wait.

Chapter Twenty-One

MARLO

MARLO WOULD'VE GIVEN anything to freeze the last couple of days in time. She and Jude barely emerged from his room. She knew this phase couldn't last forever, but she wanted to cling to the uncomplicated bliss for as long as possible. Soon enough, reality would stomp in, and they'd have to face the consequences of their spontaneous hookup.

Jesus, she hadn't even made it a day sharing a house with Jude without leaping into bed with him. She glanced over at him, still sleeping. Just look at him—no one could fault her weak willpower. She might be famous but she was still mortal.

Still, she'd committed to pursuing whatever happened between them, even if it ended up short-lived and destined to go down in flames. There was an upside to having nothing left to lose.

Her phone danced on the nightstand. It was Tara. As much as she wanted to let it go to voicemail, she knew she had to answer her publicist's call.

"Hi, Marlo, how is it going at Jude's house?" Tara asked.

"It's good." Marlo slid out of bed, slipped on a robe, and stepped out into the hallway. I've been busy in his studio, getting creative."

Marlo winced at the bald-faced lie. They'd been getting busy in his bed, but she did suppose the part about getting creative was accurate.

"Great, habibti, I love to hear it. I want to run a proposal by you. Just hear me out. Don't get mad."

Marlo groaned. It was never great when Tara issued a caution like that before speaking.

"I've been thinking if we capitulate to David and do the album he wants this time, then our contractual obligations are met, and we have leverage to do your next album the way you want with a studio of your choosing."

Marlo's heart sank. If even Tara gave up on her, maybe David Stringer was right all along. No one ever wanted the real Marlo Rayhan. They wanted the fantasy of Marlo Sage—an uncomplicated girl with uncomplicated feelings—and only so long as she delivered music to them in easily palatable sound bites.

"What he wants this time is for me to not write my own music," she said. "I've never not written my own music. It's fundamental to who I am as an artist."

Tara inhaled sharply. "Yes, but given the way everything has escalated, wouldn't it be better for you to be done with him for good?"

Marlo rolled her eyes, grateful for the distance of a telephone conversation. "Not if I have to do something so outside the bounds of who I am."

"Ya Allah, Marlo Sage, you are driving me into my grave."

"I'm sorry, Tara, but I changed my name to the one they wanted, dated the boys the labels chose, wore the clothes their stylists picked out, gave their pre-scripted answers at my interviews. And look at how they treat me. The money they've made off of me is good enough to spend, but they can't honor their promises to me? What about what I want out of the career I've devoted myself to all these years?"

"I hear you, Marlo. I do. But this is a business. And in this business, David Stringer ultimately controls the purse strings, and his reach is wide, as we've seen. I am trying to find a compromise that gets you out of his clutches as easily and early as possible. Please meet me halfway."

"What if I'm done with half-measures? A half-lived life?" A half-explored identity. Saying the words aloud acted as an instant relief valve. "Why should I continue to make myself miserable if it ultimately doesn't change anything?"

The silence in response was so complete, Marlo wondered if they'd been disconnected. Maybe Tara hadn't even heard what she'd said. Marlo opened her mouth to speak, but before she could, Tara at last responded.

"One hand alone cannot clap."

Tara loved to recite random idioms in times of conflict. She claimed they were traditional Arabic sayings that she did her best to translate into English. Marlo wasn't well-versed enough in her homeland or its language to know if she spoke the truth or simply made them up in the moment.

Regardless of the true origin, her point landed its mark.

A career in the music industry was a team endeavor, and without cooperation and compromise, there was no career. No clap. The trick was not to lose yourself in the compromise. Marlo didn't dare tell Tara that the conversations about Pop Machine set off a cascade of anxiety within her. Maybe Jude was right and she was simply burned out. The possibility that Marlo might be well and truly done with her music career hung over Marlo, clouding every conversation, every thought, and every decision. The cost of leaving would be tremendous and not only financially. But right now, the cost of staying, under David's terms, seemed an even higher price to pay.

"Yes, I get it," Marlo said. "I just need time to think about it."

"Yes, of course, habibti, you can take all the time you need," Tara said, affecting that warm, gooey voice that almost made Marlo believe time was on her side. "By the way, I am going to purchase a table for the bake-off and invite some industry guests. Maybe by then everyone's temperatures will have cooled."

"Wonderful," Marlo said, trying but failing to mask the sarcasm.

Marlo wandered into the studio, still shaken from the conversation with Tara. Sometimes she considered Tara a friend. Then other times, especially after conversations like the one they had just shared, she had to remind herself that they were business associates above all else. Now, she needed to convince herself that she and Jude were involved in nothing more than a summer fling. Then her boundaries would be safely set.

JUDE

Jude, perched on stool, strummed a few chords on his guitar. He smiled when Marlo entered the studio. She always stepped into the space with childlike awe, and it sent a flare of pride through him. He set the guitar down and crossed the room to her, pulling her into a kiss.

"You're awake," she said.

"Heard the phone ring."

"Sorry, I didn't mean to wake you. It was Tara."

"How did it go?"

Marlo sighed. "I can tell she's frustrated with the whole situation with Pop Machine. But asking me to record an album written by Tim Barrow is a bridge I can't cross."

"What happens if you don't do the album?"

"Breach of contract. He already owns my masters."

Jude's stomach twisted. All he'd hoped for was a few days of uncomplicated bliss but Marlo's career was as much a part of her as the heart-shaped birthmark on her inner thigh. She continued. "Anyway, my lawyers are working on it, but everyone is telling me the easiest way to deal with it is to do the album Stringer wants and then negotiate for the rights to my music catalogue to be restored."

Jude tightened his hold on her. "I'm sorry."

She pulled away and placed her hands on her hips, avoiding looking at him.

"Did she ask how it was going living here?"

Marlo was a smart girl, she'd obviously hear the real question beneath his words: *Did she ask about us?* Jude wasn't sure why he cared. "No one knows what's going on between us other than your parents."

"How long do you think we'll be able to hide it from our friends? Your family? Colleagues?"

She shrugged. "What would we even tell people? Hey, we're living together temporarily, and we decide to fuck while we do."

His lips flattened into a straight line. "That's not what we're doing."

"What are we doing?"

Blowing out a breath, Jude shook his head. "I don't know but it's not that superficial."

"But it's also not that deep."

Aim. Fire. Wound. Marlo always had a knack for weaponizing words.

Jude's gaze drifted from her. "Penny and Kate invited us over for dinner. They're dying to get to know you."

"They know about us?"

"They picked up on the clues."

"Clues?" She stared at him, discomfort settling between her knitted brows.

"You get under my skin, and it distracts me in a way that's completely obvious to anyone who spends a second with me. Also, I've never spent this much time away from the shop."

Marlo tightened her hold on him. He hated exposing his vulnerabilities to her like this. The truth was he wanted to shout about her being back in his life from the rooftops. But he'd always been leery of heights.

"Is that so?" she asked, her features softening.

He leaned down and kissed her. "We'll tell them or not tell them whatever you want. We don't owe anyone an explanation."

"We haven't even told my family yet."

Jude laughed. "Well, I think they've guessed by now where this was heading."

Marlo pulled back a fraction, still hanging on to him. "Explain."

"Well, my mom definitely got an eyeful that first day." He chuckled, running his knuckles across the outer curve of her breast. "And then when we kind of went off the grid, well..."

She shivered at his touch, but that determined look on her face told him she wasn't going to let him distract her, at least not yet. "Well?"

"My mom may have told your mom not to worry about your whereabouts because we were last seen together. *Together* together."

Marlo buried her head at the juncture of his shoulder and neck. "Oh God, this is kind of a nightmare."

"Or a dream. They *have* left us relatively undisturbed. When was the last time you spoke to your parents?"

"Two days ago."

He laughed. "Nice."

"Well, we are thirty-one each. I think we're capable of deciding how to spend our time."

Jude kissed her again. "If it were up to me, we'd never leave my room."

Marlo smiled against his lips. "I'm open to persuasion."

MARLO

Several hours later, Marlo smoothed out the skirt of her summer dress. They were headed to Penny and Kate's house, and her nerves were strung tight.

Jude squeezed her bare knee then let his fingers slip under her skirt and drift farther up her bare thigh. "Don't stress. They're going to love you."

She nodded, trying both to quell her anxiety and temper the heat pooling low in her belly. His hand on her thigh was an automatic on switch. She looked at him from under her lashes, trying to decipher if he was trying to distract her on purpose.

"I wish we had to time to stop and at least grab a bouquet of flowers for them," she said.

His hand scooted up another half inch. Okay, it was definitely on purpose.

"Jude."

"What?" he said, feigning innocence.

"I know what you're doing." Surprised at her own breathlessness.

"I'm driving." This time, his hand moved mere millimeters, so close yet miles away from where she needed it.

She placed her hand over his, trapping it against her mid-thigh. "Not fair."

The corner of his mouth tipped up, but he still stared straight ahead. "What are you worried about now?"

"Nothing." She squirmed, trying to still his hand, but he was too strong. She giggled as his hand landed way too close to where her need grew urgent.

"Consider this your warning. If I see you getting that little furrow at your brow, I will use whatever means necessary to rid you of it."

Marlo leaned her head back against the headrest. "Promise?"

This time, Jude shifted uncomfortably in his seat. But that still didn't stop him. He slid a finger under the hem of her underwear, and Marlo shifted closer to him.

"I think we might have time for a detour after all," he said.

He withdrew his hand and Marlo stifled a whimper. A couple of miles ahead, he turned off the road into a thicket of trees.

"Where are you going?" she asked.

"I worked in the forestry service for a couple of summers."

After I moved back home. He didn't need to say it. The time they were apart constantly hovered between them.

He parked in a secluded area off the forest road, surrounded by trees, and pulled Marlo into the back seat with him.

"Jude Beckett, you are shameless."

Three quarters of an hour later, flushed and sated, and most definitely more relaxed, they were finally back on their way to dinner.

JUDE

Jude couldn't believe they just had car sex. They'd never done that as teenagers. All he knew was, in Marlo's presence, he lost all impulse control. It scared him as much as it thrilled him. He continued to sneak glances at her, admiring the post-sex flush on her cheeks and her kiss-swollen lips. Penny would never let him live this down. Because no one could look at Marlo without knowing exactly why they were delayed.

"There it is." Jude pointed at the craftsman style house at the end of the cul-de-sac.

"It's so cute."

He watched Marlo admire the cheerful blue house with a generous front porch, complete with a wicker porch swing. The hydrangeas out front perfectly punctuated the charm of the home. Jude parked and rounded to Marlo's door, but she'd already stepped out of the car, a look of childlike wonder on her face. Her beauty floored him all over again. He fought the impulse to haul her back into the backseat.

Penny, with the baby propped on her hip, waved from the porch. "Glad you finally made it."

The comment was directed more at Jude than Marlo. He gave his assistant chef a warning look, which he knew Penny could read even with the distance separating them.

"Ignore her," he whispered to Marlo. "She likes to give me a hard time."

"That makes two of us," she said under her breath. "Your house is beautiful," she called out to Penny.

"Thank you," Penny said. "Come in. I'll take you on the tour."

"Penny, this is Marlo," Jude said, "Marlo, Penny and baby Eve."

Marlo stuck her hand out, and Penny took it with gleam in her eye. The baby leaned forward, placing her chubby little hand on Marlo's wrist.

Marlo laughed. "Hello, Miss Eve. It's so nice to finally properly meet you, Penny. Jude talks about you so much."

Penny's brow arched. "There is only a fraction of truth to anything he says."

But before Marlo could respond, Eve practically leaped into Marlo's arms.

"Hey," Marlo said, looking into the babe's bright brown eyes. "How are you?"

Eve babbled for a couple of seconds, then she leaned forward, putting her head on Marlo's shoulder. Jude wasn't prepared for the sight of Marlo with a baby in her arms.

"She likes you," Penny said after a few seconds, a triumphant smile lighting her face.

After a quick walkthrough of the house, they joined Kate at the outdoor kitchen in the backyard. Penny gave Kate a chaste kiss on the lips, but the lingering look afterward was a full-blooded smolder. Marlo smiled at Jude, and he placed a kiss on her forehead and then gave baby Eve one too. Marlo stepped forward to introduce herself to Kate, immediately offering to help with any last-minute dinner preparations.

"No, please go sit," Kate said. "You entertaining Eve is help enough. These two are usually doing the cooking, so this a rare treat for me."

Marlo and Eve joined Jude and Penny at the long outdoor table. This backyard was an entertainer's dream. Again, Marlo was struck by acute awareness that she was so far behind her peers in life. Penny, Kate, and Eve were a full-fledged family.

Jude leaned forward again. "Everything good?"

She schooled her features and nodded absently. Marlo couldn't explain this feeling of losing a race against a ticking clock to Jude at a dinner party. Kate joined them, adding a large platter of grilled vegetables to the already generous spread on the table. Penny retrieved Eve from Marlo and settled her into a high chair at the opposite end of the table.

"We dabble in vegetarianism sometimes," Kate explained, gesturing to the offerings.

"It looks and smells incredible. Thank you so much for having us over," Marlo said, trying to ignore the knowing glance Kate and Penny exchanged. Marlo piled her plate with mixed grilled vegetables, caprese salad, and half a grilled portobello panini. "So, Penny, you and Jude met in culinary school?"

"Not exactly, he'd already graduated, but he was the mentor I was assigned. All the girls and most of the boys in my year were pretty jealous."

"Penny, stop," Jude said, giving her a playful warning glance.

"No, it's okay. I want to hear it all." Marlo placed her hand over Jude's mouth, only to be met with a slobbery kiss to her palm. She wiped her hand on the front of his shorts. "Eww."

He arched a brow suggestively at her.

Damn him. Warmth flooded her cheeks, and by the way Kate and Penny were smiling, it was accompanied by a visible flush.

"Frankly, I was disappointed by the assignment. I thought, what is this washed-up bargain Justin Timberlake going to teach me about becoming a pastry chef?" Penny laughed, dodging the asparagus spear Jude launched at her with admirable accuracy.

"No food fights in front of Eve," Kate play-scolded. The baby cooed and clapped her chubby hands.

The tension between Marlo's shoulders eased. No wonder Jude loved these women so much. They exuded familial warmth and love. She grazed his jawline with her fingers. He held her gaze and smiled in that way that made her heart swoop.

Then Jude returned his attention to Penny. "Admit it," he said, "being my mentee was the best thing that ever happened to you."

Penny smiled, turning to Kate. "Second best."

It was Kate's turn to blush. "Sorry, Marlo, I'm not sure we'll ever stop being newlyweds."

"No need to apologize," Marlo said. "All of this is so lovely. Thank you, again."

Jude squeezed her shoulder, and Marlo suddenly needed to look away from them all for a moment. She was overcome with emotion—gratitude, happiness, and strangely, melancholy. It was difficult to be around people who'd figured out so much about themselves and lived comfortable in the knowledge, while she still struggled to keep everything in her life from imploding. Even with the invitation from Jude to move into his place, she was still so far from the life Penny and Kate had built.

"Excuse me," she said. "I need to use the restroom."

Marlo fled toward the house. The tears came fast and hot. She ran into the bathroom, flipped the lid down on the toilet, sat down, and let herself sob. She couldn't even explain to herself what was happening. It wasn't envy—she didn't begrudge Penny and Kate or even Jude any of their happiness. It was just, against the measure of their success, her lack was impossible not to see. She'd sacrificed so much for a career which refused to love her back. Her existential crisis had her by the throat.

JUDE

Jude stood outside the bathroom door, listening to Marlo's sobs. He was unsure whether to give her a moment or to step in and comfort her. Everything had been going so well. He racked his brain for the moment it changed, but he couldn't pinpoint anything.

Unable to bear another moment of hearing her cry, he knocked softly. "Are you okay?"

She blew her nose. "Yeah, sorry, I don't know what happened out there."

"Do you want to let me in?" Jude leaned his head against the door, fighting the urge to tear it from its hinges.

There was a long pause. Then he heard the lock disengage.

Marlo stood in the doorway, eyes red-rimmed. "I'm sorry. I'm so embarrassed."

"What happened?"

She shook her head, and her rapid blinks telegraphed that she was fighting back fresh tears.

"Talk to me, Marlo."

"I think maybe I'm having a quarter-life crisis." Her lower lip trembled.

"That's okay, happens to all of us."

"I don't know." She gestured to the backyard. "You all seem to have it pretty figured out."

"Come sit with me for a minute."

Marlo hesitated for a moment then followed Jude to the living room. He pulled her into his lap as he sat down on the couch. He brushed the hair away from her face and caught her lingering tears with his fingers.

"Shouldn't we go back outside?" She glanced nervously toward the patio door.

"We will, but let's talk first."

Jude bent his neck and kissed the top of her shoulder closest to him. He wanted her to feel safe enough to share what troubled her. He wanted her to know he was in her corner. This time, he wanted her to know she couldn't push him away.

"Do you know what David Stringer said to me after my first Grammy win?" she asked.

Jude tensed. The mention of that name set his teeth on edge. "No."

Marlo laughed mirthlessly. "The sooner you peak, the sooner you fall. Brace yourself, sweetheart."

"I've told you what I think of David Stringer," Jude said through gritted teeth. He hated that the prick had poisoned every one of Marlo's achievements. "What does that have to do with today?"

"I just look at what you and Penny have achieved with the shop and the life Penny and Kate have built as a family and…"

He hugged her into his chest. "And?"

"I feel like I'm losing the race."

Jude couldn't help himself—he chuckled. Marlo stiffened in his arms.

"No, sweetheart, sorry," he said. "I didn't mean to laugh. It's not a race. But even if it were, you've sold millions of records, sold out venues across the world, and you think somehow you're losing?"

Marlo pounded a fist against his chest. "I'd give it all away in a heartbeat to have what they have."

He captured her hand and held it against his heart. "Stop letting David Stringer dictate the narrative. You've been chasing his approval all these years, and you know you're not going to get it. But that doesn't mean your accomplishments don't exist. Nor do your achievements preclude you from having any life you choose."

She sighed. "Do you realize how few artists achieve the staying power of Beyonce or Dave Grohl? And how fewer of them started as teen pop stars? All I do is write songs about heartbreak."

"Listen to yourself. Your songs about heartbreak are what people all over the world turn to for comfort. Love and grief are universal."

"I don't know. It just feels like if I gave it all up tomorrow, no one would care."

"You're wrong. But the only person you should be worried about in that scenario is you. If you gave it all up tomorrow, would *you* care?"

Tears spilled down her cheek. "I don't know. Tomorrow and beyond is a mysterious haze, and I can't see what's next. It terrifies me."

Jude hugged her tight again. He didn't realize just how deep the wounds from David Stringer had scarred her. He hated that anyone, but especially that awful man, made her doubt herself.

"Let's start with right now. We can make our apologies and leave, or we can go back outside, finish up dinner, and drown out the world with wine, good friends, and better dessert."

Marlo wrapped her hand around his neck and pulled him down for a kiss. "I'm sorry. Did you expect me to behave like an adult?"

He laughed and gave her another peck.

"Now that I've fully humiliated myself in front of your friends, let's get back out there." She paused. "I really was having fun before the meltdown."

"Happens to the best of us."

Jude scooped her up against his chest and stood, carrying her in his arms. Marlo squealed in surprise.

"Put me down," she said, laughing, finally some lightness returning to her voice.

"Never."

Chapter Twenty-Two

JUDE

AFTER THE INCIDENT at Penny's dinner, Jude and Marlo avoided the subject of the future entirely. They didn't discuss relationship plans or career plans. They lived day by day, Marlo working with her collaborators, whom she'd flown into town, during the day and then rehearsing for the bake-off performance in the evenings. Any free time they shared, they pretty much spent testing out the sturdiness of the various surfaces in Jude's house.

Though he was living the life of his dreams, a persistent doubt nagged in the back of his mind. Summer wouldn't last forever. He didn't intend to push her, but after the conversation they'd had at Kate and Penny's house, he wanted to encourage her to consider what she truly wanted in the years ahead.

And he only prayed he somehow figured into the picture. He'd lost the ability to envision a life absent her presence.

On his drive home, Jude received a phone call. Suze's voice, breathlessly excited, boomed through his car speakers.

"Jude, darling, I have news."

"I have some news for you too," he replied. He debated pulling over for the discussion, but he was so close to home. By the end of the day, he was always eager to return to Marlo.

"You're being considered for the role of a guest judge for a televised international baking competition. Think Project Runway but with baking, a different expert judge every week."

He regretted not pulling off to the side of the road. "Suze, I didn't audition to judge for a baking competition show. I would *never* audition for any part of a televised show."

"Oh, hon', I know, which is why I submitted you for consideration. It would be two to three days max of filming. It would put your name back in the general consciousness, beyond just the culinary world. You're already a great mentor to new chefs. It would be practically the same thing. If you're still serious about writing a cookbook, we should be focused on building a platform beyond a few feature spreads in culinary magazines. Let people see you in action."

Jude gripped the steering wheel so tight his fingers whiten. "The charity bake-off will be livestreamed, isn't that enough?"

"No, that's just a start. This show will be televised internationally. It's a way bigger platform than a local charity event."

"This is so uncool."

How would he explain this to Marlo? To Penny? He couldn't leave them in the lurch to chase the dream of publication in such a circuitous route.

For a moment, Suze quieted.

"Jude, I'm your manager, and if you have certain business-related goals you wish to achieve, I have a responsibility to make your wishes into an actionable plan. Sometimes, that plan will include certain aspects you may not like."

He exhaled. "I just wish you would have spoken to me about it first."

Suze laughed. "Yes, because you would have been so open-minded about the opportunity, right?"

Now, Jude sat silently. She was right but he was still irritated. He didn't want to put himself back under the scrutinizing glare of that level of fame to achieve the new goals he'd set for himself. Plus, now with Marlo back in his life, being thrust back into the public sphere had additional implications.

Suze wasn't aware of the new turn in their relationship. Besides, he couldn't expect her to factor Marlo into the opportunities she presented to him. He was being unfair, but he was angry all the same. He wanted it all—a cookbook, Marlo for keeps, and privacy—only he didn't know how to pull it all off.

Suze cleared her throat. "So, what is the news you have for me?"

Jude pulled into his driveway and put the car in park. He wasn't sure how to best deliver this information especially now. He laid his head back against the seat and closed his eyes.

"Marlo and I have been seeing each other."

"Oh."

He waited for a beat. "Oh? That's it?"

"Well, I wasn't exactly expecting it, but it also isn't entirely surprising. The chemistry was still combusting. Anyone with two eyes could see it." She sucked in her breath. "Are you sure this is a good idea?"

The question hit him right in the sternum, bringing the whispering doubt to the surface. Part of him wanted to hang up on her. He had no fucking clue if being with Marlo was the smartest or the stupidest thing he'd ever done.

All I know is I cannot live without her.

"Suze, my personal business is just that, personal. As my manager, I'm giving you the courtesy of sharing it, but I will not answer to you or anyone else about the wisdom of my choices. I simply wanted you to have a complete picture in case that may impact the direction we take things next."

"Jude, are you telling me that you may not pursue opportunities you've been busting your ass for because of Marlo? You hear how that sounds, right?"

He groaned. "People make concessions and compromises for the sake of relationships all the time, and we call it growth. Why can't I do that for Marlo?"

Suze's took in a sharp breath. "A relationship between you and Marlo will never just be between the two of you. There are legions of shippers that still kindle the flame of hope that you'll find your way back to each other. There are news outlets that will literally try to kill each other to land the first pictures, the first interviews. Every professional step you take from here on out will be in her shadow. That's the reality and you know it."

Jude put his hands over his face. How had they arrived back at this place so soon? They'd barely had time to enjoy each other in peace. Even after all these years, their relationship remained cursed—the minute it was exposed to air, it spoiled. Now it was Suze naysaying, but if he courted the opportunities she wanted him to pursue, soon it would be the whole world weighing in. What relationship could thrive under the bright, hot scrutiny of the public and the media? He just wanted some more time to figure everything out for himself.

"I know you are looking out for me," he said, "but my privacy in this matter is of the utmost importance to me. You may have doubts about Marlo, but I do not."

He hated the way his voice tensed. He didn't need Suze hearing his doubt.

"I don't have doubts about Marlo or about you," Suze said, "but if you don't discuss these opportunities with her openly and instead act on assumptions and your own delusions, you'll end up exactly where you did last time. You know what they say about insanity."

"What?" His volatile emotions made it difficult to follow everything she said.

"Doing the same thing and expecting a different result is the very definition of it. At the end of the day, you call the shots, hon'. I'll email you the details about the show. We'll set up time to circle back later this week once you've had time to think it through."

Suze ended the call. Jude still white-knuckle gripped the steering wheel, even though he was parked in the garage. The door from the house to the garage opened, and Marlo stepped out. Her smile faltered, and even from a distance, he knew she sensed a shift from his usual mood.

Jude exited the car and forced a smile. "Hey, Marls, I missed you."

He pulled her into his arms and kissed her. Despite her immediate response to him, the tension remained lodged between his shoulders. Jude squeezed his eyes shut tighter and deepened the kiss. He needed to lose himself in this embrace, needed to forget about the conversation with Suze. He needed more time.

MARLO

Marlo tried to keep her hold on reality, but getting lost in Jude's arms was so easy. He kissed her as though he intended to steal the oxygen from her lungs. The security system alerted her when Jude pulled into the garage, but when he didn't enter the house immediately, she worried. She'd noticed his pained posture the moment she stepped into the garage. It wasn't his usual demeanor when he returned home from work. She fought between the battling urges to pry or give him his privacy.

Doubt edged her thoughts, no matter how she tried to squash it. Jude had been nothing but attentive and doting. Still, she couldn't shake the sensation of waiting for the other shoe to drop. Moments ago, he'd looked distraught, and now he kissed her like his existence depended on it.

Marlo pulled away. "Hey, that's quite a greeting."

Jude smiled but it didn't reach his eyes. "I missed you."

"Is everything okay?" She moderated her voice, hoping her outward calm demeanor would encourage him to open up to her.

He sighed. "Yeah, it's nothing. I'm starving, are you?"

She stilled him. "Jude, are you sure nothing is going on?"

"It's just some work stuff. All I want to do is eat, put my feet up, and snuggle with my baby." He leaned forward and kissed her again.

Marlo studied his face. A deep line creased his forehead, and the half-moons under his eyes were darker than usual. Maybe he was just tired after a long day at work. And even though he loved it, surely running a business was stressful. Still, her instincts warned of danger ahead. She followed him into the house and waited for him in the kitchen while he changed out of his work clothes.

She idly scrolled through social media when her attention snagged on Jude's name. Marlo read the post several times.

M & J fans prepare yourselves: Our sources are reporting that Jude Beckett is in final negotiations to star as a guest host in WebFlix's newest baking competition show.

Is this what he was hiding from her? How long had he been keeping this secret?

Marlo set her phone down and gripped the edge of the counter. Her breaths came in rapid, shallow bursts. Now she understood his insistence about her move-in and their relationship being temporary. He knew he was leaving at the end of the summer.

She had to give him credit—he was a far better actor than she ever realized.

Jude walked directly over to her, placing his large hand on her back. She resented the comforting gesture now that she knew the truth. But no matter what her brain told her, her body remained primed to respond to his touch.

"Hey, what's wrong? What are you reading?" he asked, gesturing to her phone.

Marlo looked up at him, and as angry as she was, she laughed. "Seriously?"

"Yes, seriously, what's wrong? It looks like someone punched you in the gut."

She laughed again. He was truly unbelievable. Didn't he realize he was the one who'd dealt the fatal blow?

"Why don't you tell me? All this time you've worried about my plans for the end of the summer, but you never even shared your own." There was no calm left to summon. Her voice sounded shrill even to her own ears. She didn't care. This moment deserved shrill.

Jude pulled his hand away and turned her in her stool to face him. "I was going to talk to you about it. I needed a minute to gather my thoughts."

So, he'd withheld information from her, waiting until she found out on her own and confronted him.

She nearly choked on the stench of cowardice. "I'd prefer to hear about my boyfriend's latest career coups from his own lips instead of a gossip site."

"What are you talking about?"

Marlo grabbed her phone and pulled up the post, turning the screen to show him. His eyes widened, and then the actual color drain from his face. He leaned on the counter and his mouth gaped.

"Care to start explaining now?" she asked. "Exactly how long have you known about this?"

"I literally just heard about this on my drive home," he said. "Suze called to tell me I was in consideration as a guest judge. I was angry at her for submitting me as an interested party without even asking me first."

Her anger partially deflated. Was he telling her the truth? Judging by his reaction, it seemed possible, but now she questioned her own instincts. While yes, he deserved a chance to mull it over, she also deserved not to be left in the dark about decisions that could impact their future. Especially not when she might hear about it from other sources first.

"I thought…" She wasn't even sure how to finish her statement. Ugly thoughts raced through her head. She'd been ready seconds ago to walk right out his door, never to return.

His hands were on her again, pulling her out of the chair toward him. He crushed her in a hug. And damn it if she didn't soften into it.

"You thought I knew and hid this from you, oh God." He slumped against her.

"I didn't know what to think. You wouldn't talk to me, then I saw that post, and I just…I just don't know."

Jude brought his hands up to her face, cradling her cheeks. "Marlo, I would never lie to you. I would never hide anything from you. I was so mad at Suze I could barely see straight, and I knew I needed to calm down before talking to you."

She stepped back out of his reach. "This is a big fucking deal in so many ways."

He dropped his chin to his chest. "I know. Fuck, I know."

Tears pricked the back of her eyes. She wasn't ready to lose him again. Not yet, not so soon. She wanted to stay in their private bubble forever. And if not forever, at least for a few more weeks. Panic built in her chest again. It was bad enough trying to figure out who she was without her music, but what did it say about her if she lost Jude again?

"You told me you left music because you didn't like the scrutiny of fame," she said, "and now you're going to do a TV show? You've been doing photo shoots and magazine interviews. I'm confused. I may not have a right to be, but I am."

"Marlo—"

"No, did you leave because you didn't like the spotlight or because you didn't like sharing it with me?" She hated the way her voice shook, almost more than the traitorous tears spilling over her cheeks.

Jude stepped closer again. "Marlo, listen to me. I've never liked being in the public media circus. Not now. Not then. Not ever. Suze wanted me to do the shoots and the interviews and even this show so we can build support for the cookbook I want to write."

Marlo wrapped her arms around her middle, nodding.

"I'm proud of the work we do at the shop. As the boss, it's incumbent on me to promote my business. What I'm doing with the bakery is no different than what you do for your music. I wish I loved performing as much as you do. I wish we could have done that together forever. But I was lying to myself and to you."

"Logically, I understand, but in my heart…"

Suddenly, the reality of their rushed reconnection sharpened into focus. They were pretending at a real relationship. They'd never even clearly defined their status. She called him her boyfriend because she didn't think "fuck buddy" was socially appropriate, even if it was more accurate. She wasn't really his girlfriend, was she? Or his roommate? His long-term, easy-access booty call was more like it. Great sex alone unfortunately didn't a relationship make, and obviously neither did sharing a residence. Marlo and Jude were always great at playacting love, but real had never been their forte.

Clearly, some things never changed.

Jude further closed the distance between them. He reached out for her but she flinched away from his touch. He looked wounded. She wasn't trying to hurt him. She just couldn't keep her bearings if his hands were on her.

"Marlo," he started, "please don't let this misunderstanding derail what we've got going here."

"What do we have going on other than a prolonged booty call?" Her filter disintegrated.

"Come on, you know it's more than that. You've been living here, for fuck's sake." Jude ran his hand back and forth through his hair, and Marlo longed to reach out and set it to rights. The magnetic pull between them was damn near impossible to resist.

"Have I? I mean, yes, I've been staying here. But do I live here, really? I barely knew about the cookbook, the show. What else don't I know?"

"You know everything. I want to write a cookbook. You want to write and record your own album. We want to be together, despite the odds. It doesn't have to be so difficult."

Marlo laughed. The sound rang hollow. "I didn't know it was such a chore to be with me."

"I'm not the one saying it is a chore."

"You're impossible."

He groaned. "You know exactly what I mean. Stop looking for trouble where there isn't any."

"Yes, every girl's dream is to find drama to stir up with her lover." Nope, that moniker didn't sound any better. If she couldn't even name what this thing was between them, it didn't signify great hope for a shared future. "I mean, they don't call us hysterical for nothing. How could I forget?"

Jude stepped forward again and grabbed Marlo, bringing her into his arms. He held her tight, even as she lightly struggled. They both knew it was more a show of pride than a true protest. Finally, she stopped squirming and brought her arms around his neck. She hated herself for being so weak where Jude Beckett was concerned. When he touched her, she responded automatically, melting into his warmth, seeking his comfort.

"Marlo, I don't want to lose you." His gaze fixed intently on hers.

The truth of his words echoed in her bones. A silence stretched between them, his heart pounding against her chest.

"I don't want to lose you either." Her cheeks dampened again as new tears fell.

Jude cradled her face in his hands, brushing away her tears with his thumbs. "I was so afraid just now that you wouldn't want anything to do with me once you found out about the show. I won't do it. I'll turn it down."

"No," she said, tightening her grasp on him. "No, you have every right to the career you want to build for yourself. I was wrong to imply otherwise. I just want you to be honest with me. That's all I ask."

He bent his head down and brushed his lips against hers once again. "I will never lie to you, Marlo Sage."

"Don't forget, you carry my heart," Marlo replied. "Be gentle with it."

They stared at each other. A moment suspended in time.

Then Jude kissed her again—an encore to the frenzied kiss in the entryway earlier. It was a devouring, a claiming, and Marlo happily surrendered to it. She'd much rather succumb to this man's passions than to feed the thread of worry wrapping itself around her heart. They'd hit a bump in the road, panicked, and then worked a strategy around it. That was what a mature relationship was meant to be—a compromise, a dance, a way to navigate turbulent waters together. Right?

Marlo sighed into his mouth, and he took it as an invitation to deepen the kiss even further. Soon, they sank to the cool tile floor, fumbling to free each other from their clothing. They didn't bother with any lengthy interlude—he entered her in one quick thrust, and she moved against him in a frenetic pace. He met her rhythm, and they continued kissing hungrily as their bodies collided against each other. Their need for each other in this moment was feral. Sex might not be the solution to any of their bigger problems, but it was the only thing that existed solely between them. A language all their own.

JUDE

Later, they laid tangled together on the kitchen floor. Jude cradled Marlo's head against his chest. He felt guilty for taking her on the unwelcoming tile like a crazed beast. She deserved better. Not that she hadn't been an enthusiastic participant, but on the heels of their fight, he shouldn't have acted on pure animal lust. He wasn't sure why it was like this between them, a force of inexplicable gravity drawing him to her. The need to be touching her and be touched by her consumed him when she was near. He was addicted to her and it scared him. If Jude lost her this time, he wasn't sure he'd ever recover.

Marlo stirred against him. He wasn't sure what to say or do. An apology seemed inadequate. Whispered sweet words seemed contrived.

She looked at him, a sleepy smile drawing up the corners of her mouth. "Well, that was new."

His eyes drifted to her lips. And there it was again, the insatiable need to consume her.

He forced his gaze back to her eyes. "I'm sorry. You just do something to me I can't explain."

Marlo sat up, bringing her knees to her chest, and resting her chin on them. "Why are you sorry?"

Jude sat up too, running his fingers up and down the knobs of her spine. "I kind of tackled you just now."

"I didn't object. And I get what you're saying, you do something to me I can't explain either."

"Well, at least we're on the same page here." He dropped his head on her shoulder.

She spoke so softly Jude would've missed her next words if he weren't innately attuned to her. "I hope so."

The thread of doubt wormed back into his consciousness. Marlo still questioned him and his sincerity, and nothing broke his heart more. The specter of past pain always lingered between them at the periphery. Could they build a future on so shaky a foundation? He wanted a full life with her, but he also wanted the career he'd spent the intervening years building. He knew she wasn't asking him to choose between them, but he wasn't sure he had the bandwidth to commit fully to both. He'd give everything up to keep her, but that didn't mean he wouldn't resent it.

Chapter Twenty-Three

JUDE

JUDE SPENT EVEN more time at the bakery. Since their last argument, he distanced himself from Marlo. It was lot—sharing his life and his home with her so soon after she reappeared in his life. He wasn't blind to the obstacles between them. He just hoped over time they'd work it out. Lucky for them, the fates aligned, and he didn't end up getting the guest judge role on the baking competition show. He was equal parts disappointed and relieved. Which was strange, since he hadn't actively pursued the opportunity in the first place. The prospect of getting his cookbook published seemed impossible, but at least he and Marlo were granted a temporary reprieve from the heaviness that recently settled over their relationship.

They fell back into their old habits, Jude working daily at the bakery and Marlo taking advantage of his home studio. He saw the evidence of her creating new music, but she had yet to share any of it with him. Not even when he asked. Marlo always had an excuse—she was still working out the bridge or the melody needed work.

"Soon, I'll be ready to share soon" had become the common refrain.

So, Jude sought reassurance in a perfectly turned-out pâte brisée or a remarkably airy soufflé. He'd mulled over a new pie recipe for a while, and last night, it came to him. A rosemary-infused apple pie topped with a scotch caramel drizzle—tart, sweet, earthy, and smoky flavor bursts on the tongue. He'd call it Tart Dreams. Licking his lips, he rolled out the dough. In the kitchen, he measured out flour and sugar and butter and transformed it into something magical. Every time. If he couldn't share his conflicted emotions with Marlo, then at least he folded them into a pastry or whipped them into a flavor infused cream.

Jude settled his delicate pie dough into his favorite set of pie dishes. He'd make six of these pies, take an Insta-worthy photo, and post it on the bakery account. Usually when he publicized a limited, seasonal offering on his social media, it sold out within the hour. It was such an honor that people in the community took his efforts so seriously and were so devoted to his shop. There were many gratifying aspects of baking, but the joy it brought to his customers was definitely the best part. He was granted a free pass into people's happiest, celebratory moments, and it was fulfilling in a way his music career never was to him.

"Jude," the shop clerk called out. "Phone."

"Thanks, Trudy." Jude had fallen deep into the pie zone, and it always took him a moment to reintegrate. He wiped his hands on a clean dish rag and picked up the extension in the back. "Jude Beckett, how can I help you?"

"Jude, this is Catherine Howell from *Farm & Table*. Do you have a moment to talk?"

He cleared his throat, steadying the phone in his shaking hand. Catherine Howell was the Anna Wintour of the culinary world. Getting a call from her was as far beyond his dreams as owning a pet unicorn—it simply didn't happen to mere mortals.

"Hello, Ms. Howell, how can I help you?" He cringed at his own feigned calm.

"The talk of food influencers everywhere is your shop. We would love to do a feature. I know you shy away from media attention, but I would really appreciate the opportunity to sit down with you."

There was a long pause. This call was every chef's dream come true, but he and Marlo just barely survived the WebFlix debacle. How long before a journalist, especially the caliber of journalists that worked at *Farm & Table*, realized that Marlo lived with him? Once that story broke, there would be no putting the genie back in the bottle. Suze was right. News of his relationship with Marlo would always eclipse all his work, the pastry shop. He might end up with the cookbook deal, but it would be offered for all the wrong reasons.

"A magazine article?" he asked, his mind whirling. He still hadn't completely processed that he was speaking to Catherine freaking Howell.

"Well," she paused, "a feature yes, but we are also thinking more."

More? What did she mean "more"? A cookbook collaboration?

Farm & Table published a celebrity chef cookbook every couple of years, and it was an esteemed honor to be included among the contributing chefs, even if it wasn't exactly what he'd dreamed about. He was getting ahead of himself, trying to clear hurdles that hadn't yet materialized.

Jude hadn't quite reached celebrity chef status. Former teen celebrity, yes. Chef, yes. But a celebrity chef was another entity unto itself. He was just passed over as a guest judge, for Christ's sake. And there it was again, the odd push-pull of wanting the recognition and opportunities but shying away from the media glare. And if he was perfectly honest, he didn't just want to be a guest judge or a featured chef. He wanted his own book, his recipes alone standing on their own strength.

"What does 'more' mean?" he asked.

“We were thinking of a long-form intimate portrait of America’s heartthrob-turned-chef. Video portrait.”

“What do you mean ‘video portrait’?”

“A series of five- to ten-minute video reels that are a combination of personal diary and baking tutorial.”

He considered the proposal. So they intended to make him a pastry influencer? He wasn’t sure he was interested. “And what, you’d send camera crews to my house?”

“No, we have our own studio in LA. So no one would be intruding on your private life. It would simply be a way for readers and viewers to get a more in-depth picture of America’s up-and-coming favorite pastry chef.”

“Why would this be of value?” He tried to moderate his emotions, but the question came out barbed with tension.

Ms. Howell chuckled. “You’re an attractive former pop star, and now you’re turning the culinary world on its ear. Our readers are dying to know everything they can about you. They’re fascinated. We practically had to devote a special team to handle the letters to the editor about you.”

Jude rolled his eyes. This was exactly what he didn’t want. His work mattered on its own merits, not because he’d once been linked to the world’s biggest pop star. Was he truly doomed to live in Marlo’s shadow forever? And this was all without public knowledge that they’d rekindled their romance. Once that bomb dropped, there would be no escaping Marlo’s orbit.

“I don’t think this is an avenue I’m interested in pursuing,” he said through gritted teeth. “But I’m honored you considered me.”

“Before you dismiss it altogether, think of what you can do with the stage we’re offering you. We can help you expand your outreach efforts. Bring the elite pastry world to the less privileged.”

At least Catherine Howell had done her homework. Jude and Penny had launched a scholarship program to help disadvantaged youth pursue an education in pastry arts.

"I appreciate the offer, but I really think it's best to focus my attention on the shop."

"Jude Beckett, I did not become the editor-in-chief of *Farm & Table* by giving up at the first no. The offer stands. I will send over the details, contract terms. Look over everything in writing, review it with your manager, your lawyers, and don't let me down."

This time, Jude laughed. "Ms. Howell, I walked away from a music career with the girl...my best friend at the height of our success. I didn't get to where I was without a bit of fortitude either."

"Touché, Mr. Beckett. I'll be in touch."

MARLO

Marlo paced in the entryway, waiting for her dad to arrive. She'd grown increasingly restless by the day. Alone, there was too much time to think, and her mind cycled through everything. All the time. Obsessively circling thoughts about herself, her life, and questioning what it all meant. She couldn't understand why anyone studied philosophy—existentialism exhausted her. She'd invited her dad over because she couldn't stand another hour alone. Finally, the doorbell chimed.

"Dad, welcome." She flung her arms around him.

"Hello, habouba, we've missed you. The house is so quiet with you gone."

"Come in. I'll take you on the tour."

"First, I want to talk to you," he said, concern knitting his eyebrows together.

"You can talk while we tour." Marlo started walking away from him, but he was quick on her heels.

"Marlo, aynee, Mom and I are worried. Did you rush into this? We know you needed to move, but maybe a place of your own would have been better."

She whipped around. "Can you stop treating me like a child? I'm thirty-one."

"You're our child, no matter what age you are or how many records you sell. We love you and we worry about you."

Marlo stopped in front of the studio. "Stop worrying. I want to show you something."

Her dad's mouth gaped, and a flash of fear darted across his eyes. "What, something?"

She opened the door to the studio, and her dad exhaled audibly. What did he think she was going to show him?

"Come in," she said, "Let me show what I've been working on."

Marlo shut the door behind him. She picked up an oud and sang him a few bars of her newest composition. There were layers of traditional Middle Eastern music melded with her characteristic modern pop sound with a dash of alternative rock—it was entirely a new sound direction for her.

When she looked back up, she caught him brushing tears from his eyes.

"Dad," she said, drawing the word out gently.

"Mashallah, habibti. I'm so proud of you."

"See, I'm doing okay here. I've been taking oud lessons online. I'm making music again. You and mom don't need to worry."

He glanced around the room before his eyes came back to rest on her. "There are times like this when I wish your bebe and jidoo were here to see the amazing young woman you've grown into."

She swallowed against something thick in her throat. "You don't think I would disappoint them?"

"Disappointed them, laysh?"

Marlo shrugged, setting the oud back into its cradle. "I don't know. I mean, I've never been to Iraq. I don't know how to speak Arabic. I changed my name because the one you gave me was too hard for people at the label to pronounce. I feel like by the time…if I ever have kids, they won't even have a clue as to their heritage. I barely do."

Her father gave her a small smile, his eyes focused beyond her. "I suppose that's all my fault. It was tough when I was growing up here, so removed from our homeland, our culture. We didn't have a big Arab community here back then. Worse, I resisted their efforts to teach me about it. All I wanted was to fit in." He shook his head. "It sounds so shallow now. I had no idea what I was sacrificing for supposed ease."

Marlo had never talked to her dad about this before. Strangely, his admission of his own struggles with their Arab identity made her feel better, even though she heard the sad echo in it.

"Plus, we couldn't easily travel back and forth, like so many people from other ethnic groups can," he said. "We were isolated here, our movements and the movements of our family limited by harsh immigration and travel restrictions, to speak nothing of decades of wars and violence."

"I never really thought about it that way before."

Even if they'd wanted more of a connection to the land of their ancestors, it wasn't readily available to them, and by the time she could afford to make the trip, it was unsafe for her to go.

Maybe someday.

"The diasporic dilemma," her father continued, shaking his head. "Not quite of this place but not quite of another."

"Nomads looking for a place to call home," she added. Existing between two worlds was something she understood intimately, not only due to her heritage but also because of her celebrity.

Her father's eyes glistened, awash with fresh tears.

"You really miss them," she said.

"I always will. Aside from you and your mother, they were the only family I had."

Another problem that often plagued the diaspora—the distance from extended family intensified the connection to the nuclear family, making their loss so much more acute.

Marlo rose from her stool and walked over to him, wrapping him into a hug. He cried on her shoulder. She hadn't anticipated a reversal of their roles this afternoon.

Her dad put his hand over hers. "Don't stop making music, even if it's just for you. You have a gift and it would be a waste not to use it."

JUDE

A few hours after his conversation with Catherine Howell, Jude's phone buzzed in his pocket. He looked at the screen for a second before realizing Marlo had sent him a voice memo.

He texted her back. "What's this all about?"

"Listen to it." She wrote back.

He pressed play, and Marlo's voice filled his head. But this voice and accompanying sound was different from the effervescent one typical of her prior albums. It was soulful and sultry. Grown up. She played the oud and sang. He pressed pause and retreated to his office in the back of the bakery to connect his phone to the Bluetooth speaker. He pressed play again.

Marlo sang something about finding love again.

But it wasn't about him. It was about the music.

Jude knew she hadn't yet worked out all the lyrics yet because she hummed over missing words. Then she stopped playing, and he heard her soft breath on the microphone before she spoke.

"It's not perfect yet, but it's getting there." Her voice was bright and cheery and not in a fake way. "Let me know what you think when you get home."

He smiled and played the voice memo a couple more times. So things weren't perfect and they had a lot to work out, but they could do it. He just needed to remember to be patient with her and with himself. Marlo tended to come to things in her own time. He knew this about her. Jude had walked away once when things between them grew too complicated.

He wasn't going to do it again.

MARLO

Marlo's phone buzzed in her hand. Jude finally texted back.

I love it, and yes I'm so happy. Let's celebrate tonight. I'm leaving the shop early, and I'll pick up some bubbly on the way home.

She smiled. Things had been tense lately between them, and her relief that they found their way back to each other was immeasurable. She was tempted to share the entire new album with him in its raw, unfinished state, but this work was so different from anything she'd done previously. It was pared down, bare, full of angst and longing. It referenced her ancestors, her existential crisis, her career. Marlo wouldn't be able handle it if he didn't approve. This album was so close to her heart, vulnerable in a way she'd never dared to be before.

If Jude agreed, she planned to hire back some of her touring band and record her new album herself in his studio. Mr. Beckett, Jude, and her dad were right—she needed to make music for the reason she started doing so in the first place, for the love of it. Maybe she'd release her new songs for free to her fans. She didn't really need more money. She had plenty to live comfortably for years. She loved her new material and couldn't wait for the molasses-slow traditional album publishing to share it. Tomorrow, she'd call Tara and ask how she could legally make her own music at her own cost and release it for free.

Marlo sent Jude a picture of herself making a kissy face and wrote, *Come home soon.*

He immediately sent back a picture of car keys in his hand.

She exhaled. She'd been so worried about Jude and her falling into their old relationship patterns that she's stopped paying attention to what had improved between them. They were older and more mature, and they were ready for this new phase, bumpy road and all.

Chapter Twenty-Four

JUDE

JUDE ARRIVED HOME a quarter of an hour later. He couldn't remember ever leaving the bakery so fast. Penny agreed to close up for him but not without a little gentle ribbing. She insisted that he bring Marlo over to her and Kate's house later in the week for dinner again. He'd agreed just to expedite his departure. He kicked his shoes off in the mud room and walked straight to the bedroom, but Marlo wasn't there.

He walked back out and poked his head into the office, but no Marlo there either. Then he smiled to himself—of course, they'd just talked about it after all. He walked to the opposite end of the house and pressed the button to the left of the studio door that triggered a flashing signal light. The door opened, and Marlo yelled, "Surprise," as she flung herself into his arms.

Behind her, Jude saw a space cleared in the middle of the floor where she'd spread a picnic blanket. Candles dotted the room. A couple of champagne flutes and an ice bucket sat in the center of the blanket.

He gently tapped his forehead with his fist. "I completely forgot to pick up champagne."

Marlo laughed. "I'm certain we can find a bottle in that massive wine fridge." She hugged him tighter. "Get comfy. I'll be right back."

Jude gave her a quick kiss before releasing her. He lowered himself to the floor and propped himself up on a couple of the throw pillows she'd thoughtfully placed throughout the room. Then he noticed the music playing.

It was Marlo's new songs. He leaned back and closed his eyes, letting her words wash over him. He couldn't understand why the label would ever deny her the opportunity to innovate. The songs were laced with so much emotion and raw power. She'd evolved, and they were trying to pin her in place—a butterfly frozen in time and space. The thought struck him right in the gut. It was exactly what he'd done to her years ago. Was he doing it again? He heard the door open softly and opened his eyes.

"My god, Marlo." His eyes scanned up and down and back up again. She wore a black lace corset, lace underwear, and a black silk robe and held a bottle of champagne in her hand, giving him a half smirk.

"Surprise," she said again, but this time in a soft whisper that sent a tingle up his spine.

Jude sprang up, took the bottle from her, and practically threw it into the ice bucket. "We'll have to wait for it to chill."

"It came from the wine fr—"

Jude placed his finger on her full lips. "If you expect me to sit here and drink a bottle of champagne while you're dressed like that, you are a mad woman."

He pulled her in, and his hands roamed over her body, moving from lace to bare skin to lace and back again. He pushed the robe gently off her shoulders as he kissed her. It pooled at her feet. His lips traveled from hers to her jaw then to the soft skin at the junction of her neck and shoulder. He continued downward until he reached the swell of her breast.

Jude undid the first hook-and-eye closure and kissed the mound of her partially freed breasts. He continued in a downward progression, each closure opened then followed by a trail of kisses. Soon, the corset fell behind her, and he was on his knees before her.

Marlo ran her fingers through his hair and murmured his name.

He kissed her over the sheer lace underwear, reveling in the hitch of her breath. She sank down to her knees too, bringing her face to his level.

Jude hadn't seen the sparkle in Marlo's eyes for too long. Now, he was the one struggling to draw in enough air. She was so beautiful. He couldn't believe she sat before him, half nude, her soul bared to him as her new music serenaded them over the speakers. He should tell her about the conversation he'd had with Catherine Howell from *Farm & Table*, but he didn't want to dispel the magic of this moment.

Marlo leaned into him, wrapping her arms around his neck, her breasts now pressed delectably against his chest. "Hey, where did you go?"

He chuckled. "I was just in my head for a second. I still can't believe you're here, with me. I dreamed it for so long, and the reality of it takes my breath away every time."

"I think you're wearing too many clothes." Her hand reached beneath the hem of his T-shirt and then danced up his back, sending a wave of gooseflesh over his skin.

They'd talk later. Marlo deserved a celebration, and Jude was determined to give it to her.

The outside world could wait.

Jude unwound his arms from around her and yanked his shirt over his head. Marlo sighed, and the sound of her soft exhalation sent a tingle straight to his cock. He pulled her down so they laid side by side. He ran his hand down her side from her ribs to her hip.

Then he leaned forward and kissed her again, a deep plundering kiss that left no doubt as to his intentions. She curled her fingers in his hair, drawing him closer. His hand traveled to the sweet swell of her bottom, and he brought her forward so she was pressed right against the hard length of him. They both moaned at the contact.

Marlo pushed him onto his back, straddling him as she fumbled with the button at the top of his jeans.

And, Jesus, the sight of her breasts softly bouncing as she attempted to undo his pants was one he'd never forget. He reached his hands up and gently cupped her, and for a moment, she stilled. He squeezed gently, his thumbs circling her nipples. Marlo bit her lip, and she rubbed herself teasingly against his trapped erection. He reflexively squeezed her breasts tighter, and she again rode him.

"I need you," she said.

He tipped his hips up against her, rolling her nipples in his hands. "I'm right here, baby."

She closed her eyes. "Inside me."

He flipped her over onto her back and shed every last stitch of his clothing. Marlo's eyes gleamed and she widened her legs. He lined himself up at her opening, a delicate layer of lace separating them from joining. She wrapped her legs around his hips, drawing him closer.

Jude felt the beckoning warmth of her through the thin fabric. He teased her again, and she bucked her hips. He looped his fingers around her underwear, and she helped him remove them.

"That's better," he said as he sat back on his heels.

Marlo laid before him, a feast for the taking.

His fingers traced up the sensitive flesh of her inner thighs. He smiled at the way she squirmed from the gentle tickling. He leaned forward, dropping a kiss on the birthmark he adored.

"Jude," she pleaded.

"Yes, baby," he said as his fingers neared their intended target. She wiggled her hips a little, trying to direct him to where she wanted him.

Jude kissed her sweet, warm center. "Is this what you want?"

"Yes, please."

He parted her folds with his fingers, and this time gently suckled her nub. He felt the shiver that erupted through her. He blew on her heated flesh, and then his tongue circled and alternately sucked. Soon, she joined the rhythm, grinding into his mouth. He smiled against her, lapping her up. He loved that she trusted him enough to completely come apart in his arms. She stilled then shuddered as her muscles flexed around his fingers. He gave her one last kiss there and then trailed kisses up her abdomen, lathering attention at both her breasts until she grabbed him by the jaw and brought him up to her mouth.

They kissed again, limbs frantically tangling. Then Marlo reached for him, delivering a few strokes before guiding him to her entrance.

"Please," she whispered.

"Anything for you," he said as he slowly pressed into her, enjoying each pleasurable millimeter.

She lifted her hips up and he laughed.

"So impatient." He thrusted into her and she sighed.

"Finally." She rocked against him and found his mouth again.

They kissed and moved against each other in an electrifying dance. Even though they were joined, he still couldn't get close enough to her. He wanted them to subsume each other.

"Jude," she groaned. "Oh, Jude, I need—"

"Shh," he cooed. "I know, baby."

They needed each other in a way that probably frightened her as much as it did him. He'd never felt the frenzy of desperation during lovemaking like he did with her. Their pace increased, his body pursuing its own agenda while his heart wanted to make this moment last forever. He couldn't shake a nagging suspicion that things would change irrevocably after this joining. A finality hung in the air around them, and Jude simply wanted to shut his eyes, plunge deeper into Marlo, and never reemerge.

Was this normal?

Marlo dug her nails into his back as she tightened around him. She was close. He was close. He slowed trying to delay the inevitable.

"Oh, God, Jude, you're killing me."

He kissed her. "I don't want this to end."

There, he made the admission. It was up to her now.

She placed her hand on his cheek and stared so deeply into his eyes he swore she could see right into his soul.

"Me either," she said.

The world spun slower. They continued holding each other's gazes. It was a benediction of sorts. A promise. Things might not be easy between them, but sometimes what was worth having was worth the fight.

They crescendoed together and then collapsed against each other. Jude shifted off her gently so he didn't crush her, but they remained entwined, sweat pooling between them.

Marlo brushed a damp curl back from his forehead and kissed the tip of his nose. Jude curled into her, and she wrapped her arm around him. They fell asleep folded together, the outside world forgotten.

MARLO

Marlo's eyes fluttered open some time later. They'd really fallen asleep on the middle of the studio floor. It was hard to tell the hour in the windowless room. She shivered and Jude stirred. She stared at his beautiful face and watched as his thick fringe of lashes beat against each other, struggling to open. He gave her a sleepy smile.

"What time is it even?" There was a husk in his voice that made Marlo tingle.

She kissed the tip of his nose again. "I have no idea, but I do know that I am freezing."

Jude sat up suddenly, alert. He pawed around behind himself and her until he located his shirt and her robe. He held them out to her.

"Should we go to bed?" He stood up and stretched. The studio spotlights highlighted the planes of his muscles.

"To bed or to sleep?" Marlo waggled her brows, quoting one of her favorite books.

"I never managed to perfect a Scottish brogue or so I've been told," he teased back and held out his hand.

"Your efforts are appreciated."

He was truly a glorious specimen of man. Marlo still couldn't believe she'd resisted returning to him for so long. Something had deepened between them a few hours ago. If she lost him now, it would hurt in a way she couldn't even imagine. She shivered again.

"To bed, lass," Jude said in his best imitation of a Scottish accent.

Marlo laughed. "You're right. Don't ever do that accent."

Once they reached his room, he pushed the robe back off her shoulders, took his shirt off of her, and tucked her into bed before following after her. He pulled the covers over their heads.

"I have a few ideas of how to warm you up."

She saw his smile even though they were surrounded in darkness.

"I'd like to see you try," she teased.

"Lassie, you know I rise to every challenge."

Marlo groaned. "Did you just make a sex pun in the bad accent?"

"You know you love it." He pinned her to the mattress, bringing every one of her nerve endings to life again.

She did love it. She loved him.

And it terrified her because she couldn't shake the feeling that they were nearing the end of something. Last time she'd experienced this premonition, it proved true.

Marlo closed her eyes. The doubts and fears could wait. Right now, this delicious man deserved her undivided attention.

Chapter Twenty-Five

JUDE

THE CHARITY BAKE-OFF was mere weeks away, and it loomed more and more like an expiration date. Every moment they shared carried a sense of finality. Summer would soon end, and the obligation they committed to together would be completed. What would happen after that? Marlo planned to return to LA, and Jude needed to return his focus to the bakery. They'd stopped fighting about any of it. By all appearances, everything was going well, and yet Jude couldn't shake the nagging feeling in the pit of his stomach. Probably because he still hadn't told her about the offer from *Farm & Table.* If they were headed to a natural end, there was no point to telling her anyway. The conclusion of the blissful summer would be difficult enough without any added complications.

When Jude entered the house, Marlo was speaking in hushed tones on her cell phone. There was something unsettling in her voice, and he wondered who was on the other end.

Jude turned in the opposite direction and got into the shower instead. If she wanted to talk to him about it, then she would. Still, it bothered him that she'd been secretive about her own career while getting upset with him when he did the same. Though she'd finally shared her new music with him, she still hadn't told him anything about her intentions beyond the charity concert. True, he still hadn't told her about the call with Catherine Howell, but it wasn't the same. He spoke with Catherine once a couple of weeks ago and no formal offer was made, so it seemed silly to bring it up. It would simply lead to another fight, and it wasn't worth it at the moment.

Marlo had been even more on edge lately. Negotiations with her label weren't going well, but she hadn't discussed further details. Jude wanted her to trust him enough to share everything with him, the good and the bad. Plus, he still didn't trust David Stringer. As long as she remained beholden to that man, nothing good could come of it.

He closed his eyes and lathered shampoo into his hair. Then he heard the shower door unclick.

"You didn't invite me." She fake-pouted as she joined him in the stream of warm water.

"You were busy." He tried for levity, but his words fell flat.

Jude usually invited her into the shower with him. It was a running joke between them. She didn't accept most of the time. Today, he wanted a moment alone to process his swirling emotions. Since Marlo had moved into his house, he was never alone. He went from work to her and back again, and the lack of time to himself wore on him. It was also entirely possible that he withheld the invite for no other reason than a petty act of passive aggression. He tried to be mature, but sometimes childish impulses won out.

"I'm never too busy for you." She soaped up her hands and lathered his chest. "I missed you. We haven't had a lot of time together since our little celebration two weeks ago."

"We've spent every night together the last couple of months."

He tried to focus on the things he wanted to say to her, but it was so hard when she stood there wet and naked in front of him, touching him. Speaking of hard…

Marlo's hand drifted down his abdomen, and then her hands encircled his shaft. He was already at full attention, but the pressure of her hand around him hardened him more. He closed his eyes and relished the sensation of her hand pumping up and down, slick skin to slick skin. He gasped and braced himself on the shower wall when her tongue encircled his engorged tip. His eyes flew open. She'd bent down over him, hair pooling around her shoulders, taking the length of him farther and farther into her mouth. He traced the knobs of her spine and barely contained his threatening orgasm, but her tongue swirled and flicked, her teeth placing gentle pressure as she moved her mouth up and down, suckling him.

"Marlo," he groaned. "I can't hold back much longer."

She straightened and smiled at him with a look in her eyes that shot straight back to his cock. Marlo wrapped herself around him, her soft breasts pressing deliciously into his chest.

"Tell me what you want," she breathed heavily into his ear.

Jude lifted her up and gently backed her up to the shower wall. He slid her down to where he could easily enter her. "I need to be inside you."

She nodded, tightening her legs around him and wrapping her arms over his shoulders. She was hot and wet, and she sighed as he pushed inside her, her muscles stretching to accommodate him. It was fantastic. He thrust deeper into her, and she matched his rhythm in a gravity-defying feat of acrobatics. Jude was surprised how much he needed this, a moment to escape and feel alive in a way only Marlo made him feel.

MARLO

Marlo remained in the shower for a few extra minutes after Jude exited.

She used the excuse of needing to shave her legs, but really, she needed a moment to calm her fretful mind. Jude had been angry with her when he came home today. She'd read it in the tense set of his jaw and his bunched shoulders. It was even more obvious in his clipped tone and the way he'd avoided eye contact with her. He practically ran past her, straight into the shower. She should've given him some time to collect himself, process whatever he was feeling, but she instead she'd panicked. Her day had been awful, and she just wanted to lose herself in the comfort of his body.

Her call earlier with Tara had not gone well. David Stringer was now threatening legal action if Marlo didn't comply with his exact demands for her next album. Tara said he still refused to listen to the sample of new songs she'd sent last week. Marlo naively thought she had time to convince him to reconsider his initial edict, but this latest move showed just how low he was willing to go to bring her to heel. Her Pop Machine contract remained an albatross around her neck. She'd been too foolish, young, and hungry to know that she could and should negotiate the terms to protect herself and her future prospects. She'd given up so much control to protect the boy she loved.

Tara explained that, upon review by Marlo's own attorneys, the contract didn't stipulate that her albums had to be written or even approved by Marlo. So they were left with no solid legal footing to fight it. Marlo might be able to walk away from the studio and remain financially stable for years if she broke her contract. But she wouldn't have enough money to survive a prolonged legal battle to retain control of her masters. Her only option, as Tara outlined it, was to do the record as David Stringer demanded. Then at least she would've have fulfilled the terms of her contract, and the masters would revert back to her. The cost exacted would be compromising her standards, giving David Stringer the win, and putting her name on a record she hated.

Marlo couldn't stomach the notion of David winning this battle over her. All because she'd chosen to speak truth to authority. The cutthroat music mogul, known for speaking horribly to his clients, was so thin-skinned that the easiest of insults at his expense transformed him into a monster. It would never cease to amaze her. The worst part of all of it was the thought of just how disappointed Jude would be if she went along with the studio's wishes for her next album. All those years ago, he'd stood on principle and walked away. There was no way he'd think of her as anything but a coward for not doing the same.

Her return home and to this relationship with Jude were supposed to be her grand escape from reality, but the real world continued to creep into her little bubble.

Marlo turned off the water and grabbed the towels Jude left for her, wrapping one around herself and winding the other around her damp hair. Eventually, she'd have to talk to him about it. He'd keep asking, keep pushing, and her distraction tactics would stop working.

She stepped into the bedroom. Jude sat on the chaise in his pajama bottoms with a guitar in his lap. He gently strummed and sang under his breath. Relaxation washed over her at the sound of him singing. She took his pajama top from the bed where he'd laid it out for her and slid it over her head. Wiggling into the briefs Jude had also set out for her, she sat cross-legged at his feet. He glanced at her for the first time since she'd entered the room and smiled.

"What are you singing?" she asked.

"That day in the studio, when you started playing your new song." He strummed again. "I haven't been able to get it out of my head. I keep trying to recreate it."

He tried again, and the chords this time sounded more familiar. She stood up and took the guitar away from him.

"Let's go to bed." Marlo set the instrument down, out of his reach.

"We have to talk about whatever else is going on with you." He tried to capture her wrist, but she danced out of his way.

"I know, but not now." She leaped into the bed and pulled the covers up to her chin.

Jude hovered over her for a moment, but she refused to look up at him. If he gazed at her with that question in his eyes, she'd cave. She couldn't have the conversation about her music right now. All she wanted was the safety and comfort of Jude's bed and his arms holding her close. She heard his retreating steps as he circled back the other side of the bed.

"Good night," he said under his breath.

Marlo couldn't ignore the strain in his voice. She wished he wasn't hugging the edge of his side of the bed, keeping maximum distance between them. She wanted to say something, anything that would bridge this divide between them. Instead, she let her tears quietly fall on her pillow until eventually she fell asleep. It was the first night in Jude's bed that didn't end in some form of physical connection.

~

The next morning, Marlo padded into the kitchen. She was sore in the worst way possible. Sore from being adored and lavished with affection one minute and then being shunned the next. She'd hugged her own edge of the bed so tightly she'd woken up with a kink in her neck and dull throbbing centered behind her eyes. She turned on the espresso machine, checking that there were enough whole beans in the reservoir. Push-button fresh espresso felt like cheating, but she loved that it was the one thing in the kitchen she couldn't mess up.

Jude's phone on the counter lit up and started bouncing up and down as it danced toward her. She shouldn't answer it, but she couldn't help herself, especially when she saw a woman's name crawl across the screen.

"Jude Beckett's phone," she answered in an obnoxious sing-song.

"Oh, yes, this is Catherine Howell from *Farm & Table*. Is Jude available? I wanted to circle back after our talk earlier this month."

Farm & Table.

The hipster millennial foodie bible? The magazine was the culinary equivalent of *Rolling Stone* or *Vanity Fair*. It was huge if they were asking to interview Jude. Why hadn't he told her they'd reached out to him? That sinking sensation that she was on the verge of losing something returned stronger than ever.

"Hello? Are you still there?" The woman sounded just as you would expect someone from her caliber of magazine to sound, confident with a dose of self-importance.

"Yes, sorry, let me check." Marlo pressed the mute button. She entered the still darkened bedroom and gently nudged Jude awake. "Jude, there is a call for you."

He blinked a few times, trying to dislodge the sleep from his eyes. "My dad?"

"No."

Jude stared at her for a moment, a question hanging in the air between them. She didn't know how she'd answer it if he voiced it. She wasn't sure why she'd answered his phone, or even if she suspected why, she hardly cared to admit it to him.

"Catherine Howell from *Farm & Table*," she said.

He looked stricken, confirming Marlo's suspicions. He'd knowingly kept this from her. Just like before. All so…what? He could fuck her senseless in the shower, in the kitchen, in the studio, demand she open up her soul to him, tell him all her secrets while he didn't reciprocate and share his big news with her.

Jude held his palm out to her and hit the unmute button.

"Ms. Howell, hello." He paused and glared at Marlo.

He demanded privacy. Privacy from her. He was keeping secrets again, and it felt as horrible as the first time.

Marlo walked back to the kitchen. Would things between them ever feel like anything other than an exercise in contradictions? He wanted her here, or so he said, but then he dropped a curtain, keeping her at a distance. To be fair, she did the same with him to some degree, but at least she'd earnestly tried to let him in. She'd shown him that she took his advice to heart, working on her music again. But he continued to hold her at arm's distance.

She paced the kitchen. Minutes ticked by, and she wondered if he was still on the phone or if he was simply avoiding her. She moved into the great room and plopped down on the couch. She attempted to distract herself with mindless TV, but her heart raced. The last time Jude had pulled away from her like this was just before he'd left her. She leaned her head against the back of the couch and closed her eyes.

She wouldn't be left behind this time. This time, she'd leave first. Marlo wouldn't back out of the charity concert, but she'd put an end to whatever relationship play had transpired between them. She got up and grabbed her phone off the kitchen counter.

"Hey, Carla, how are you?" Marlo rolled her lip between her teeth as her personal assistant yammered on about her dogs and her boyfriend.

"Anyway, how are you? Can I help with anything?" Carla asked at last.

"Yes, can you find me a home to rent in Cascade Falls? Preferably something furnished and ready to move in."

"You got it. I'll be in touch."

"Thanks. Please find me something quick."

Marlo pressed end on the call and looked up to see Jude staring at her, gaping.

"What was that all about?" He folded his arms across his chest.

"Funny, I should ask you the same thing."

"Do you mean, you overstepping your bounds and answering my calls?" An unpleasant edge crept into his voice.

"Overstepping my—"

"How would you feel if I answered your phone?" He cut in.

"I'm not hiding anything from you. You're my boyfriend. I'm fine with you answering my phone." She dug her nails into her palms. "What is it you are trying to hide from me now, Jude?"

"Nice deflection."

"Yeah, tell that to yourself."

"So, what? Things got tough, and you're running away?" The muscles at Jude's jaw jumped.

"What can I say? I learned from the best."

It was if someone hit a pause button. They were suspended in time, barely breathing.

Then after a few beats, Jude ran his hand over his face and through his hair.

"You're welcome to use one of the other rooms until you find a new place." He turned on his heel and walked away from her.

Her heart shattered into a thousand pieces. Away from the tears which pooled in her eyes.

"Fuck you, Jude," Marlo said under her breath before grabbing her purse and keys and heading to her car. Thankfully, she hadn't brought too many things over to Jude's place, and frankly, she could easily replace anything she left behind. *Thank you, pop star bank accounts*. Replacing the hole gaping in her heart was a completely separate issue.

Chapter Twenty-Six

MARLO

THE FOLLOWING DAY, Marlo woke to a text from Jude. It took her a second to regain her bearings. She was in a sterile hotel room. Right back where she started—alone, pining for a life that wasn't meant to be hers. She pulled up the message.

Forgot I was due to meet some vendors in Napa this weekend. You're welcome to stay at the house. I'll be back Sunday night. We'll talk then. Love you.

Marlo stared at the message for a while. Jude planned to travel to ostensibly one of the most romantic places on earth, and he didn't even invite her along. Not that they cared to risk being seen together on a romantic getaway, but she still wanted him to ask.

Anger and sadness churned through her. He expected her to accept that he'd continue to hide parts of himself from her, and she was supposed to return to his house and await his return like a good little obedient girlfriend. It was singularly infuriating.

She deleted the text and headed into the hotel room shower. She alternately sobbed and scrubbed her hair and skin with barely tempered fury.

Now what?

The question taunted her again. She could return home.

Marlo almost laughed. What home? Her family home? LA? Neither felt anything like Jude's house did.

The realization rocked her. She'd started thinking of his place as home, a quiet refuge from the storm of her professional life. Marlo had few rules for herself, but the top of that list was never to grow dependent on anyone. Yet here she was in a hotel room in her hometown, feeling alone and unwelcome. She was hundreds of miles north of LA, hiding from her record label and manager. She sank to lower and lower levels of pathetic with every passing day.

That was enough. Marlo wasn't built to lose. Once she found her own place, she'd get back to work. She wasn't going down without a fight, consequences be damned.

An hour later, her phone buzzed. It was a text with links to several rental properties available.

After checking them out, she called Carla. "Thanks for the text. Can you check if the three-bedroom on Vista Clare is still available? It's the top of my list."

"Of course, give me a few minutes."

"As soon as I can get in to see it would be great." Marlo tried to school her voice, but urgency came through anyway.

"Okay, I'll call you back in a few."

Thankfully, Carla called exactly seven minutes later.

"It's still available," Carla said, "and the agent can arrange a walk-through later today."

Marlo smiled, even though Carla couldn't see her. "Great. Thank you so much."

A new sense of triumph filled Marlo's chest. Next, she called her mom to give her a heavily redacted version of the story. Her mom objected lightly, but Marlo knew, as much as her parents loved her, they'd settled happily into their empty-nesting routines and she'd been an unexpected disruption.

Afterward, Marlo called Jude. Her call went to voicemail immediately.

She tried not to read too much into it and decided not to leave a message. He'd given her a couple magical months, and maybe that was enough. It wasn't meant to be more than a summer diversion anyway. Marlo wouldn't stay just for them to grow truly resentful of each other. She'd rather leave it as a happier than not memory. She'd done them both a favor.

JUDE

Yes, he'd run away like a coward after their big blowout, fleeing to Napa on a lie about a business meeting. The truth was he needed a break. He needed to clear his head. They were on opposite career trajectories. He once hoped both their curves would level off and they would travel together on parallel courses, each finding their own professional contentment. Currently, that didn't seem possible.

But he didn't count on coming home to Marlo gone. Completely gone.

Barely a trace of her remained, except the faint hint of her signature scent of jasmine and citrus on her pillow and her hair products in the shower.

He shouldn't have withheld information from her or fled like he did. He owned that. But she also shouldn't have just walked away without giving him a chance to talk to her. She wasn't returning his calls or responding to his texts. In a moment of true desperation, he even reached out to Tara about her whereabouts, which went exactly as he should have predicted.

"If Marlo had wanted to share her current contact information with you, then she would have," Tara said. "I know it hurts, but this is likely for the best."

Jude hated the note of satisfaction in her voice. She'd probably always disapproved of their relationship, but she didn't have to be so obvious about it. His eyes stung, but he tried to ignore it. He couldn't believe Marlo just left like that and refused to speak with him.

He collapsed on his bed, Marlo's scent filling his head, and tried to ignore the ache in his chest.

For a brief minute, everything had been so perfect between them. They finally turned the corner on the pain of the past, or so he'd thought. He replayed the scene from that ill-fated morning in his head, trying to pinpoint the exact moment it all went to hell, but he couldn't. He'd planned on talking to Marlo about the *Farm & Table* offer eventually and even asking her advice. He'd simply needed time to process it for himself first, but Marlo unknowingly forced his hand. Now, Catherine Howell had really turned up the heat on him, and at best, he had a few more days before he was due to give her an answer.

Fuck.

Marlo was part of the reason he'd originally planned to turn down Catherine Howell. No, that wasn't fair. His pride had been bruised when Catherine implied their interest in working with him was only because he'd once sung pop songs with Marlo Sage. In the second call, Catherine clarified her interest. Like Suze had told him, it wasn't wise to put his success on the line for a relationship that was doomed from the start. He wanted to call someone to talk it out, but the only person who came to mind was Marlo. But she'd moved out like the last couple of months between them hadn't happened.

One big fight and she'd left.

Jude stood and tore the sheets off the bed. He'd wash her out of them, get the smell out of his head. He couldn't think straight when she consumed his consciousness.

A raw, aching sensation burned in his chest. He loved her so much, and for whatever reason, he couldn't seem to convey that to her. They always ended up back in this place of mutually assured destruction.

He grabbed the laundry tote from his closet and shoved the sheets into it. Seeing his home devoid of signs of her devastated him. Marlo's presence had seemed so real, so permanent, he'd never realized how little she'd actually moved in. Maybe she'd never intended to stay. Maybe he was always meant to be her temporary distraction while she licked her wounds from the tabloid assault in LA.

He'd been foolish to think otherwise. Marlo Sage wasn't going to move back to her hometown in Northern California, forsaking her career, for any reason, least of all him. And there wasn't enough of Marlo Rayhan left to make her stay either.

"God, you're a fucking idiot," he muttered to himself.

Jude needed to grow up and let go of his childhood fantasies. Marlo and Jude never got a happy ending. That was the whole draw that held their audience on tenterhooks, unfulfilled longing. It was about time they stopped trying to force something that wasn't meant to be. He'd been happy before her. He'd be happy again after her too. Eventually.

He picked up his phone and typed out a text. His finger hovered over the send button for several seconds, his heart lodged in his throat, before he finally pressed send.

MARLO

Marlo tensed when she saw the notification of a text from Jude. Maybe he'd cooled down and was ready to offer both an apology and an explanation of his completely irrational behavior. She opened the text and blinked in long, slow beats, reopening her eyes, hoping to see the letters on the screen reassemble into more of an apology and less of a final goodbye.

J: Marlo, I am sorry about the other morning. What can I say? We tried and we failed. I wish you would have given me a chance to explain everything to you.

It was no use—*We tried and we failed* was seared into the back of her eyelids.

Just like before, the slightest bit of hardship, and Jude took the opportunity to bail out. Things between them would fundamentally never change, no matter how old they got. Marlo knew it was foolish to entangle herself romantically with him, but she'd done it anyway. She was incapable of escaping her own self-destruct mode. She might have moved out too hastily, but she didn't want him to resent her. Plus, she didn't want to grow to be disappointed by him. And she'd already struggled not to feel that way, given his recent behavior.

M: I left your spare key at the guard house. Good luck with your new endeavors.

She hit send immediately after composing the text. It was petty and immature, but she was not feeling particularly gracious toward him at the moment.

Jude had hurt her, pushing her away when she needed him to hold her close the most. She'd lost everything she'd worked so hard for her entire life, and she'd just wanted a companion to tell her it would all be okay. If only he appreciated how difficult that dynamic was for her.

No matter what she'd lost, she'd found her spine. If relationships, professional or personal, didn't suit her needs, she'd no longer stay in them.

Marlo remembered a conversation she once had with David Stringer when they'd argued over which single should be the first release from her first solo album.

"The thing you don't understand, sweetheart, is that your ambition is going to be your downfall. The public wants cute. It wants sweet. It wants nice. What no one can stand is an angry, ambitious woman behind a microphone."

She shuddered at the thought. All the ugly things that man had said to her were permanently woven into her memories. She wished she could exorcise him from her consciousness. But the part of herself she hated the most would always wonder if he was right. Maybe her life would be easier if she wanted less for herself. But then she wouldn't be herself.

Her phone buzzed again.

J: What about the charity show?

M: Of course, I'll still fulfill my promise there. I'm not an asshole.

J: Thanks

Marlo stared at her response. It might not have been wise to continue with the bake-off, but she'd made a commitment in honor of Jude's dad. At least all her years working for David Stringer taught her to perfect her acting skills—Marlo could swallow heartache with the best of them.

Chapter Twenty-Seven

MARLO

MARLO WAS ABOUT to power her phone down when it rang in her palm. It was her personal assistant again.

"Hey, Carla," she said, feigning nonchalance, even though her heart thundered after the exchange with Jude.

"Great news, Marlo. The property manager confirmed the meeting at the rental later this afternoon. If you like it, then it's yours for any amount of time you want it."

Finally, something this summer went Marlo's way. "Thank you so much."

Several hours later, Marlo drove to the house, and much to her appreciation, it sat on the complete opposite side of the development from Jude. Given the large, two-acre-plus lots, it was a whole galaxy away.

The house itself was quite stunning. Marlo parked in the driveway, waiting for the property manager to arrive. She decided to walk the perimeter of the home to investigate further. The side of the house opposite the driveway was nearly entirely glass, which gave it the feel of an extravagant treehouse. Even from outside, she could tell the interior of the house was luxurious.

She returned to the driveway when she heard the crunch of tires on the gravel.

The property manager parked alongside Marlo's car and emerged with a wide grin on her face.

"Thank you for meeting me so soon, Ms. Sage." She extended her hand to Marlo as she spoke. "My name is Zainab Daniels."

"Zainab, thanks for showing me the property, can't wait to see inside."

The raven-haired woman used her phone to release the actual key from the realtor safety box. She held the door open for Marlo. "This property is seven thousand square feet, three stories, and completely eco-friendly with solar power, recaptured and filtered rainwater, LED lighting, and smart home technology. It is furnished and available for immediate move-in."

Marlo followed the petite woman through the house as she gesticulated and pointed out every detail, from the light fixtures to the flooring to the high-tech features, in every space. Marlo intended to rent the house no matter what and wanted to tell Zainab she didn't need to pitch it so hard. But the realtor's passion for her job was evident, so Marlo simply listened, taking stock of the many amazing features the home offered.

When they arrived at the third story main suite, Marlo gasped. This was no simple bedroom. It was a penthouse in and of itself—a bedroom, exercise room, a closet practically the size of her childhood home, an office, and a reading nook all with a near 360-degree view of the forest around her.

Zainab smiled. "The pièce de résistance."

"Certainly is. I'll take it."

The realtor laughed. "We haven't discussed the price."

Marlo waved her hand dismissively. "Whatever the price, I'll take it."

"If only my job was always so easy."

This house with its incredible view was nearly inducement enough for

Marlo to embrace a hermit lifestyle, swallowed near whole by the forest. After the terrible day she'd had, standing here among the treetops just outside her window allowed her to exhale. She turned back to Zainab, fighting back the tears pooling in the corner of her eyes.

Marlo fished out her personal assistant's card and handed it to Zainab. "My assistant, Carla, will handle the paperwork with you, and I am available at any time to sign whatever is needed."

"If you have an hour free, I could stay here and finish up the paperwork, and then I'll be able to turn the key right over to you."

"That would be fantastic, thank you."

"I'll head downstairs. Make yourself comfortable." Zainab excused herself.

Marlo walked out to the balcony outside the bedroom and sat down. In the distance, the birds and insects traded harmonies. She inhaled deeply, her nose filling with scent of pine needles and fresh earth.

She desperately wanted to call Jude to tell him about the house.

Marlo brought her knees to her chest and wrapped her arms around her shins as sobs racked her frame. She imagined waking up wrapped in his arms as the early morning light filtered through the green trees.

She wiped her eyes with the back of her hands. She and Jude were nothing more than a beautiful dream. Marlo gave herself permission to mourn the loss, but after today, she promised herself not to shed another tear for him. She needed this time for own healing. She had to reevaluate her priorities and make a new plan for the future, her own future. Marlo knew better than to let her happiness depend on a man, even a man as great as Jude, or her career. She needed to source the well from within. Until she did, she'd never build the life she deserved. She'd spent the last couple of years wandering through life as a ghost of herself. It was time to start living again. She needed to embody the energy her new music unleashed.

Marlo rose from her balcony chair and reentered the bedroom, *her* bedroom. She splashed cold water on her face in the bathroom and blinked at herself in the mirror. She still looked puffy and splotchy from crying, but she didn't care because, for the first time in a long time, she saw something in her own eyes—the wisdom of her ancestors and a glimmer of hope.

"Love is for fairy tale princesses," she said to her reflection. "You don't need love."

She paused and repeated the last part.

"You don't need love."

Inspiration struck like a crack of lightning. Marlo fished her phone out of her pocket and started hurriedly typing fragments of lyrics. It was what was missing from her album—the anthem. There was always one anchor song that tied the collection of songs on a record together, and she'd just stumbled on the one. Maybe it would even be her new album title. Marlo was so caught up in her fevered spark of creativity that she didn't hear Zainab return.

"Ms. Sage," Zainab called out. "Ms. Sage."

Marlo emerged from the bathroom.

"Yes, sorry, I was lost in writing a new song." She smiled weakly.

"Sorry to be unprofessional for a moment, but oh my goodness, my daughter is going to die when I tell her I was in the room when Marlo Sage started working on a new song."

Marlo laughed. "I can do you one better. How about I promise to let you two be the first to hear it?"

Zainab squealed, transforming into a fan girl before Marlo's eyes. She remembered why she loved her job so much in the first place. Nothing intoxicated her the way connecting to fans through her music did. It was the beating heart of what she did, and she needed to find her way back to that purity. It wasn't about album sales, talk show appearances, awards, or any of the other trappings of celebrity. She didn't need industry blessing. She simply loved entertaining people.

"Well, the paperwork is ready," Zainab said. "I have emailed you all the forms, so if you e-sign them now, we can complete the walkthrough and I will turn over the keys."

"I cannot thank you enough. You're a life saver."

Zainab's cheeks darkened. "Just doing my job, Ms. Sage."

"Please call me Marlo, and I am serious—I was desperate for a place, and you made it happen within hours. I appreciate it more than you can know."

After an hour of signing page upon page of electronic documents and walking through the house and generating a list of minor repairs, Zainab removed the lockbox and handed Marlo her new set of keys. Marlo called her parents and invited them over for dinner and drinks later that evening, then she made a list of groceries and sundries. She spent several hours between the home goods store and the grocery store, and she couldn't remember the last time she'd shopped like this completely on her own. By most people's standards, it was nothing, but Marlo relished how accomplished she felt. Today, she'd adulted the hell out of herself.

Her normal existence kept her so sheltered, shielded from regular daily activities of life. Although some of her fellow shoppers and the store clerks did double takes or verbally recognized her, for the most part, they left her alone. It was a relief just to be moving through the world without a throng of paparazzi or publicists and without worrying about her appearance.

By the time the sun dipped low in the sky, Marlo had nearly completely settled into her new house. She'd washed and folded all her new linens, washed and organized the dishware and flatware she purchased earlier in the day, and had a chicken roasting in the oven.

Oud lessons weren't the only classes she'd taken online. She'd also taught herself how to cook this summer. She'd suffered a lot setbacks over the last couple of months, but she'd also made progress.

A British voice announced the approach of guests to the house, and

Marlo laughed. Getting accustomed to all of the house's technological advances would take some time.

"Mom, Dad," Marlo squealed as she opened the grand front door. "Welcome to my new house."

"This is a big surprise," her mom said as she hugged her tight.

Her dad glanced around the house wide-eyed. "Are you planning to stay in Gold Hills?"

"I'm renting month to month, so it's not that huge of a commitment," Marlo said. "I'll stay as long as I want."

Her parents exchanged a look. The one that always preceded a lecture.

"Honey, this place is amazing." Her mom glanced at her dad again before continuing. "It's just a bit rash, and on the heels of moving in with Jude, we're just worried."

"It's not like I chose to move in with Jude. The circumstances kind of forced my hand."

Her mom and dad both pursed their lips.

"And then the circumstances changed again." Marlo's ears prickled with heat. She tugged at the collar of her T-shirt, which suddenly felt too snug around her neck. "I'm fine."

Her parents didn't look convinced.

"Listen," Marlo said, "I didn't invite you over here to talk about Jude."

"Habeeba, what happened between you two?" her dad asked gently. "You know you can talk to us about anything."

Tears pricked the back of her eyes. She wasn't ready to have this conversation with her parents, not right now. She wanted them to be proud of her first true steps of independence. She longed to tell them that she'd hired back her touring band and one of her favorite producers. Once she found new studio space, she'd start the process of laying down tracks of a fully new album, all financed by her. She'd finally grown up and she was desperate for them to see it.

"We broke up, okay?" Marlo said. "Tale as old as time."

"Honey." Her mom reached out to her.

But Marlo stepped away. "Mom, I don't want to talk about it. Will you guys just come inside and let me give you the tour."

Her parents exchanged a look again and then nodded in resigned unison.

Marlo led them through the house, parroting what she remembered of Zainab's tour. Her parents oohed and aahed appropriately, and the tension between her shoulders eased. When they returned to the kitchen, she poured them each a glass of wine and sat them at the island while she finished up dinner. She pulled the chicken out of the oven, allowing it to rest, as she prepared a salad.

"I don't think I've ever seen you in the kitchen," her mom teased.

"Yeah, I guess Jude inspired me." Marlo shrugged, hoping her parents didn't see how much the admission stung.

"I'm surprised, after everything between you two, that you wanted to stay in this neighborhood," her dad said.

Marlo set the salad tongs down and looked at her dad. "Do you see this place? I had no idea a neighborhood like this even existed here." She paused. "I should buy you a house here or one of the other neighborhoods nearby."

Her parents both started to object.

"No, seriously," Marlo said. "You never let me buy you anything. And you saw what happened when the media descended upon your house."

Her mom dismissed her with a flick of her wrist. "You do plenty for us. You paid for the roof replacement a few years ago."

"And the kitchen remodel," her dad chimed in.

"You deserve so much more," Marlo said. "And I want to make sure you're safe as well. Whether you like it or not, you belong to me."

Her mom dismounted from her stool and came around the wide island to Marlo's side. "You've earned every success yourself, and you deserve to enjoy it for yourself. You don't owe us or anyone else anything."

Her dad joined them, folding them both in his arms. "We're so proud of you, habibti. We just want you to be happy. It's an honor enough that you're our child."

Marlo swallowed back tears. As much as her parents sometimes annoyed her, she wouldn't trade them for the world. They never used her as a vehicle for their own missed dreams or as a lunch ticket. They advised her as wisely as they could as outsiders to the industry. They supported her every step of the way. Her gratitude for them knew no bounds.

"Okay, that's enough cheesiness for one evening," Marlo said. "Yella, let's get this food on the table and eat."

Her parents laughed and followed her to the dining table. They spent the remainder of the evening reminiscing about the past. All talk of Jude and the future was forgotten. It was a simple family dinner, exactly how Marlo needed to end her tumultuous day.

JUDE

Jude drifted through his halls like a lovesick ghost. Marlo's absence left his house large and looming, devoid of warmth. It had been a home before her, a home with her in it, but now it was an empty shell. Much like his heart. He called his parents and invited himself over to their house.

"Oh, sweetheart, what a lovely surprise," his mom said, as she wrapped him in a hug.

He felt small again in her arms, and he relished it, not wanting to leave her embrace. He needed his mom to tell him everything would be okay because then maybe he'd believe it.

"Sorry to intrude on your plans," Jude said, as he straightened to his full height.

His mom waved her hand. "No plans. We're day two out from his last infusion. Our only goal today has been to keep your dad from puking his brains out."

Guilt knifed through Jude. Since Marlo's reappearance, he'd hardly seen his family. When his dad first started undergoing treatment, he'd been by his side around the clock, but eventually, his parents urged him to resume his normal routines, focus on growing his business. Marlo stepped up as she'd promised. After the initial paparazzi craze calmed down, she took his father to a couple more of his appointments. She'd made a game of it, wearing outrageous wigs and giant glasses and roping his dad into her hijinks.

Jude hated to admit it, but he was grateful for the reprieve. It was tough seeing his dad transform from a bulwark of quiet strength and gentility into a husk of his former self, hairless and wearied. The impact on his mother was near impossible to ignore too. She tailored her eating habits to his dad's and had lost a tremendous amount of weight herself. Jude tried to ply her with sweets from the shop, but if his dad was too nauseous to eat or everything tasted too metallic, his mom didn't eat either in some twisted sense of solidarity.

"Sorry I haven't been around much," he said.

His mom's eyes sparkled with that mother-knows-best twinkle. "You and Marlo have been busy reconnecting. We understand. How is she?"

Jude stiffened. His parents didn't know that he had fucked things up with Marlo again and she'd moved out. He'd been hoping they'd heard it from Marlo's parents. But now he'd have to tell them himself and open himself to their judgment.

"Where's Dad?" Jude asked instead, delaying the inevitable.

Luckily, his mom didn't notice, too busy with kitchen prep. God, he was a coward.

"His favorite spot, the old recliner in the TV room. We discovered if he's seated at just the right angle in that thing, he can stave off most of the nausea. Go on in, honey. I'm grabbing a few things from the kitchen, and then I'll be right there."

"Can I help you, Mom?"

She shook her head and nodded in the direction of the family room.

"Pops," Jude said, stepping into the darkened room.

His dad shifted in his chair as if trying to get up.

"No, no, I'll come to you. Stay put." Jude gave his dad a kiss on the cheek, momentarily taken aback by the sensation of thin and papery his skin against his lips. "How are you?"

His dad shrugged. "Handsome as ever, don't you think?"

Jude smiled and pulled a chair right up against his recliner. "Are you eating anything?"

"Yeah, I eat enough. Don't you worry, at least not about me. Your mom's the one doing all the work around here lately." His dad gave him a weak smile, and Jude hated seeing the cracks at the corners of his lips. "She's the one who needs to rest."

"Drinking enough water?"

"Come on, son, you're sounding like your mom." He patted Jude's knee.

Jude blinked back tears. "We have a right to be worried about you, you know."

"I want to hear about you. How's the shop? How's the lady? Tell me everything."

Jude ran his hand back and forth through his hair.

"Oh dear," his dad said. "That bad? Talk to me."

"We broke up, I guess." Jude's stomach clenched in a fist. Saying the words aloud deepened his pain.

“Want to talk about it?” His dad’s sunken eyes studied him.

“I don’t know. I don’t really know what went wrong.” A shameless lie—he’d overreacted and driven her away. “It was great and then it wasn’t. But I still…”

No, he couldn’t say those words aloud.

The admission that he still loved her would destroy him.

“Maybe you two just needed to readjust, nothing wrong with that. Your mom called off our first wedding two months before the date, and at first, I felt so betrayed and so angry I couldn’t even hear the wisdom of what she was saying and feeling.”

“What?” Jude sat stunned. “You never told me that. Have you been holding out on me all these years?”

“No one likes to hear the ugly parts of a love story.” His dad laughed. “In the end, all that matters is that you get there.”

“Hold up. I need more information. What the fuck happened?”

“Language,” his mom called out, as she set down a tray of freshly cut fruit and cheese cubes.

“Where do you think he learned that from?” his dad asked, winking at his mom.

She gently swatted his arm as she handed him a protein shake.

“I was just telling the kid about how you called off our first wedding,” his dad said.

His mom placed her hands on her hips. “Oh yeah, did you tell him the part about what an immature little asshole you were too?”

They both laughed, and she leaned down, placing a kiss on his dad’s lips. The love between them was palpable, and it was the exact dynamic he hoped to achieve with his partner one day. He thought he’d found it with Marlo.

His mom perched on the armrest. “We had more growing up to do. We just weren’t ready yet.”

"Yeah, I definitely had some growing up to do," his dad said, "but something like that lights a spark under your ass to get it right. So, maybe this thing with Marlo is the spark you need."

Jude nodded. Maybe his parents were right. Maybe they had to take a part of their journey separately in order to find themselves together again. But they'd already done that once, and it blew up in their faces again. He didn't want false hope, but he couldn't resist the promise of it. He preferred it to the alternate reality where he was a selfish jerk who chose his career over love. The exact thing he'd accused her of doing years before.

"Life," his dad continued. "It just has a way of sucker punching you when you least expect it."

Jude watched the new look exchanged between his parents. His dad tightened his grasp on his mom's knee. They'd suffered the turbulence of young love only to land in a place where their hard-won efforts and wisdom might be whisked away from them in a moment's notice. Jude, though grateful for the perspective, wanted to scream about the injustice of it all. He vowed to be more present for his parents and to be more present for himself too. He needed to stop simply seeing the circumstances of his life as events happening to him and to be a more active, engaged participant.

Chapter Twenty-Eight

MARLO

MARLO RESUMED WORK on her new album. Her assistant helped her locate a nearby studio where she could record her music. Thankfully, it was only a forty-five-minute drive away. She spoke to Tara about her plans to proceed with the new album, regardless of whether Pop Machine objected and threatened to sue her for publishing it. After several contentious arguments, Tara agreed to support Marlo in her new endeavor and promised to continue working out an amicable way to end her relationship with her current label.

Despite everything career-wise finally moving in the proper direction, a gaping hole remained in Marlo's chest. She particularly noticed it at night, alone in her bedroom. Other than texts exchanged about upcoming rehearsals for the charity show, she hadn't heard anything from Jude. She hadn't seen him since she left either. The first of the rehearsals was scheduled for tomorrow at his home studio.

Marlo tried to avoid thinking about the last time they'd shared the space. It was the night that had started off magical but morphed into an extended, slow-playing nightmare that eventually spelled the end of them.

She closed her eyes tight, willing sleep, which refused to come. Breaking up with Jude had been inevitable. All the signs she'd refused to acknowledge glared at her in retrospect, but that awareness didn't lessen the loss of it all.

You lost your best friend.

Marlo hated her stupid inner voice. She'd lost her best friend a decade earlier. Prior to the karaoke reunion, they'd barely spoken in years, so what was the difference now? They clearly weren't meant to be lovers, and they clearly didn't even have a foundation of true friendship. Everything between them had been a lie, a sweet one, but a lie all the same time. Or maybe a dream—an ideal if everything else in their lives had aligned, but they'd never been on the same path. Not even when she thought they were. Jude always kept his deepest self closed off to her. He didn't trust her with his deepest fears and wants. That was what always remained broken between them—his refusal to open up to her. Marlo punched the pillow next to her and groaned in frustration.

Then she turned and flipped on her bedside lamp. With sleep determined to elude her, her only other option was to distract herself. She picked up the weathered novel on her nightstand. It was a historical romance she'd stolen years ago from her mom's collection. She read it anytime she yearned for comfort. She knew every beat of the story, but the emotional journey still walloped her with every reread—a roller coaster of highs and lows, miscommunication and misunderstanding, which coasted into the sweet, satisfying happily ever after that evaded her in her real life. If those two dummies could finally figure it, maybe there was hope for Marlo yet.

JUDE

Jude tossed and turned in his bed. He'd finally see Marlo again tomorrow. It had only been a couple of weeks, but it felt like years. He'd checked his phone so many times, hoping to see a missed call or text notification. He'd even written her a few texts which he deleted before the temptation to press send grew too great. In his desperation for things to work out between them, he hadn't noticed how much they'd drifted apart until it was too late. Obstacles obscured every step in their paths, even before they took the romantic turn. Of course they'd been doomed for failure. They were the Titanic headed straight for the iceberg of past hurts and mistrust.

After several conversations with Catherine Howell and Suze, Jude decided to take the *Farm & Table* offer. He'd film a large portion of the show in LA, but they decided to film some of the shoots at his bakery and his home. Since he no longer shared the space with Marlo, letting the crew into his personal sphere wasn't a big concession. Catherine Howell agreed to write it into the contract that Jude would not be asked anything about his relationship with Marlo and that his pop career would only be referenced as he saw relevant to his current endeavors.

In other words, for once, he'd retain control of his own narrative.

Jude couldn't wait to tell Marlo about it tomorrow. Not to gloat but to share a proud achievement with one of the people he respected most in the world. Also, as a heads-up. He wasn't sure how long she intended to stay in Gold Hills, but sooner or later, someone would discover that they lived in the same neighborhood. He'd learned that detail from his parents. His emotions about the revelation remained mixed—there was a strange comfort in knowing she remained nearby, but it was torture just the same. If the media floodlights returned to their lives because of him accepting the *Farm & Table* gig and someone connected the dots, he'd at least be certain to give her advance warning. The irony was there would probably be speculation about a romance brewing between them. His stomach tied itself in knots. He flipped over onto his back and stared at the ceiling.

"Fuck," he groaned.

He pushed himself up into a semi-seated position and grabbed the TV remote. He aimlessly flipped through the channels until he landed on a screening of *When Harry Met Sally*. He didn't openly admit this to anyone, but he loved rom-coms, especially when he was stressed or in a dour mood. He'd grown up watching them with his mom and then with Marlo. He'd memorized every line of this movie, and he'd still never tire of it. Harry's anguish when he lost Sally and his desperation to run back to her resonated with Jude viscerally every time he watched it. He settled against his pillows and lost himself in the movie. Tomorrow would be tough, even more so without sleep, but at least the next couple of hours he'd be distracted.

Chapter Twenty-Nine

MARLO

THE NEXT MORNING, Marlo bashed her phone alarm with her closed fist, desperate to quiet the incessant chiming. Best estimate, she'd slept for about five minutes. But the phone continued dancing and bleating out an obnoxious tune on her nightstand.

"Damn it," she said, sitting up and blinking furiously against the bright morning sun trying to sear her eyeballs. "I'm awake. Just please stop."

She finally grasped the phone and silenced the alarm. It was early, but she doubted she'd be able to sleep any better now than last night. Marlo grabbed a change of clothes and headed into the shower. She sang herself one of the new songs she'd been working on, as the warm water revived her. Anything to drown out the drumbeat in the back of her mind—

You see Jude today, you see Jude today, you see Jude today.

Marlo piled her wet hair on top of her head and secured it with a large clip, and then padded into the kitchen.

"How about an omelet?" Living alone had many perks, but she had picked up a bad habit of talking to herself. Depending on the phrasing of her statements, the techie house sometimes responded to her, and then she made it a game of confusing the artificial not-so-intelligent system.

As she cracked the eggs into a bowl, her mind drifted to the morning a lifetime ago when Jude first taught her how to make an omelet after she'd graduated from scrambled eggs. Her developing prowess in the kitchen proved a point of pride for her. Jude's lessons, combined with Pinterest and YouTube videos, made it possible for her to subsist on her own cooking in a way she'd never done before. She'd even wowed her dad by learning how to make dolma and baklava the Iraqi way.

Marlo whipped the eggs and cream in a bowl, while a pat of butter melted in her frying pan. She poured in the egg mixture, allowing it to firm up as she sprinkled in salt, pepper, goat cheese, and chives before gently folding it in half. She slid the omelet onto a plate and moaned as she took the first steaming bite. She might not be a professional, but she'd mastered the omelet. She bet even Jude would be proud.

"Yeah, right." She laughed to herself.

She hated how he crept into her thoughts so often. A phantom she doubted she'd ever exorcise. It would be even worse after seeing him today. Marlo shook the thought away. She rinsed off her plate and placed it in the dishwasher.

If she couldn't predict how the afternoon with Jude would go, she could at least control how she'd look, and she intended to look fierce.

If you look your best, you'll feel your best. Her mom's mantra was one that never failed Marlo before. When she was in school, she'd dress up for every test. To this day, Marlo loved to let her clothing speak for her.

And today, Marlo would look her best. Because right now, she felt like a mess of nerves, and she wasn't about to let Jude see that.

JUDE

Jude took himself on a punishing dawn run and then spent another hour lifting in his home gym. Neither dissipated his building anxiety about the afternoon ahead. Thoughts of Marlo chorused in his head like the worst jingle stuck on loop. The cold water of the shower sluiced down his sweat-drenched chest, and it hurt almost enough to make him forget about her for a moment. He reached out to grab his shampoo bottle but ended up with hers. He cursed under his breath. Memories of all the glorious showers they'd shared flooded him. He flipped open her shampoo bottle and took a deep inhale.

That scent was indelibly printed on his soul. He poured some into his hand, and the fragrance filled the air. His cock stirred.

"Fuck," he groaned.

He lathered the shampoo in his hands, and the scent invaded every part of him. Now his cock stood at full attention. This wasn't the prelude he needed before seeing her again today. He couldn't help himself. He stroked himself with his sudsy hand and closed his eyes, letting his mind fill with pictures of her. His hand moved with increased speed and urgency. His release wasn't nearly satisfying enough. He rinsed away the evidence of his weakness for Marlo. Maybe he'd done himself a favor. When he saw her in a few hours, he could rest easy knowing he'd discharged whatever sexual tension might remain between them.

Jude washed himself thoroughly, but he couldn't erase the smell of her from his memory. He threw Marlo's shampoo bottle away to avoid the temptation of replaying that shameful moment of self-indulgence. He wasn't ashamed about pleasuring himself, but pleasuring himself with his ex's shampoo as he pined for her was a level of desperation he wasn't ready to revisit.

He needed to bake to clear his mind. He dressed quickly and then drove to his shop. Jude wiped down the cool surface of his prep table. He wasn't sure what to make yet, but he enjoyed trusting himself to follow whatever creative spark hit him to its inevitable conclusion. Sure, sometimes it turned out disastrous. But those times it proved magical were worth all the failed starts. This method had led to his most celebrated creations.

Jude recalled the scent of Marlo's shampoo, and the fuse lit. Lemon chiffon cupcakes with honey and jasmine-infused buttercream frosting.

He prepared all his dry ingredients, carefully sifting and weighing the cake flour. This cupcake needed to be light as air, a wisp of a memory, and it should leave a slight tangy aftertaste—a bittersweet longing. Once he had the dry ingredients measured and mixed, he set to work preparing the wet ingredients. He grated lemon zest into his flour mix and into the frosting he prepared.

Penny stepped into the kitchen from the front of the bake shop.

"Oh hey, I didn't think you were coming in today." She walked over to the schedule printout on the wall and squinted.

"No, I'm not officially here, just had an idea I needed to work out."

She studied him, and the corner of her mouth tipped up. "Oh, babe, you've got it bad."

"What are you talking about?"

"As if you don't know. Stop being foolish." Penny laughed.

Irritation flared. "Whatever you think is going on is not going on."

"Jude, some people eat their feelings, others run them out, but you… you do this." She gestured to the work surface between them.

He held up his hands in mock surrender. "Fine, guilty. Remind me, why did I hire such a smart-ass sous chef?"

"I think you answered your own question. I'm smart and I *kick* ass in the kitchen."

They both laughed. Jude knew exactly why he'd hired Penny—she had a savvy business mind and was an amazing pastry chef, but moreover, they worked well together. They'd always shared a collegial relationship that allowed them to bounce ideas off each other with complete trust and support.

A realization struck him—working with Penny in the kitchen was how it used to feel working with Marlo in the studio. He'd never made the connection before.

Obviously, there was nothing romantic between him and Penny. She'd been with her partner since before she started in culinary school. Penny and Kate were the real deal. They loved and supported one another and were the proud parents of their baby girl. Every minute Jude spent with their family reminded him of his ultimate relationship goals.

"Okay, you've gone to that distant creative genius place, so I'll leave you to it." Penny walked into the office they shared.

Jude lost himself again in the process. A couple of hours later, he iced the last cupcake. They were a beautiful pale yellow with a swirl of golden honey laced through the buttercream frosting on top. He placed a small sprig of lavender in each one and stood back admiring them. They'd be a great seasonal item to add to their menu. They just needed a name.

Lemon Longing.

He liked it. Jude plated one of the cupcakes and brought it to Penny.

"May I present you with Lemon Longing, a lemon chiffon cupcake where sweet meets tang." He half bowed.

Penny's camel-brown eyes brightened. "It's almost too beautiful to eat."

She picked up the cupcake and sniffed it, a soft sigh escaping her lips. Then she took a hearty bite.

"Oh my god, Jude," she said after swallowing. "I taste it. I taste the bittersweet yearning. This is divine. I can't decide if I want to smile or cry. You are a sugar sorcerer."

Heat crept into his cheeks. Penny often complimented his recipes, but he couldn't remember her eyes gleaming quite like this before.

"I almost feel like you should just call it Breakup Cake or The One that Got Away," she said.

Jude playfully punched her in the shoulder.

Penny continued. "You should give her one."

"So, a seasonal offering?" he asked, hoping to steer the conversation away from Marlo.

She studied him again. "I don't know. People experience loss year-round. I think we should make it a permanent offering."

Jude nodded. Another ode to Marlo to haunt him. His earlier buzz from the creation of something new faded. No matter how often they walked away from each other, would he ever really be able to quit her? She was as much a part of him as his own limbs. He glanced at the clock. He only had an hour before she was due to arrive at his house.

"Hey," he asked, "can you do me a favor and box up a couple of those for me while I clean up the back?"

Penny nodded. Jude tried to ignore the I-told-you-so sparkle in her eye.

After half an hour, he retrieved the boxed cupcakes from Penny and headed back to his house. The drive between had never felt longer. He'd created such a mess of things with Marlo. He should've left everything distant and professional between them.

Whoever the fuck said it was better to have loved and lost was a goddamn asshole.

An ache gnawed in his chest. They weren't good together. He knew it. She knew it. But then why did it still hurt so much? Would he always carry a Marlo-shaped hole in his heart? Jude slammed his hand on the steering wheel. He should've called her and rescheduled.

No. The only thing worse than seeing her was not seeing her. He'd been a shadow of himself the last couple of weeks. Tomorrow, he was due to fly to LA to meet with Catherine Howell, and he wondered if she'd still be interested in working with him once she saw him in his current state.

Speaking of Catherine Howell, he had to tell Marlo about the project today. He'd literally waited until the last possible minute. Another wave of dread washed over him. It promised to be a rough afternoon for a million reasons, but at least he came armed with cupcakes.

MARLO

Marlo arrived right on time for their rehearsal. Standing at Jude's door brought a tide of mixed feelings—anticipation, dread, and as much as she wanted to deny it, hope. She wondered if she'd always see him through a lens of possibility. The heartache filter that rendered him in a hazy azure of promises unfulfilled.

He opened the door. She attempted to school her features, but it wasn't easy. He wore a fitted black T-shirt and dark jeans, nothing particularly breathtaking, but it was the way his clothes hugged and highlighted the planes of his body. Half of his mouth quirked up into a smile before fading all together.

She could never mask her thoughts from him. He always saw right through her.

"Thanks for coming over today," he said, his gaze flitting away from her.

"No problem, we're neighbors now so it's not much of a trek." She blew out her breath. She'd hoped to see some kind of reaction from him, maybe even an apology.

But he avoided eye contact as he turned and walked toward the studio.

Marlo followed him, a wide distance separating them. She fought the urge to turn around and run out the way she'd come in. But the charity bake-off took precedence over her heartbreak, and she wouldn't deliver a half-ass performance just because of what a shitty girlfriend she'd been. Jude held the door to the studio open for her, and heat radiated off him even as she tried to flatten herself against the opposite side of the doorway to avoid brushing against him.

JUDE

Jude wished he could follow Marlo's lead and act normal. Instead, he diverted his gaze in every direction but hers. She'd dressed up for the occasion, and perversely, it filled him with pride that she still cared to make the effort. Her hair fell over her shoulders in large, loose curls, the right side pinned back showing off her cute ear. *Cute ear?* What the fuck was wrong with him? Since when did he admire someone's ears? He rubbed his hand over his face.

Marlo stepped up to the microphone, and the way she grasped it made his lower abdomen clench.

He excused himself from the room. "Oh, hey, I forgot something. I'll be right back."

Marlo's eyes widened, but before she could say anything, Jude ran out of the studio. Jesus, fuck, he needed to calm down. He marched into the kitchen and gulped down a glass of cold water. Then he grabbed the cupcakes so he wouldn't seem like a complete psycho.

He coached himself to walk back slowly and give himself time to slow his heart rate. Before he reached the studio, Marlo stuck her head out the door.

"There you are. I was worried." She smiled.

Jude held out the pastry box. "I made these for you today."

Marlo studied him. "For me?"

He swallowed. Everything he'd created was for her, about her. He couldn't believe he ever tried to pretend otherwise. His entire second act was a tribute to her. Anger flared in his chest, and he attempted to tamp it down. He wasn't upset with Marlo but with himself.

"Just a recipe I'm trying out," he said.

Her smile faltered, and Jude immediately felt like an asshole. He'd given her a gift and then yanked it away. It would've cost him nothing to let her think it was an act of kindness for her specifically, but pride and a wounded ego interfered. If all he wanted was to be seen by her, then he needed to stop placing so many barriers between them. Why not let her see just how much he thought about her, how much he admired and cared for her?

"But, yes, for you," he said, softening. "Inspired by you."

His eyes drifted down to her mouth. Marlo's lips parted ever so slightly, and he'd never wanted to kiss her more. He longed to paint her lips with frosting and lick it off of her.

"Trying to poison me?" She laughed, but the hurt lingered in her eyes.

"No, I was trying to capture that feeling of the first few days of spring when the world is bright and full of potential."

She nodded. "Before it all shrivels up and dies."

"Marlo—"

"No, never mind. I didn't mean it."

Marlo took the box from his hand and walked over to the piano. She set it on top of the baby grand, taking one of the cupcakes out. She smelled it, and then she licked the peak of the frosting off.

The sight of it shot straight to his groin.

Marlo took a bite, and she closed her eyes and sighed. Her reaction was nearly identical to Penny's. She turned to him, a single tear tracing down her cheek. He yearned to cross the room and wipe it away. He hadn't meant to upset her, at least not so soon.

"It's perfect," she said. "Devastatingly perfect. Springtime Sadness."

That was it. That was the name. Springtime Sadness. Marlo had always been the one with a knack for words.

"I think you just named my cupcake," he said, trying to lighten the mood.

"It's delicious but it also sucks." Marlo set the uneaten half of the cupcake back in the box.

He quirked his head, trying to understand. "What do you mean?"

"It sucks that this is what you think of when you think of me."

His newest creation might have a name, but this look on her face…he had no words for it. Marlo gaze held his with a wild desperation.

Anguish. Anguish he'd caused.

"And the cake, the one that was sold out the first day I went into the shop?" she said. "Remind me what it was called."

Jude swallowed hard. She didn't have to rehash it all now, at literally the worst moment.

"I mean, not just the cake, the whole fucking shop." Now a flare of anger erased the anguish.

The muscle at her jaw tensed, and her eyes glistened with unshed tears.

"It's all just a memorial to what a bitch I've been to you." She laughed, but the sound echoed hollow around them. "Oh my god, I am so fucking stupid. You spelled it all out for me, and I still somehow thought I could earn your forgiveness."

"Marlo—"

"No." She held up her hand. "No, I don't want to hear it. You didn't carry a torch for me all these years. You carried a vendetta, pure resentment, and you used that resentment to build a shrine to just how much you hate me."

Her words came so fast Jude couldn't even decide which argument to refute first. Marlo had to know he didn't hate her. He never had, never could.

"It's nothing like that, Marlo."

"Isn't it? No wonder you're letting all those journalists sniff around. What better coup than getting to share your hatred of me on public platforms. All this time, I thought it was pining, but really it was trolling. You're no better than Cliff Rochester."

His stomach roiled. Her accusations pierced his heart. If he told her about *Farm & Table* now, Marlo would simply see it as confirmation of her worst suspicions.

Then her face paled. "The charity show..."

Jude crossed the room to her and grabbed her by the elbow. "No, there is no grand plan, no ulterior motive."

Her mouth gaped but no words emerge. He needed to fix this.

"Listen to me," he said, his fingers pressing into her soft skin. "Is the shop a tribute to you? Yes. You have always been a huge part of my life. I have complicated feelings about you. I've always been honest about this. Do I have an ulterior motive to destroy your reputation? Absolutely not. Nothing could be further from the truth."

He took a deep breath.

Marlo hadn't stepped away from him or tried to escape his grasp. He loosened his hold on her, and still, she didn't move.

"The truth is, I ache for you. I always have. Even standing in the same room with you, I miss you. I don't know how to explain the effect you have on me. Unlike you, words fail me. You consume nearly every thought I have, and the only way I can process the big feelings I have for you is by baking."

MARLO

Marlo exhaled sharply. They were caught in a disastrous push-pull. But she couldn't bring herself to walk away from him. He radiated the warmth she craved. She wanted to fold herself into his strong chest and have him wrap his muscled arms around her and tell her everything was going to be okay.

But they'd both outgrown fairy tales. There was no happy ending here.

As much as it hurt, the realization freed Marlo. *Sometimes you have to hit bottom to bounce.* Love wasn't always enough. She'd love him forever, but ultimately, they were incompatible.

She took a shaky breath and finally stepped away from him. "You know what? We don't need to rehearse. I've already memorized the cues. I'll perform the five songs I sent over."

Jude stared at her, his eyes wide and disbelieving. "Marlo, don't be ridiculous."

Marlo smiled tightly. "It's not ridiculous. Singing and performing are the path I chose. I am a consummate professional."

He shook his head.

"We've made our choices. Now we just need to act like grown-ups and accept them. The past is over. There's no reclaiming it."

Jude stared at her, his mouth gaping.

"Thank you for the cupcake," she said. "It was a truly magical way to say goodbye to sugar."

"You're giving up sugar?" he asked.

Marlo laughed. After everything she'd said, that was the only objection he saw fit to raise? She was making the right choice now. She'd never been so sure of any decision in her life. Choosing herself was always the fail-safe option.

"Goodbye, Jude."

She walked right past him and out the front door and didn't look back once.

Chapter Thirty

JUDE

JUDE LEANED HIS head back against the leather seat. Catherine Howell had insisted on sending a chauffeured town car to pick him up from the airport for their meeting. She also insisted on meeting at her home in Santa Monica for their discussion. It was less formal than an office. The repetition of the scenery soothed him—buildings, palm trees, traffic. The repetition also gave him time to think, something he enjoyed decidedly less.

His mind drifted to Marlo. He'd become the textbook definition of a one-track mind. She occupied every beat of his heart, and the intensity of his feelings for her frightened him. He shut his eyes for a moment.

Yes, the intensity of his feelings for her frightened him. So, each time he and Marlo grew close, he either shut down or fled or some combination of both. His chest tightened. It was such a simple, obvious observation, and yet he'd never made it before.

He'd pushed her away because he was afraid of losing her, but in doing so, he lost her anyway. He invented excuse after excuse just to convince himself no future with Marlo was possible. Because if he tried, really tried, and still failed, he couldn't survive it. Yet here he was without her, surviving. Maybe not thriving, but he functioned. Just as he did when he'd left her years ago. It broke his heart to lose her but he wasn't broken. The epiphany rocked through in a revelatory chorus.

He didn't *need* Marlo in his life, but he wanted her in it. He chose her. All he had to do now was to ask her if she would choose him as well.

But was it too late? Could he salvage a relationship with Marlo after hurting her so spectacularly?

Jude shifted in his seat, opening his eyes again and lightly groaning in frustration. He took a deep breath and sat forward, staring out the window. They had to be nearing their destination. The density of palm trees increased, and the sight of them transported him to an entirely different moment.

A late night in Florida with Marlo after one of their shows. They'd picked up key lime tartlets from the hotel and sneaked off to the beach. Palm tree leaves gently swayed in the warm breeze in the distance. They'd been so busy rehearsing, performing, and attending to interview requests that they hadn't had time to visit the beach yet. Marlo kicked off her sandals and pulled her dress over her head. Jude tried not to ogle her bikini-clad body, but it was not an easy task for a teenage boy. Her suit was fluorescent green, and it perfectly highlighted her tan skin even by moonlight.

There was a light, warm breeze, and Marlo waded into the water. She was yards away from him, but the water still only lapped mid-calf.

"Oh my God, I get Florida now. You wouldn't believe how warm the water is." Marlo looked over her shoulder, beckoning him in.

"What if there are sharks or other scary sea creatures?" he asked, only half joking. The ocean and its possibilities terrified him.

Her laugh carried on the breeze. "If there are, you wouldn't be able to see them anyway."

Jude jogged out to her, the warm water spraying behind him.

"I wish I had a camera," she said, watching him.

"Why?"

"You look like an ad for cologne. Muscles rippling in the moonlight, sea spray in your wake."

Jude was thankful for the darkness around them. He hoped it shielded his no doubt flushed cheeks. Marlo teased him sometimes about his looks, but he could never quite tell if she was revealing how she truly felt or if she was just needling him like a childhood friend. But he didn't have any other friends who made out with him in dressing rooms, tour buses, or in secret corners of hotel lobbies. This had become a new game for them lately, and he wasn't sure what it meant to her. But he lived for those stolen moments.

"Muscles, huh?" He stopped and flexed his arms, kissing each bicep, and before he could look for her reaction, he was doused with salt water.

Coughing and sputtering, his eyes burning, he bent down and generated his own wave in what he could best tell was Marlo's direction. Her screech vindicated him. He heard splashing moving toward him, and he tried to turn and run in the opposite direction. He didn't get too far before he was waylaid by Marlo launching herself on him. They both toppled into the water.

Marlo laughed, and Jude tried to ignore the feeling of her breasts pressed against his back for one delicious moment that did not last nearly long enough. He wrapped his arms around her, bringing her to rest against his abdomen, her legs stretched out along his.

"Jude," she said, softly.

He couldn't tell if she said his name in objection. He loosened his grasp on her, but she didn't move. She leaned back against him and turned her head up toward the star-speckled sky.

"This water is amazing," he said, a bid to gauge her mood. "You're right. It feels just like a bath."

He'd never been in this much contact with so much of her bare skin, and if it were possible, he would stay right in this spot forever. Not even his innate fear of ocean creatures made him want to move.

"I can't believe how shallow it is for so far out," she said. "I love it. I love this."

I love this.

Jude fixated on the phrase. This closeness with her. This attraction. This love. No, they were too young for love. They sang about it on stage every night. They pretended for the audience, but it wasn't real. He had to remember it wasn't real.

Still, he silently let the words roll on his tongue. *I love you.*

David Stringer had warned him not to get confused. "Don't be fooled by these feelings you have for a pretty girl. It's just born out of proximity. Best to forget all about her, distract yourself with some groupies or an up-and-coming starlet."

Jude always found it strange for the label president to engage him in such a conversation. They'd never spoken about any personal subjects before, strictly business. Sure, they'd posed for photos together, usually with Marlo between them, but before that moment, Jude hadn't even realized David Stringer knew his name.

Marlo pushed off his lap, and Jude missed her warmth and weight immediately. He wondered if she'd figured out the tenor of his thoughts. She turned, and to his surprise, she sat back on his outstretched legs, now facing him. She scooted dangerously forward and wrapped her legs around his waist. If she moved one more inch, she would feel exactly the reaction she elicited in him.

Jude tried to think of something that would settle him. He chuckled awkwardly. "What are you doing?"

She loosely hung her arms around his shoulders, not releasing his gaze.

"Marlo—"

Before he could say anything more, she leaned forward and kissed him. He was so stunned he sat completely still, lips unyielding.

Marlo sighed in frustration. "Why don't you like me like I like you?"

He wanted to scream because it was not like—it was love. If he kissed her back right now, he wouldn't be able to hide the emotion behind it. Marlo would know it was love, and that terrified him even more than the thought of sea creatures lurking near in the darkened waters.

"I do," he said.

She shook her head, and even in the dim moonlight, he could see the hurt in her eyes. "I am always the one who pursues you, kisses you first."

"No, when we were twelve, I kissed you first."

"We were thirteen." She sighed again.

Jude hated seeing her sad, especially if he was the source of her unhappiness.

Something clicked in his brain. He brought his hands to her bottom and pulled her forward so there could be no doubt how he felt about her. Marlo's eyes widened, and she gasped, giving him the perfect opportunity to claim her mouth. He brought one hand behind her head and kissed her deeper than he ever had before. She wrapped her legs around his waist even tighter, and Jude thought he'd die from the contact. They were only separated by thin layers of swimsuit material. His erection throbbed against his swim trunks, seeking the release that was so close by.

Jude pulled away, breathless. "See, I like you. I always have."

I love you.

Marlo giggled softly and brought her head to rest on his shoulder. He wrapped his arms around her back and shifted her because, if he didn't, he thought he might bust through both of their bathing suits.

"I have to go on a date tomorrow," she said into his skin.

Those words were the off switch he needed. He nodded, unsure what to say. He'd been at the meeting with their managers and the studio executives when the Marlo publicity plan had been rolled out. Jude wanted to blurt out, "No." Instead, he sat on his hands, studying the grain of the wood table. He could feel Marlo's eyes burning trails on his skin from time to time. But David Stringer's words were on replay in his mind. He'd basically warned him to stay away from her. Why? So they could now offer her up on a silver platter to every other famous teen.

Jude's lack of protest at that meeting was probably something Marlo hadn't forgotten either. That was why she'd kissed him before telling him about the date. She had to ensure his devotion, even though she was about to be trotted out with all the hottest teen celebrities.

"Who's the lucky guy?" He tried to restrain his pain, but he heard it. He knew Marlo heard it too because she sat up straighter.

"Shouldn't it be you?" she asked.

Jude was seated well above water, but he felt like he was drowning all the same. It should be him. He wanted nothing more, but he wanted it to be something between them only. Private. He didn't want to share her with the rest of the world. He didn't want to date her as some publicity strategy to sell more records. He wanted to keep her to himself.

Marlo stood up, a siren straight from the sea, and he wanted to pull her back down and tell her exactly how he felt about her. Instead, he watched her walk away from him. Whenever he needed them most, words abandoned him.

First, she stepped farther out into the water, and then probably after she grew tired of waiting for him to say something, anything, she headed back to shore. She stepped widely to skirt around him. He followed her, but the window he'd had to change anything shut.

"Wait," he called after her as he gathered his things.

Marlo didn't turn around. She didn't acknowledge him talking to her. She just kept walking.

"Marlo, stop." He finally caught up to her, and he cut in front of her.

"You don't need to explain," she said. "I get it."

"You get what?"

She looked on the verge of tears. "You've had so many chances, so many opportunities, and the only reason you haven't taken any of them is because obviously you're not interested in me."

Jude reached out to touch her, but she stepped away again.

"I can't do this anymore," she'd said. "Wondering, waiting. I'm not going to feel guilty about my date tomorrow night and all the ones that come after because now I know."

Now I know.

The first fight and the beginning of the end. The funny part was, after that first date with the guy from the vampire show, she'd ended up back in Jude's hotel room.

He'd answered the door surly. "Did you get lost on your way to your boyfriend's room?"

Marlo pushed past him, flopping on the bed. "Please, don't make this harder than it needs to be."

Jude followed her into the room. He paced at the foot of the bed, unsure what to say or do. He was angry. He felt betrayed and he knew she did too. Marlo was right—he'd had every opportunity to claim a relationship with her, and instead he'd pushed her away.

She pressed up on her elbows and watched him move back and forth across the tight space. "I really hate you sometimes."

He turned to face her, completely stricken. "You hate me?"

"Yes, I hate that I want you so bad and that you don't want me back. I hate that I spent the night on a date with every girl's dream guy, and all I could think about was leaving and coming back here. And I hate that I'm here, waiting for you to see how much I love you."

Jude wasn't sure who moved first, but they collided against each other, tumbling back against the mattress. He was so impatient, trying to get her dress off her, that he ripped it. Marlo laughed against his mouth.

He sat back. "Oh God, Marlo, I am so sorry."

She shook with laughter and struggled to speak. "No, it's fine. It's just like the books I steal from my mom."

She grabbed the torn part of the dress and yanked the rest of fabric apart.

Jude pulled her in again. "Marlo, I love you too."

Marlo stilled, her hand lightly tracing his jaw. "You do?"

He nodded and then kissed her again.

That was the night they'd lost their virginity to each other and start of their short-lived secret relationship.

Jude had gone to see David Stringer after that and offered to be the one who dated Marlo publicly, but David had laughed in his face.

"You stupid fool. I told you to stay away from her."

Jude's blood boiled. But he was taught not to talk back to adults, and David Stringer exuded a don't-fuck-with-me attitude.

"Listen, son, I've seen this play out time and again. It always ends in disaster. I will not have my chart-topping duo break up over stupid teen drama of their own making."

No, you'd rather craft the teen drama yourself and use it to line your pockets.

"I love her," Jude said, fists clenched at his sides.

"Then I'll make you deal."

Jude took a step back, a warning thrumming through his veins.

David's eyes had narrowed, and he grinned like a serpent. "Marlo's getting a little loose with that tongue of hers. I don't need her delivering soliloquies about feminism, immigration, or whatever nonsense of the week she's spewing. I don't need her posting that shit online either."

Jude swallowed, still unable to speak.

"I will only allow the two of you to date on two conditions: first, you agree to be photographed together on dates, sneaking into and out of each other's rooms, making out in dark corners."

Jude shivered. This sounded like a threat. It sounded like he knew every single one of their secrets and might already own these photos.

"And second, you muzzle that mouth of hers. Encourage her to stop yapping on about subjects no one wants to hear a dumb girl talk about. Got it?"

Sweat trickled down Jude's spine. David chuckled, still holding him in that grossly hypnotic stare. As much as Jude wanted Marlo, he couldn't agree to what David demanded. He couldn't ask her to be someone she wasn't. He loved Marlo Rayhan—brash, principled, outspoken Marlo Rayhan. Jude would not forge himself into a tool of the patriarchy to be wielded against her.

But Jude had also known in that moment that he also couldn't stay and watch Marlo fake date other guys. It was his broken heart versus hers.

Jude shook his head to dislodge the memories.

If only he'd told her the truth then. They might have had years together. Instead, he'd walked away, and Marlo had been left to face David Stringer and the rest of the assholes at Pop Machine alone.

He didn't regret the life he'd built without her, but her absence hung over him all the same—an aching chasm that no amount of pastries with clever names could fill. All those years ago, he'd made a choice—inaction, and then worse escape—and it had cost him the love of his life.

Now, he could make a new choice. An active choice.

Marlo deserved to know she was deeply wanted, perceived flaws and all.

MARLO

Marlo pulled her earpiece out, wiping the beads of sweat from her forehead. She popped into the control booth. "What do you think?"

The producer studied her for a minute before responding. "It was just right."

Marlo exhaled. She'd felt that too as she sang. There were times when she was recording that were pure magic everyone could feel, and they'd just achieved that heady alchemy. She wanted to call Jude to tell him about it, but her heart skipped. They were not at the call-at-will stage of the breakup. Everything was still too raw. She'd never been more grateful to be working on a new project that was simply her own. She needed every distraction she could get.

What she really needed was a class in how not to push her love interests away. Marlo was getting too old to be so unsuccessful in relationships. People acted like women were tough to understand, but all the women she knew were confident in what they wanted from a relationship and unapologetic about asking for it. It was the men who were confusing. Emotionally stunted men who couldn't name their feelings, much less discuss them.

"I think we should do 'Undeserving' next," Marlo said, folding and unfolding her hands. "I'm feeling it."

The producer nodded. She gave Marlo a few notes, and then Marlo returned to the recording room. The guitar started hard and unyielding on this one, and Marlo felt the rhythm deep in her bones. She didn't think through a recording strategy in the prescribed way she normally did. She just allowed the music to pulse through her and sang it as it came. In the moment. Marlo needed to stop looking back or trying to predict what came next. Her focus belonged on the here and now. The bridge, so full of angst, allowed her to dig deep into a primal part of her voice—the essence, hungry and raw.

The last line was near whispered, which heightened its punch.

"The undeserving don't even realize what a treasure you are until they've lost you."

The tears streaming down Marlo's face surprised her.

The studio fell perfectly silent, and her producer said nothing for what felt like an eternity. Marlo couldn't move, rendered inert by the aftermath of the emotional performance. Finally, the overhead speaker clicked on.

"Marlo, that was incredible. My god," her producer said.

Marlo glanced behind her at the musicians who had played so beautifully, and new tears dropped as she scanned their awed faces. The bass guitarist clapped, and soon everyone else joined in, giving her a mini standing ovation. Her cheeks flushed, and she dropped her gaze. She had no idea where her emotional intensity came from.

No, she knew exactly where it came from—all her, unapologetically Marlo Sage. Correction. Marlo Rayhan.

"Well, I think that's a wrap for today," the producer said. "This album is almost done! Thank you, everyone, for all your time and energy. Thank you, Marlo, for allowing us to work on such an amazing piece of art."

Marlo smiled, still shaken. Little aftershocks of emotion reverberated through her. She needed to be alone to process what had just happened. Scratch that—she needed to be alone, immersed in a hot bath with a glass of white wine.

An hour later, she finally sank into her hot bath. She was as spent as she'd been after the one marathon she'd run a few years ago just to prove to herself she could. Her muscles turned to jelly in the hot water.

She leaned her head back against the brim of the tub and closed her eyes.

The warmth of the water reminded her of Florida. The first time she'd ever enjoyed a beach there was with Jude. It was also the first time they'd fought about their confusing relationship. Marlo swallowed hard and opened her eyes again. It was also the first time he'd rejected her. She'd asked him to be the one to date her to save her from the ridiculous PR plan that would have her trotting out with new celeb boyfriends every other week. The plan that eventually earned her a reputation for being promiscuous, which haunted her to this day. A plan that begot its own host of flak from the very PR team that had conceived it in the first place. An unearned reputation Cliff Rochester capitalized on to make a quick buck.

"I should have said no," she whispered into the curls of steam rising above the bath water.

Her first reaction when they'd proposed the plan was to say no. But she was a lone teen girl sitting in a room of middle-aged men who literally controlled the fate of her career. They'd laughed at her, made crass jokes. She'd never felt so simultaneously invisible and stripped bare.

David Stringer had leaned forward in his conference chair and tilted his head, studying her as if she were an alien. "Sweetheart, we handle the business. You do as we say."

Anger flared inside her. She was young, she was inexperienced, but she wasn't stupid. She knew all along it was a flawed idea. How many times had everyone seen these forced celebrity pairings crash and burn in the media? Her career was supposed to be about her music, not her dating life. She wondered if they planned to discuss a similar plan for Jude. The entire time, he sat ram-rod still, avoiding her eye contact and not betraying a single emotion.

Her stomach clenched. Marlo couldn't stand the thought of Jude dating anyone else. She hadn't told him about the shift in her feelings toward him, even though she'd shown him, sneaking him off any chance she got and shamelessly throwing herself at him. He always reciprocated but never initiated.

Jude was the one she wanted to be dating.

Marlo began panicking. There had to be another way. She kept nervously glancing at Jude, waiting for him to speak up and offer her rescue. But he didn't.

"The goal is to keep your face in the magazines," David said.

She gripped the armrests of her chair so tight her knuckles whitened. *Jude, please look at me.*

Another executive spoke next. Marlo couldn't even remember most of their names. They all looked roughly the same to her, sneering older white men wearing varying shades of gray suits. Part of her marveled at why men who viewed her with such contempt invested in her career at all. Then she remembered—she and Jude made them enormous amounts of money. She straightened her spine.

"Well, apparently my input is not needed, and Jude has none to offer." She placed her hands on the table and stood up, the conference chair sliding out behind her. "Thanks for the meeting."

She had walked out, hoping they couldn't tell she was trembling inside. They might act like they were doing her a favor by "allowing" her this career she'd worked so hard for, but she would not forget ever again that she was the talent and that she held value.

They were nothing more than gatekeepers. Without her, they had no content to sell.

Marlo held her breath and dunked her head under the water. She didn't want to think about how that night ended. It was the beginning of the end for them, and it had given the studio executives the leverage that poisoned her career in the aftermath of Jude leaving.

That ill-fated night in Florida had rippled through so many aspects of her life for so many years. She had allowed that night to rock the foundation of her beliefs about herself. She believed Jude was right to refuse her because she wasn't worthy of him. She believed the studio was right to coerce her into relationships she didn't want. And worst of all, she believed the tabloid headlines that screamed she was a promiscuous hack who kept releasing the same variation of her songs. She believed all the negative charges leveled at her, and she'd stopped questioning them because, the one time she had, she lost everything.

The most ridiculous part was that the night after Jude rejected her at the beach ended up being the night they lost their virginity to each other. They started sneaking into one another's rooms every night, and for a brief moment, it had been heaven sent.

Marlo resurfaced and sucked in a deep breath. Despite what she told herself for months, she hadn't lost everything. Only a piece of herself.

But she'd survived without Jude before. She could do it again. Now, she intended to use her platform to call out the hypocrisy of the treatment of her and other women in the media versus the treatment of the male celebrities she'd been casually associated with.

Starting with Cliff Rochester.

All she needed to do was to post a few texts and pictures from her phone, and he'd see how swiftly she could counteract the lies he'd been spreading. David Stringer might have media contacts, but her social media reach would eclipse them. She didn't need an interview with a snooty magazine or a condescending news anchor—she simply needed to post a video to her social media accounts.

It took far too long time to get to a place where she'd even consider saying no to the record label and their PR team. But she'd say no now, and that was growth.

Her new music was a departure, a much needed one, and she was proud of the work she'd done. She had enough of a nest egg for herself that she had the privilege to choose not to be reliant on the traditional patriarchal business model once they released her from her contract. She'd leverage social media and her fan base to force their hand.

If they thought her a nightmare diva before, they had no idea what was coming.

Marlo would continue to hire her own production teams and musicians and make her own albums. She'd release them straight to streaming and return to making music for the sheer joy of it. It was all within her grasp.

Except Jude.

Yes, she'd build herself a wholly independent life and she'd find contentment, but part of her would always regret the loss of Jude as her partner. If only they could get to a place where they could be honest with each other and commit to compromising, they could find happiness.

At the end of the day, Jude was her soul mate. There was no denying it.

He understood her in a way no one else did. History wasn't all they shared. They also shared values and passion and respect. He would never question her commitment to music, and she'd never question his to baking. He left to save himself. Marlo saw that now. He'd walked toward something he loved.

The realization stunned her.

He hadn't left her all those years ago. He'd walked away from the risk of losing her.

Fear dictated that he protects his heart above all else. The great irony was that they lost each other in the machinations of celebrity anyway. The pain was shared, but their response to it was vastly different.

Marlo ran headfirst into fear. That which could not be named and confronted could not be vanquished, and she had to destroy fear before it sank its teeth in her. But Jude was the opposite. He fled from fear. His self-preservation instinct was over-primed. He'd rather walk away from something great than risk losing it.

She pulled her knees up to her chest. It was such a clear, obvious dynamic. She couldn't believe she'd never seen it before. They were wired to confront fear differently, so of course all those years ago on the beach, they'd collided and bounced away from each other in completely opposite directions. She'd resented him unfairly for so many years, but now, looking back on that night through the lens of distance and maturity, she saw the trap they'd set for themselves.

The trap David Stringer had baited for them.

Marlo stepped out of the bath, leaving a trail of water behind her as she crossed the bathroom for her towel. She looked over her shoulder and laughed. It would've driven Jude crazy that she'd left behind a wet spot in the bathroom. He'd lecture her about the risk of a fall, an overprotective impulse from the same place, fear of losing her. When he looked at the world, he saw the potential for things to go wrong, and he tried to protect proactively.

A wave of gooseflesh erupted across her skin. If she'd been able to see these tendencies earlier, she would've understood how to deal with him differently. They could have developed strategies together to avoid each other's triggers. They could have taken care of each other.

She dressed slowly as her mind continued to whirl.

Maybe it wasn't too late. They still had a chance to salvage their relationship but only if they both equally wanted to.

Marlo sat on the edge of her bed, cradling her head in her hands. She believed in their relationship. She was ready to fight for it.

But he needed to want the same for it to work.

She grabbed her phone, but she wasn't calling Jude. There was something else she needed to take care of first. The phone rang about four times, and just as she was about to hit end, she heard the rough scrape of a familiar voice.

"Hello?"

Marlo cleared her throat. "Hey, Cliff. It's Marlo."

She was met by utter silence on the other end.

Marlo continued, "I need to ask you for a favor."

"Me?"

"Listen, you've done a lot of shitty things to me the last couple of months, but I'm feeling gracious. I'm willing to forget if you help me out."

"You're willing to forgive me?"

"No, I'll never forgive you, but I'm willing to forget about you. I know you were in a bind. You've squandered every opportunity you've been handed on a silver platter, and you needed cash quick. If my suspicions are correct, David Stringer offered you a deal."

"I... Bloody hell, what do you expect me to say to this?" Cliff slipped into full Hugh Grant-style flustered Brit.

It was just where Marlo wanted him. "Don't choose wrong, Cliff," she warned. "I didn't have to doctor the damning photos I have in my possession."

Cliff sucked in his breath.

"If you want any chance of getting cast in anything ever again, it would behoove you to help me forget about you and the dossier I have on you."

"Fuck me."

"Let me know what you decide."

"I'm listening."

Marlo shared the rough outline of her plan and his part in it, should he choose to accept it. Either way, she still had enough evidence to build a compelling case. Cliff must have recognized the chord of determination in her voice. He capitulated with barely any effort.

Now, she could shift her attentions to Jude.

Chapter Thirty-One

JUDE

SLEEP CONTINUED TO defy Jude. Nighttime ushered in the past, playing across the movie screen in his mind. Memories of Marlo and how he failed her haunted him night after night.

The bake-off was days away. He rolled onto his side, bringing his knees up and curling his body into a fetal position. It would be impossible to share a stage with Marlo, even if he wasn't singing with her, and not be transported right back to the emotions of it all. Jude flipped onto his back. He was also due to return to LA soon for more *Farm & Table* special filming. The emptiness inside him gnawed at him. Not even baking dulled the edge anymore.

The phone on the nightstand rang. Jude ran his hand over his face.

"Fuck," he groaned at the ceiling before answering in as cheery a voice as he could muster, all things considered. "Hey, Catherine."

"Jude, sorry to call so early, but I knew you were eager to hear about the final call schedule." She sucked in her breath, and Jude already figured what she'd say next.

His exact fear come to fruition.

"I really tried to advocate for you," she said. "I know how important the show at the end of the month is to you and your family, but the cost of delaying production was simply too much. Plus, the director and a handful of the crew are expected on other projects."

He blinked up at the ceiling. "I understand. Thanks for trying."

There was a pause.

"If there is anything else I can do for you, let me know."

"Will do."

Catherine said a quick goodbye, and Jude pulled the covers over his head. Now there was truly no way to avoid telling Marlo about the *Farm & Table* segment. He sat up, untangling himself from his covers.

Jude glanced at the clock. It was too early to call her. He got out of bed, dressed in his running gear, popped in his earbuds, and took off.

His feet kept pace with the racing music on his playlist. The cold morning air stung as he gulped in breaths. The first few minutes always involved an internal conversation about how much he hated running until the endorphins kicked in and his body switched to cruise control. His mental fog lifted too. He'd stop by the bakery and whip up something for Marlo, then he'd personally deliver the treats and drop the bomb of his absence from the show that his family had basically coerced her into doing along with him.

He suspected she wouldn't take his last-minute cancelation well. It wasn't the best plan, but it was a plan all the same. He couldn't shield her from this by not telling her about it. The right thing to do was to put it all out there and then figure out a way to work it out together. His breathing regulated, and the tension between his shoulders eased at last.

Jude turned the corner and, in the distance, thought he saw Marlo jogging toward him.

He blinked, attempting to dislodge the mirage. But no, it truly was her.

All his hard-earned calm evaporated. He slowed to a walk, removing his earbuds. Marlo mirrored the movement. Because they both slowed, it took them longer to reach each other.

Marlo's lips curved up at one corner, and Jude swore her pink cheeks darkened a shade. His lips slipped into a smile. He couldn't help himself—no matter how often he remembered how things soured between them, he still missed her. He swallowed.

It was more than that. He loved her.

The thought knocked the wind out of his lungs all over again.

He still loved her. He'd always loved her. But now, as a man, he loved her, and his future wouldn't be the same without her in it.

Jude stopped walking.

MARLO

Marlo stutter-stepped when Jude stopped dead in his tracks, the ghost of a smile on his lips but now with brows furrowed. When she first saw him running toward her, her heart leaped into her throat. No matter what happened between them, she'd always love him and crave his company. The last few weeks of barely seeing him left a gaping hole in her heart. When he'd smiled at her, she thought maybe he felt the same, but now she wasn't so sure.

She looked back over her shoulder as she considered turning around and running back the way she came but decided it would look foolish.

Marlo waved at him. "Hey, how are you?"

He cleared his throat. "I'm good."

The silence between them settled in again as she stepped up to where he was rooted to the ground. She looked up at him, urging herself not to reach out to sooth the furrow at his brow. She wanted to wrap her arms around him and squeeze him tight. She longed to press her mouth against his and forget everything that had gone wrong between them.

No, to forgive it.

"The bake-off is only a few days away," Marlo said, racking her brain for something to alleviate the awkwardness between them. "Wild."

Apparently, it was the wrong thing to say because Jude's forehead crease deepened, and he took a step backward.

"Jude?"

He looked down and shook his head. "I didn't want to tell you like this."

Her heart bottomed out at her feet. The earth shifted beneath her. The only other time he'd looked at her like this was when he'd announced he was leaving their pop duo and going home. Marlo wrapped her arms around her middle, giving herself the hug she'd need once he told her.

"Catherine called me this morning," he said.

"Catherine?"

"Catherine Howell, from *Farm & Table*."

Marlo nodded.

"The thing is…" His voice drifted into another silence as he shifted his weight.

"Please just tell me." She hated the sound of desperation in her voice. "I'm a big girl."

"After we broke up, I accepted her offer. For the video series she proposed."

"And…" Marlo spun her wrist in impatient circles.

"Well, the filming schedule was changed, moved up to accommodate the director's other commitments, and I tried to change things, but ultimately it would be too costly so…"

Marlo tried to fill in the gaps for herself. Filming schedule changed. Then it hit her—the bake-off.

"Oh my God, the show, for your dad." She braced herself on her knees. trying to gulp in air.

Jude's feet entered her line of vision, then the heft of his hand was on her back. "I really didn't want to tell you like this."

She straightened, forcing him to pull his hand away. "Oh yeah, how did you plan to do it? Were you were going to deliver the news with a side of dessert?"

His face reddened.

"Oh my fucking god, you were weren't you?"

"I was going to sit down with you, talk this out like adults. And because I'm me, yeah, maybe some dessert would be involved. I was hoping you'd understand."

Marlo's immediate impulse was to make a snide remark about him abandoning her on stage again. But instead, she took a beat to think before she spoke.

He was clearly distraught about this conflict in his commitments. He didn't need her piling on simply because she was disappointed about losing an opportunity to work with him. Plus, she'd been right where he was many times. Pursuing a dream often meant making difficult choices and even harder sacrifices.

She could help.

"I do," she said.

"You don't..." Jude paused. "Did you say you 'do' understand?"

"Yes, and we'll figure it out. Don't worry." Marlo glanced at her watch. "Will you be home in about an hour?"

"Yes. Why?" His eyes remained wide as saucers, staring as if trying to solve a riddle.

"I have an idea. I'll tell you all about it soon." Marlo turned on her heel, waving bye behind her back as she took off in the opposite direction, back to her house. Her feet pounded the pavement, fueled by the excitement.

"Marlo," he called out after her.

But she didn't stop. She had to fix this for him so he could just enjoy the *Farm & Table* opportunity without any self-flagellation. When she reached her house, she stood in the driveway to cool down before entering, sweat tracing rivulets down her face. Marlo looked up at the trees, branches reaching overhead in a protective cocoon, and smiled.

Success was within her grasp and not at the cost of Jude's dreams versus her own.

JUDE

Jude remained frozen until Marlo disappeared from sight. He'd expected his admission to be met with anger, maybe even tears. Instead, she took it in stride. Literally. That thought jarred him into action again. He moved swiftly in the direction she'd run. He hoped to catch up to her and ask for an explanation. He'd never run faster in his life.

He wasn't sure if he should be impressed or depressed that his absence from the bake-off was met with positivity bordering on enthusiasm. He had his apology speech prepared. But Marlo always had a way of subverting his expectations.

Jude skirted through the driveway he saw her turn toward, but she was nowhere in sight. He jogged up the steps to the front door and pounded on the wall of solid wood slab.

"Marlo, let me in."

His eagerness to see her nearly made him feral.

He pressed his ear against the door, but it was too thick to hear anything through. Then her doorbell security system clicked on, and her voice came through tinny and small.

"I'm on a call," she said. "Give me a few minutes."

Jude turned to face the camera. "No, let me in. Please, I can explain."

"I promise I'll be with you in five minutes."

"Let me in now, or God help me, I'll strip naked on your doorstep and livestream it all."

There was a long pause. She was really going to make him do this.

Jude shook his head and then kicked off his shoes and peeled off his shirt. It wasn't until he looped his fingers into the waistband of his shorts that he heard the lock mechanism turn. The door opened, and Marlo glared at him with her hand over the mic of her phone.

"You are an impatient bully," she said. But there was no heat behind the words. She grinned at him, her gaze lingering on his bare chest. "It's Jude," she said to the caller. "Okay, sure."

Marlo held the phone in her hand between them, putting the call on speaker.

"Hey, Jude," said Penny.

"Penny? Why are calling Marlo?"

Penny laughed. "Jealous?"

"Go ahead and tell him," Marlo said.

"It would be my absolute honor to replace you as the host of the bake-off," Penny said.

His gaze flicked up to Marlo.

She was still grinning. "Told you I'd take care of it."

Jude dropped to his knees before her, and he prayed she could read the devotion in his eyes. "I am so sorry for every time I ever hurt you. It kills me inside."

"Yes, my man, grovel that ass off," Penny yelled through the phone speaker. "Please tell me that boy is on his knees."

"He is, which is my cue to go. Thanks, Pen!" Marlo said, ending the call.

She sank to her own knees in front of Jude.

"I hurt you too," she said, "and I'm sorry too."

"I'll spend the rest of my life making it up to you," he vowed. "I love you, and I cannot live another moment without you."

It took so few words to admit the secret he'd carried in his heart for so long, and now that he'd spoken them aloud, the fear surrounding them dissipated. In its place, hope took root.

Marlo lips parted, but no sound emerged.

"I love you," Jude repeated. "I am sorry about the charity bake-off. I am sorry I agreed to do the *Farm & Table* thing in the first place without talking to you about it first. But I'm not sorry about doing it. It's an exciting opportunity for me and the shop and Penny."

"Don't be sorry. Every obstacle was a step on the journey to bring us here," she said. "But from this moment forward, there can't be anything hidden between us. We have to work as team, as equals, as partners."

"And lovers?" he asked in jest.

Marlo play swatted him.

"We wasted a lot of time, Jude Beckett," she said, unable to stop smiling.

His eyes flared as he stared into hers. "Do you trust me?"

"Yes."

Jude pulled her into his arms and kissed her the way he'd wanted to since he first saw her this morning. She placed her hands on his bare chest, not to push him away but to steady herself. He deepened the kiss, and she leaned in closer, bringing her hands to rest around his neck. Everything else melted away except the feel of her in his arms, the warmth of her mouth.

When they finally separated to take breaths, Jude sensed something shift between them. He'd opened up, confessed all his thoughts and feelings to her. And that kiss. That kiss was an opus composed of promise, hope, and…love.

Love, the real adult kind.

MARLO

Marlo wouldn't recover from that kiss for a long time, but at the same time, she felt more grounded than ever. They were no longer the same teens who crooned poppy love songs to each other. They'd both grown up. So had their talents, and at last, so had their love.

"I'm proud of us," she said.

"For restraining ourselves?" He smiled that mischievous boyish grin that revealed the dimple in his left cheek. Then he tugged her down so they laid side by side, staring up at her coffered foyer ceiling. Jude slipped his hand into hers. "I'm proud of you. You've been working so hard, and today, you blew me away with your maturity."

Marlo laughed. "How do you know what I've been doing in your absence?"

"I have my sources."

"Also, I'm mostly mature, but sometimes I get so heated I react before I completely hear you out."

Jude chuckled. "Where's a recording device when you need one?"

She fake-punched him in the arm. "I won't always react coolly or calmly. You have to know that about me by now."

He turned on his side toward her, wrapped his arm around her waist, and pulled her in close again. "It's one of my favorite things about you. That fiery Middle Eastern passion. You feel things in their full enormity. I wish I could be that free with my emotions sometimes. You're the most courageous person I know."

Marlo cupped his face, running her thumb across the plane of his chiseled cheek. "And I wish I could tuck those big feels away sometimes."

"I guess we're the perfectly matched pair then."

She smiled as she stared into his dark eyes. "Can we at least agree to be honest with each other?"

"Of course, and honestly, if we're not naked in bed in the next couple of minutes, I might just take you here."

"Promise?" She laughed.

There was still a lot of work ahead, but she knew now that they could do it. They were both invested, and that counted more than perfection because it was the chance to wake up every day to this man and consciously choose him as her partner again and again. She stood up and took Jude's hand, leading him upstairs to her bedroom. They peeled the sweaty clothes off each other with the urgency of teens who had an hour tops before their parents came home.

Jude pulled Marlo to the bed and pressed her back against the mattress while he let his eyes rove over her for a few seconds before joining her. He hovered above her for a moment in a semi-plank while he kissed her. Marlo wrapped her arms and legs around him, bringing his delicious, strong body down against hers. She'd never tire of the feeling of his weight pressing into hers. The kissing intensified, heat and tension pooled low in her belly.

She grazed his bottom lip with her teeth, and he rewarded her with a deep growl that instantly made her melt inside. His hands skimmed over the curves of her body, and then his lips followed the path. Marlo quivered as he continued his downward progression. She squirmed, her need for him building. He teased the inside of her thigh with his fingers and then his tongue.

"Jude, please." Marlo wriggled again.

"Always so impatient, baby." He gently nipped the inside of her thigh.

He parted her folds and placed a kiss at the apex. Marlo sighed. He circled her nub with his thumb as his two fingers dipped in, and her nerves sang to life. He continued to stroke inside her, as his tongue replaced his thumb.

Marlo moaned. Her muscles clenched, and her eyes squeezed so tight small stars exploded against the back of her lids—a premonition of what was to come. Jude alternated between sucking and licking, and she hovered at the edge of completely breaking apart. She anchored her hands in his hair. He squeezed her thighs and continued his mouth play.

The wave of sensation crested, and she let out a full-throated cry as her body shuddered.

Jude placed sweet, soft kisses down the length of both of her legs as she reacclimated. He settled next to her and traced his fingers along her bare abdomen.

"Thank you," he said.

Marlo turned toward him and brought his face down to her. She kissed him and rolled him on his back, straddling his hips. "I should be thanking you."

"God, you are so hot," he said in a gravelly voice as he cupped her breasts. "There's something about seeing you naked, framed by trees."

Marlo glanced over her shoulder. "It's a pretty spectacular view."

He stared right at her. "My favorite."

She ground down on him. They moaned in unison. She positioned herself to accept him as he lifted his hips. Marlo sank down until he buried himself inside her to the hilt.

His eyes darkened. Marlo leaned forward and kissed him as they moved in the rhythm they'd perfected. She felt stretched full of him, surrounded by him, and most especially, tenderly loved by him.

"Marlo," he growled. "God, Marlo, I love you so much."

Unbidden tears sprang to her eyes, true, honest-to-God tears of elation. She grasped his hands, pinning them to the mattress above his head. "I love you too."

They slowed their speed, holding one another's gazes. It was simultaneously sexy and sweet, and the shell she'd built around her heart finally fully cracked. They belonged both to each other and to themselves, and it was glorious. They'd work out all the details later. Right now, she'd enjoy each moment as it came. And they came.

Chapter Thirty-Two

MARLO

MARLO SAGE HAD performed at concert venues around the globe to audiences numbering in the tens of thousands. Granted after Tara's brilliant idea to sell online streaming tickets as a further fundraiser, her performance at the bake-off would likely reach millions tonight. Still, Marlo had never felt such intense pre-show jitters. Jude would've been at her side if he could, but she wished he was here all the same. She looked at the rack of designer looks her stylist pulled, and none of them seemed quite right.

Marlo was used to shows with multiple outfit changes, laser light effects, and rotating stage sets, but this evening, she'd take an intimate stage with her guitar, her oud, a piano, and her voice alone. It seemed wrong to wear a slinky, fresh-off-the-runway number. She wanted something simple, something cozy, something that would evoke the mood of her contemplative, raw new music.

"What do you think of this one?" Heather held out a shimmering red dress.

Marlo scrunched up her nose. She was so grateful to at least have her friend here with her.

"I'm not sure why you're asking my help. No one really aspires to kindergarten teacher chic." Heather laughed.

"Wasn't Princess Diana a kindergarten teacher?"

Heather rolled her eyes. "What did Tara suggest?"

Marlo held up a floral purple jumpsuit and scrunched her nose before setting it back on the rack.

"Even I know that's a no," Heather joked.

"She's been distracted. I'm not sure if anything else is going on," Marlo said.

She flipped through the outfits again. Tara ended up inviting other Pop Machine stars, as well as executives from other labels. She'd gifted a ticket to David Stringer but warned Marlo not to expect him to show up.

"This one?" she asked Heather, pulling out a black silk sheath.

Heather quirked her head. "Simple, elegant, I guess it works."

"Accessorized of course," Marlo said, handing Heather the dress and darting into her closet.

She frantically searched through items on hangers, folded stacks of clothing, and neatly organized drawers until she finally found what she's looking for—an old, baggy, midnight blue cardigan with interwoven threads of silver and gold, which made it look like she'd wrapped herself in the night sky.

"Bring me the dress," she yelled. "Please."

"Yes, princess," Heather said, laughing. She stepped back out into the main bedroom so Marlo could change.

Marlo shimmied into the black sheath dress and then slipped the cardigan over it. It was the perfect counterpoint to the fitted sheath, and Marlo twirled in front of her full-length mirror. She rolled up the loose sweater sleeves up to her elbow then settled on a pair of chunky-heeled, black lace-up moto boots.

"What do you think?" she asked as she emerged from her closet.

"I love it." Heather clapped her hands together.

Her stylist, Emma, who'd just returned from fetching a glass of water downstairs, eyed her silently for a full two minutes.

"This shouldn't work." She walked around Marlo in a slow circle.

Marlo clung to the hopeful lilt she heard in Emma's voice.

Emma drummed her finger against her lips. "But for some reason, I kind of love it."

Heather squealed. "It's perfect!"

Marlo grinned. She gestured to the racks of clothing behind her. "I mean, there are some beautiful items there, but they just didn't quite feel right for tonight."

Emma nodded. "Let me pull some jewelry, and then we can get your hair and makeup done."

After ten minutes of trying and discarding several items, Emma and Marlo settled on a mix of silver and gold bangles on one of Marlo's wrists, large simple white gold half hoops for her ears, and a thick black leather woven silver chain necklace long enough to loop around Marlo's neck twice.

Emma stood back and took in Marlo's whole appearance. "I have an idea."

"Uh oh, I've heard that before." Marlo glanced nervously at Heather, but the truth was Emma had never let her down. Her last-minute additions were usually the most praised aspect of Marlo's looks.

Emma turned to Heather. "You should get ready too. We'll head out about an hour after Marlo and Tara."

"Okay, break a leg, my love." Heather blew Marlo a kiss.

"Feel free to borrow anything you like, new or old," Marlo said.

"Okay, break it up," Emma said. "Let's get a move on."

Marlo spent the next hour mentally rehearsing while a hairstylist tamed her thick, frizzy mane into a simple, "messy" knotted braid that rested behind her right ear, with tendrils of loose curls framing her face. Then it was on to makeup.

There were many parts of fame that sucked, but Marlo loved all the primping and prepping, even with all the people buzzing around her, talking about her as if she were an inanimate object. It was oddly soothing. Just enough white noise to lose herself in a nearly meditative state.

Her makeup was done in a fairly simple palette, perfectly executed eyeliner wings, and a deep berry lip.

But the wow factor was thanks to Emma—a silver glitter star outlining her left eye.

Marlo wasn't sure how it would look, but now as she stared at her reflection in the mirror, she was awed. "It's perfect."

Emma smiled and high-fived the makeup artist. "I told you it would work."

"Speaking of work…" Tara leaned into the guest room, which had been converted into a dressing room for the afternoon. "Wow, you look amazing."

It was rare for Tara to lose track of her thoughts, especially where business was concerned.

Marlo took it as further evidence that she looked as great as she felt. "Thank you. What can I say? Emma's a genius."

Emma swatted her hand in Marlo's direction. "Nonsense. Marlo did most of the heavy lifting this time. Hopefully it doesn't go to her head."

"Well, we need to get to the venue to go through the sound check, and make sure everything is set up right," Tara said. "Ready?"

Marlo nodded. "Thanks, everyone. See you tonight."

She had purchased tickets for all the support staff as a thank you.

Tara reached out and grazed her fingers on the arm of Marlo's sweater. "Who is this by?"

"Noor Ahmed," Marlo replied, grinning.

Tara gave her that look that usually made Marlo snap into focus.

"My bebe," Marlo said. "She knitted this for herself. It was one of the things my father saved for me when she passed away."

Tara smiled. "It's gorgeous, and it looks like a decadent hug."

"It is that. I should learn to knit so I can make you one." Marlo nudged Tara's shoulder with her own in the backseat of the rented car.

Tara sat up straighter. "We should have them made, for the cancer patients, and then we should sell a limited release of them on your website, all proceeds donated to the L&L Society."

"That's actually a brilliant idea."

"Habibti, don't act so surprised." Tara laughed.

When they arrived at the venue, Marlo was shocked to see the seemingly endless line of news vans, from local stations to international media.

"Whoa, that's a lot of press," Marlo said, sinking back into her seat, grateful for the dark tint on the windows of the town car.

"Of course it is. You've been MIA for months, and people are excited to have you back in the spotlight." Tara went back to typing on her phone. "Okay, so I have a designer and manufacturer on board. We need to take pictures before your sound check, and then we might be able to announce it at the end of your show."

Marlo nodded, unable to focus on Tara's words. She wasn't sure why she hadn't expected this much attention for her little concert. She swallowed hard.

Her phone buzzed in her hand.

J: Miss you, wish I could be there.

She smiled. It was as though an invisible thread connected them and he could sense her need no matter how many miles separated them.

M: How is the shoot going?

J: Good. Ee hit a bit of snag earlier, but back on schedule, so I should make my flight no problem.

Marlo sighed. If Jude couldn't be back in time for her show, she at least wanted him back in time to take her home.

M: There are so many media vans here. It's nuts.

J: I am not surprised. Marlo Sage is always big news.

M: Hopefully the good kind this time.

J: Your new songs are going to blow their minds. I'm so proud of you.

M: Thanks, babe. I love you.

J: Love you too. Gotta run, getting the LOOK from the director.

"Jude, I take it," Tara said.

"That obvious?" Marlo laughed.

"You've mooned over that boy for as long as I've known you and, from what I've heard, even longer than that."

"That's the truth. I tried to fight it for so long, and now that just seems like the silliest thing."

"We're not always mentally prepared for the gifts the universe graces us with, but with time and a little luck, we figure it out." Tara stared wistfully out the window as the car neared the private entrance at the back of the property.

Marlo gaped at Tara. She sounded oddly Zen, almost maternal, and that wasn't a side of her Marlo had ever seen. She wanted to ask a follow-up question, but before she could, they were whisked into the venue by security. After a quick tour of the facilities, Marlo was ushered into sound check.

There were two stages, which faced each other. One, small and sparse, featured a single black piano, a dark heartwood oud, and Marlo's black glittered guitar. The other was significantly larger and featured several baking stations. The room was larger than she expected, and the tables were so close together there was barely room to walk between them.

"Ms. Sage," one of the production staff said, drawing her attention. "Could we film a little teaser? That way, we can check if there are any glitches with the livestream."

Marlo glanced around, looking for Tara to ask her advice, but she wasn't anywhere to be found. Weird, thought Marlo. It wasn't like Tara to be MIA at such a moment.

She shrugged. "Sure, why not?"

He pointed her to the proper camera to address and handed her a mic. When they gave her the signal, Marlo met the camera with a wide smile. "Hello, hope you're able to join us tonight to raise money for the Leukemia & Lymphoma Society. We've got a special show planned."

"That was great, thank you. Everything is in working order."

"Great, thank you for your help." She excused herself to the refuge of her dressing room.

The room was nicely decorated with a welcome sign and a generous spread of food, including a giant bowl of white and red M&Ms as well as a giant bouquet of red and white roses. Still, Tara was nowhere to be found.

M: Hey, are you okay? You disappeared on me.

T: Yes, sorry, there was one last detail to button up. I'll be right there.

Marlo had never known Tara to be so distracted. Tara had every right to be a full-fledged normal human with other clients and a life outside all this madness. Still, something felt off, but Marlo couldn't place it.

"Are you ready?" Tara asked when she finally entered the room.

"Are you okay?" Marlo replied.

"I'm fine. Let's focus." Obviously, Tara was back to her taskmaster self.

"Okay, well, sound check is done," Marlo said. "Guests are being seated, and I will be on in about an hour for song one."

"Are you nervous?"

"No, I was a little earlier, but I think now I'm just excited."

"Did I tell you David Stringer is coming after all?" Tara blinked at Marlo innocently as if she hadn't just dropped an atomic bomb on her.

"Are you kidding?"

"Didn't I mention it earlier?"

"No, you did not."

"I'm sure I did. I told you people from the label are coming."

"Yes, people from the label, but you told me not to count on David Stringer showing up."

Marlo's palms grew slick. She stalked over to the spread of food, picking up a napkin so she wouldn't inadvertently destroy her dress. Excitement pulsed in her veins. After the cruelest summer she'd ever endured, she'd finally get to address her nemesis face-to-face and torpedo his career while he sat, powerless, forced to listen to her.

Surprisingly, she had Cliff Rochester to thank. He'd come through with mounds of damning evidence against David.

"I'm surprised he decided to come," Marlo said after a moment.

Tara shrugged. "Probably to show that there's no bad blood between you two, plus the whole donating to charity angle, as if that alone can absolve him."

Marlo flipped around to face Tara again. "I told you everyone knows what I said is true, even you."

"Yes, but I told you in confidence, not in front of an audience armed with their phones."

What would Tara say if she realized Marlo intended to pull another stunt designed to upset David Stringer?

"Excuse me," Marlo said. "I need to make a call."

She stepped out into the hallway and dialed Jude's number. But it went straight to voicemail. Damn it, she needed to speak to someone she trusted. Was tonight the best venue to pursue her vendetta against David?

Marlo leaned against the wall in the hallway and looked up at the ceiling.

She'd let David Stringer ruin enough of her big moments. He didn't get this one. This was hers and hers alone. She'd worked on it all summer.

Marlo Rayhan would step out on that stage, sing the songs of her heart, and reclaim her life, her name, and her reputation from the clutches of David Stringer. It didn't matter if her actions led to her spending every single year of the rest of her life embroiled in lawsuits with him. She'd survive. And out of spite, she'd find a way to thrive.

Besides, she'd already won the prize—she'd made a damn good album, and she'd nabbed her true love.

Marlo grinned. She'd waited so long to break free from David's hold over her, just to realize he only held as much power over her as she allowed him to.

"Fuck you, David," Marlo said aloud, the perfect exclamation point to her catharsis.

She reentered the dressing room.

"Tara, I need to tell you something," she said. "Well, show you something."

Marlo swore Tara turned green before her eyes. Marlo fished out the manila envelope bursting with copies of incriminating photos, emails, and text messages.

"I added a special surprise to the end of the setlist," Marlo said.

Tara's eyes practically bulged out of her skull as she flipped the contents of the envelope. "Ya allah."

"I'm exposing him tonight."

A heavy silence descended between the two women. Marlo wasn't sure what to do. She wouldn't alter her intended course. She wasn't asking Tata permission, simply giving her the opportunity to step away if she didn't endorse Marlo's plan.

"So?" Marlo finally asked.

Tara stared at her for a moment, then she smiled. "Get that prick."

Marlo clutched her chest. With Tara on her side, in addition to Heather, Jude, their families, and the other artists who'd agreed to come forward to attest to David's bad practices, Marlo felt buoyed. She could get through anything coming her way after the show.

Tara wrapped Marlo in a hug. "Go out there and show them what you can do. They'll never see it coming."

"Thank you, Tara. I could never have found the courage without you in my corner."

"Nonsense, you did this all on your own. We both know I probably would've tried to talk you out of it but ultimately failed."

They both laughed at that, and Marlo blinked back her tears. She refused to ruin her flawless look now. Yes, damn it, she was proud of herself. She'd poured her heart into her latest songs, and even if no one but she loved them, the fact that she did was enough. More importantly, she'd already raised a quarter of a million dollars for the L&L society, and the night hadn't even kicked off yet. She wouldn't announce it publicly, but she intended to match the final donation amount.

The stage manager popped her head into the dressing room. "Ms. Sage, five minutes."

"Thank you," Marlo said.

"I need to go take my seat," Tara said. "I heard Penny is killing it as host. Great pick."

"Of course she is. See you soon! Say hi to my parents for me."

Once alone, Marlo performed her warm-up vocal exercises, touched up her lipstick, and then took a selfie making a kissy face and sent it to Jude. After an eternity, the stage manager returned to escort her to the stage, much to Marlo's relief.

Marlo stepped out on the stage to thunderous applause, and her heart leaped into her throat.

"Thank you for showing up for the Leukemia & Lymphoma Society with such enthusiasm," she said. "These patients spend months at a time in the hospital and at infusion clinics for life-saving treatments. Your donations will help support the exorbitant cost of treatment, housing near treatment facilities for families, and research."

She played a couple of chords on her guitar, and the audience fell completely silent.

"You may have heard I got myself into some hot water a few months ago. Again." She gave the crowd a sardonic face with a perked eyebrow.

The audience laughed.

"Apparently, you're not supposed to rant about your boss in public."

This second statement was met with a tense silence. Marlo had the audience exactly where she wanted them—baited on tenterhooks.

"Well, I guess I needed that crisis to remember what really mattered. Thank you, Gold Hills, for welcoming back your prodigal daughter. Over the summer, the time I spent here let me rest, reassess, and most importantly, create. You were promised a tour through Marlo & Jude past hits, but I hope you'll indulge me in allowing me to perform some new material while our chef contestants take well-earned breaks between challenges."

She paused again, looking out into the crowd, almost seeing the pulse of excitement in the room. Marlo spotted Heather right away and waved excitedly to her friend.

Then she looked directly into David Stringer's narrowed eyes.

"What do you say?" she asked the audience.

They exploded into a triumphant roar.

She smiled, gaze still fixed on her label president. Fury ignited behind his eyes.

Just wait.

"Mr. Stringer, this one is dedicated to you." Marlo played the opening chords of "Ancient History" on her guitar.

Suddenly, a piano accompaniment joined her. She glanced over her shoulder and praised herself for years of practiced professionalism because seated at the piano bench was none other than Jude Beckett.

He winked at her. Marlo didn't miss a beat, even as her heart swelled, fit to burst.

Marlo blinked back tears. She couldn't believe he'd made it back in time for the start of the show and that he'd learned to play her new material. Tara's last-minute distractions explained. Marlo owed her one.

She turned back to the audience and started singing.

You said I owed you my life, but that isn't a price
I am willing to pay.
Your relevance is ancient history, and I'm here to stay.
You're ancient history. I'm here to play.
My debts to you, tenfold, have been paid.
Best, if you take the opportunity to walk away.

Marlo watched David Stringer stand up and exit the room. She smiled, and Tara gave her a thumbs-up.

To Marlo's surprise, Jude joined her, singing on the chorus—a long overdue catharsis.

Don't even bother with a wave, your exit is long overdue.
Don't even say goodbye. You're gone and I'm hardly blue.

Marlo sat on the edge of the piano bench, facing the opposite direction, turned toward the audience, and they finished the song in harmony. She couldn't have orchestrated a better ending for her and Jude than sending off David Stringer in a lyrical fuck-you.

She rose and returned to her stool and mic stand, this time with her oud. “Thank you, it’s always nerve racking to share new songs for the first time.”

The audience applauded so loud her ears rang.

“How about a round of applause for my handsome piano accompanist. Thank you, Jude Beckett, for making all my dreams come true, then and now.”

The crowd let out a collective *aww*.

“Okay, ready for another?” Marlo turned to look at Jude.

He mouthed *I love you* to her as she started playing the oud, and she couldn’t mask her grin. She didn’t even want to. She swiveled and performed the second song to the same enthusiastic reception from the audience.

An hour later when she closed out the set with her final song, the audience rose to their feet. They gave Marlo and Jude a standing ovation that lasted at least five minutes. Marlo saw Heather dabbing her eyes and blew her kiss.

Jude pulled Penny on the stage with them. “Please, another round of applause for our evening’s host and my business partner, Penny Garner.”

The crowd went feral once again.

When Jude and Penny turned to Marlo, she gave out the last parting words.

“Thank you all for indulging me. It was such an honor to be invited to such an incredible event and one I’ll hold near and dear to my heart. James Beckett, I dedicate tonight to you.”

Marlo held her hands in a heart and scanned the room until she located the table the Becketts shared with her parents. Jude’s father smiled bigger than she’d seen him do in months as tears streamed down his face. She blew him a kiss.

“As you may have gathered from earlier in the evening,” she continued,

"I have experienced some trouble with the management at my record label. And I'm not alone in those struggles."

A website link and QR code flashed on the screen behind Marlo.

"In work separate from and not endorsed by the Leukemia & Lymphoma Foundation and thanks to my colleagues and my friends, I've gathered evidence I'd like to present to you for your own judgment. This website will remain live until Pop Machine releases me and the other artists who wish to leave from our predatory contracts and allows us all to negotiate a price to buy back our masters. The ball is in your court, David."

Jude slid his hand in hers. Here they went, everything out in the open, including a very clear gesture of togetherness.

Marlo was done hiding. "Thank you from the bottom of our hearts. We'll never forget this night."

She beamed up at Jude. No truer words were spoken. Tonight wasn't an ending. It was just the beginning of a life reimagined.

Chapter Thirty-Three

One year later

MARLO KICKED OFF her shoes in the mudroom. She didn't even bother getting her bags out of the car. She'd been gone for so long she couldn't wait one more second to be back home in her own bed. After a few more singers came forward last autumn with allegations of harassment against David Stringer, Marlo was finally freed from her contract just in time for the release of her highly anticipated new album last January. The video clips from the charity bake-off went viral, and fans clamored for the new songs. So, she joined forces with the other women whose careers had been threatened or sabotaged by David Stringer and they formed their own label, Red Records, their logo a simple red period. They were a collective of women whose femininity had been wielded against them, but they'd survived and come out stronger. Every stop on Marlo's tour had sold out within minutes of ticket sales opening up. Being able to reclaim her career on her own terms was an incredible gift.

Still, nothing brought her as much joy as being home.

Construction on the new addition to Jude's house had finally completed a couple of months ago, but it still smelled of new paint. It turned out even better than she and Jude dreamed. Their very own third-story mega-suite with almost a 180-degree view of the trees. The house was dark. If Jude knew in advance she'd planned to take the earlier flight home, he would have left lights on, her own runway markers leading straight to him.

Marlo tiptoed through the house, not wanting to wake him before she reached him. In the room, she heard him softly snoring.

She stripped off her clothes and slipped under the covers, wrapping her arms around his solid frame. He sighed, and then he stiffened. His lashes fluttered as he tried to adjust to the lack of light in the room. Marlo brushed a curl of his hair away from his forehead and placed a kiss there.

"I came home early," she whispered.

"Thank God because for a minute there I thought I'd been caught in the strangest home invasion." His voice was still thick with sleep.

"I missed you," she said, this time brushing her lips across his shoulder.

His eyes widened as his hand traveled down her side. "Marlo Sage, are you naked?"

She smiled and pressed in closer to him. "I said I missed you."

Jude pulled away from her and yanked his shirt off before wriggling out of his shorts.

"Not one to waste time, huh?" She laughed.

"The way I see it, we have so much wasted time to make up for, why wait?" He tugged her close and gazed at her with indisputable love in his eyes. "I want to know all about the tour, but first…"

He devoured her mouth, and Marlo met him stroke for stroke. The kiss unmasked their deeper hunger. He nudged her onto her back and settled between her thighs. He reached above her and turned on a bedside lamp.

She blinked furiously. "What are you doing?"

"I need to see you in all your glory. I want to see you come apart for me." The husk in his voice was no longer from sleep but from desire.

Marlo's cheeks flushed. It didn't matter how often they'd made love—every time felt as exciting and brand new as the first time. Loving him was so easy. It amazed her that she'd resisted it for so long. Jude ran a finger along her cheek. She lost track of where she ended and where he began, and that was exactly what she wanted in this moment. A complete union.

After he gave her a full welcome home, he held her and softly sang to her. She loved that the new songs he composed were for her ears only.

He brushed his lips against her neck. "Would you like a slice of cake? And then you can tell me about the tour."

Marlo untangled herself from him. "Only if you serve it to me nude."

"There will be no clothes worn in this house for at least a week." He smiled and then kissed her.

Jude rose, and Marlo stretched out across the sheets, luxuriating in their bed. There was a time when her dream of a life with Jude felt too delicate, and she hadn't dared believe in it. But that's the thing about pastries—you couldn't build a delicate layer without a strong foundation. Now Marlo knew better than to second-guess her dreams. They'd always been well within her reach.

The End

Acknowledgements

First and foremost, if you've made it this far, I owe you, dearest reader, my deepest thanks of all. Your time is precious and you have a plethora of entertainment options available, it is a true honor that you chose to give my story your valuable attention. I appreciate you beyond measure.

Secondly, I must thank my family for navigating this wild ride of writing and publishing alongside me, cheering me on when all I wanted to do was curl up in a ball and cry, and especially for keeping me well fed on hummus, dolma, candy, coffee, tea, and whatever other writing-related cravings arose. Thank you for calling me a writer before I ever dared to myself. I wouldn't have achieved any of this without you.

Without further ado, I must find a way to thank the myriad writing friends and professionals that helped me get here. While drafting and revising a book can be a lonely endeavor, the writing community is a loving and supportive group that saw me through the many obstacles I faced on this journey to publication.

Amongst the earliest writers I met on social media, who I now have the honor to call friends, were Alexandra Overy and Amelinda Bérubé. They have been by my side since the early days, encouraging me and sharing their expert insights.

In 2017, I had the good fortune, following Amelinda's urging to apply, to be accepted into Nova Ren Suma's YA Writing Workshop at the Djerassi Resident Artists Program in Woodside, CA. There in a magical collection of cabins in the woods, I met writers who inspired me beyond measure including Nova Ren Suma, herself, Alison Cherry, Kim Graff, Sara Ingle, Imani Josey, Nora Revenaugh, Randy Ribay, Leigh Shadko, Rachel Lynn Solomon, and Cass White. The following year at the reunion workshop, I finally got to meet Amelinda in person as well as Bree Barton, Shellie Faught, Jacqui Lipton, Melissa Mazzone, Wendy McKee, Catey Miller, and Rachel Sarah. It's no exaggeration to say these writers changed my life and I remain forever indebted to them.

Next I must extend my gratitude to TJ Ohler, Melissa Mazzone, Alexandra Overy, Sara Ingle, Cass White, PJ Gardner, and Kelly Coon. Thank you for always being a DM or text away, thank you for your sage career advice, and thanks for cheering me on even when I've been at my lowest lows. There aren't words big enough to capture the depth of my love for you all!

I could dedicate an entire novel's length of acknowledgements to the inimitable Kristin Dwyer. She is one of the most generous writers I've ever met and an even better friend. I'm so honored I got to watch her career blossom and I wish her every continued success in the world.

Thank you to the Northern California writers (past and present) who folded me into their midst without hesitation—Kristin Dwyer, Adrienne Young, Stephanie Garber, Jennieke Cohen, Joanna Rowland, Shannon Dittemore, Jessica Taylor, Kim Culbertson, Jenny Lundquist, Margie Fuston, Jenny Lundquist, Deb Crossland, and Autumn Lindsey. For a girl with wallflower tendencies, being invited alongside you to launch events and dinners meant the world to me.

More recently at a castle on the southwest coast of Scotland, I had the incredible privilege of participating in Adrienne Young's Storyteller's Retreat where again I had the good fortune to meet incredible writers that I will count as lifelong friends. Thank you, Marissa Firlight, for being the best bedmate a girl could ask for! Thank you, Shannon Arnold, for always having Kleenex on hand for your weepy retreat mates. All my love to my Just the Tipple gin tasting girlies! And to my critique group, Trevor's Storytellers, we made magic tucked into Trevor's cozy bar in the back corner of the estate. Thank you, Adrienne Young for sharing your story sorcery with us, and thank you, Marielena Torres Browne, Jamie Kenny Clark, Rachel Goodson-Hill, Deanna Kalk, Francesca Magini, Rachelle Gonzales Morrison, and Catharina Natalie Wandrup for being such a stellar collection of both writers and women. I want to be each and every one of you when I grow up!

To all the online writing friends I've made along the way, thank you for commiserating with me, exchanging Hamilton, Outlander, and Swiftie memes with me, and most of all encouraging me along all the dips and valleys of publishing life. I root for your success behind the screen of my phone like it's my own! This list is nowhere near exhaustive enough, but special thanks to Jeanne Renee, Jessica James, Gretchen Schreiber, Moniza Hossain, Inez Lozano, Elora Cook, Diana Quincy, Diana Wallach, and Taj McCoy!

To the experts whose services I engaged for the completion of this book, thank you for wisdom and professionalism—Jen Prokop and Jeni Chappelle (editing), My Lan Khuc (cover design), and Vivien Reis (formatting). Thank you, Sean Wing, for allowing me to interview you about your boy band days, your insights were invaluable to the creation of this book, and any inaccuracies are purely my fault!

Lastly, I would like to thank my dearest friend, Rachelle Hodson, who I first confessed my dream of becoming a writer to. She stuck by my side as I tortured her with crappy first draft after first draft, her belief in me, unwavering. I owe you years of your life back!

Milton Keynes UK
Ingram Content Group UK Ltd.
UKHW042046041024
449101UK00004B/398

9 798991 123402